KJ Burrage

Fires of Retribution

Paperback ISBN: 978-0-6459722-1-4
Hardcover ISBN: 978-0-6459722-0-7
eBook ISBN: 978-0-6459722-2-1

Published by Valiant Heart Publications

Cover Design and Artwork by the fabulous Chicklen.Doodle on Instagram

instagram.com/chicklen.doodle/

Chapter Headings and Ornamental Breaks done by Etheric Designs

facebook.com/groups/282998856658696

Fires of Retribution is written from multiple character points of view. Each chapter begins with the character's name and their location. At the back of this book, you will find character, location and language indexes for your convenience.

Content

Fires of Retribution is a New Adult fantasy standalone. While some of the marriages are unhappy, all romance scenes are written fade to black. The story includes themes including alcohol consumption, blood and corpses, branding, death, executions and murder, grief, physical abuse, mentions of past infant loss, slavery, violence and torture.

To my dad, Glenn Stevenson, the history nut,

who passed his interest to me.

This book and my coffee addiction is your fault.

Any dry humour found between these pages can also be attributed to you.

Contents

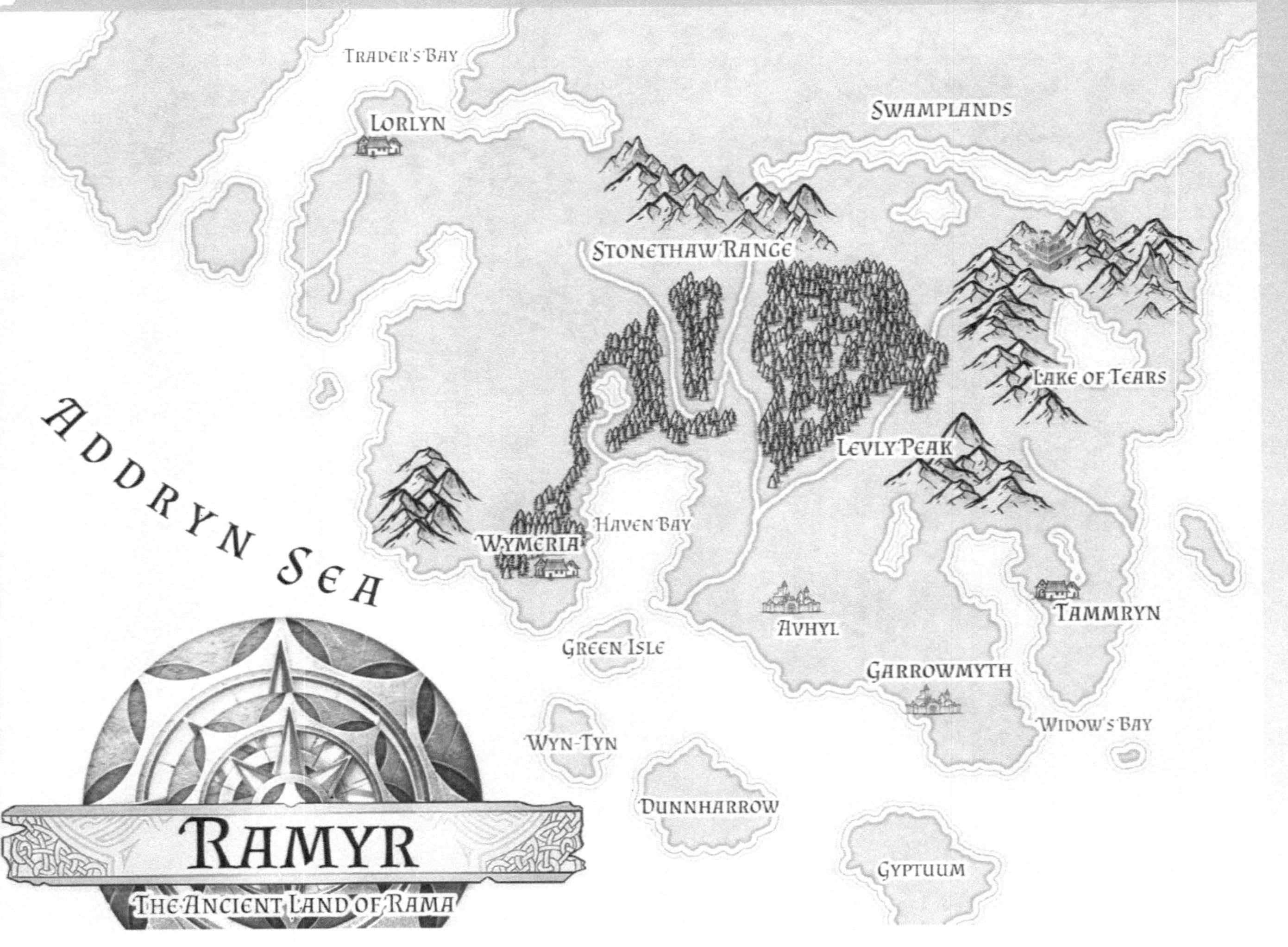

Trader's Bay
Lorlyn
Swamplands
Stonethaw Range
Lake of Tears
Levly Peak
Addryn Sea
Wymeria
Haven Bay
Tammryn
Avhyl
Green Isle
Garrowmyth
Widow's Bay
Wyn-Tyn
Dunnharrow
Gyptuum
Ramyr
The Ancient Land of Rama

CHAPTER ONE

Pyrah

THE GREEN ISLE

Humans thrived on chaos. Throughout their short mortal lives, they scuttled about their quaint villages like ants preparing for a thunderstorm. No matter how hard they toiled, they could not avoid danger, pain and hardship. Perhaps this was why the *vehyl*, the free humans of Ramyr, were such strange creatures.

For Pyrah, time and experience had not made living among them any easier. Her husband's own fighting men squabbled like children; their barbed tongues were coated with untruths and empty threats.

She bent and untied the laces of her impractical slippers that her husband, Luthur of Wymeria, had gifted her last high winter. The wet sand beneath her feet was firm, and she stepped into the refreshing foam of the sea. Her power hummed, warming the blood in her veins. Longing to stretch out her arms wide and command the waves, she lifted her eyes to gaze upon the calm waters of the bay. From her vantage point on her secluded Green Isle, she could see the mainland.

Along the southern coastline of Ramyr, Pyrah was known as the Green Lady, the patron of calm seas and safe harbours. Chieftain Luthur of Wymeria, her husband, enjoyed the protection that she could provide but did not appreciate her less than human attributes. In fact, he refused to look upon her reptilian form. Humans were such weak, suspicious beings, easily swayed by their leaders. The villagers of Wymeria enjoyed the fruits of her immense powers, but because she was an interloper, they would never fully welcome her.

After unlacing the strings of her gown, Pyrah discarded her outer layers on the sand. Unashamed by her *vehyl* body, she stood on the beach in her thin chemise. She let the water caress her ankles and hitched up the hem of her chemise. The water retreated, taking with it the excess sand between her toes.

"Do you remember the lazy summer days we used to play on the white beaches of Artroth, *sudunyn*?"

"I remember those days well." Closing her eyes, Pyrah did not have to see her twin in order to sense the irritation pumping through his blood. Elryk was eager to leave. "We have stayed too long, *sudunah*."

Pyrah tilted her head back and let the sun beat down on her face. Born into the ruling draconic family of Artroth, she had known the privilege of power. But privilege was a two-edged sword.

The emerald dragon inside her growled in impatience as she turned towards Elryk. He was taller than her. His bronze skin was marred by the three scars that ran horizontally across his face. Serious green eyes stared back at her, and she knew he understood her better than she understood herself. He was as handsome as any of their kind. But he was dragonless.

Traditionally, when an Artrothian child was able to sustain both a dragon and power, the first manifestation occurred. Back home, the physical ability to transform oneself into a beast of power was the transition from childhood to adulthood. The day she had manifested and Elryk had not, she spent pleading for her twin to try.

Their father, Parlyn, a renowned healer in the emperor's court, had grasped Elryk's shoulders. She could still see her brother wince, his knees buckling under the rough handling of their father.

"I'm sorry, *Aluel*, I have no ..." This was the only time Pyrah witnessed Elryk cry. Despite having a strong affinity with fire magics, he had no dragon.

Pyrah stomped her foot. "Try harder!"

"Not all who are born with power have dragons," Parlyn, their father, said. "Your brother is—"

"Empty ..." Elryk choked on the word. He knew he had no dragon, and he kept it secret from her. To this day, the thought still stung. "I'm going to die ..."

"Lullah." Pyrah remembered whispering the word with a fresh wave of horror. Their mother, Latunya, was the sister of the emperor of Artroth. She would not keep a son who failed to manifest a dragon. The shame would be too great.

Those who weakened the dragon bloodlines were destroyed. It was the way of nature. In purging the lacking, future generations were not polluted by their wrongness.

"You will not die," their father said. "We will flee ... Your mother is busy at the palace ..."

And so, they fled their homeland, hoping to escape the sacred laws of their kind. In the span of a few short hours, Pyrah went from princess to fugitive. She never wanted her twin brother to die. But Ancient One's Talons, she cursed him for many nights for the disappointment of his emptiness. If only he had a dragon of his own, she would have remained in the emperor's royal court.

Their father, Parlyn, brought them to Ramyr. Here in this new land, he made a pact with Chieftain Luthur before disappearing. Luthur safeguarded Pyrah and Elryk's identity, and in return, she married into the chieftain's bloodline. The protection of the coast was something extra she gave the ungrateful *vehyl* of Wymeria.

Pyrah told herself that she married for duty, for Elryk's and her own protection. She gave Luthur two healthy daughters, but still her dragon beckoned for her. The seas cried out for her to escape the small world she was trapped in.

She longed to break free and fly away. To leave Ramyr ... to leave safety. It was an impossible dream. She could not leave her vulnerable daughters behind. The mother dragon within her would not allow it. Although it was not within her capacity as a dragon to understand them, her heart still beat for her defenseless hatchlings.

"The sun will set soon." Elryk continued to watch her with his penetrating gaze. He turned his face towards the sea breeze. His long, dark auburn hair danced in the wind. "We should go."

Pyrah splayed her fingers and gestured at the sea. Her power sung and bubbled forth, halting an incoming wave. As more seawater gurgled, joining with her power, the wave grew in size and intensity. She continued to hold it.

"Pyrah." Elryk was rarely impressed with any display of her gifting. He jumped nimbly from his rock and collected his discarded boots. "We don't want to be caught by your husband. Not again."

Pyrah gritted her teeth, slamming her hand down so that the growing wave imploded. Water churned around her feet and drenched her chemise, which clung to her thighs.

She crossed her arms against her chest, studying how her brother's face went from unimpressed to furious. It had occurred to her that if she had not married Luthur, she would have been able to become a hunter as well. The dragon within her longed to stalk the skies. She was more capable than her husband's fighting men and women, including Elryk.

"A dragon bows to no one," Pyrah said, stepping further into the water.

"We need to go." Elryk's voice deepened into a warning growl. A trait he inherited from their mother. "And you're wet …"

Bending, Pyrah let her fingers touch the water. She lifted them to her mouth, tasting the salt. "I don't want to go back."

"Pyrah …" There it was. The head tilt and softening of his expression. He was coaxing her back to their small world of Wymeria. In that moment, she hated him.

"Swim back if you must."

Elryk frowned. He might be a broad-shouldered man, but he feared the sea. The awe he had for the ocean was the wisest thing about her twin. Too many men took advantage of the waters while they were calm, withholding reverence for the raging currents under the surface.

The only way Elryk would return to the mainland was astride her back. He'd be cursing his decision to come with her.

"You might be immune to your husband's punishment, but I am not." Elryk ground his teeth. He strung his boots around his neck and waded into the water.

"What are you doing?" Pyrah asked. She watched him slosh through the water, his head turned stubbornly away. "You'll drown."

Keeping his eyes on the far horizon, Elryk remained silent. His strides held no hesitation. She would have been impressed if she didn't already know his fear of the ocean and how weak his swimming skills were. Their shield-fire father had been too compassionate; he refused to force Elryk to face his fear of water.

"Elryk!" Pyrah bent, placing her hand into the water. The currents heeded her call and pushed against Elryk, forcing him closer to the shore.

Blinking the water out of his long lashes, Elryk turned to face her. The waves were now around his waist. Although Pyrah knew his heart would be wildly beating in his chest, he gave no outward indication that he was terrified. He always said he would prefer to meet a boar or a horde of raiders than swim in the sea. Foolish man.

"Are you going to force my hand?"

Still Elryk said nothing and fought against the current. He knew she would not use her power to topple him.

"Fine!" Pyrah snapped. "Typical that you would blackmail me back to my prison."

Pyrah turned her back to the siren call of the ocean and waded to the shore. She stopped by her clothing and shook the sand from her skirts.

Elryk watched her dress from the ocean. She plucked up the useless circlet of shells and shiny stones, then rammed it onto her head. She had the sudden urge to command the waters to sweep her brother under, but she resisted the temptation. That would have been unnecessary and cruel.

It wasn't Elryk's fault. He spoke truly. They needed to return to the village.

Her husband didn't have the courage to punish her; the foolish man had learned that lesson well. But there were ways he could make Elryk's life a living misery. That she was dissatisfied with her place in the world was not her twin's burden to bear.

Sand and salt clung to the hems of her skirts. She didn't mind. She was the mistress of the sea. Much better the smell of salt than the grime of everyday human life.

Grimacing at his wet hunting leathers, Elryk returned to the shore. "Charyss is eager to show her mother her newest garden."

Pyrah turned her face away in shame. Her eldest, twelve-year-old Charyss, was a complex puzzle to her. She showed some aptitude for gardening and was a quick study, but the child was frightened of her own shadow. It seemed ironic that her firstborn was a mouse. Quiet, submissive and terrified of any type of conflict, Charyss hadn't inherited the strength of dragons.

Pyrah had begged Elryk to drill her daughter to ready her for the hunt, but Charyss lacked the required skill and confidence. The child hated having her hair pulled back in the hunter's braids. Instead, she preferred to let her hair cascade down her back and walk barefoot among her plants.

"She wants to please you, Pyrah," Elryk said. "She's a sweet girl who's kind, intelligent—"

"Sweet girls don't rule," Pyrah snapped. "When Luthur passes from this world, I intend for one of my children to take the chieftain's place. Sweet Talons, she's missed all the attributes of her dragon bloodline."

Elryk's eyes hardened, his voice lowering to the growl he used when he was less than impressed. "She's your daughter."

"So is Vallah. It's in her I must lay my hope."

Where Charyss failed, Vallah excelled under Elryk's tutelage. She was strong, fast and determined. Conflicts didn't frighten her. Ten years old, and she took to the sword and bow as if they were extensions of her arms. Despite lacking a dragon, Vallah would grow into a woman who was beautiful and frightening.

Elryk shook his head. "One day, you may live to regret your dismissal of Charyss."

Pyrah tied the useless strings of her slippers and brushed her hair from her face. She scowled at her brother, who thought he understood her daughters better because he was dragonless. "Don't go telling me I don't love that girl because I do. I haven't deluded myself into thinking she might grow into something she's not."

"You might love her," Elryk replied. "It doesn't mean you haven't injured her."

"The world is cruel. Charyss will learn that she can't rely on a sweet temperament to survive. She needs to learn to take initiative and fight for herself."

"She has some abilities, Pyrah," Elryk reminded her.

"With plants. What good are blooming flower crowns? Tell me, what devastation can plants have in a battle?"

"Not all battles are fought with the sword or spear." Elryk sighed heavily and turned on his heel. He looked up at the sky, his brow furrowing. "Do you hear that?"

Tilting her head to the side, Pyrah listened. The wind whispered of another dragon. She could feel the air disruption as he tore through the sky. The Wind Song heralded the approach of a large bull dragon. No doubt he was Artrothian.

"Dragon!" Pyrah said. "Take cover."

Elryk was already powering his way up the beach before she finished speaking. Sand flew underneath his enormous feet as he fled. Hiking up her skirts, Pyrah followed him. Thick forest surrounded their private cove, making it perfect for instances such as this. Unless the other dragon was actively seeking them, they should remain hidden.

Elryk reached the edge of the vegetation first. He dove into the shade and laid himself flat in the shadows. Pyrah squeezed in beside him. Wedged between her brother and the trees, she let her traitorous heart slow down.

Torqui, her dragon half, rumbled within her own mind. *It's one of us.*

Pyrah's guts clenched at the thought of another dragon so close to her home. Excitement and worry warred within her as she stole a look at Elryk's stoic face. In the last decade, Ramyr had become a shelter to more Artrothian refugees. Although she didn't see them often, she knew them all by sight. Many of those who had fled the reign of her uncle flew to the northern reaches. She had heard of no rumours of any other dragon flying in their region. The incoming dragon was coming in from the sea ... not from the mainland.

Very few dragons flew over the oceans to hunt. Those who feared the wrath of Artroth kept their hunting grounds over land, close to places to hide.

"He's near ..." Elryk whispered, shifting in the sand. Dragonless, he had good reason to be afraid. Pyrah reached out and grabbed his hand, giving it a reassuring squeeze.

The incoming dragon was almost overhead before Pyrah spotted him. His light blue scales were almost white and camouflaged him well. Her stomach cramped. Rage and fear coursed through her veins, and she took a chance to check her brother's reaction.

Elryk's eyes were cold. He lay perfectly still. She could sense his muscles tensing, ready to spring into action. A futile wish. If Elryk attacked a dragon, he would surely die.

Hatred followed the rage, and she trembled from the force of it.

Rhodys, the Winter Storm, was in Ramyr.

"Where do you suppose he's heading?" Elryk's voice was soft. He already knew the answer, but Pyrah replied anyway.

"Wymeria. We're the only dragons for miles around."

Normally, Elryk would hiss and spit like a hatchling that he wasn't a dragon. He must be too preoccupied with thoughts of Rhodys.

"Do you think Luthur is stupid enough to entertain him?"

Pyrah laughed, bitterness joining her rage. "My husband, in all his glorious wisdom, would see a dragon visit as a great honour for Wymeria and not a threat. He doesn't seem to understand he is easy prey."

"Maybe you should eat him," Elryk grumbled. "He's only human."

"I am a princess of Artroth. We do not lower ourselves to eat the *vehyl*," Pyrah answered primly. "We need to get back to the village."

"Finally, you are speaking some sense," Elryk replied, wriggling his wide shoulders from their hiding place.

Pyrah followed him. Her green dress was now covered in fine granules of sand. Her long, auburn hair was loose as befitting her station as the chieftain's wife. It stood frizzed from the seawater. It wasn't the first time she wished she had the right to pull it back in a huntress' braid.

Elryk was just as filthy. As a hunter, he didn't seem to mind a bit of dirt. Stepping past him, Pyrah closed her eyes and felt power flowing through her. Her blood warmed as her shoulder blades tingled and her skin rippled. Fragile human skin morphed into hard, glittering emerald scales. Large, leathery wings burst from her shoulder blades, her face elongated, and her dragon, Torqui, the Green Lady, was free once more.

Over the years, Elryk had seen her manifest many times. As her bronze talons gouged into the soft sand, he was already hefting himself onto her back. She felt him settle, his large, calloused hands tapping the side of her neck to signal he was ready.

"Shall I hide you somewhere close by?"

Only death would follow the arrival of an Artrothian dragon. She was under no illusion; she would die right beside Elryk and her children. If the dread dragon, Cilvryn, found out about her daughters sired by a human, she would be named a traitor and guilty of polluting Artrothian bloodlines. She would fight for her family until the breath of life was torn from her lungs and she fell into eternal sleep.

"I'll stay by your side and weather the tempest that is to come," Elryk replied. "I'm with you until the bitter end."

"Never run," Torqui murmured, a vicious smile gracing her scaly lips.

"Never surrender." Elryk's voice echoed his calm, enduring nature. He was the only man she could trust who would never abandon her.

Chapter Two

Pyrah

Wymeria

To avoid offending the delicate sensibilities of the humans, Torqui landed in the dense forest surrounding the village of Wymeria. The *vehyl* of Ramyr had strange ideas about dragonkind and the danger they posed to natural born mortals. So she hid her scales, claws and teeth like they were a shameful secret. Best not to give the humans fuel for their tall tales.

Over the years, she had heard whispers of how Luthur greeted her father with a thrust of a spear. As a healer of great renown, the injury to his ribs didn't bother Parlyn. Despite the aggression shown by the humans, her father arranged an advantageous marriage for her.

She had been furious, but she understood what her father wanted. As an Artrothian, Parlyn understood the importance of dominance. The only way she and Elryk would be safe was to have a position of power. Thanks to their long lives, dragons were patient. The plan was simple: marry the most powerful man, give him children with dragon blood and replace the human leadership with her own. Failing that, she had two daughters who could potentially take their father's place.

While she might disparage her husband's intelligence from time to time, Pyrah didn't understand why he agreed to marry her. Thanks to his frequent bouts of drinking, she knew Luthur was not blind to her father's scheming. When she was still young, only thirteen years old, he was content to ignore her existence. However, on her eighteenth birthday, he proclaimed they would marry within the season.

Pyrah could tell Luthur was less than enthusiastic about their marriage vows. During the ceremony, his ugly scowl didn't leave his face as he watched the skies. At the celebrations, Luthur got very merry on mead and couldn't stand the sight of her. When they were ushered to his chambers, he grabbed her forearm and dragged her close.

"You'll tell your dreaded father we did our duty." Luthur's voice trembled with more than drunkenness. "The monster made it quite clear he required grandchildren of dragon blood."

It comforted her she wasn't the only unhappy spouse in the marriage.

Nostrils flaring, she scented the clearing. The air smelt of a summer storm rolling in from the coast. During the glorious warmer months, rain was a constant feature in Wymeria. It was drizzling now; cool drops of water ran down her scales.

Elryk jumped off her back, the soles of his boots pressing into the soft mud. Without looking back at her, he grasped his spear and the game he had placed nearby. To fend off her suspicious husband, he accompanied her anytime she wanted to manifest into her dragon. They used the excuse that he was hunting while she was gathering mushrooms or herbs.

The humans of the land saw it as her duty to help provide for her people, which was the perfect excuse to leave the village. Today she had been in a hurry and didn't lay out any herbs. After manifesting into her human body, she grabbed a handful of wildflowers and yanked.

Elryk grunted in disgust at her haul. "Luthur might be daft, but he won't believe that."

"Do you have a better idea, brother of mine?"

"Tell him you fell in the river, *sudunah*."

Pyrah scowled and threw her long, wet hair over her shoulder. It was already curling. "Mother!"

Surprised, Pyrah spun on her heel, watching in disbelief as her eldest daughter ran towards her. Charyss' dark hair was loose, and a crown of leaves sat upon her head. Yellow flowers and bright crimson berries were woven between the leaves, giving the child a sunny, cheerful look. Her soft leather slippers, which were not suitable for a trek in the woods, were wet. Streaks of mud caked the hem of her skirts and ankles. Her long, dirt-stained fingers clutched a wicker basket to her heaving chest.

"Charyss, daughter of Luthur!" Pyrah said, a scolding tone entering her voice. Internally, she winced; she sounded like her mother.

Emerald eyes brimming with tears, Charyss stopped a few feet away from her. Her button-like nose, dotted with freckles, wrinkled. She held out her basket to Pyrah. "Mother, I bought herbs so you can tell Father you have been busy foraging for the village."

"Bless you, child," Elryk replied. Pyrah wanted to wipe the indulgent smile off her brother's face. He was much too lenient.

"No!" Pyrah snapped. "The woods aren't safe. She has mastered no weapons."

"Mother, the trees will tell me if there is any danger," Charyss said, twirling a dark strand of hair around her finger.

Slowly, Pyrah closed her eyes and reached out for the basket of herbs. She needed to soften her tone. "My thanks, dear one."

"I brought you a clean overskirt too."

Pyrah looked down at her ruined dress and chemise. The rain hid most of her misadventure, but a newer one would ensure her husband did not spy the sand. It would not do to be found lying to the chieftain.

"Very clever," Pyrah said to her daughter. Elryk was right. For her lack of courage, the girl had a good head on her shoulders. She thought of everything, and this aided her in getting out of trouble. If one had the stomach for it, intelligence was also a weapon.

Charyss beamed up at her. The child lived to please, and that was what Pyrah truly feared.

"You are most thoughtful," Elryk said. "Now go, find your sister and stay out of trouble."

"There's a dragon with Father," Charyss replied.

"We know." Pyrah cursed her husband. "Now do as your uncle has bid and hide."

Charyss eyed Pyrah wearily, chewing her bottom lip. "Father had me serve him refreshments."

Pinching the bridge of her nose, Pyrah longed to scream. Would her husband's stupidity know no bounds? If a dragon was in the village, he was putting his daughters' lives at risk. To have their soft-spoken child serve a dragon ...

Beside her, Elryk stiffened.

"The stranger asked me who my mother was," Charyss said.

"What did you tell him?"

"Father was in the hall, so I had to be polite." Charyss' pale cheeks reddened as she spoke. "I told him the Green Lady of Wymeria was my mother."

Elryk and Pyrah exchanged glances. In rebellion against her husband's strong dislike of her dragon, Pyrah wore emerald to remind him what colour scales she had. While Charyss had been smart enough not to use her mother's real name, it was a title the humans used to refer to her.

"A reasonable answer," Elryk finally said. Charyss beamed up at him. "Clever and polite."

Pyrah shook her head, the shells and stones of her circlet clinking together. She unlaced her outer skirt and let it fall to the ground. Charyss bent to pick it up, and Pyrah watched her daughter fold the ruined skirt with great care. She shimmied into the clean overskirt and knotted it into place.

"Take that and go hide," Pyrah said. "Your father and I need to have a discussion."

Charyss frowned.

Such a sensitive child, Pyrah thought.

After Luthur's horrible hunting accident, Charyss tended to him day and night, hoping for his approval. She used her plant knowledge and magic to help him. She failed, and Luthur walked with a lurching gait.

Luthur was a fool. Charyss was only a child, and she had gotten further than the old cantankerous herb woman in the village. But Luthur, once a healthy, powerful man who loved the hunt and battle, was permanently wounded. And for that, he blamed Charyss.

Instead of the praise she craved, Charyss only received disdain from her father.

The boar should have gutted him that day.

"You've done well," Pyrah said. "Now do as I have asked and hide."

Charyss turned upon her heel and skipped away. Pyrah could not help but watch as her daughter disappeared among the trees.

"She needs boots," Pyrah said, straightening her skirts.

"She'll never wear them," Elryk replied. He nodded curtly, hefted his spear and stalked towards the village. "She prefers barefoot. Many that have an affinity with the earth do ... Don't you remember them in Artroth?"

Pyrah sent her brother an irritated glance. Many that had powers over plants and earth in Artroth had the shield-fire instead of battle-fire. They were the nurturers of the community and the young. "If she were only born a dragon, she would have shield-fire."

"Artrothian society needs both the shield dragons and the battle dragons. I remember liking the shielders more." Indeed, as a young boy, Elryk had made many friends among the shield-fires.

"Life isn't about being liked."

"Our father was a shield dragon."

"Look where that got him ... exiled. No one has seen Parlyn Life-Giver since he dumped us here."

"He gave his life for me," Elryk replied. His voice lowered, taking on an emotion Pyrah didn't quite understand. "Without him, I would have died. He protected a son that could give him nothing in return."

Pyrah followed Elryk from the forest and at his words, she felt shame wash over her. She had been so angry lately, so caught up in her own discontent that she had not thought about how her words affected her twin. It had been nineteen years since they had seen their father. She knew Elryk had hoped Parlyn would return when she married Luthur. They never spoke of his absence, but they both knew what it meant.

Parlyn Life-Giver had been captured. There was no doubt in Pyrah's mind that her father was dead. Once captured, his fate was sealed. He would have been executed as a *shakhyr-levly*. The second death of a corpse-lizard was a gruesome affair. Parlyn's human heart would have been dragged before the emperor and his court, tortured and executed. But the suffering didn't stop at the time of death. Once his human had breathed his last, his dragon would have manifested, free from its prison of human flesh. As a dragon, Parlyn would have been tortured and executed a second time.

"I miss him too," Pyrah said.

"He would have loved your daughters," Elryk said. "I know he would lay his life down for them as he did for me."

"Do you suppose the Otherworld exists?"

"I know it does," Elryk said, his gaze fixed firmly ahead as they entered the village. "I've *seen* it."

Pyrah clinked her teeth shut. The village wasn't the place to discuss their family drama, especially if there was another dragon in their midst.

The village of Wymeria was in an uproar. The humans huddled in groups, eyeing the meeting hall with some trepidation. Ramyr boasted several dragon families, and because of their nature, they quickly rose to places of leadership among the humans.

Although dragonkind valued family and clan systems, out of necessity, they didn't cross over territories. No one wanted to draw the attention of Artroth.

It seemed the peace from Artroth was finally over. For many years, the mother-country had done little to pursue their refugees. Now it looked like they were to be hunted.

Pyrah had always thought their uncle, the emperor, was too lazy to do such a thing. She left the incessant worrying to Elryk.

They moved through the village, avoiding those known for gossip. Pyrah could see it in their expressions; they expected her to give them answers. Even if she had them, she wouldn't have shared her knowledge.

The large wooden building that served as both her home and the community meeting hall loomed in the darkness. Pyrah lifted her skirts and carefully made her way up the slippery steps. Motifs of sharks and fish carved into the entrance doors stared down at her with soulless eyes.

Elryk followed her like a grim shadow. He glanced at her, then put his shoulder against the heavy doors and pushed. Neither of them would cower in the face of danger. It wasn't the Artrothian way.

Elryk stepped back, allowing her to enter first as Lady of Wymeria. Luthur's servants were noticeably absent. Had Luthur had the good sense to dismiss them, or had they been frightened off?

Thankful that Elryk was at her side, Pyrah tossed her damp hair over her shoulder and glided through the silent halls. She entered the main meeting hall, piercing Luthur with a stern gaze as she did so. It was here the men of the hunt and battlefield met with her husband.

Pyrah stepped further into the room, noting the absence of Luthur's arguing fighting men. Even her husband's closest advisors were nowhere to be seen. He was alone with their visitor. His lips twisted into a scowl when he saw her, which deepened as he looked to Elryk over Pyrah's shoulder.

Under normal circumstances, Elryk would hang back as a sign of respect for the chieftain. Not today. He followed her as she walked along the benches that were used during feasts.

Luthur gripped the intricately carved armrests of his throne-like chair. From between his clawed fingers, Pyrah could see the woodsmiths' interpretations of waves during a winter's storm. She had to admit, for something carved with human hands, it was remarkable.

Eight years older, Luthur had seemed powerful when they first married. He was a broad-shouldered man who was too proud of his physical prowess. Secretly, she was glad when her daughter could not heal the muscles in his legs. The chieftain of Wymeria was humbled. One day she would replace him, and then the humans would see her true value.

Pyrah tore her eyes away from her husband and focused on their visitor. It had been many seasons since she had seen her cousin, Prince Rhodys. Eyes as cold as ice, his gaze landed on Elryk, and a sneer transformed his arrogant smile.

Rhodys was the youngest son of Emperor Cilvryn. A dragon born of winter, he was revered and doted on from birth. As a child, he had been spoiled, and she doubted time had softened him.

"Fair cousin," Rhodys said, sweeping into a bow. His eyes returned to her wet chemise and her ruined hair. "I knew it was you."

"Did you?"

"You've a beautiful daughter," Rhodys replied. "She has her grandmother's colouring. Stunning little creature. She speaks with an Artrothian lilt. Pity her temperament is not more like her mother's."

"She's more intelligent than you give her credit for," Elryk said.

Rhodys' lips quirked. "Cousin El! How I have missed our games. Luthur was telling me you were one of his finest fighting *rokun*."

Pyrah flinched at the Artrothian insult for human. To Elryk's credit, he didn't react to the inflammatory words.

"How is our mother?" Elryk asked. It was a sore point for Elryk that their mother never came to search for him. They might have left Artroth, but Pyrah knew that her twin prayed that their family might be reunited.

"Losing her children was devastating," Rhodys replied. He took a few swift steps towards a table and plucked up a goblet of wine. He made a show of inspecting the wooden cup before lifting it to his lips. "Your father's demise cured some of her ache."

"Glad she's doing well," Pyrah said. She couldn't help the bitterness creeping into her tone. The casual confirmation of her father's death left her feeling cold inside. She blinked rapidly against the rising tide of grief in her gut.

"What do you want?" Elryk snarled.

Pyrah felt her twin's pain as if it were her own. His anger mingled with guilt. She wished she had the power to comfort him and rip Rhodys to shreds for giving them knowledge of their father's death. Hope that their sire still lived was shattered.

"Your clansman has an interesting offer." Luthur stood up from his seat and limped down the steps onto the open floor. Clapping Rhodys on the shoulder as he passed him, he approached the seething twins. Rhodys frowned, tilting his cup to better study his wine.

Biting her lip, Pyrah hid her amusement at Rhodys' discomfort at being touched by a human. She swallowed her nasty reply. It wouldn't do to provoke Luthur into anger—yet.

"My father, Cilvryn of Artroth, would like to extend an offer of protection. I'm here as a peaceful emissary," Rhodys said.

"*Peaceful?*"

Pyrah shared her brother's disbelief. Rhodys, like most young males, began his training for the battle and the kill at seven summers old. He had excelled. He was the type of dragon that enjoyed bloodshed, and his winter born status made his powers unpredictable.

Rhodys was a master of storms. His calmness was a front. Behind his cool façade, he was ready for a fight.

"I have signed Emperor Cilvryn as co-heir with my daughters. Once I am gone, the emperor will have a partial rule of Wymeria and her lands. In return, we've protection from a brewing force of dragons who seek to infiltrate Ramyr."

"No!" Pyrah shouted. "You fool."

"Men in Artroth have trouble controlling their wives as well," Rhodys said. He took another drink from his goblet. His cold eyes studied Pyrah from over the rim.

Infuriated, Luthur rounded onto Pyrah. "Quiet, wife!"

"Of course, you'll both receive full pardons."

Pyrah ignored her cousin, wishing she could wipe the smirk off his face. "Destroy the document, Luthur."

After picking up a piece of parchment, much finer than the humans of Ramyr had, Luthur rolled it up and tucked it away into his tunic. "No."

"It seems you're too late, Princess," Rhodys said.

Under her skin, Torqui roared in fury. She reached out and slapped Rhodys, raking her nails against his pale skin. He reared back, his face twisting in fury at her defiance. Along his high cheekbones, she could see scales rippling underneath his flesh. She bit down a sigh ... It looked like she would have to manifest into Torqui and fight his dragon.

What a shame.

"Keep that lizard under control!" Luthur commanded.

Rhodys jeered at Pyrah, not deigning to look at the chieftain. "He calls you *sais-levly*, and you let him?"

Pyrah snarled.

"Very well. Soon you will be *shakhyr-levly*. You have chosen your path."

"I am not dead yet," Pyrah said.

Leering, Rhodys' face rippled once more under the pressure of his scaled hide trying to burst forth. Pyrah bit her tongue and schooled her features to remain perfectly neutral. Rhodys was unable to manifest into his fearsome dragon.

Elryk nearly doubled over in laughter at his cousin's confusion. "You can't manifest in the village. It's protected by *vehyl* magic."

Pyrah sent her husband a warning look, threatening him with extreme discomfort if he gave the game away. Human magic did not protect the village. Something else was at play.

"Release me from the spell!" Rhodys hadn't changed. He expected Pyrah and Elryk to grovel at his feet and give in to his demands. He was going to be disappointed.

"Can't." Elryk crossed his arms against his chest. Pyrah couldn't blame him for enjoying the show. Watching an arrogant dragon struggling to manifest was entertaining. That it was Rhodys, of all Artrothian upstarts, made it all the sweeter.

"Can't!" Rhodys shrieked. "What do you mean, you can't?"

"I can't undo the spell," Elryk said. He shrugged his broad shoulders. "I'm not a human mage."

Swearing, Rhodys unsheathed the thick blade at his side. The blue-white scales on his face became more pronounced as his anger grew. He lunged toward Elryk, and Pyrah knew he meant to kill her twin brother for his mirth. Rhodys was the master of storms, wild and unpredictable.

Pyrah had enough of this nonsense. She grasped the handle of Luthur's sword and drew it.

"Woman!"

Pyrah ignored her husband, spun on her heels and intercepted Rhodys. As her blade clashed with Rhodys' sword, Elryk's lips peeled back into a leer. A flickering tongue of flame danced over her twin's overturned palms. Elryk the Empty never ran from a fight. Not like her dim-witted husband, who retreated the moment she relieved him of his weapon.

"You'll draw a weapon on a visitor, Princess?" Rhodys asked, pushing his blade against hers.

"You can only reasonably expect violence from me," Pyrah replied through her gritted teeth.

Rhodys nodded, abruptly stepping away. He had expected her anger. And Pyrah knew she was a fool. He wanted her to react. Baiting his opponents into violence was a favourite game of his. Spoiled by the emperor, he was never reprimanded for any of the fights he started. If Pyrah came home with tales of cousin Rhodys, her father would tell her she needed to control her temper and outsmart him.

"You are charming as always, sea-mistress." Rhodys sneered at her simple circlet of shells and gems. When he spoke again, it was in Artrothian. *"Duryl, the Master of Wind Song, would have made a better mate than this rokun scum. You would have had a brood of sturdy sons by now."*

"I'm happy with my fate," Pyrah snarled, trying not to think of Duryl, the young male dragon her mother had hoped for her to marry. He cared little for rules or regulations and would have allowed her to do whatever her heart desired. He was handsome, from a good family.

"Are you?" Rhodys whispered. "*Aluel* executed him."

"Did he, now?" Pyrah's stomach cramped at this unwelcome news. While she had no interest in Duryl as a mate, he had been good company, known for his generosity and wit. With him she would have been happier than she was with Luthur.

"Duryl was fond of you. He had a contact in Ramyr, a dragon renowned for deceit, and he received word of how you were faring. He made the mistake of betraying Artroth and keeping his silence."

"Go, Rhodys." Pyrah let the point of her sword dip. Spitting venomous words would not help the situation.

The smile didn't leave Rhodys' face. "I'll be back to meet your daughters and find out whether they are fit for *Aluel's* court. I'm sure he'll find them quite amusing."

"You will not!" Elryk growled, leaning forward. The snarl on his lips made him look feral. "You'll not lay one hand on those girls."

"Charming."

"Stand down, brother by marriage," Luthur barked. "They're girls. They'll go where their chieftain sees fit."

Pyrah lifted the tip of her sword once more and slowly advanced upon her husband. "You hand my daughters to my uncle, and you'll face retribution fire of the likes you have never seen before."

She spun on her heel, ignoring Rhodys' mocking laugh as she stalked from the meeting hall. She needed to think. Her time was running short. If Rhodys was here, she knew the emperor had already set his plans into motion.

Her temper and non-human attributes meant she had very few allies among the *vehyl*. And truthfully, what could the *vehyl* do against a dragon?

"Not much. They would become dragon food," Torqui whispered in her mind. *"We need allies."*

Without glancing behind her, she stomped out into the rain. The weather had made the paths little more than mud, and not for the first time, she cursed her luck at being married to a human, a chieftain of a small, inconsequential village.

"Rhodys is playing us," Elryk said.

Pyrah snorted. "He's never been one for listening to orders. Not sure why Emperor Cilvryn hasn't put him in his place."

"The question is, how do we respond to Rhodys' threats?" Elryk was right behind her.

"With decisiveness," Pyrah replied. "We'll make Rhodys and Luthur regret underestimating us."

CHAPTER THREE

Elryk

WYMERIA

Elryk scowled at the grey storm clouds that hung low over the village. The rain now fell in cold curtains. For this misery, he blamed Rhodys. Hunching his shoulders against his cousin's subtle threat, he followed Pyrah down the steps of the meeting hall. She relished the falling water and strode ahead with her face raised to the sky.

One day soon, Luthur would regret underestimating his dragon wife. She was a clever woman, and when the occasion called for it, his *sudunah* was ruthless. The Green Lady of Wymeria was not a dragon to make your enemy.

With a slight gesture of Pyrah's fingers, the rain split. It was enough that he could walk and remain dry. Pyrah glanced over her shoulder at him, smiling playfully. He nodded his thanks. Otherworlds, he hated water.

When they were young, Pyrah was the one who swam in the seas of their homeland. The ocean was full of carnivorous fish, creatures with poisonous glands and treacherous currents. After he almost drowned, he preferred to keep his feet dry.

In his nightmares, Elryk still felt the burning pain in his chest as he drew in seawater into his lungs instead of air. It was always the same inky blackness and numbing cold. Once the darkness cleared, he would walk among those that were dead. Pyrah never believed him, but the day he almost died, he entered the Otherworld. Near death, he felt their wispy fingers along the soft skin of his cheek, and he heard their harsh voices.

Empty, they hissed in his ear, *worthless child*.

There had been another voice in the dark, a quiet rumbling. It whispered to him in a pleasant bass, and Elryk felt the warm puff of air from dragon breath. *Not all dragons have scales. Arise, my son; face the world with defiance.*

His near death wasn't an accident. His uncle, the emperor, had invited his family to join him on his royal barge. He sat on the rail of his uncle's ship, observing the human slaves working on the shoreline.

When he was young and didn't know any better, he thought them strange, foreign creatures. His elders taught him how humans were weak-minded beings, easily corrupted and created to serve those who were born into greatness. Life had since humbled him.

Confident he wouldn't be reprimanded, Rhodys pushed him into the water. Giant oars that churned the water pulled Elryk under the surface. The more he struggled and screamed, the more disorientated he became. In his frenzy, he couldn't tell which way was up and which way was down.

The incident had enraged his father, Parlyn. After he dragged Elryk's limp body onto the deck, he grabbed a gloating Rhodys by the scruff and delivered a dozen stinging swats to his backside. It was the wailing of the prince that got the emperor's attention.

For his insolence, Parlyn was taken into custody. Elryk was too bewildered to protest when his father's dragon was forced to lie belly down in the middle of the slave markets. He cried as the membranes of Parlyn's wings were nailed into the ground and an enormous cuff was set about his neck. The emperor's guards encouraged the bystanders to poke Parlyn with spears and to spit on him.

Elryk went to the slave market every day to sit beside his father to defend him. After Parlyn's week of torment was up, he was publicly flogged in his human form. To add insult to injury, Rhodys was consoled with a new stallion, paid for by Parlyn's own purse.

From that moment, Elryk hated Rhodys and the emperor. His hatred only grew as he got older.

At first Pyrah had merely sniffed at their father's treatment. One did not lay a hand on a royalborn and expect to escape punishment. But then came the day Rhodys permanently scarred him. From that day, she had become a fierce adversary of Rhodys.

Elryk was ten summers old, and Rhodys was fourteen. Sick of being mistreated, he reacted and challenged Rhodys to a spar. The shocking death of Rhodys' mother was the only thing that could wound the young prince. That was the barb that Elryk used.

"Poor Rhodys … he got no mother. She couldn't bear to see the coward son of hers, so she went and died!"

Rhodys' face paled, his strange grey eyes glinting. One insult, and that was all it took for his cousin to attack. He was talented and was already skilled in weaponry. It was not a fair fight, and Rhodys was not in the mood to show mercy. Elryk screamed when his cousin slashed his face, narrowly missing his eyes. Warm blood seeped through his fingers as he clutched his bloody face.

Parlyn was once again the adult dragon who intervened. Elryk looked to him for vindication. But his father's furious gaze was on him. Proud of his disfiguring of Elryk, Rhodys watched on, amused, as Elryk's backside was punished. Rhodys was never scolded for his part in Elryk's wounding.

Pyrah had bristled at Elryk's unjust punishment. But Elryk understood his father's lesson. The punishment was for making a challenge he couldn't win against an enemy that had no mercy. Not for fighting. The emperor's sons were untouchable.

"*Rshon mahthyt*! I hate water."

"Must you swear with those words?"

Elryk grinned at his sister. "Dragon or no, *sudunah*, your dung smells no different from mine."

Pyrah scoffed, and they continued to trudge through the mud. One would have thought being the brother by marriage to the chieftain meant he lived nearer to the meeting hall. But they gave him a small wooden hut right on the outskirts of Wymeria to keep him away from the normal humans.

Typical.

In Artroth, when his dragon had failed to manifest, he was an oddity and not nearly dragon enough to deserve life. In a land primarily filled with many *vehyl* groups, he was too dragonish, too powerful and intimidating to be welcomed. Pyrah was forced into a mate-bond with a human while they left him on the fringes. It was a lonely existence.

Kicking open his rickety door, he paused and unlaced his boots. He heard Pyrah tutting at him, but honestly, he didn't want water through his home if he could help it.

He was greeted by the giggling of his nieces, which usually meant that one or both of them had been up to something naughty. Glancing at his sister, he had to wonder how much she was aware of her daughters' antics.

"I gave him the herbs," Charyss said. The sound was muffled, like she had placed her hand over her mouth. Elryk stepped further into his home, ushering Pyrah inside. "If he tries to manifest, he'll fail."

Ah, Elryk thought, *Charyss has more sense than her father.*

That his niece made a strategic move and fed a stranger a herb that would strip away his advantage did not surprise him. The suppression herbs were meant to control and dampen a dragon's power. Used only in Ramyr, they were unknown in Artroth. Rhodys and his minions would be woefully unprepared for their use. Dear, sweet Charyss was more dangerous than everyone thought.

"I wish I was there to see him," Vallah replied. She sighed wistfully. "Who showed you the herbs?"

"Ruethea. They are suppressant herbs that make it impossible for a dragon to manifest."

"The old medicine woman? She's so *blergh*!"

"She's old, Vallah," Charyss replied. "One day you might look like that."

"I hope not. She looks like Uncle Elryk's old, stinky boot. What else has she taught you?"

Charyss dissolved into fits of giggles. "Oh, poor Papa!"

Elryk leaned forward, interested in finding out where this was going. Pyrah laid a hand on Elryk's forearm to stall him from announcing his presence. Turning his head to look at her, he noticed the proud sheen in his sister's eyes first. Then the firm, straight line of her lips. Listening to her daughters unseen was amusing to her.

"Charyss! What did *you* do?"

"Well—I ..." Charyss sounded embarrassed. "I know father takes other women ..."

Pyrah's smile melted into a cold frown. He could see the muscles working in her jaw at the thought of Luthur with his human mistresses. Dragons were loyal to their mates, even if it wasn't a love match.

"Takes 'em where?"

"So I slipped him a little something that ensures he doesn't make any male heirs ... or rather, no more babies from him."

Elryk wasn't sure if he wanted to shake his niece until her teeth rattled or hug her. Luthur siring a son on another woman was something he was concerned about. There was no love lost between him and Pyrah, and his daughters could be in danger if he produced a living son. But it also meant that Pyrah would have no more opportunities to have a child.

"Does that mean no more babies for Mama?" Vallah asked.

"She doesn't need sons," Charyss answered. It was one of the few times that his eldest niece sounded confident. Pyrah let out a small huff that sounded like a laugh of agreement.

"She has us. I'm smart and can work with people, and you can lead the men into battle. We're a perfect team."

"I think you should have asked Mama before poisoning Father," Vallah said.

"I think you should mind your own business," Charyss replied.

Elryk stomped his feet.

"Shhh," Charyss hissed. "Someone's coming."

"Are you here, girls?" Elryk called out.

"In here, Uncle," Vallah replied. "We are making some spiced wine to ward off this nasty weather."

Pyrah moved around Elryk and entered first.

"Mother!" Vallah cried. "You're here."

Elryk stepped into the room, watching as his two nieces exchanged concerned glances. Giving no indication that she heard about Charyss poisoning Luthur, Pyrah sat at his table, looking elegant despite her wet clothing.

"Off the table," Pyrah said.

Vallah obediently ceased swinging her legs back and forth and jumped from her perch. It came as no surprise to him that Charyss was crouched beside the fire, stirring a large pot. She looked up to greet them, and his heart twinged in sadness. Rhodys was right; she favoured her grandmother. As he watched, she dusted the surface of the spiced wine with powdered herbs.

"Wine, Uncle?"

"Thank you," Elryk said and sat himself opposite Vallah.

Pyrah watched both of her daughters in contemplative silence.

Charyss seemed blissfully unaware of her mother's study of her. She picked up the ladle and filled four of his wooden cups to the brim with her spiced wine. Picking up two, she then carefully walked across the room and handed him a cup.

"Lord Uncle," she said, with a sweet little smile and a curtsy.

Elryk grunted. He was no lord. At one time he was a minor prince, but that was buried in his past. The corners of her lips twitched, and he knew his niece was teasing him. He took the offered cup and grunted again.

"Lady Mother."

Pyrah smiled at her daughter; the lines around her mouth looked taut. Perhaps she was considering the merits of admonishing Charyss for poisoning her father or congratulating her.

Once she served the adults, Charyss handed a cup to her little sister and then took one for herself.

Lifting the cup to his lips, Elryk drank. Charyss had been making her own spiced wine from the time she could walk. She had her own little patch of earth in his garden where she was free to walk barefoot and tend to her precious plants. Pyrah didn't want her growing things where her father might notice she held power. Luthur had never laid a hand on either of the girls, but he was well-known in the village for his greed. Worse, he could be unpredictable and take action without listening to advice from his own fighting men and women.

"It's a bit tart," Vallah said, screwing up her button nose.

"Hush," Pyrah said, leaning back in her chair. "It's perfect."

Which was Pyrah's way of saying she was pleased.

Vallah poked her tongue out at her sister. Grinning at the praise, Charyss turned away and searched through his cupboards for something to eat. This was how it always had been. His sister's children had free rein in his home. Here it was safe to take what they needed.

Elryk lifted his cup again and drained it, relishing as the warmth spread through his body. He closed his eyes, pretending it was the burn of power flooding his veins. Under the table, he clenched his fists. It was there. Below the surface of his skin. He was a Fire Mage. Even denied a dragon form, he could bend and manipulate fire at will. This was another reason he had been relegated to a secluded place in the village.

Humans, the strange little creatures, were afraid of fire.

This was why Pyrah didn't hold on to hope that her children might have a dragon. When he, born of two dragons of pure Artrothian blood, failed to manifest, what chance did her daughters have with a human for a father?

At first, when Charyss showed potential with plants, Pyrah had been hopeful. But as the girl grew, her temperament seemed too sunny, too sweet for her to have a dragon. And Vallah. Little Vallah had never shown any sign of power.

"Would you like more, Uncle?"

Elryk didn't open his eyes to look at Charyss. "No, thank you. One cup is more than sufficient to warm your old uncle's heart."

"You're not old!"

He chuckled at Vallah's outburst. "I feel old."

"I need paper," Pyrah said.

Opening his eyes, Elryk studied his sister. She had risen from the table and was pacing, and her teeth worried her bottom lip. "Paper? What need do I have for paper? I'm but a lowly human."

Pausing, Pyrah glared at him. "I know you have paper."

"Charyss, assist your mother, please."

Charyss stood from her crouch by her pot and rattled through one of his chests, which consisted of hunting daggers, belts and boots. She found old parchment, which was crinkled with age, and a small bottle of ink. As one of Luthur's fighting men, he didn't need many personal effects.

"What are you up to, Pyrah?"

"We need allies." Pyrah exhaled a slow and deliberate breath. "If our uncle, the emperor, has found us, we need dragon allies."

"You're sending a bird north." Elryk swallowed, unable to hide his displeasure.

"We've no choice."

"And what of Luthur?"

"He'll have to be persuaded to behave himself."

"I could make him sick," Charyss said. Everyone stopped and stared at her.

Elryk dropped his cup to his table with a heavy thunk. Poisoning a chieftain was a serious crime. If Luthur were to discover that Charyss had been using her herbs on him, the consequences would be severe. Daughter or not, Elryk feared that his brother by marriage would kill her or send her away to another chieftain to tame. He couldn't decide which punishment was worse.

"Don't you dare, Charyss, daughter of Luthur," Elryk growled. "If I find out you've done something to your father's wine, you'll be a sorry little girl."

"She could put it in his mead," Vallah said.

Elryk sent her a withering stare, and Vallah shrunk back.

"He won't be sick for very long. He'll be bedridden for a few days." Charyss' face fell. Elryk knew that her father mostly ignored her, and her mother failed to see her penchant for trouble. From toddlerhood, Elryk had often stepped in, fathering both of his nieces.

"Leave your father to me," Pyrah replied. She was still looking at Charyss as if her daughter had two heads. Then she slowly turned to Elryk. He could see the shadow of her dragon lurking under her eyes. Pyrah's dragon was most pleased that her firstborn was showing some backbone.

Moving over to her mother, Charyss spread the parchment on the table and smoothed it with her small hands. They were the hands of a healer, Elryk mused, but enemies beware. Healers could be notoriously tricky to deal with when vexed. He couldn't help wondering if Charyss had the courage to take someone's life under the guise of 'healing'.

"I need a quill, girl," Pyrah said.

"Got one!" Vallah was headfirst in the chest, a bent quill held up in the air.

"You need to look after your things, brother."

Elryk grunted.

By the time Pyrah finished composing her letter, it had stopped raining. Elryk led them to the back of his ramshackle hut where he had his messenger birds he kept in cages.

Orange, beady eyes watched them approaching. The birds he used as messengers were brightly coloured fiends with vicious hooked beaks. They were mischievous animals and would destroy anything in sight, which was why he kept them in cages.

Elryk opened a cage and offered his arm. His favourite, an intelligent bird of blue and green, hopped eagerly onto his arm. Hoping for a treat, the creature clicked his beak while Elryk swiftly tied a small leather pouch around its ankle. Out of necessity, he had fashioned these pouches to carry important messages. He had spent years developing his birds' skills. With one simple command, they would know where to fly.

"To Ayrahylse."

Pyrah wrinkled her nose as if a terrible smell wafted under her nose. Ayrahylse was the self-made dragon queen of the northern mountains. She was a legendary beauty who had taken a large male dragon as a life-mate. The stories about her shy husband all said his *vehyl* brothers loved him. But among the other dragons of Ramyr, he was known as the Deceiver, and Elryk had reason to not trust him. He very much doubted that Rhodys' warning about a contact in Ramyr, a deceiver, had been a flippant remark.

Elryk did not wish to make a scene in front of his nieces, but he had to wonder what Pyrah had felt at the Deceiver's mention. Was it with hatred or anger that her heart burned upon hearing those words?

The bird on his arm ruffled his feathers, looking put out by the delay. A smile twitched on Elryk's face as he pulled a nut from his pocket. His feather messenger reached out delicately with his claws to grasp at the treat. After cracking the nut with his powerful beak, the bird devoured the inside and looked to Elryk for another.

"Don't be greedy, Nix."

The bird inched forward, tilting his head to stare at him with pleading eyes.

"Off you go." Elryk lifted his arm, and the bird launched into the sky with an indignant squawk.

"Do you suppose it is safe to send him?" Charyss was biting her bottom lip again. Elryk knew she was worried about the bird coming to harm, not her mother's letter.

"Dragonkind would not think to send a message via bird. Much too primitive for them," Elryk said. He smothered his hand over his grin. Any Artrothian dragon would expect messages between them to be sent through mental bonds. When it came to lurking Artrothian foes, it was best to have a quiet mind.

"Sometimes the simplest method is the best," Vallah said, taking her mother's hand. "I wouldn't want Mama to fly away. Not with that other dragon around. And Nix is smart."

Tilting her chin to look up into the sky, Charyss announced softly, "I'll go and make some more suppression herbs."

The two girls walked off hand in hand, and Elryk waited for Pyrah to speak.

"You should leave."

"No."

"If you stay, you'll die."

"Then I die." Exhaling, Elryk turned away from his bird cages and headed towards his home. He needed to wash up. "This isn't the time to retreat. This is the time to make a stand. If we kill Rhodys, Artroth will still come. We knew this day was coming. Artroth is here to take us all back. They can't let us live outside their borders and their control."

Pyrah sighed. "Who do you think betrayed us?"

"You know who I think it was ..." Elryk said bitterly. His mind went to the time he caught his still unmarried sister in the arms of another dragon. "Rhodys is a conniving, boastful monster. He mentioned Duryl's contact. That's who betrayed us."

"Torryn, the dragon of Deception ..."

"Hopefully, Ayrahylse leaves him at home," Elryk muttered.

"Where do you think he came from?" Pyrah asked. "He has never mentioned his family ... but he must be Artrothian. He's a dragon."

"His power is somehow mixed with deceit. I doubt anything he says holds any truth or worth," Elryk replied. "He had you fooled once before. Be careful around him if he comes."

Pyrah's face split into a grin. "It is Torryn who needs to be careful, brother."

CHAPTER FOUR

Torryn

THE STRONGHOLD

The lake at the base of the Stronghold Mountains was a place of reflection for Torryn. Today, however, the peace he craved eluded him. On the opposite bank, the village carpenter and his small son strolled along the water's edge. Even though he stood on the shore in his human form, Torryn's superior dragon eyesight clearly saw the way the wind tousled the youngster's hair and how the child's face lit up as he scurried around looking for little treasures. The child bent to roll up his tattered trousers and waded out into the water.

Hands hung loose at his side, Torryn continued to observe the pair. His stomach felt leaden, and yet he could not force himself to look away. Life was cruel. His own son would have been the same age as the child, but he was gone.

"Neo, don't go too far." The carpenter waited on the shoreline while the boy splashed in the water.

Torryn knew he should leave. But it was addictive imagining his own child playing with the small *vehyl*. He longed to walk among the humans freely, as he once did before he took Ayrahylse as his life-mate. Some of the humans might trust him enough to allow their children to clamber on his back. He yearned for the opportunity to take wing with a young one and show them the wonder of the world from the sky.

"Impossible," his dragon grumbled. *"It'll upset our female. There's no reason to stoke the fires of her envy."*

As if sensing him, Neo lifted his head. The wind stirred, and Torryn could hear his laughter. His skin was a pleasant bronze, a perfect blend of his mother's pale flesh and his father's deep ochre complexion. He had to be the most handsome boy in the known world.

"You're only saying that because he looks like yours."

Torryn raised his hand in greeting and watched as father and son turned away. The boy protested, tugging against his father's hold. The carpenter ignored his child's pleas, and soon they disappeared from sight. The carpenter wasn't the only human wary of Ayrahylse, and by extension, him.

Disappointed, Torryn stretched before manifesting into his dragon form. A quick swim in the lake might help him forget his melancholy thoughts and loneliness. The summer sun was pleasant, and the lake was calm.

Torryn plowed forward into the lake, and cool water lapped against his blue scales. Strong claws raked the smooth pebbles and mud of the riverbed. A rumble of satisfaction came from his parted lips, and he continued into the lake until he reached its deepest parts. Here, in the middle of the lake, he could fully submerge his dragon body. Torryn was an excellent swimmer. Even his wings moved in a parody of flight.

Of all the places in Ramyr, the lake was his favourite.

When Torryn had been forced to flee the wrath of the Artrothian Empire, it was by this lake that Torryn landed, exhausted and afraid. Only fifteen summers at the time, he was a vulnerable dragon without clan or protection. It was a long, arduous journey, and the lake was his symbol of hope. He remembered crawling across the sharp pebbles so he might quench his thirst and looking down at his reflection in the eerily still water. His deep brown skin marked him as a stranger in a region full of fair-skinned humans. Some of the *vehyl* even had curious brown speckles dotting their flesh. He despaired that he had not flown far enough to find safety.

When his hunger became too much to ignore, Torryn gathered his courage and approached the human settlement. The humans of the north proved to be curious. They accepted his story that he had come from the western coast looking for a den away from the hustle of the port cities. A chieftain even invited Torryn to live among them. The man told him that a sentient being shouldn't be all alone.

So Torryn found purpose among them as their stonemason. His dragon power over earth and rock made him popular. He worked long hours and volunteered when extra hunters were needed. His willingness to help won him the respect of the people. And he was happy.

Then Ayrahylse entered his life. Torryn was entranced by the beautiful female dragon with her buttery yellow scales and big doe eyes. He assumed the fluttery feelings in his stomach were love. Such was his infatuation that he took her to be his life-mate, willing to dismiss her strong Artrothian beliefs.

It did not take him long to realise that despite her promises, she used her power against him. In his adoration of her, he made the mistake of letting down his guard, and she manipulated his emotions like he was a puppet on a string. After years of being together, Torryn had developed an awareness of when she was using her powers. But it had taken time and experience to grow this skill.

Ayrahylse had begged Torryn to use his influence over the humans to try and sway them into making her their queen. Torryn was horrified. He valued the compassion and kindness of his human neighbours, which in turn infuriated Ayrahylse. Soon he found himself caught in a rift between his dragon mate and the humans of the north.

Ayrahylse's goal to become Queen of the North was ambitious and short-sighted. Humans were not creatures to trifle with. They might lack scales and claws, but they had their own ways of seeing the world. Each village had their own chieftains, customs and laws. They wanted no queen. And they made no secret they did not want Ayrahylse ruling over them.

The relations between Ayrahylse and the humans continued to sour and deteriorate after the death of their son. So much so that Torryn was no longer welcome among his *vehyl* brethren. He was forced to give up his stone masonry to please both the human chieftains and Ayrahylse. Walking away from his purpose felt like a piece of his soul had died.

It was with these thoughts of abandonment that Torryn surfaced. He propelled himself through the water, allowing his body to come to a float so that his back spines and wings could catch the gentle breeze. Ayrahylse would be expecting him to return to the den soon. She had hinted that she had news to relay this morning before she flew out for a 'hunt'.

Which was interesting, because Ayrahylse didn't lower herself to hunt. That was Torryn's job.

When Torryn returned to his home high in the mountains, Ayrahylse was waiting for him. From the sky he could see her gleaming yellow scales as she prowled outside their den. Torryn landed beside her, disturbing the rock on the ledge they used to sun themselves.

"Where have you been?" Ayrahylse rounded on him, snapping her jaws.

"I cannot see how that is any of your concern," Torryn replied, his nostrils flaring.

Ayrahylse lifted her snout, scenting the air. Her eyes narrowed. "You've been to that lake again. Torryn, you know that when you see the humans, you come home in a foul mood."

"It's a hot summer. A refreshing dip cools one's scales." Torryn stepped around her, easily avoiding an angry nip of her fangs. He was larger than Ayrahylse. His physical labour only strengthened his dragon. "A kind word from my life-mate might sweeten my mood."

"*Ketur*, you'll never be one of them."

Torryn flinched at the dragon use of 'beloved'. He tried to be a dutiful husband and live peacefully with his wife. Resentment now beat in his human heart. He yearned to return to his work as a stone mason. Using his skills as both a human and dragon brought him joy. Ayrahylse refused to hear his desires, and he was sternly rebuffed. It simply wasn't the Artrothian way.

"I don't desire to be human," Torryn said, the lie coating his tongue. "I would like to exist in a world where I can use my full potential."

"Dragons don't work for humans," Ayrahylse said. "It was bad enough that you hunted for the lazy two-legged beasts last winter."

"They were starving ..."

Torryn didn't listen to Ayrahylse's reply denoting the might and glory of Artrothian dragonkind. Instead, he released a slow, weary exhale and nodded in appropriately timed places during his wife's rant. He gazed up at the home he had created to celebrate their union. He did not provide her with a simple dragon's den. No, he poured in every ounce of his dragon power over the earth to carve out an austere palace. The artwork had been fashioned after the Artrothian style. Motifs of fighting dragons, their eyes decorated with semi-precious gems, winked at him as he lumbered over the threshold of his home. An eternal celebration of war and the survival of the fittest. They simply called their home the Stronghold.

"Your reputation is damaged enough as it is ..."

Torryn flinched, rounding onto her. "You are the one who betrayed me! You spread stories ..."

"If you had only done what was required." Ayrahylse lurched forward, nipping his hindquarters. Torryn ignored the blossoming pain. "Your lack of control, your untruths are not stories ..."

Digging his powerful claws into the hard rock of the ground, Torryn dragged in a slow breath. After a particularly nasty argument, Ayrahylse had left their den and revealed to other dragons Torryn's most shameful secret. He had been forced to flee because he used his power to kill, crushing unfortunate souls under mountains. She told them how he lied and cheated his way into Ramyr to escape justice ... The damage to his reputation was immediate. He was branded as untrustworthy and ostracised from his own kind.

Dragons were often bloodthirsty, proud creatures. But they had little tolerance for deceit and a lack of control. Fear was what fueled his uncontainable power that day. Fear was another sign of his weakness. Of his failure.

Torryn returned to his human form, glancing over his shoulder as Ayrahylse did the same. Her long blonde hair hung loose over her slender shoulders. A crown of steel studded with diamonds sat upon her head. She had been his bright golden one in their youth.

"Don't be angry with me," Ayrahylse said. "You're the author of your own discontent. It is your actions that you now face the consequences of."

Torryn growled. If she had kept his secrets ... If he had been able to control his fear and power ... If he hadn't killed so many people ... He bowed from the waist. "Apologies, my queen."

"I want your worship in another way." Ayrahylse flicked her hair back, a sultry smile on her lips. She stepped forward, tenderly cupping his cheek. "It's been too long that you have graced me with your presence in my bed."

"You've seemed disinterested in me these last few seasons." Torryn lifted an eyebrow, surprised by the sudden demand. "I was a dutiful husband and left you be."

Ayrahylse pressed her body against him, reaching up to kiss him on his cheek. "You've been so melancholy of late. I've missed you. I yearn for you."

Torryn grasped his wife's hands in his own. Her skin was warm. A shiver of desire that he did not wish to acknowledge wound its way up his spine. "I'm sorry. I am ..."

"You're a shield-fire," Ayrahylse said earnestly. "Give me a son, and you'll stop mourning for what you can't have."

"I don't think I'll ever stop mourning," Torryn replied.

"It's been six years, Torryn. He was sickly, and no dragon lived within him. He died." Ayrahylse lifted her hand to rest it on his chest. There was no doubt she was beautiful. That was the case with Artrothian blood. His gut clenched, his dragon curling tightly with arousal. "There is no point grieving for what was weak and lost. Give in to me, and I can make you forget your sorrow."

Torryn swatted her hand; he could feel her power tingling over his skin. "I have no desire."

"Liar," Ayrahylse said, with a slight laugh. "We need a son. A child with his father's strength ... horns of gold like his sire. This one will survive, I know it."

Torryn turned his face away, even as his inner dragon rumbled with need. Ayrahylse grasped his chin. Her nails, like deadly talons, dug into his human flesh. Against his will, Torryn felt himself melting as she pulled him into a kiss. She ran her tongue along his lips, asking his permission. His hands gripped her around her waist and pulled her closer. He deepened the kiss, thirsty like a man who had been too long without water. Was it so terrible to indulge himself, to let Ayrahylse mask his torment so that he might feel whole if only for a little while?

He could feel Ayrahylse's breasts pressing against him. And he wanted her. He wanted her so badly that he thought he might burn bright until he was consumed by his desire.

"No." Torryn stepped away, shaking his head to clear his thoughts. His dragon whined at the loss of contact.

Ayrahylse's smile didn't falter as she reached out and clasped his hand. "Come, husband, there's nothing wrong with desiring your wife."

"I don't want another child."

"You're lying to yourself," Ayrahylse said. "You want your wife, and you want a child, Torryn Shield-Fire. You want an heir, and the only way you'll father a child is with me."

"A child of my blood." Torryn knew he shouldn't be tempted. He knew he should remember his poor dead son ... but his mind whispered traitorous thoughts. If he were to have a child of strong dragon blood, they would be safe. The ever-welling grief in his heart had overwhelmed him, dulling his love for his life-mate and his willingness to be a good husband. And now his dragon heart was pumping with that love once more. Torryn wasn't fooled; Ayrahylse had broken down his wall once again.

"Forget the past." Ayrahylse stood on her tiptoes, peppering hot kisses down his jawline. "Live for the future."

Torryn's dragon purred.

Sensing her victory, Ayrahylse unlaced the cuff of his sleeves and tugged his shirt. Her eyes shut as she reached up to cup his cheek with her hand and her lips pressed against his own. "I love you, *ketur*. Your disdain for me and dragonkind is an arrow to my heart."

"Forgive my weakness," Torryn replied. "I do not mean to be so cantankerous."

Ayrahylse's hands travelled the planes of his chest. "My big, strong man is sensitive ... but now I want to see his bull dragon, to whom no other can compare."

Torryn growled, while his dragon inwardly preened at her praise. He felt the tingle of the truth of her statement wash over him, and his blood boiled and bubbled with desire. He stepped forward, crashing his lips against hers. Her eyes widened in shock at the strength of his passion. They fluttered closed as she lifted her hands to grip him behind his neck. His lips never left hers as he hitched up her skirts.

"Be careful what you wish for, *ketur*."

Eyes lidded, Torryn trailed his fingertips along the pale flesh of Ayrahylse's arm. He watched delightedly as gooseflesh dotted her skin. "I take it you are quite sated, *ketur*."

At Torryn's rumble, Ayrahylse tilted her head back to look at him. She winked and rose from their shared bed. Padding across the dark chamber, she draped a soft gown of light blue over her body. It gave Torryn an odd sense of satisfaction, watching her twine a gold belt around her waist. Wrapped in the colours of his scales and horns, his wife was a beautiful sight to behold.

"I've had a message from the south of Ramyr." Ayrahylse turned to regard him. "Your old lover, Pyrah, wants our help."

"Pyrah? What exactly does she want?" Torryn rolled to his side, using his elbow to prop his head up. He could still remember that glorious summer he spent with the dragon princess who was destined to marry another. He had fallen hard and fast for Pyrah and had foolishly daydreamed that she would fly away with him. It wasn't to be. She chose to marry her chieftain.

"Artroth has found her."

Torryn felt an unexpected pang of fear for his first love. True to her Artrothian roots, Pyrah had expected him to remain loyal and unattached after she married Luthur of Wymeria. When Torryn had dared to take Ayrahylse as a life-mate, she sent him a strongly worded missive. Torryn attempted to pen a reply, but anything he wrote seemed sad and pathetic. Like a coward, he never sent the letter. "She wants to fight Artroth?"

"Potentially. She's asked me to come to a dragon summit in her quaint human village."

Realising that the invitation had not been extended to him, Torryn felt like a hot knife had been driven through his gut. Artroth was his enemy too. Or had Pyrah so conveniently forgotten?

"You'll of course accompany me as my consort." Ayrahylse's tone brooked for no argument.

"That will not please Pyrah," Torryn commented, unsure why he didn't like the twisted smile on his wife's face. "How severe is the Artrothian threat?"

"Significant," Ayrahylse answered. "They've contacted me."

Torryn's mouth went dry. He blinked rapidly, wondering in what world his wife would not immediately inform him of this very dangerous development. "Who has contacted you?"

"One of the emperor's spies." Ayrahylse strode forward, running her long nails down his jawline. "Fret not. The Artrothians are desperate for new dragon blood. Our kind is on a steady decline. To earn Emperor Cilvryn's forgiveness, all I have to do is provide him with a young one to serve the realm."

"So this had nothing to do with your desire for me, or for a child." Torryn removed her hand and leaned away from her seductive touch. "But a way to serve the emperor we both hate?"

"Torryn, *ketur*, this way you have the child you crave," Ayrahylse said. "And I'll get the forgiveness I have sought for so many years. I thought you would understand."

"What makes you think the emperor would forgive you even with a babe in your arms?" Torryn said, ignoring the way his inner dragon writhed in discomfort. Years of being blackmailed and hiding had made his dragon untrusting.

"All I am asking for is a child. Refuse, and I'll have you dragged to Artroth in chains. I'll use your dragon's golden horns and talons to fashion myself a new throne."

"She doesn't love us," his dragon whispered. *"Ayrahylse is a danger to us. Any child that we manage to sire with her will also be in danger."*

"What does your dragon whisper to you, *ketur*?" Ayrahylse, like most dragons, could sense when another's two halves were communing with one another. She watched him openly, her clear blue eyes expecting him to answer.

"He's excited to live free," Torryn answered, the lie stuck in the back of his throat. "He wishes to go hunt for his life-mate. I'll be back soon, beloved."

Torryn crouched beside the reptilian body of his kill. Bored of hunting deer, he had flown north to the swamps. Home to the fearsome snapdragons. He relished the challenge of the hunt; snapdragons were predators that preferred to stalk their prey from the murky depths. Once a snapdragon latched onto its victim, their jaws did not open until the thrashing ceased. Some hunters underestimated the snapdragons, assuming that they were slow upon the land. They dragged their bellies along the ground with their stumpy, clawed feet. But snapdragons were aggressive and could dart forward at astonishing speeds on the land.

Spotting snapdragons in the sludge and slime of the swamp waters was easy with his keen dragon sight. Torryn had learned to ensure that his dives were tight. His talons needed to hit the hard ridged back of his prey, breaking its back. A snapdragon that wasn't immediately paralysed still had the ability to bite him or topple them both into the murky water.

Today's hunt gave Torryn no pleasure. Discontent echoed in both his human and dragon thoughts.

It was quite possible that if Ayrahylse had gained favour in Artroth's eyes, she needed to prove her value. A female dragon with strong offspring was a good start. She may be very beautiful and sly, but she wasn't wise with her words. Her dire threat sounded an alarm in Torryn's head. Life-mates did not threaten even in great moments of anger. He could only hope that her words had been idle.

Torryn was reasonably sure that the Artrothians did not yet know about him. His sins against the empire were too great for him to expect any type of forgiveness. Ayrahylse couldn't reveal her association with him without endangering herself. So which bull dragon did Ayrahylse plan on telling Artroth was sharing her den, if not him?

The thought soured his stomach. Shock and betrayal left him feeling numb.

Another spike of fear coursed through him. Ayrahylse wanted a child. She still lived by the old ways of Artroth. Nothing was more important to an Artrothian than the procurement of strong dragonkind children and the solidification of one's legacy.

Torryn's mind went back to the day of his child's birth. He recalled his simple belief that they needed to have faith. Although their son had been born early and he was small, Torryn prayed he would grow in time. Ayrahylse's voice had been void of emotion as she told him that the child would never survive.

"Tell me what to do," Torryn begged, pressing the whimpering child to his chest. He knew he would do anything for his newborn son. His dragon sung, wanting nothing more than to curl up and nuzzle his hatchling. He had seen many hidden dragon young in his travels. He thought he felt a soft hum, no more than a gentle note of power from the babe. What if the child were allowed to sleep and soak in the radiant warmth of his parents' scales? Could he become strong in power and might?

The expression on Ayrahylse's face was pinched. "Go hunt. I need to feed so he can."

It was with great reluctance that he handed his son back to the care of his mother and left the cave to hunt. Every fiber of his being told him to stay to protect Ayrahylse and his vulnerable child. He wished he had listened to his instincts.

By the time he returned, the child was dead.

Overwhelmed, Ayrahylse would not look at their babe. So Torryn bundled up their son and flew him to the highest peak of the mountains and buried him there. He stayed by his son's side until sunset, casting the blame on his own shoulders. For it was likely his weakness that caused his child's death. He had heard the dire warnings from his mother's people ... A man like him wasn't meant to sire a child. His bloodline was weak. Tainted.

"I can't have a child," Torryn said, shaking his head. He cast his gaze along the carcass of his kill, a plan formulating in his mind. The teeth, claws and the soft, leather-like underbellies of the snapdragons were valued by humankind. "My dragon bloodline isn't strong enough to sire a healthy child."

"I can't go through the pain of losing another hatchling." His dragon echoed his sentiment.

Brandishing a knife, he skinned the belly of the snapdragon. Once that job was complete, he cut it into portions. The belly meat was particularly sought after, and

Jilearah, the witch in the woods, was fond of snapdragon meat. For good measure he removed the sharpest teeth.

Cleaning his knife on his trousers, Torryn left the majority of his kill behind in order to seek help from the old woman. She was an odd character he had met by chance after injuring himself on his first snapdragon hunt. He had been lying half in the swamp, delirious with pain when she revived him.

Instead of manifesting into his dragon form, he set at a steady pace through the swamp. He was close by to her hut, and his human body could do with the exertion of walking.

Torryn was not at all surprised when Jilearah was standing outside her front door waiting for him. Her frazzled grey hair formed a halo around her head. Her skin was bronzed and wrinkled from her time in the sun. While humans did not seem to have the same affinity for power as dragonkind, Torryn had learned to be ready for surprises when it came to humans. Jilearah seemed to be able to see events in the future. No doubt the old crone had been waiting for her snapdragon meat.

Striding up to her ramshackle home without speaking, Torryn handed her the packet of meat, the belly skin and three teeth.

"Such a good boy you are," Jilearah said in way of a greeting. "Tell me, of whom did you dream last night?"

Torryn cocked his head to the side. What he had failed to tell even Ayrahylse was that he suspected he had a secondary power. Comfortable with the strange human woman, Torryn had confided in her about his dreams.

"The white dragon." From the tips of black horns to his inquisitive silver eyes, he could still see the white dragon as if he were standing before him. Torryn had witnessed an almost grown boy straining to manifest his dragon. He experienced the white dragon's thrill of his first flight. Other times he felt a foreign weight prohibiting the manifestation. And oh, how that had hurt him, growing but imprisoned in his human body. "I am not here to talk about the true Winter's Dragon, the one born upon high winter's morn who will end the draconian empire. He's a fairytale."

"Artroth will fall one way or another," Jilearah said. She weighed the meat in one hand and, apparently happy with her prize, turned and entered her house.

Torryn followed, ducking to avoid hitting his head on hanging pots and drying herbs. The old woman lived simply with a small cot and an open fire for cooking. He watched as Jilearah sunk slowly into her only chair, her old bones creaking. He suspected the lack of furniture was to encourage unwanted guests to leave.

"Ask what you will, Torryn."

Torryn shifted, trying to avoid Jilearah's keen gaze. She gave him the unsettling feeling she could see right through him.

"I must not have a child," Torryn said.

The smile on Jilearah's lips told Torryn she had been expecting this. "Really, scaly-one, why not punish Ayrahylse? You could become a wonderful father."

"I don't think you know me well enough to make such a bold statement," Torryn said. "Please, before I lose my nerve."

"Ayrahylse will betray you," Jilearah said. "She'll go to another bull dragon."

Torryn shook his head, even though he had already thought the same thoughts. "Ayrahylse is my life-mate. She will not go to another. It's not in the nature of dragons."

Jilearah's smile was sad. "I cannot dissuade you?"

"No," Torryn said firmly. "I am ... I am of undesirable blood. Any child I conceive will die."

"Torryn ..."

"Either they die in infancy or are taken by Artroth, or they live a life in fear because of who their father is. Please, I cannot take more heartbreak."

Jilearah had the vial in her ratty cloak. She was ready for him, knew what he would ask of her. Without a word she stood, hobbled over to him and pressed it into his palm.

"I still believe you are being a stubborn fool, dear boy," Jilearah said, patting his cheek.

"I won't change my mind."

Jilearah sighed and turned away from him. "Go quickly. A storm is coming, Torryn, but I know you have the strength to weather it."

Clutching the vial to his chest, Torryn nodded his head and left the old woman's hut. Still striding towards a clearing, he uncorked it and swallowed the bitter mixture. It stuck to his tongue, and his heart ached with regret. It was for the best. He couldn't risk bringing a child into the world.

CHAPTER FIVE

Pyrah

WYMERIA

If Pyrah were to bring any of her kind into the fold against the Artrothian threat, tonight needed to be perfect. The only way to impress dragonkind was a display of wealth and power. It was a terrible thing indeed to be found weak by one's enemy, but it was worse still to be found lacking by allies. This was what Pyrah feared above all.

Although Elryk's feathered messengers had done their duty, most dragons had either fled Ramyr or ignored her. Only a small handful had replied they were willing to hear what she had to say. It was imperative that these dragons were convinced to join her in her crusade. Otherwise, Pyrah would find herself fighting Artroth alone.

It was with a heavy heart she returned to her personal chambers. A fleeting thought swept through her mind. Maybe fleeing Ramyr was her only option ... She could distract Rhodys, and Elryk would slip away with her daughters. Pyrah dismissed the daydream. In order to taunt her, Rhodys would hunt down her brother and children.

A soft light greeted Pyrah when she stepped into the sanctuary of her rooms. Dozens of tall votive candles set in their wrought iron stands emitted a pleasant orange glow. She found herself pleased by the welcome, remembering when she was a girl the collection of candles and oil lamps in her mother's rooms. Dragons were creatures of heat and light.

Gangly legs tucked closely to her body, Charyss was curled up in an armchair. A delicate shawl of pink, taken from her dresser, was wrapped around her shoulders. Her fingers paused in their braiding of another crown of fresh herbs. She looked like an ethereal spirit with the golden light brushing across her pale skin. There was a small smudge of dirt on her nose, and in her loose braid she had added sprigs of herbs.

"I picked out a gown I think will be suitable for tonight," Charyss said. "I hope it pleases you, Mother."

Pyrah swept across the room, brushing her hand down Charyss' dark locks as she passed her. The gown her daughter had laid out on her bed was black with an emerald underskirt. She exhaled, feeling a weariness in her bones. She longed for a time when she could burrow underneath her furs and close her eyes to ward off the worries of this world. When her girls were small, they would often join her, giggling and tickling her with their chubby fingers. But this wasn't the time for daydreams. The sun was setting, and she needed to prepare herself to meet her guests.

In silence Pyrah tossed her day dress and shift on the bed and dressed. Charyss came to her side, smoothing out the black silken skirts. She had chosen well. The black dress clung beautifully to Pyrah's curves. A split ran to her groin. It would flash the emerald underskirt as she walked. Sheer lace trimmings accentuated her breasts but already itched in the summer heat.

"Discomfort is the price of power." Charyss turned to study her.

Pyrah's long, nimble fingers tightened the laces on her bodice. Her daughter had an eye for beauty and for items that spoke of power. "You've been listening to your father, girl."

"It's as true for women as it is for Father's fighting men." Charyss' eyes shone with admiration. Her daughter's next words made her heart swell. She knew the adoring look was for her, not the men in the village. "You look dangerous tonight, Mother."

If only her daughter knew how dangerous she was. Pyrah glided towards her dresser and cupped Charyss' chin, pressing her lips to her daughter's cheek. "Don't let any man tell you you're weak, child."

Settling herself into the wooden chair at her dresser, she allowed Charyss to brush her hair until it shone. She then inclined her head to allow her daughter to fit her shell circlet on her head.

In the pane of silver metal that her husband had gifted her, Pyrah's reflection scowled. A mirror had been an extravagant gift to celebrate the birth of her first-born child.

"He wasn't always so difficult."

"Mother?" Charyss' expression was one of reverence. Her fingers repositioned a stray shell.

Swallowing back a sense of overwhelming guilt, Pyrah twitched her lips as she attempted to smile. She reached out and touched the cool, beaten surface of the mirror. "Sometimes your father found it in his heart to be kind. He's lost his way."

"We all lose our way from time to time."

"When did you get so wise, daughter?"

"I'm not a child anymore."

Pyrah lifted her gaze to Charyss' reflection. From the moment her newborn daughter had been swathed in clean swaddling and laid on her chest, this was what she had been afraid of. A girl child grew into a woman. And one way or another, she would lose her. No doubt Luthur was already looking at the eligible young men to wed his daughters. If he couldn't sire his own male heir, he would search for a way for his daughters to give him a grandson. Once Charyss was betrothed, it would not be long before Luthur's fighting men would look to Vallah.

"Stay out of sight."

"I was hoping to meet the other dragons," Charyss said. She fiddled with a loose thread on her sleeve.

"Do you want to be betrothed to a dragon, little flower?"

"No, Mother." Charyss shook her head.

"You are your father's eldest. You must remember you're playing a game of survival. Now go, find your sister and stay hidden."

Pyrah turned away from Charyss' pouting expression and arranged her cosmetics on her dresser. Hearing her chamber door softly open and close, she breathed a sigh of relief. With steady hands, she painted her lips a dark red and added kohl around her eyes.

On a whim, she opened her dresser draw to look at a treasure she rarely indulged in wearing. Once upon a time, she had been a girl in love, and her former lover had given her a heavy necklace of gold, crafted into a snapdragon. She let her fingertips rest upon the predatory animal. "Otherworlds, give me courage."

Hanging it around her neck, it felt heavy as it rested on her collarbone. It made her feel powerful.

There wasn't much time left. She snatched up a leather pouch she always kept on her. It contained a vial of clear liquid that she had acquired to add to her cosmetics. Closing her fist around the pouch, she knew what she had to do. She took the vial carefully between two fingers and uncorked it. The liquid had a strong odour, but she ignored it in favour of adding it to her nail paints. She mixed the liquids together and then added more colouring to her left hand.

"Pyrah! Are you ready, wife?"

"A moment, husband." One last glance in her looking glass, and Pyrah knew she was ready for her summit. Forcing a pleasant smile onto her face, she swept from the room. She might have trouble connecting to her strange dragonless daughters, but they were hers. Luthur had no right to make decisions on their behalf.

She opened her chamber door to find Luthur lounging against the wall. He eyed her appreciatively, and she noticed he already had a full goblet of mead. Around his shoulders he had draped his most expensive cloak, which was clasped together with a pin fashioned into the likeness of a fish.

"Do not embarrass me tonight," Pyrah growled. It had taken all her womanly wiles to convince him to allow the summit and behave himself. The bastard thought the meeting of dragons was his own idea.

Luthur inclined his head. "Bring more dragonkind into our fold, and I'll be most pleased."

Pyrah narrowed her eyes. "If it pleases you so, husband, rip up your contract with Artroth."

"There's no reason to upset Artroth ... They have forgiven your father's crimes."

"I think you'll find forgiving the dead is an easy task."

"Then we have no reason to worry about further consequences." Luthur shrugged carelessly, and Pyrah gritted her teeth to stop herself from slapping sense into him. "Under the contract with Artroth, you're permitted to remain here, Elryk won't be hunted, and our daughters will be matched to a young male dragon when they are ripe for marriage. I see this as a stunning victory for you, my dear."

"Ripe for marriage?"

"They have a few years yet before I'm willing to give them." Luthur shrugged again in his infuriating, self-assured manner. Pyrah clenched her fists, careful not to break her skin with her nails. "I have done no different than your over-glorified father."

"My father had no choice."

Luthur's eyebrows lifted, and he chuckled. "Let it be known, my dear, that your sainted father didn't negotiate. He offloaded you and your cursed brother and flew into the sunset."

Gritting her teeth, Pyrah could feel Torqui, her dragon, rippling under her skin. She felt a savage sense of pride as Luthur stepped back in fear, knowing he saw the dragon reflected in her eyes. "Be careful, husband."

"Nevertheless, the contract with Artroth makes Emperor Cilvryn co-heirs with Charyss and Vallah. Imagine the bother you would have saved if you only gave me a male child."

"You don't deserve them."

"And you do, my dear?" Luthur chuckled darkly. "Your guests are arriving."

Lifting her chin, Pyrah stepped around her husband and made her way to the entranceway of the meeting house. Luthur followed her, still chuckling. She schooled her features to seem unaffected by her husband's mirth.

Elryk was already on the top step of the meeting house, watching the horizon. Hearing Pyrah, he pointed out two incoming dragons.

"Are you ready, *sudunah*? Ayrahylse has brought her consort with her."

As a pure dragon, Pyrah was blessed with a superior sense of sight. Elryk's announcement was unnecessary. She could see for herself the glimmering yellow scales of Ayrahylse and the brilliant blue and gold of her elusive mate.

She exchanged a weary glance with Elryk. Torryn would be someone to stay clear from. From the rumours that sprouted from Ayrahylse's own lips, Torryn lacked both control and wits. The most damning of Ayrahylse's complaints was Torryn was prone to telling untruths. It was said his tongue was coated with lies. Rhodys hinting that a deceiver had given him her location pointed to Torryn betraying her. Her blood warmed at the force of the emotions she valiantly tried to keep hidden.

"Laelyth the Speak Mind and Gahryk the All-Knowing."

From the west was the rose-gold form of Laelyth, a younger female dragon who could not only speak into the minds of others but control them. Pyrah had heard that she was afraid of her gift and fled Artroth when Emperor Cilvryn's generals turned their attentions to her.

When she reached Ramyr, she was taken in by Gahryk, a cantankerous old dragon who normally preferred to be left alone. It was said that his power of Sight was unparalleled. Whatever he saw back in Artroth had compelled him to leave the land of dragons and seek a life in Ramyr. In the past, Pyrah had tried to weasel out answers from the steel-coloured dragon, which ended with a vicious tongue lashing and Gahryk telling her things about herself she didn't wish to know.

"Uxhyn the Tracker." Luthur stepped forward, tilting his chin to stare up at the gigantic black dragon. Despite his size, Uxhyn had been able to approach in the shadows, undetected for far longer than the other dragons. His power was at work. "Make sure he joins us, wife."

Pyrah rolled her eyes. Uxhyn, despite his name and his gifting, disliked killing. He was about as useful as the wart on Luthur's backside. The black dragon preferred to be left alone. A gentle giant, she was surprised to see him respond to her request. She exchanged a glance with Elryk.

Ground quaking under his weight, Uxhyn landed first. Pyrah couldn't help but startle at the thick white scar that ran down his face. In the place of the black dragon's left eye was milky white tissue. His right horn was damaged, cracked almost to the root. The scales on his flanks were puckered from scarring. The pacifist had been in a fight.

From his back, a human dismounted.

"Nahilya!"

Pyrah pursed her lips, watching as Elryk rushed forward to greet the healer with more enthusiasm than she thought was appropriate. Nahilya was like Elryk, born of Artroth, and had a power but no dragon. She had fled to Ramyr alone and lived in a humble hut in the forest. Over time she had grown a reputation as a trustworthy healer.

Returning her gaze back to Uxhyn, Pyrah wondered if that was why the healer was with the big black dragon. Had Uxhyn required help? Why hadn't he fled if he had a certain distaste for bloodshed?

"Lady Pyrah," Nahilya said after kissing her brother on both of his cheeks. Flicking her hunter's braids over her shoulder, she sauntered up the steps to the great log house. She was outrageously dressed in leather hunting gear. Pyrah caught Elryk eyeing the healer's plump rear end as she walked ahead of him.

"A pleasure, as always." Pyrah glared at Elryk for his flagrant rudeness.

But Nahilya glanced over her shoulder and winked at him. "The pleasure is all mine."

Pyrah wasn't the only woman looking at Nahilya askance. Landing lightly, Ayrahylse tucked in her wings and shook her slender head at the healer's presence. The dislike was clear in the yellow dragon's eyes. "What are you doing here? You have no dragon."

"*Ketur*, she has power. She is of Artroth." Pyrah had marked Torryn's landing, noticing with a savage satisfaction that he hung back as if he was unsure of his welcome. "She has the right to hear what Pyrah has to say just as much as you do."

"Thank you, Torryn, but I can defend myself." Nahilya smirked at the yellow dragon. She was completely unbothered by the northern beauty's disdain. "If there is to be a fight, you may be glad of my presence, Lady Ayrahylse."

Uxhyn grumbled under his breath, swaying his head back and forth to look at Torryn. "Welcome, brother," he said. "I would not have thought the father of lies would be keen to show his face."

Cocking his head to the side, Torryn didn't look at all flummoxed by Uxhyn's rude statement. "We all have a place, scale-brother."

"You're no scale-brother," Uxhyn replied.

This time Torryn looked stunned by the retort.

"A certain Artrothian warned me about you," Uxhyn continued. "Right before he plucked out my eye."

Torryn's gaze lingered over Uxhyn's injuries. "I'm terribly sorry to hear of your misfortune."

Nahilya returned to Uxhyn's side and touched his foreleg. "We can talk more inside. Come."

Uxhyn's gigantic body shuddered, and moments later, in the place of the black dragon was a middle-aged man with greying hair. The injuries carried over to his human half, who Uxhyn simply called Hyn. Uxhyn was one of the few dragons, apart from herself, that didn't give up his human identity.

All the while Torryn watched them. His gaze never wavered, not even when his wife manifested into her human form beside him. Ayrahylse dragged her fingers along her husband's scaled side. She run her tongue over her teeth, licking her painted pink lips in Pyrah's direction. When she moved, her light blue gown floated after her. Her golden hair was woven into an intricate braided design of the old country, and upon her head was a crown of iron and diamonds.

Swallowing thickly, Pyrah took the crook of Luthur's arm and stared back. She fought to keep a grimace off her face as Ayrahylse stood before her.

"What a quaint crown," Ayrahylse said. "And what a strange necklace, wing-sister. Snapdragons are of the north."

Pyrah's fingers touched the jaw of the snapdragon around her neck. She opened her mouth to reply, but Luthur tugged her to his side. His fingers clutched her waist, and he glowered down at Ayrahylse.

"Pyrah is the beautiful wife of the chieftain of Wymeria. We recognise no queen of the south or the *north*." Luthur's voice took on a low, gravelly tone. He squeezed Pyrah closer, but his eyes did not shift from Ayrahylse. Pyrah suppressed a shiver as Luthur pressed his warm lips to her neck. He could be very protective when the mood took him.

Ayrahylse met Luthur's gaze coolly and turned away from him. "Manifest, husband."

Torryn obediently showed his human form. He was tall, and unlike most of their kind, he kept his parentage secret, but he must have inherited his warm brown skin tone from somewhere. Maybe he was descended from dragons of the more flung off isles of Artroth. He was as handsome as she remembered. Seeing him again after all these years was like a kick in the gut. Torryn's expression faltered in recognition of the piece of jewellery around her neck.

Pyrah felt her heart pause. She had been young and naïve when she left him on the beach among the fishing boats. Torryn had disobeyed her. She was so sure that he would listen to her commands to stay unattached. However, a few short years later, he replaced her with Ayrahylse. Which meant any hope of being together in their dragons' lifetime was all but impossible. Even now, her blood simmered at the thought of his rejection and betrayal. A human life was a short time to wait; Torryn had scorned her the first opportunity he got.

With his knowing gaze on the necklace around her neck, Pyrah found herself wanting his arms around her. She wanted to bask in the warmth and power that only came from a bull dragon's embrace.

"I believe you know my husband, Pyrah?" Ayrahylse asked. Her smile held a hint of a warning.

"I meet many people," Pyrah replied. She tore her eyes away from Torryn as Luthur's fingers dug possessively into her hips. "I can't say I remember him."

"You would remember if you met with a dragon with golden horns." Ayrahylse laughed. It was clear to Pyrah that she knew of their tryst. "Your last letter to Torryn was certainly entertaining."

Eyes widening, Pyrah felt a flash of bitter disappointment and betrayal. Torryn stiffened and looked away. He had never answered her letter that declared her love for him and berated him for his choice of life-mate. Had he been laughing behind her back with his pretty little wife all these years? Was she a mockery in the north?

Torryn nodded politely; his incredible dark eyes drifted to stare at the spot above Luthur's head. "It would be better if I dismiss myself."

Luthur cleared his throat, and Pyrah knew he was going to voice his agreement with Torryn's sentiment.

"Nonsense!" Gahryk said. "You'll provide plenty of entertainment tonight."

Torryn scoffed, crossing his arms against his chest.

"You'll be a distraction for us to blame instead of our own actions," Gahryk continued.

"Wonderful," Torryn muttered. He marched up the stairs, his dark eyes resolutely staring ahead.

Laelyth licked her lips as Torryn passed her. Lowering his head, Gahryk nudged her forward. Her rose gold scales shivered, and before Pyrah was a young woman with long brown hair and deep, soulful eyes. "Torryn isn't the only one who holds surprises."

Gahryk rolled his eyes. He would listen to the discussion through the slatted windows. His human heart had died over a century ago, so he no longer had a mortal form. "We're all trying to survive the best we can in this imperfect world, Laelyth."

"Gahryk, Laelyth, a pleasure, I'm sure," Pyrah said.

Gahryk smirked in her direction. "Destiny is at our fingertips tonight."

Whatever Gahryk might have thought, it did not feel like the evening held any sort of promise of destiny. Hyn spent most of the dinner either sulking or snapping. A stark contrast to the easygoing man Pyrah once knew. His main target for his ire was Torryn, who seemed to take each insult and comment with grace.

But Pyrah knew better. She was watching the vein throbbing in Torryn's neck, waiting for him to lose his temper. During their short and tumultuous affair, she had witnessed his anger on more than a few occasions. She put it down as him being a young, jealous male dragon.

Meanwhile, Elryk's attention was firmly fixed on Nahilya, who was trying to soothe an agitated Hyn with soft, calming words. Pyrah had to wonder how she hadn't noticed the depth of Elryk's fondness of the healer. She knew Elryk ventured into the forest to spend time with Nahilya, usually with a gift of a new fur or dagger. Pyrah was getting an inkling that her brother was more than fond of the recluse.

Laelyth sat at the table, overlooking everything like a well-satisfied empress. She watched imperiously from the sidelines but did not contribute.

Too young, too proud, too vain, Pyrah thought. *Gahryk should have left his little pet at home.*

Gahryk was watching Laelyth through one of the large arched windows, a sly smile on his face. With all the bickering at the table, no one else noticed the all-knowing dragon wasn't participating. It was slightly disconcerting to see little response in his facial expressions. Pyrah shifted in her chair. Surely it was an ominous sign if Gahryk was content to watch and wait.

She had contemplated not inviting Gahryk to her table. Seers were notoriously untrustworthy. He had served the Artrothian Empire for many years and was legendary in her uncle's court.

The moment Gahryk defected, he made it clear that his goal was to be instrumental in destroying the empire. Cold and calculating, he would discard anyone he saw as having little purpose for his objective. This made him dangerous.

Shifting in her chair, she caught Elryk's eye. Her twin raised his eyebrow and grabbed his goblet, then drained it in one gulp. His glance swept over Gahryk, and his lips curled back in a snarl. Elryk had been fond of Aunt Sussette. Clearly, he too was thinking of Gahryk's involvement with her death.

She remembered well the day that the Empress Sussette was dragged into the throne room by Gahryk and dumped at the emperor's feet. Even as the empress lay prostrate in front of the throne, she had requested that the children be dismissed. Pyrah could still hear her aunt's steady tone, clear and confident, reverberating in the audience chamber. She was ready to die for her sins.

Her father grabbed Pyrah about the waist to stop her going to Sussette when Gahryk proclaimed her a traitor. Neither Cilvryn nor Gahryk had pity on the beaten queen. Cilvryn handed a long dagger to his youngest son, Prince Rhodys, and bid him to dispatch his own mother.

"You promised me protection!" Sussette shrieked in horror, and her golden eyes bored into Gahryk. Pyrah felt ill to her stomach and nestled closer to her father. As young as she was, she understood that Sussette believed she was embroiled in a plot against the emperor with Gahryk. Unfortunately, Gahryk sided with the emperor.

"Dry those tears, boy. No son of mine sniffles like a coward. Do your duty."

At his father's command, Rhodys wiped his eyes on his sleeves. He reached forward with trembling fingers to take the blade from the emperor. Unbidden tears slid down his flushed cheeks, and he stumbled forward.

"You cannot do this to my child!" Sussette turned her imploring eyes to her husband. "Please, let me die as a *shakhyr-levly*. Let me die the second death. But please, I beg you, Glorious One, don't do this to our son."

"A strong son does what is required for the good of the realm," Cilvryn replied. The emperor's eyes were cold and unfeeling. "It is time he learned the bitter weight of leadership."

"Please!" Sussette cried. "I implore you, husband. Have mercy on your child."

Caught between his weeping mother and his stoic father, Rhodys halted, staring down at his own reflection in the blade. Rhodys' eldest brother, Xavryn, stepped forward and nudged him.

Sussette lifted her hand to Rhodys in invitation and smiled through her tears. She drew him close to her and then bowed her head forward. "Come, dear one, do what your father asks of you."

Rhodys was frozen in horror.

"Base of the neck, *sudunyn*," Xavryn said with a nod and nudged Rhodys into action.

Years later, Pyrah realised the mercy Sussette's eldest had given her. The blow, even from her youngest, killed her quickly; her suffering was not prolonged. Without blinking, Xavryn took charge and killed his mother's dragon before she could finish manifesting after her human body's death. He left the chamber, leaving bloody footprints in his wake. The next morning, he was banished to the furthest island of the realm for stealing Cilvryn's right to torture Sussette's dragon.

Overnight, Rhodys' spiteful demeanor spiraled into something more sinister than before. His hand in his mother's death irrevocably changed him, morphed him into something that resembled his cruel father. Her father urged her and Elryk to be kind and patient with Rhodys, for their cousin was consumed with self-hatred.

Not long after Sussette's death, Gahryk fled, vowing he would not lay his head down and die until the day the Artrothian Empire was toppled. The whispers at court spoke of how Rhodys and Empress Sussette had been nothing but pawns in Gahryk's plotting.

"The mead is excellent." At the head of the table, Luthur observed everything around him. His fingers flexed around his cup, but his eyes never left those gathered as he drank.

"One last chance," Pyrah said, leaning over to speak in Luthur's ear. She pressed her body a little too close and let her hand linger on his arm. It was best to distract him from his plotting when he drank. "Give me the contract with Artroth to destroy."

Luthur didn't bother to look back at her as he replied, "It's done, wife. Let's take what we can from the situation."

"Very well," Pyrah said, her words clipped. She dug her fingers into his arm. One last warning. "Have it your way."

A self-satisfied smile curled on her husband's lips. He thought he won the argument, when in reality he had sealed his own fate.

Torryn stood, raising his goblet of mead as his chair clattered to the ground. He walked around the table until he was standing before her. Pyrah shivered as his dark eyes bore down into her own. He breathed in deeply, and she could see him attempt to unclench the stiff muscles in his jaw.

"What is it you want, Lord Torryn?"

To answer Pyrah's question, Torryn sculled his drink and placed it before her with a thunk. Offering his hand, he glanced sideways at the mute bards who had been watching the feast and argument with growing concern.

Pyrah openly stared at the empty cup. Torryn was initiating an Artrothian custom. In the emperor's court, the first dance was reserved for non-mates. Depending on what was most beneficial, Artrothians used that time to forge alliances with one another or make threats. By draining his cup and presenting it to her, Torryn was asking her to be his first dance partner.

"A dance, Lady Pyrah, to cool your frazzled nerves?"

Ayrahylse twined her blonde hair around her finger and eyed Hyn. Grinning back, Hyn drained his cup and handed it into Ayrahylse's clawed hands.

Pyrah would have rather poked her eyes out with heated irons than accept Torryn's offer, but Hyn and Ayrahylse were already standing, and she had delayed too long.

Face flushed, Luthur brandished his dagger at Torryn. "What is this insult you bring to my table?"

Torryn calmly regarded Luthur and then Ayrahylse, who was drawing Hyn close.

"Forgive me, Chieftain Luthur. In Artroth, it is customary that the first dance is reserved for non-spouses. It encourages forming friendly bonds between families," Torryn replied.

Pyrah stood, smoothing her black skirts and offering Torryn her hand. His palm was pleasantly warm, much like their kind. Not cold and clammy like a human. Her heart fluttered in her chest as his hand closed over her fingers. "It also has the benefit of keeping enemies close."

The smile on Torryn's face was tight as he led her to the middle of the floor. When she was still a young princess in the court of her uncle, the emperor, Pyrah had learned to not think during the dancing. She numbed her mind to a pleasant fog. The music would flow over her in waves, and in the haze, nothing could touch her.

The bards began to play, and Torryn grasped her waist and drew her closer. The press of him against her ruined her chances of ignoring her racing heart. Under her skin, Torqui stirred, reminding her of how she pined for this man. "If we're to dance in tandem, we need to pretend that we like each other."

Pyrah's lips tightened into a thin white line, and she let her feet follow the steps she had known since she was a girl. "A pity I'm not an actress."

"Still contrary, I see." Torryn's nose crinkled as he fought to hide his chuckles. The dark pools of his eyes shone with amusement. He pulled her closer, and it took everything within her not to push him away.

"Your fear of your cousin is well founded." Torryn's breath was warm on her ear. His fingers gripped her tightly. The casual observer wouldn't notice anything amiss.

"Did you betray me?" Pyrah hissed.

Torryn's fingers tightened their grip around her waist. "A great danger is coming ... Whatever you are planning ... please ..."

"Rhodys warned me about you, Lord Deceiver. As does my heart."

"Who would you rather believe? The man you rejected or the relative that would see you burn?"

Pyrah's gaze lifted to Ayrahylse and Hyn. Torryn's wife was elegant and beautiful. Her eyes shifted to Luther, and Pyrah's stomach clamped with envy. "I trust neither of you."

"Perhaps that is smart," Torryn conceded with a nod of his head. It might have been the light of the hundreds of candles in the room or the mead, but Pyrah noticed the dragon in Torryn's eyes regarding her with open desire. A moment later the emotion was gone, and Torryn's expression returned to cold and cordial. He lowered his voice as he whispered in her ear, "One day soon, you may find yourself in need of help. Remember me, I beg of you."

"If I must stand against Rhodys alone, then I will."

Torryn's steps faltered slightly. "Then you'll lose your children and your life."

"Are you threatening me?"

"A mere observation," Torryn replied. "Consider it a warning."

"A warning?"

"I know you, Pyrah. You're about to tip the scales," Torryn said. "Is open warfare what you want?"

"I'm here to strategise against Artrothian interference."

"Your stubbornness will be your own undoing."

Pyrah pulled away from Torryn, and this time he let her go. She felt a tug of disappointment when he didn't protest. Stalking across the hall, she caught sight of Elryk cuddled up with Nahilya and sniffed in irritation. Hyn caught her eye and raised his goblet in salute. The scarring on his face churned her gut, and she turned away from him.

"Come, wife," Luthur said, grasping at her around her waist. Her husband's strong hands pulled her off her feet and into his arms. On his breath, she could smell the mead that he favoured. His arms snaked round her, pressing her flush against his body. She ran her hands over his chest, savouring his muscular tone. Luthur worked hard to keep in good health after his hunting accident. His lips descended and pressed against hers.

Letting a moan escape, Pyrah parted her lips in invitation, and Luthur deepened the kiss. His calloused hands grasped at her backside, giving them a playful squeeze. There were many things that could be said of Chieftain Luthur, but he was generous in sharing pleasure.

"Maybe I'll put a son in you tonight, wife." Luthur abandoned her lips to press a trail of kisses down her neck and along her collarbone.

If only he were a good man. Then Pyrah would gladly have given him another child that night. But she had other plans.

"Kiss me again, husband," Pyrah growled and nipped Luthur's lip, enticing a chuckle from him. His lips returned to hers to devour her. Very slowly, she lifted her hands to cup his cheeks, and sighing, tightened her grip.

"To bed, wife," Luthur said. "I beg of you."

Pyrah pressed down with her fingernails, scratching the skin on Luthur's cheek. "Later," she whispered. "We wouldn't want to offend our guests."

CHAPTER SIX

Torryn

WYMERIA

Disgusted by Pyrah and Luthur's passionate display, Torryn frowned and turned away. He wasn't fooled by their pretense.

The aroma of roasted meat and vegetables roused the interest of Torryn's dragon. He salivated, eyes lingering on the banquet and all that Wymeria had to offer him. In the days leading up to the summit, he had been unable to hunt or eat.

Determined to find something tasty to satisfy his hunger, Torryn's fingers found the bone handle of his hunting dagger. He plunged it into an untouched roasted river goose. A ripple of satisfaction ran through his dragon.

In the corner he spied two serving girls gossiping in the shadows. They huddled together, whispering and nodding in his direction. He glowered at them as he cut a generous portion of meat. Scandalised by his open stare, the women fled back to the kitchens. He watched them go, chewing slowly and deliberately.

"You look monstrous doing that." Full of judgement, Hyn's voice echoed in Torryn's mind. *"Was it necessary to taunt innocent maids?"*

Torryn licked his lips and cut himself a second helping. Dragonkind favoured succulent meat bursting full of flavour. Pyrah's kitchen staff had done well. The meat was juicy, seasoned with combination of tangy spices. He swallowed thickly, and with a soft moan of pleasure, rammed a third piece in his mouth.

"Are you going to ignore me?"

"The maids were foolish enough to challenge me." Torryn felt his dragon raise his head in irritation. *"You bring me only hurt, scale-brother. I doubt we have anything cordial to say to one another."*

"Stay away from Pyrah," Hyn said. *"I know you want her for yourself, plain as the horns upon your head."*

Once again, Torryn's eyes were drawn against his will to Luthur and Pyrah. The chieftain was a man fueled by jealousy. He had little love for his wife but hated to think that another might show her affection.

"What once lay between me and Pyrah is dead," Torryn said. His teeth tore through another piece of the bird savagely. *"I have a life-mate, and I am happy."*

Luthur might have boasted earlier to him he had control over Pyrah and her dragon, but the man was a fool. No one controlled a dragon. As her husband made humiliating remarks about her over the feast, Pyrah seemed to remain impassive. Torryn had sensed her tightening muscles and her dragon rippling in fury below the surface. The green dragon was plotting. And Torryn feared she was going to take them all down with her.

A good general rule about dragons was that they were dangerous at the best of times.

Now that her safety was no longer guaranteed in Wymeria, Pyrah would look for a way out. It was painfully apparent that Luthur was in favour of allowing Artroth access to his town and his family. Her hatchlings were in danger. A mother dragon would always protect the young over the father. If it came to choosing between Luthur and Pyrah, Torryn knew he would happily rip out the chieftain's throat. Pyrah would only have to ask him.

Luthur's only ally among those at the summit was Elryk. Although he hated the chieftain, he still respected his status. But Elryk was far too preoccupied with Nahilya to rein in his sister if she did something unexpected.

During his time of silent observations, Hyn continued to speak into his mind, but he hadn't taken in a word of what was said.

"You're not happy, Torryn."

Snatching up a goblet full of mead, Torryn made eye contact with Ayrahylse, pointedly ignoring Hyn's glare. His wife stood close to Laelyth, a look of deep contemplation on her face as she listened to what the younger woman was saying. Interest piqued, Torryn raised his cup and took a sip. During their open meeting time, Laelyth had very little to contribute, but now it seemed she had a lot to say.

As he continued to observe them, Laelyth's lips curled into a sly smile. There was something distinctively predatory in the young woman's expression. Ayrahylse touched Laelyth's upper shoulder, and over the music, Torryn heard his wife's tittering laugh. In that moment, their gazes locked. She lifted her fingers and pressed them to her lips to contain her amusement. Laelyth's expression was instantly cold.

"You're not the only liar here ... "

Torryn gulped the rest of his goblet down. Having a large bull dragon spirit within him meant he was blessed with an extraordinary resistance against alcohol. The batch that Luthur proudly poured in his halls tonight was a pleasant mix of sweet with a strong burn.

"Hyn, I think you'll find that under the right circumstances, life makes a liar out of us all."

Having enough of Hyn's nattering conversation, of the gossip and false façades, Torryn turned upon his heel and strode into the cool night air. He'd let Ayrahylse charm the others.

From the top step of the meeting hall, he stared out over the village of Wymeria. It was late. The humans had all retired to their beds. Not one of the house's windows held any light. For a quiet moment, he was grateful. He liked to be alone with his thoughts.

Artroth's actions made very little sense. While he was glad the great emperor himself had not bothered to fly over the country, a winter's dragon was a concern. Especially one as heartless as Rhodys.

His wife had been strangely tight-lipped about what she knew about the high society of Artroth. Ayrahylse had made it clear the emperor expected her to give children into his service so that she might be pardoned.

Her crime was different from the others. Early on in their courting, she confessed that she had been cornered by a young bull dragon one day while training. He antagonized her, pushing her to fight. Unfortunately, her opponent died. Worse, he had connections to the emperor's court, and experienced battle-dragons concluded her victim died as a result of an unprovoked attack.

While the murder of an ordinary dragon was not something noteworthy in Artroth, the slaying of a dragon with connections in the emperor's court was a different matter. Apparently, the parents of the young male were vocal about justice for their slain son. In a panic, Ayrahylse fled Artroth. To the emperor's court, this confirmed her guilt.

If it hadn't been for this severe miscalculation, Ayrahylse would have married a mate worthy of her, and she would not have remained without an heir.

"You'll have a son." Torryn jumped and whirled around. Cloaked in shadow and mystery, Gahryk was watching him closely with his hawklike gaze. "You will have two. One to bless our land and one to betray it."

Torryn looked up into the starry night sky so that he might ignore the all-seeing one. He had a theory that if one looked at Gahryk, he saw more. "The solution is simple. I'll have no son."

Gahryk tutted. "You'll be given very little choice in the matter."

So much for being the all-knowing one, Torryn thought bitterly. The taste of the foul substance that made him impotent still lingered on his tongue. "You don't know who I am or what I've done."

"I didn't say you would have a child of your own body," Gahryk replied. "Indeed, it was foolish for you to consume poison."

"I cannot bear more heartbreak." Torryn's hackles rose.

"Endure it you must." Gahryk nodded sagely. "I see more than you give me credit for, Torryn. And I know you see things as well. The white dragon stirring, rising for the greatness of dragonkind—"

"You're not to harm him," Torryn snapped, surprised by the anger in his own voice. For a dragon he wasn't sure existed, he felt deeply protective of him. Gahryk said nothing, merely tilted his head and smirked. "You're better off making sure Pyrah doesn't do something reckless and doom us all."

Gahryk barked with laughter. He flashed his teeth. In the dark, the all-knowing one's eyes gleamed with the hope of violence. Torryn had heard rumours that Gahryk was once an adviser to Emperor Cilvryn's father and had given up his role to flee. "Torryn, you don't need the Sight to know Pyrah is up to no good. It's already done. This is the beginning of the end. I'm here to watch history unravel."

"And Laelyth, why bring her? She's not your usual type to hold your interest. Do you plan to sell her back to Artroth to save your own scaly hide?"

Gahryk hummed, a strained little smile on his face. "I let her follow me. She has a role to play in all of this, just as Elryk does."

"Elryk? Dragonless? How?"

Gahryk exhaled. "Parlyn was the only Artrothian that saw the great potential of his son. He died hoping that Elryk would have the chance to realise his value."

"Parlyn didn't have the Sight."

"No. But he knew how to look."

Torryn shifted his weight, glaring at Gahryk in the dark. "Why have you come?"

"You have hidden well. Your father—"

"I have no father."

Gahryk smiled. "He has protected you, my friend."

Torryn huffed through his nose. "He hunted me."

"Then how has the emperor's spymaster and general failed to catch you?"

Torryn inhaled, held his breath and slowly released the air from his lungs. "I am clever."

"Clever enough to know he let you go," Gahryk replied. "Clever enough to know the hatchlings are in danger."

"Hatchlings?"

That was the trouble with dragons. The conversation could jump from one topic to the next. Sometimes those with great mental abilities left Torryn dazed and confused. True to his seer nature, Gahryk was speaking in riddles. Torryn wondered if it was a deliberate act or if it was simply his way.

"Yes. Pyrah's nest is under attack."

Gahryk left him there, and staring up into the night's sky, Torryn wished he were drunker than what he was. He meditated, trying to calm his frazzled nerves. Seers rarely spoke to hear their own voices. Gahryk had his reasons for seeking him out. The trouble was deciphering what the old dragon's motives were.

Torryn looked at the silvery disc of the full moon, tempted to shed his human skin and fly off into the night. If he flew off now, Ayrahylse would be angry with him. With his head tilted to the sky, he noticed shadows drifting across the light of the moon. Dread curled in his belly, and he fled inside.

Gahryk had tried to warn him, but he was too focused on himself to notice.

Elryk and Nahilya were in the greatest danger. He needed to get word to them first. He skidded to a halt by the wooden doors where Ayrahylse met him. She took in his distressed expression and raised a delicate eyebrow.

"Artroth is here!" Torryn gasped.

Ayrahylse's face hardened. She lashed out and gripped his bicep painfully, pushing him back outside. "Time to leave."

"We need to warn—"

"No time."

"The hatchlings. The dragonless ones."

"Leave them to their fates," Ayrahylse hissed, tightening her grip. He felt the pulse of her power bleeding into his mind, attempting to give him a sense of urgency. "Think about us for a change."

Angry voices rose from the feasting hall. Torryn couldn't make out the words over the din they were making. He shook her hand from his arm.

"If we are found here, they will brand us traitors."

"MURDER!"

A cold sensation washed over Torryn. The shouting in the feasting hall increased. Who had died?

"Go," Torryn gasped, taking her hands in his own. Ayrahylse's skin was so smooth and delicate under his touch. "There's no redemption for me. I'll stay and help."

Ayrahylse's featherlike touch on his cheek was tender. "Artroth knows. Don't you see, Torryn? The emperor wants to meet you, to let you join his ranks. He wants to learn about your powers. You're our freedom, and if we are found here, it will all be for nought."

At his wife's mention of Artroth, Torryn stiffened. "Impossible."

"Not for me."

"My father ..."

"The emperor will protect you. All Cilvryn asks is for your obedience and our daughters."

Torryn knew the offer seemed too good to be true. "Our daughters?"

"We can keep our male children."

"And if I sire a dragonless one?"

Ayrahylse stepped back, studying him with her bright blue eyes. "*Ketur*, you know the way of the dragon."

A shiver of horror snaked its way up his spine. Indeed, he knew of what happened to the unfortunate sons and daughters who were born in a dragonless state. Grasping his wife's hand, he tugged her from the front door and into the dark village. His heart thudded in his chest. With Ayrahylse in proximity to him, he had a strong urge to protect her. It was the influence of her power.

Letting his gaze roam over her, Torryn knew he had to decide soon whether he could trust his life-mate. The trouble was he had no one to turn to for help. If Artroth was in the skies, it might be too late for him to flee without detection.

Even as he heard the heavy thumps of three Artrothian dragons landing, Torryn dragged his wife behind a hut that looked like it belonged to a blacksmith. He peered around the corner.

"Prince Rhodys," Ayrahylse whispered in his ear. She pointed to the largest dragon.

Rhodys swayed his long neck. He rumbled at his two companions that flanked him on either side before manifesting into his human form. His dark cloak billowed out behind him.

"Remember, we're to cajole our prey into giving themselves over to us," Rhodys said, giving each of his bodyguards a hard stare. "We're here to find Pyrah's hatchlings. The emperor desires to study all progeny to see what potential they might serve."

"I thought Pyrah's daughter had little to offer," one of the guards muttered.

"She's dragonless, but I sensed something under that meek little mask she wore. I wish to tear the child's defenses down and see exactly what type of young Pyrah has birthed," Rhodys said. "It seems when bred with a dragon, *rokun* can produce offspring that have a use we can extract."

Torryn's breathing hitched; his stomach clenched. He had heard from Pyrah of the cruelty of her cousin. How far would he stoop to glean information from a child?

"Let's go," Ayrahylse whispered, her mouth close to his ear. "We can contact Artroth in a few days and tell them what we know."

Torryn shook his head, his fists balling at his sides.

"Torryn, we can trade our knowledge on the matter with Artroth."

"Along with our children ..."

Even with Ayrahylse at his side, Torryn had never felt so alone. He glanced over her dark shadow. She thought he was trapped in her web of seduction, unable to leave her side. The steely glint and anticipation on her face told him everything he needed to know. It was time.

Feeling like a coward, his first step was to remove himself from her power's reach. When he made his move, he needed to be sure that she could not manipulate him. His thoughts and feelings must be his own.

"Go hide in the forest," Torryn said. He licked his lips and pressed his hands against his thighs so that his jittery hands would not betray his true intent. "Artroth won't be pleased to find you here, and it's dangerous to fly. I'll cover your tracks. I'll meet you back at the den."

CHAPTER SEVEN

Pyrah

WYMERIA

Luthur flinched back, his large, calloused hands clasping Pyrah's fingers against the coarse stubble of his cheek. Doing her best not to wrench away from him, Pyrah licked her lips and kissed his face. The scratch wasn't deep, but she was pleased to see the tiny ruby beads of blood on the broken skin.

"Feeling feisty tonight, my dear?"

"It's the drink," Pyrah replied.

"I should find you another." Luthur pulled away, a lascivious smile etched on his face. He paused as he turned. "Looks like your troublesome brother has found a woman who'll have him."

Pyrah swivelled her head around to glare at Elryk, cursing him under her breath. Of all the nights for her standoffish brother to decide he might like some female company. She needed him alert for what would soon transpire. Watching Elryk's hand grasping Nahilya's waist, Pyrah had to bite her tongue. It would have been wise to forewarn Elryk instead of assuming he would watch the proceedings, brooding and silent.

"Come my dear." Forgetting that he was apparently getting her another drink, Luthur returned to her side to pepper kisses down the hallow of her neck. "Don't begrudge your brother a woman's embrace."

Luthur's lips returned to hers. He pressed his body against her, his hands roaming over her back and then down to squeeze her buttocks. Pyrah gasped in protest as Luthur deepened the kiss. She had no choice but to allow her husband's invading tongue in her mouth. Pyrah comforted herself that it wouldn't be long now ...

Luther pulled away with a pained groan. She watched, detached, as his brows knitted together. His eyes fluttered as he swiped his hand across his face.

"Husband, what is wrong?" Pyrah asked. Lifting a hand, she beckoned for a server to come and give Luthur something to drink. A startled boy, no more than fifteen summers, stumbled forward. He had one cup of mead on his tray.

Perfect.

"I'm well, wife," Luthur gasped, his large fingers pressing against his throat. A look of horror swept over his expression.

After plucking the cup from the tray, Pyrah handed it to him. "Nonsense. Here, drink."

Luthur snatched the cup from her hands and sculled the drink. He swallowed, his lungs heaving for more air. Pyrah watched eagerly as he studied the mead. His eyes took on a glassy sheen. He knew.

"Consorting with dragons only brings death." Luthur broke off into rasping coughs. "Your father never gave me a choice."

"I beg your pardon?" The question came out more clipped than Pyrah would have liked. Her stomach cramped. Did Luthur already suspect her?

But Luthur rallied his strength and leered up at her. "I should never have defied him ... your father. He's a murderer ... Ruellea, my first wife, her blood is on his claws." Spittle flew from Luther's mouth; his smile was dangerously ugly.

Pyrah stomped down any sympathy that she had in her heart for Luthur. Her father had simply done what was required. Neither of them wanted the marriage. She was aware that Luthur already had a woman, and she assumed that her husband sent her to another chieftain so that she wouldn't get in the way. He had moped for weeks, often flying into rages. Then he became cold and disinterested.

Luthur's left hand clawed at his throat, leaving a trail of scratches. His bronzed skin turned grey, and Pyrah admired the furious blue tinge appearing around his lips. The whites of his eyes stared at her in horror. His chest heaved under the strain of his panic; his lungs would be burning with the effort to draw breath into his body.

"Husband?" Pyrah asked. She tilted her head to the side, determined to act the politely confused but concerned spouse. She needed to play her part flawlessly for her plan to work. "What's wrong?"

"Poison!" Luthur wheezed, falling to his knees.

Whirling around, Pyrah let her skirts flare out dramatically. It was time to channel a distressed wife.

The servant clutched the tray to his chest, eyes wide and shaking his head in disbelief. He was perfectly positioned for the next part of her plan. Sometimes one had to sacrifice a pawn in order to play the long game.

"Help!" Pyrah cried. She knelt beside her husband and looked around the room tearfully. "Someone, help my husband."

Lifting a shaking finger, Luthur pointed at the servant. "Murderer," he gasped.

Pyrah dropped to her knees and assisted him to lie down. She brushed the hair away from his sweaty face, a parody of a loving wife. His lips trembled. She leaned over his body and looked into his eyes as he fought to remain conscious.

Very delicately, she pressed her lips to his. "You should not have put our daughters in danger," Pyrah whispered, and she kissed him a second time. Maybe she could force tears to fall when Luthur was proclaimed dead.

Luthur's eyes widened. "No ... no ... you ..."

Pyrah rocked back as both Elryk and Nahilya came to the chieftain's side. The healer closed her eyes and summoned her magic. Pyrah could only hope that Luthur was too far gone to be helped. She had not considered that Nahilya would be here tonight.

Elryk's face was pinched as he took in Luthur's state. His eyes swept over to the small scratch on his cheek and then to Pyrah's impassive face.

"Get the girls. Take them to my hut," Elryk said gruffly. "They shouldn't see this."

Translation: *get the girls out of the village. I know what you have done.*

Nahilya was no fool. Pyrah could almost feel the moment the healer called back her gift and looked to Elryk for guidance. Shaking his head, Elryk gave the silent command. *Don't help him.*

"Help me with him, Elryk," Nahilya said. "We'll take him to his chambers, where he can be more comfortable."

"Mine are closer ..." Pyrah interrupted. She needed Luthur's chambers to be empty so she could commence her search for the contract with Artroth.

Again, Nahilya looked to Elryk for confirmation. Pyrah felt a flash of annoyance that the healer would look to her twin instead of her. Sensing her irritation, Elryk glared up at her, his green eyes ablaze. He jerked his head to the door, gesturing that she should go before Luthur's death could be discovered by his loyal men.

"Our friends from Artroth are here." Gahryk's dragon eye peered through the window.

Behind them, Hyn, who had been quiet, cursed and stalked out of the room. "Poison, mark my words."

Pyrah felt a flutter of panic. Artroth could not be here. They would ruin it all before she could find the cursed signed document. She needed to take control of Wymeria so that she could protect her family, and Luthur wasn't dead yet.

"Murderer!" the server cried, pointing his finger at Pyrah.

"How dare you!" Pyrah cried, swiftly standing and wiping her hands on her skirts. "I am the Green Lady ... I am not the one serving drinks."

"*Rshon mahthyt*! Dragon dung, woman!" The servant thrust out his chest in challenge. He scooped up a goblet of mead and sculled it. "The drinks are safe! The chieftain was in trouble before he took the drink from me. How would I have known that you would call me to serve?"

Gahryk chuckled. "That's the problem with dragons. Always underestimating the quick intelligence of humankind. Your doom is knocking at the door. Laelyth is already in Artroth's embrace. Now all that's left to do is to help poor, unfortunate Luthur die while the threads holding dragonkind together unravel."

Elryk looked down into Luthur's pale face. The chieftain was thankfully unconscious. "And what of you, Gahryk?"

"I'm here to simply watch history happen. It's all very fascinating."

"The servants?" Nahilya asked, sweeping her eyes through the gathered minstrels and servers.

"I highly recommend them leaving now and hiding in their homes before Artroth arrives. One does not want to be questioned by an impatient Artrothian." Gahryk's words were all it took for the servants to disperse.

The boy Pyrah accused of poisoning Luthur continued to stare at her. "I want to be questioned by Artroth."

Elryk shook his head. "Go. Do what you must, *sudunah*."

Not sparing her husband a backward glance, Pyrah dashed from the room. She did what she had to. Her slippered feet hit the floorboards with a hollow sound as she ran towards her husband's room. Wrenching the door open, she entered.

Behind her, she could hear raised voices. Her heart hammered in her chest. She had to work quickly. A servant, disturbed by the shouting in the feasting hall, ran past. He must have spotted her; he skidded to a halt.

"Mistress ..."

Pyrah lifted her head to look at his stricken face. She recognised him as Luthur's most loyal servant. "Go quickly. Find your master's children and take them to Elryk's house and hide them there."

The man stared at her with wide, frightened eyes.

"Don't you understand?" Pyrah demanded, her voice cracking. "Artroth is here. If they find my children, their lives are forfeit."

"Mistress, the master said—"

"What would my husband know of the terrors of Artrothian dragons? What do any of you humans understand? Get my children out. *NOW*!"

One last glance at her, and the man turned tail and ran in the opposite direction. She could only hope he was smart enough to hide her daughters quietly. There was no choice. She went back to her search.

When scattering all the parchments on Luthur's desk was fruitless, she turned over every piece of furniture. Then she set her sights upon Luthur's cloaks in his wardrobe and his blanket box. Puffing, Pyrah swallowed down a curse word.

She grabbed a nearby hunting dagger and, frustrated, stabbed at Luthur's mattress over and over again. Feathers and downing fluttered about as she slashed at her husband's bed. There was something cathartic about the act of destroying Luthur's things. No document would stop Artroth taking Wymeria. But her husband's signature gave Rhodys a legitimate claim to her daughters. As it was their chieftain's wish, Luthur's men would hand Charyss and Vallah over without raising questions.

She had given humankind half of her life. No more. No more hiding. No more pretending to be one of them.

Panting, she noticed the shouting from the feasting hall had quieted. She turned back to the mattress; it was a mess. Admitting defeat, she was resolved to take her young and leave. She would start again. Ayrahylse and Torryn had both started from nothing. Maybe they could live like Nahilya, hermits in the woods.

Chuckling, she made her way to the hallway. The shouting had started again. If she were to escape, she needed to keep her wits about her.

"You there!"

Swivelling her head around, Pyrah noticed the man who had spoken was no man at all. Even now, she saw the rippling of scales underneath his cheeks.

Pyrah turned and ran.

If Artroth wanted a fight, a fight they would get.

First, she had to get clear of the building.

She dashed along the hall. Smaller than the Artrothian male, she relied on her speed and agility. The sound of guttural swearing followed her through the halls. Her dragon sense tingled, telling her he was enjoying the chase.

Ignoring everything around her, Pyrah ran, bursting out of one of the side entrances, and stood under the starlight. She shed her human form, relishing the feel of her hard scales covering her reptilian body. She unfurled her emerald wings and took off ...

Needle-sharp pain shot through Torqui's spine, and she crashed down to the earth. The ground shook under her weight. Dazed, she rolled to her side. The Artrothian was quicker than she had given him credit for. Manifested into his battle dragon, he loomed over her. Golden, pitiless eyes studied her with an air of contempt. His scales were such a deep red that he looked black under the moonlight.

"Going somewhere, pretty scales?" The Artrothian flicked his tail.

Torqui turned her head around and lunged at him, aiming for his snout. The dark red male boomed with laughter, as if she were no more than a bothersome hatchling.

She growled, lunging again. Her fangs found purchase on the Artrothian's shoulder, and her foe roared with delight. While she wrestled with the Artrothian, dozens of humans came out of their homes. What dim little creatures! They stood in the dark, their faces in various expressions of disbelief.

"Leave her."

Torqui swallowed a displeased rumble. Looking immensely pleased, standing on the topmost stair of the meeting house, was Rhodys. He sauntered forward, the humans parting before him. Laelyth drifted a few paces behind.

"You'd betray your own kind, scale-sister?" Torqui asked.

Unabashed by Torqui's outrage, Laelyth returned Torqui's glare.

"My father sent my sister-in-law to Ramyr before our vanguard to infiltrate the ranks of refugees, and when the time was right, flush you out," Rhodys replied. His grin widened. "It was the perfect plan. When you sent your little letter, she informed me immediately."

Panting in the dirt, Torqui once more turned her eyes to Laelyth. Dressed in a gown of pink and adorned with bronze jewellery, the young woman did not look like a princess of Artroth. "*Her*? She's a mouse."

"I am Laelyth the Puppeteer. Tonight, you danced to my tune and into Artroth's trap."

Rhodys laughed. "Poor Pyrah. So secure in your own confidence, you couldn't see that the mouse was a serpent."

"She was with Gahryk," Torqui gasped.

"I think you'll find that Gahryk is a law unto himself. He does as he pleases," Rhodys said. Torqui wished she could remove the smug look from her cousin's face. "He is neither for nor against us. Tonight, his actions played into our hands. Tomorrow, they might be in yours."

Sick of hearing her cousin lording over her, Torqui freed herself from the Artrothian guard holding her. She lowered her horns and charged. Rhodys rippled into his dragon form, and they clashed.

Torqui clamped down on Rhodys' neck with her sharp fangs. Wrenching her head around, she shook Rhodys. The coppery taste of dragon blood slid down her throat, and Torqui resisted the urge to gag on the hot liquid.

Rhodys rumbled with laughter, and Torqui remembered that even as a child, her cousin relished pain and injury. Pain amused him, and he welcomed it during a spar. Torqui cursed, withdrawing to lunge at a more vulnerable target to incapacitate Rhodys. A dragon who enjoyed being hurt was difficult to gain mastery over.

Rhodys rarely took any prisoners during a fight. Rather than aim for her flanks or her neck, he took her wing into his jaw and chomped down.

Agony swept through Torqui's body. She roared and instinctively pulled back, tearing her membranes. She roared again. With a flick of his head, Rhodys brought her to heel.

"You!" barked Rhodys' dark red guard, pointing at the blacksmith with his black talons. "Get chains, nails and tent pegs. Quick, or it's your family."

"Don't you dare!" Torqui growled. She lay panting on the ground, helpless before her enemies.

The blacksmith's gaze darted between Torqui and her tormentors. She could see the whites of his eyes and the tremble in his legs.

"We'll hold her down, sire."

Another Artrothian appeared at the top of the steps. Resisting the urge to curse, Torqui knew she should have suspected that Rhodys would have more than one other dragon that escorted him into Wymeria. Torqui would have taken the silhouette, broad-shouldered and tall, to be a man if she had not already heard the voice. The Artrothian woman came closer, moving with a predator-like grace. A long dark braid hung down to the middle of her back, a savage grin twisting her comely face.

"Yirys, take her shoulders and neck," the male on her back said. "I'll hold her rump if necessary."

The Artrothian woman, Yirys, rolled her eyes and manifested into a speckled bronze dragon. Her claws and horns were a pitch black. She made for quite a striking opponent. Yirys carefully stepped over her. She placed each of her front claws on Torqui's shoulder blades and pushed down. The bronze dragon then grasped Torqui's neck in her mouth and lightly squeezed, enough to let Torqui know that struggling was a terrible idea.

Once Torqui was secured, Rhodys turned his back to her. "Izzur, go and gather all the *rokun* and bring them here."

"As my lord commands," Izzur murmured. His hungry gaze left Torqui.

"Why chase us down?" Torqui snarled. "We've lived peacefully here for years."

Rhodys sneered and knelt on the road so that he could look straight into her face. Torqui wriggled under the bronze dragon's grasp. Her cousin was so close. If she could just …

Yirys rumbled and tightened her grip.

Rhodys' lips twitched. "The prevalence of half-breed wretches and empty dragons are weakening the might of Artroth. We must fight against the spread or subdue them before our kind becomes extinct. Whatever may come, the empire must survive."

"So it is true. The empire is falling. That's welcome news."

"*Ri rshon hanoch!*" Rhodys swore. "Careful, cousin. The great Emperor Cilvryn's dragon is weakening. I'll be the next emperor."

"Don't flatter yourself."

Torqui tried to quench the flutter of hope she felt hearing her uncle was unwell. She rejoiced at the thought of his death. Over time, she had come to loathe her uncle and everything he stood for.

Yirys released her neck to speak. "You have plenty of older brothers to stake a claim."

"I am Winter's Dragon!" Rhodys snarled. "I have the birthright via the rule of the greatest power. My brothers will either bow or be destroyed. You are merely a battle dragon of mid rank. Be silent."

"Then prepare for war, my prince." Yirys scoffed, and Torqui felt her shrug. She could only assume that this guard holding her had served Rhodys long enough to have weathered his temper before.

"My brothers have underestimated how hard I'm willing to fight for my people. Under my rule, our kind will have dominion once more. I'm not afraid of war." Exhaling heavily, Rhodys turned and snapped at Izzur. "Get the *rokun*."

As Izzur ambled away, Torqui could hear him mumbling under his breath. Rhodys watched him and then walked away. "Let me know when you're ready."

Through the claws digging into her shoulder, Torqui felt the rumble of Yirys' reply.

Chapter Eight

Elryk

Wymeria

Fighting the urge to scream, Elryk gritted his teeth. His sister had put him in a precarious position. The *vehyl* had a particular way of handling justice. Many of the chieftain's loyal men resented Luthur's dragon-born wife. It didn't take a good imagination to see how Pyrah might be accused of murder. If found guilty, she would not see the dawn. Worse, her daughters would likely share her fate.

Thankfully, Luthur had succumbed to unconsciousness. He would not be able to speak of what happened in the hall. Resting his hands on his knees, Elryk murmured a quick prayer for him. The chieftain's face was flushed and twisted in anguish. Had Pyrah known what suffering she was inflicting on her life-mate?

"Elryk, he's dying," Nahilya whispered at his side.

Luthur was beyond help. This was the only opportunity to intervene and give Pyrah time to escape.

Elryk swallowed and spoke to the servant, whose cries of murder had ceased. "Flee. Trust me, once Rhodys finishes questioning humans, he kills them."

"Elryk ... we have to do something." Nahilya's plea was soft. Her fingers burned as she rested her hand on his elbow.

Elryk turned his face towards the young servant. If he had any sense, he would slit his throat so he could not speak of what he had seen this night. He decided to show mercy; the servant was just an angry boy. "Close the door behind you."

"Letting a man die goes against everything I stand for," Nahilya said.

Waiting for the servant's footsteps to fade, Elryk chanced a look at Nahilya. Over the years, they had built a trust between them. He could see it in her eyes; she didn't understand, but she would do as he asked.

The muscles in Elryk's jaw tightened. He dragged in a deep breath, forcing himself to relax. "I know, Nahilya. I'm sorry, but we're implicated."

"It's wrong."

"I know ..."

Nahilya's eyes widened, looking towards him as heavy footsteps approached.

"Run!" Elryk grasped her hand and ran for the windows. He jimmied the wooden slats open, then grabbed Nahilya by the waist and hoisted her through the opening.

"Elryk ..." Nahilya crouched low over the roof, halting to stare back at him. He had no doubt of her survival. She was both quick and sly. One had to be to live alone in the forest.

"Run!" Elryk commanded.

Cursing Pyrah's lack of foresight, he swung his legs over the ledge to follow. Before he made it through the window, Nahilya jumped from the roof and disappeared into the night. He also crouched low, moving stealthily across the clay tiles. Where the roof was lower to the ground, he leapt and sprinted into the shadows.

He reached the safety of the headhunter's hut and tried to calm his racing heart. Had Pyrah escaped? Where were his nieces?

Nahilya's nimble fingers caught his jacket, and she jerked him forwards, pressing her soft lips to his. Elryk groaned, wanting nothing more than this nightmare to be over so he and Nahilya might be left in peace.

"You should have gone on without me," Elryk said.

"Never ..." Nahilya answered. Despite the danger, her voice was laced with desire. "Marry me and be free of all this."

"I ..." Elryk took her slim hands in his, his brow furrowing. Surely this wasn't the time to have this discussion.

"We could live close by," Nahilya said. "You can keep an eye on your nieces and protect your sister as you promised your father."

His father's parting words rang through Elryk's mind. He owed his twin his life. It was because of his shortcomings they were exiled from Artroth. If it weren't for him, she would have lived a carefree life without Luthur.

Looking down in Nahilya's glimmering eyes so full of hope, he ached. For years he had longed to be with her.

"I'll marry you, Nahilya of the forests. But please, go," Elryk croaked. "I'll catch up. They aren't expecting you here."

"I won't go far." Nahilya cocked her head to the side, the corners of her lips turning down.

She turned to disappear into the furthest edges of the village and into the forest but hesitated.

"I love you, *ketur* ..." Elryk said.

"That's for dragons only," Nahilya whispered.

"I might be empty," Elryk replied. "But I love you as fiercely as any bull dragon might."

Nahilya's eyes clouded over with unshed tears. This wasn't how Elryk wanted his eventual marriage proposal to happen. He had imagined something ... more.

"Go," Elryk said. "Before it's too late."

This time Elryk didn't watch as Nahilya disappeared into the dark. He turned and jogged towards his own hut, careful to remain out of sight. The girls. He couldn't forget his girls. Reaching his home, Elryk could see the doorway was lit by a single candle outlining a silhouette of a man. He bit down on his angry shout and snarled.

"Quiet!" the shadow barked, stepping out of the gloom. Torryn the Deceiver was in his home. Elryk wasn't sure if he was relieved or furious. "Inside, quick. Artroth is here."

"I know. Gahryk warned us in the feasting hall." Elryk shouldered his way past Torryn. Relief washed over him the moment he saw his two nieces huddled together at the hearth. They looked pale but unharmed. Charyss held a second candle in her hands. Torryn followed him and set his candle onto the table, then wearily sat down with a soft grunt.

"Where's Ayrahylse?" Elryk glared suspiciously at Torryn.

"I told her to fly back to our den," Torryn said, staring into the flickering flame of the candle. The inflection in Torryn's tone was evidence that his unwelcome visitor had not told him the full truth.

"Then what are you doing here?" Vallah asked, raising her chin and puffing out her chest. "Go be with your she-dragon."

"Vallah, that's rude." Charyss admonished her sister with a sharp shake of her head

"A good question, I say," Elryk snarled, throwing his twisted huntsmen braids over his shoulder.

"While your lips were locked onto the lovely Nahilya, Gahryk told me the hatchlings were in danger," Torryn answered. "I saw them coming this way in the dark, so I had the human servant with them leave us, and we hid."

"And you thought to use my home?" Elryk replied.

Torryn blinked, his expression showing he was not at all concerned by the accusation. Possibly as one who bartered in lies, he was used to heated conversations.

"Why would I trust you when I know what you did?" Elryk continued.

Torryn cocked his head to the side. "What is it that I have done, Elryk of Wymeria?"

"You brought Artroth back into Ramyr. You betrayed Pyrah and set everything into motion."

Torryn's face fell. In the dim candlelight, he peered at Elryk, his deep brown skin flushed. The blue scales of his dragon rippled across his cheeks. Elryk's words had hit a nerve. "Where did you get such a ridiculous idea?"

"Do you deny it?" Vallah cried out.

Torryn's expression darkened as he turned his head toward the small girl. He stood, his chair clattering to the ground, but Elryk stepped in his way to block him.

"Of course I deny it," Torryn replied. "I have shield-fire. I'm a protector. Why would I bring Artroth to a place where children are? I know what they do to young that show no promise. I know it only too well."

Elryk shifted uneasily. His eyes wandered over to his box of hunting knives. If he could get to them without Torryn suspecting foul play, he might be able to subdue him.

"I'm not who you think I am, Elryk."

Elryk sniffed.

"I came here to help you escape; I've put my own life in jeopardy. Why would I do that if I were for Artroth?"

"Who is to say why Artrothians do anything?" Elryk growled. "Charyss, stay where you are."

Charyss had moved from the safety of the fireside to stand at the window. She flicked her loose hair over her shoulder. Her freckled nose wrinkled in disgust, but otherwise she showed little concern for his words. "Uncle, everyone is leaving their homes. There's a dragon I don't recognise ... He's herding them like sheep."

"Artroth scum," Torryn muttered. "Get away from the window, girl."

Tilting her head to the side, Charyss hummed and stepped away obediently. Her eyes roved over Torryn, from the tips of his boots to his dark curls upon his head. "You have to be the first dragon I've met who's not proud of his Artrothian heritage. Even Mama ..."

"He has dark skin. Are you from the west of Ramyr?"

An uncomfortable expression crossed Torryn's face at Vallah's question. Elryk watched him shift his weight, the movement almost imperceptible to the human eye. His hunter's instincts told him that Pyrah's girls had stumbled upon a truth that they were dangerously close to uncovering.

"It'll not go well for me if Artroth finds me." Torryn cleared his throat. "We need to leave."

"There's a back door, stranger," Vallah said.

"Good," Torryn replied with a nod of his head.

Vallah eagerly jumped up from her place, gesturing for Torryn to follow her. Torryn chewed his bottom lip, looking towards Elryk as if to gauge his reaction.

Elryk exhaled, grabbing a pair of hunting daggers and a spear. He gestured for Torryn and Charyss to follow the youngest member of their group.

"Once you are clear of the village, hide with the hatchlings." Torryn leaned back to speak softly. "Don't wait for me."

Elryk grunted in acknowledgement. He hadn't planned on waiting for Torryn. He had learned to trust his hunter's instincts. Torryn was trouble.

The cool breeze of the evening brushed against Elryk's skin. His fire power moved within his body with each pump of his heart. It was tempting to unleash his gift ... but it was best to leave Wymeria without raising alarm. He glanced over his shoulder, wondering what had happened to Pyrah. His stomach knotted.

"Chieftain Luthur is dead!" someone called out in the dark. "The dragons have the murderer."

Swearing, Elryk pushed past Torryn to place his hands on Vallah's shoulder blades. His niece had stopped in her tracks, her bottom lip trembling. Vallah adored her father.

"What's happened to Papa?"

"It was Mother, wasn't it?" Charyss asked.

"We don't know anything yet," Elryk said. "Keep moving."

"Liar." Charyss' gentle features twisted into a snarl. Her green eyes bore into him. She would not be a girl for much longer. Soon she would be a woman. He could only hope that he was up to protecting her.

"Move," Torryn said, his voice taut. "We can talk when we are safe ..."

"Torryn, halt! Who is it with you? Pyrah's girls ... Charyss and Vallah, go no further. Who is the man?"

Torryn's back stiffened. He had allowed a little distance between Elryk and his nieces. The whites of his eyes were round with fright. "Silence!"

"I can't move!" Vallah cried.

Understanding hit Elryk like a thunderclap. Torryn's cry for silence was a warning. While Pyrah had been unimpressed with Laelyth, Elryk had been concerned. A dragon with an ability to impose their will upon others was dangerous. All it took was one spoken command for them to take complete control. Their power was exerted by speaking the names of those who they wished to force into obedience. Elryk's anonymity was his only defense until he was out of her range.

"Take the girls to Rhodys, Torryn." Laelyth's tone held an amused lilt as she strode forward, swaying her hips. Oh, Pyrah had thought her too young and inexperienced to be a threat. But that was a mistake. Laelyth was a snake.

Torryn's eyes slid towards Elryk, his face stricken with panic.

Elryk ran into the forest as fast as his powerful legs could take him.

"Uncle!" Charyss' cry of despair tore at his heart.

"Elryk!" Laelyth cried out in victory. He felt the insidious tendrils of the female dragon's power against his mind. He gritted his teeth, tilted his chin down, and with a groan, forced himself to plough forwards and out of Laelyth's range. His guts clenched at the sound of Charyss' sobbing, but he turned a deaf ear to her cries. If he were captured, he wouldn't be able to scheme to free anyone.

Soon, sweet niece, he vowed. *Soon I'll have all of us free.*

His fingers tightened around the leather grip of his hunting knife. He was the son of two proud Artrothian dragons, and Luthur's finest hunter. Rhodys would regret the day he made an enemy of Elryk the Empty.

CHAPTER NINE

Pyrah

WYMERIA

Torqui could feel the fierce burning of all the *vehyl's* eyes on her. Luthur hated to be reminded his wife was not entirely human, so it was a rare occasion any of them saw her dragon up close. She had little doubt that they had seen her silhouette from time to time whenever they cast their eyes to the sky. To the people of Wymeria, dragons fighting on their streets would be a terrible sight to behold.

Once she was properly secured, Rhodys approached, his grey eyes sweeping over the lacerations on her wings. "I am forever grateful for my father making me strong."

"He made you a pawn, Rhodys," Torqui said. There was something to be said for the moral victory of watching your tormentor writhe in discomfort. "You were a child who committed matricide."

"My mother was a traitor." Rage flashed in Rhodys' face, and for a brief flicker, she thought she saw pain. Good. He was still suffering, and that was the weak chink in his armour. She felt her lips twitch. Despite being his prisoner, she felt a coil of enjoyment warm her belly. "It was an honour killing. That my father—"

"Made you a murderer," Torqui whispered. The weight holding her down shifted. A blast of warm air caressed her emerald scales, and strong claws dug into her shoulders. The bronze dragon, Yirys, who weighed her down was warning her. She flicked her gaze to Rhodys, but he remained unmoved. Once he commenced her punishment, she knew he would not hold back. "A weak, pathetic—"

"I'm not weak!" Rhodys' jaw tightened, his body quivering as icy-blue scales shimmered under his human flesh. An angry dragon made mistakes.

"Do you still suffer the nightmares?" Torqui asked. When they were children, Rhodys had little control over his outbursts. Now it seemed he had learned a measure of discipline. "The crushing guilt? The pain of knowing you betrayed the only living being capable of showing a worm like you love?"

Fists clenched at his side, Rhodys leered. Here was the cousin she hated, the malice and the cruelty she had come to expect from him. "I'll tear down your nest and make garlands of your children's intestines."

"Is this what you want, cousin, to feel the pain?" Torqui said. She felt a swell of fear, but a dragon in her position could not afford to show they were afraid. "Artrothian rumours say you are mad."

Rhodys leaned forwards, spittle flying from his mouth as he spoke his next words. "Pain makes me stronger, smarter and crueler. When I am emperor—"

"May hordes of Artrothians dance naked over your open grave," Torqui snarled, using an ancient dragon curse. "May the sun rot your scales and your nest wither under the light of the moon."

Yirys stiffened. Many in Artroth believed that the ancient dragon prayers and curses held a significant amount of power.

"I have no nest." Rhodys' gaze flicked towards the bronze she-dragon. He pushed his hair away from his face. "I have no hatchling that carries my name. Now, it was a long flight, so I'm going to partake of your delicious wine over the body of your departed husband."

"Imagine the hate your mother felt for you in her last moments," Torqui growled.

"You're *wrong*," Rhodys said. He turned away from her, shaking his head.

Torqui watched him leave, hating how self-assured he was even when she did her best to pierce his heart. The pain did little to him. "How could anyone love a lizard like you?"

"I am a prince, a royalborn son of the Artrothian Empire." Rhodys paused on the top step and slowly turned his head to look down at her. "I don't require anyone's love or admiration."

He disappeared into the meeting hall, leaving her with his guard.

Torqui hated the thought of Rhodys snooping around her home, touching her things. Thanks to Luthur's carelessness, he already knew of the existence of her children. She could only hope that their humanity made them uninteresting targets. She doubted it.

Rhodys had a gift for finding things to inflict the most amount of pain on his victims. Tonight, Torqui was his to torment.

"Ancient Taloned One, protect Elryk and the children," Torqui whispered.

Yirys' claws pressed her shoulders harder into the ground as Torqui bucked, trying to free herself. Swallowing a lump, she uttered what she could only assume were meaningless pleas. The ancient ones had abandoned her family the moment their father had refused to submit.

A warm, salty tear ran down her scaly face.

"Look, Mama." A small child tugged free of her mother's grip and dashed forward to Torqui's side. Little hands grabbed the hem of her skirt and dabbed away the tear. "The Green Lady is crying."

The pressure of Yirys' weight increased as the bronze dragon lowered her snout to stare at the child with her luminous amber eyes. Nostrils flared to scent the girl while the mother gasped in shock. The woman ran forward. The freckles on her pale face stood out as she reached out a trembling hand to grasp her child.

"Leave the hatchling alone," Torqui said.

"You should keep your child away from dragons." Yirys ignored Torqui writhing under her claws and instead spoke directly to the human mother.

"Apologies, madam dragon," the woman cried, tucking her child behind her back.

"Not all dragons are as placid as me."

"Thank you, lady dragon." The mother retreated, bobbing up and down in a ridiculous show of respect.

Yirys' claws pricked into Torqui's shoulder as she turned her attention back to her prisoner. "Your mother wants you home."

"Damn my mother to the Otherworld," Torqui snarled. Yirys' words cut a wound in her heart. "Damn her, and damn Emperor Cilvryn!"

"You're a royalborn dragon," Yirys replied. "You'll be punished and returned to your uncle's household. Bloodline strength runs through the female line, and we need young."

"I have a husband."

"Had," Yirys interrupted. She chuckled darkly. "But you got rid of that little problem. Izzur is not a bad male dragon. Accept the offer Rhodys will give you tonight."

"I'd rather rot in the Otherworld."

Yirys sighed. "Even I have given the emperor a son for the greatness of Artroth."

"And what of Elryk?"

"He is dragonless," Yirys replied. "You know our customs. We cannot afford the threat of him siring children and polluting the bloodlines."

The thought of her twin brother's corpse lying sprawled on the ground and left to decay brought a sharp pain to her chest. She could imagine his lifeless body, his fiery red hair covering his face, his skin waxy in death. Struggling, she fought against Yirys' hold.

"Here comes the *vehyl* back with the nails." All of Torqui's squirming did not bother Yirys in the slightest. "Take the punishment. Know it will be over soon, and you'll be on your way to Artroth."

Torqui opened her mouth to speak, but at that moment, Rhodys returned. She clinked her jaw shut, resolute not to speak any further words he could use to harm her. His heavy human footfalls descended the stairs. Cruel eyes narrowed in vicious glee as he looked over Torqui's shoulder. "Look, cousin, our special guests."

There was the sound of the *vehyl* parting. Leading the group was Laelyth, who looked immensely pleased with herself. Torqui strained her eyes and caught sight of her children. Both Charyss and Vallah looked to be unharmed.

"Mama!" Vallah cried, her hands reaching out towards Torqui.

Alongside them stood Torryn, his eyes staring straight ahead, his expression one that could only be described as resigned. The muscles along his jawline were taut. A slight tick of a vein was all she needed to tell her he was not happy to be in the Artrothians' presence.

Striding forward, Laelyth twirled her hair around her finger and gazed with malicious delight at Torqui's sad circumstances. She had underestimated the power of sitting back and watching. Laelyth's reserved nature had not been one of disinterest, but of a predator waiting for their prey to make a fatal mistake.

Rhodys stepped up to Torryn, his grey eyes studying the taller man. "I know your secret."

"My mate told me you are aware," Torryn answered. Torqui tilted her head, noticing the way her ex-lover's posture straightened to stand upright.

"What are you doing here in Wymeria, Torryn Lie-Tongue?"

It was a trap. Despite not being too fond of Torryn, Torqui wanted to scream a warning.

"Gahryk told me hatchlings were in danger," Torryn replied. Even to Torqui, his answer sounded sincere.

Rhodys' laughter held a cruel edge. "You have shield-fire. Good. But you are uneducated in the ways of dragons."

The tick in Torryn's cheek indicated he was contemplating the merits of punching Rhodys in the face. During their brief affair, Torqui was witness to him decking a bigger man who was harassing a fisherwoman. He also floored the man's three friends who thought to get revenge.

"Pyrah's daughters have no dragon or power," Rhodys said, addressing the crowd of humans. The *vehyl* shifted; many of them did not care if the children had power or not.

"That's not true!" Vallah bunched her fists at her side. "Charyss has power over plants and healing."

"No!" Torqui yelled.

Vallah's crestfallen face turned towards her. Torqui bit her lip and tasted her own dragon blood. She should have sat down with her girls earlier and spoken to them of the dangers of Artroth. They knew bits and pieces, but she hadn't told them the entire story. She should have expected that Vallah might accidentally reveal information that was better kept secret; she was only a child.

Victory gleamed in Rhodys' eyes. "Is that so, girl?"

Vallah stared back at Rhodys, an expression of horror on her face.

"Look at me," Rhodys demanded, and unable to resist, Charyss faced him. "Is that the truth?"

Charyss remained frozen, blinking and shaking under Rhodys' stare. After a long pause, Rhodys unsheathed a sword. Torqui cried in horror, thinking that he meant to harm her children. But in the next moment, he thrust the blade through the membranes on her wing. She bucked against Yirys' weight and bellowed.

"Mother!" Charyss cried in horror and promptly burst into tears. Her daughter tried to go to her, but her feet remained fixed on the spot she was standing.

"I ask you again, pretty little Charyss, is what your sister says true?"

Charyss' lips wobbled.

"Shall I carve up your brave little sister's face?" Torqui would not have put that past Rhodys.

"No!" Charyss cried. "Don't hurt Vallah or Mother! It's true."

"Ah," Rhodys said. "The emperor could do with some new *vehyl* pets."

"*Pets?*" Vallah screwed up her nose. At any other time, Torqui might have found her daughter's sass amusing. Now it was frightening. "Father says dragons are flying vermin, riddled with disease."

Charyss hushed her sister with a harsh jab of her elbow into her ribs. "Mother's a dragon."

"Rhoddie ..." Even as she choked out the word, Torqui knew she could not expect any familial loyalty from her cousin.

Rhodys blinked, his head tilting to the side to stare at her girls. He looked perplexed by their antics. He frowned. The youngest prized son of the emperor by a good dozen years, Rhodys had always been serious. "Quiet, children! Tell me about the supposed *vehyl* magic that makes manifesting in Wymeria difficult."

At Rhodys' question, Vallah's dark eyes went to Torqui, seeking reassurance. It was clear to all around that she was confused. Torqui internally swore, remembering the lie she had fed Rhodys when he first arrived in Wymeria.

"How about you, Charyss?"

Under Rhodys' weighty stare, Charyss dried her eyes on the sleeve of her gown. Intelligence glimmered in her daughter's expression. Although she hadn't told either of the girls about Rhodys' last visit, she could see that Charyss suspected what Rhodys was referring to.

"Lord dragon," Charyss said meekly, twisting her hands in front of her. Her stance spoke of how uncomfortable and scared she was. "I'm not old enough to learn human magics. The old medicine woman lives deep in the forest. It's dark, powerful magic that holds a dragon."

Torqui was immensely pleased with her daughter's bold lie.

"Can you take me to her?" The greed on Rhodys' face was unmistakable.

Charyss looked down at her sister and then at Rhodys, her lips twisting down into a distressed frown. "She moves about the forest. If word of dragons has reached her ear, she would have moved on. We won't see her in weeks. It's the human way."

"We don't have weeks," the dark red dragon, Izzur, said. He emerged from the darkness, his eyes glaring around at the assembled humans.

Rhodys exhaled and turned towards Laelyth, who was still smiling at him with a sultry pout on her face. "Command Torryn back to his nest. I'll visit him shortly."

"Torryn, go home," Laelyth commanded.

Torryn swallowed, his eyes gazing over her two girls as if it pained him to leave them behind, even if it wasn't done voluntarily. His body shuddered as he was forced to manifest into his dragon. He cocked his head as if in apology in Torqui's direction, his golden horns winking under the starlight.

"What a magnificent bull dragon you are," Rhodys drawled sardonically.

Powerful blue wings unfurled, and as the *vehyl* surrounding Torqui screamed, he was airborne. In a matter of seconds, he disappeared. Torqui wondered how strong Laelyth's compulsion was and how far Torryn had to fly to free himself. She desperately needed an ally, but she hoped that he would not turn around for her. Torqui didn't want to examine the reason why.

"Pyrah's allies have scattered," Izzur grumbled.

"Never mind," Laelyth replied. "Gahryk is uninterested in conflict, Uxhyn is a gentle giant with no thirst for blood, and we'll catch up with Ayrahylse and Torryn."

"What about Elryk?" Izzur asked.

Rhodys licked his lips. "Elryk cannot help himself. He'll not be far. Now, dear cousin, let's get this unpleasantness over with."

Torqui closed her eyes and willed Elryk to stay hidden wherever he was.

The cold points of large tent pegs were pressed to the edges of her wings. She gritted her teeth and lay still. The pegs weren't there to keep her down. They were there for further punishment. Struggling against the pegs would tear her wings further. She had to stay still of her own volition and take whatever Rhodys had for her or risk losing her ability to fly.

A downed dragon was a dead dragon. Torqui would rather die a horrible death than live without the ability to fly.

She gritted her teeth against her anguished screams as the village blacksmith hammered the pegs through her wings. With each metallic clink of the mallet, a fresh wave of hot, searing pain shot through her body. The temptation to tear free was overwhelming.

Her daughters cried; Torqui spared them a quick glance. Vallah huddled close to her older sister's side, while Charyss had to be held back. Charyss' limbs were shaking, and she looked pale and ill. Her dark braid, entwined with her precious herbs, had come loose. Tears streaked down her face, her expression ferocious as she clawed at the hands of Izzur, who had taken charge over her. To Torqui, she had never seemed so wild, so beautiful in her own delicate way.

"It's okay, little ones," Torqui said, wishing that she might nuzzle her girls and curl her warm, scaly body around them to protect them from all harm. "All will be well."

Yirys removed her body weight from Torqui's back. "My lord," Yirys said. "If the children are to be gifted to your father, might I take them to our encampment?"

Laelyth rolled her eyes, staring at the bronze dragon. "You are hopelessly weak, Yirys."

Yirys snorted, then stretched out her wings and snapped her teeth.

Charyss stilled, her eyes glaring defiantly up at the bronze dragon. Her fingers curled around Vallah's. "I'll not let you hurt my sister."

"Enough!" Rhodys waved an imperious hand at Yirys. "Take the humans if you feel the desire to nest. I need you back on patrol tomorrow morning."

Torqui wasn't blinded by her pain. Yirys was trying to show her a kindness. No dragon mother wanted their young to see them in pain, punished and humiliated. Her mouth felt dry. If the bronze dragon was allowed to show her this scrap of compassion, her children would be removed from her. It would make rescuing them more difficult for Elryk.

Very carefully, Yirys reached out and grasped her children around their middles. Torqui froze at their desperate cries for help, wishing she had the power to save them.

"Be warned, Yirys. If we lose either of the human pets, your own child will be forfeit."

"I won't disappoint." With a graceful dip of her head, Yirys was gone.

Torqui wanted to scream and cry to the heavens. There wasn't time to contemplate the fate of her children. The first stab of a spear hit her side. She ground her teeth and took the pain as they stabbed her over her wings and body. By the tenth wounding, she was openly whimpering.

She tried to meditate through the pain. She could feel each heartbeat and the warmth of her power wishing to break free. Thick, black blood coated her wings. Her head felt foggy, and her limbs shook under the strain of staying as still as possible.

After what seemed like an eternity, the punishment abruptly stopped.

She felt the cool hand of Laelyth on her scaled shoulder and felt her scales shimmer as she was forced to return to her human body. Delirious with pain, Pyrah had no chance to fight off the human form of Izzur grasping her thin wrists in his grip and binding them. He forced her to her feet and dragged her to the pole where Luthur liked to tether his favourite mare.

"Behold the murderer!" Rhodys cried.

Pyrah could hear the disgruntled murmurs of the humans around her. They weren't satisfied with her punishment and humiliation. They wanted blood.

"She will be taken to Artroth to stand before our emperor. Now to bed with all of you. This wretch will be left tied like an animal here tonight."

Pyrah listened to her own breathing as the human crowd parted. Leaning her head against the pole, she wept.

Rhodys' footsteps approached, and he looked down at her pathetic form. "I have the document your husband has signed. Wymeria and your children are mine."

"Rhodys, please." Pyrah swallowed her pride. She'd give up all her power, live out all her days as a worm if only to spare her daughters. "Let my children go. They're nothing to you."

"I cannot." Rhodys' voice was soft. Was that a hint of regret in his tone? His next words were hard, judgement dripping with each syllable. "They have the blood of a dragon. You should never have mated with a human. Izzur is your new bond-mate."

"Yirys told me this was an offer," Pyrah gasped through the pain.

"It's not an offer." Rhodys was unsmiling as he turned away from her. Laelyth followed in his wake, leaving Pyrah alone with Izzur. "It's your only chance of survival."

"I'm not asking, Princess," Izzur said. "You're mine. You'll learn to obey."

"I am Latunya's daughter," Pyrah said.

Izzur grunted and fumbled with a water canteen at his side. He pressed it to Pyrah's chapped lips. "Are you with your late husband's child?"

Pyrah shook her head, and Izzur pushed the canteen harder against her mouth, forcing her to drink against her will.

"Good."

"Do you want this?" Pyrah asked.

"I'm a good soldier. I do as the emperor commands," Izzur replied.

Shifting her weight, Pyrah turned to stare up into Izzur's face. "Then you are the one in slavery."

Overhead, the air rumbled. Purple bolts of lightning streaked across the sky as the clouds opened to a heavy downpour. Under normal circumstances, Pyrah would not have minded the rain. She would have welcomed the drops of water running down her skin. This was Rhodys' doing. His way of further driving the point home that she was his prisoner.

"Looks like you didn't need the water after all." Unimpressed, Izzur grunted, twisting the cap back on his canteen. "I look forward to meeting our sons and daughters. You gave Luthur two strong-willed human whelps. Do you think I missed it? Your eldest girl, she outright lied to Prince Rhodys."

Pyrah never thought she could feel fear like she did in that moment. There was no telling what Rhodys might do if he discovered her daughter's untruth. Rhodys wasn't known for mercy. Even though she was of the royal Artrothian bloodline, her daughters' lives meant very little to Rhodys. They were only human, after all.

"Please." The word tumbled from Pyrah's lips. She wasn't one to beg. But in this moment, bound, beaten and on her knees, there was no choice. Izzur held her daughters' fate in his hands. "Please. Don't say anything."

Izzur brought his face dangerously close to Pyrah. "Give me Elryk, and I'll consider keeping my silence."

"I can't do that ..." Pyrah shook her head, her wet hair sticking to her face.

Izzur cocked his head to the side. She knew her reply hadn't surprised him in the slightest. With no further words, he turned on his heel and walked up the stairs into the meeting hall.

"Izzur! Don't be a fool. Once I am free, you'll pay for Rhodys' sins in blood. We can negotiate."

Izzur paused halfway up the stairs. "You were the one who fled Artroth as a traitor. The time for negotiating is over, Pyrah. Your allies have abandoned you, and you've lost."

Alone in the silence, Pyrah slumped against her ropes and breathed in through her nose. To stay a prisoner of Artroth would mean death. Escaping and finding Elryk was the only way to rescue her daughters. Elryk would know what to do. He was nearby; she could feel it in her bones. He was out in this wretched weather and waiting for the moment to strike.

When the time was right, he would come.

He had to come ...

Chapter Ten

Pyrah

Wymeria

Blood from Pyrah's wounds mingled with the rain of Rhodys' storm. She shivered, her body aching as the cold light of dawn swiftly approached. With every whisper of the breeze, her traitorous body shook. Soaking wet, she had been left kneeling in thick, oozing mud.

She fought to stay conscious through the long hours of the night. Terrified that if she slumbered, she would miss a signal from Elryk, she embraced her agony. Angry thoughts and pain kept her company and alert.

"Elryk, please, I need you." Pyrah licked her dry lips, tasting the salt of her tears.

"Hold on," her dragon whispered. *"He's your twin. The half that makes you whole ... he is coming ... he is coming ..."*

Pyrah's head lolled to the side. She let her thoughts wander back to last night, mulling over the details to keep her mind active. Concentrating on the least traumatic moment of the previous evening, Pyrah recalled the sweet taste of the water Izzur had forced upon her. Although it had been many years, she recognised the taste of home. When dragons travelled great distances, they took extra water from Artroth. They believed the waters of their homeland were a blessing. Artrothian legends stated that a taste of water from Artroth brought renewal, strength and healing. For it was from water that all life was sustained.

Pyrah cursed again. Izzur had blessed her with strength. Offering Artrothian water was an ancient way of announcing a dragon marriage. Even though she was bound, she had drunk from Izzur's hand, which meant she had accepted him as her new life-mate. The simple ceremony would be enough to make them husband and wife. Whether the large male warrior had done so as an act of kindness or domination, she did not know. She could only assume the latter.

"Would this bring you joy, lady mother, to see your daughter treated like this?" Pyrah whispered to the greying light. She curled her aching legs under her body to try to stave off her exhaustion. It was only a matter of time before fatigue and pain won.

"Your lady mother has a love of violence." Heavy footsteps sounded behind her.

Pyrah cringed, knowing even as she craned her neck, it was Izzur behind her.

"They say she licked her lips in delight as she drove a blade through Parlyn's heart."

"I guess I'm more like my mother. I've murdered a husband. You ought to be careful." Pyrah's eyes fluttered closed as she leaned against her bound wrists, taking some weight off her stiff knees and thighs.

"You're more like your father." The footsteps came closer.

Pyrah lifted her head haughtily to stare into the fathomless depths of Izzur's eyes. She pursed her lips and looked away, letting him think that like her father, she was defeated. He couldn't keep her imprisoned forever, and once she was free ...

"He was strong," Izzur said. His fingers caressed the handle of his sword. "He didn't beg for mercy."

Pyrah blinked back her tears, wondering how her parents had been driven to such madness. It was sheer folly for Parlyn to hope that Elryk might escape. She couldn't imagine her mother ramming a blade through her father's chest. But this she knew: Izzur was speaking truly. Parlyn would have met his demise with stoicism and honour.

"You are much like him, Pyrah," Izzur said. He circled her, his fingers twitching as if he wanted to reach out and touch her. "Just as proud and dignified. But I wonder, are you willing to lay down your life for your brother?"

"You know I am," Pyrah rasped, swallowing past the stinging lump in her throat.

"Tell me, my sweet, are you hungry? Thirsty?"

"I ask nothing of you," Pyrah replied.

"Ah." Izzur reached down, cupping her chin gently with his gloved hand. "You took the water of Artroth from my hand. You're my wife."

"Luthur—"

"Dead," Izzur interrupted. "How did you do it?"

Pyrah flexed her fingers, looking with sadness at her painted nails. "I betrayed him with a kiss."

Izzur ignored the movement of her hands and studied her lips. She knew traces of her cosmetic paints were still on her skin. He knelt beside her, tore the lace edging from her skirt and wet it with another canteen of water. Grasping her chin, he wrenched her neck so that she was looking into his face. He scrubbed her lips and cheeks and around her eyes.

"Am I safe from you, wife?"

"Yes." Pyrah forced herself to sound meek.

"Good." Izzur grunted, stretching as he cut her wrists free. "Time to go inside and rest."

Pyrah stood, letting her movements seem hesitant and slow. She bowed her head, letting Izzur believe that the strength had been beaten out of her. Two large fingers tucked under her chin, forcing her to look into her new husband's face.

"Do you think I'll forget what you have done to me?"

Izzur chuckled, his free arm tugging her close to him. Pyrah forced herself to be still as his lips lowered.

"Show me the dragoness," Izzur purred, his warm breath ghosting over her neck as he placed a kiss there. "Show me the fires of Artroth. Show me the strength of the royal line."

Pyrah lifted her hand as he nibbled and kissed her collarbone. She rested it on his chest, tilting her head back to bare her neck to him. Izzur hummed in delight.

Digging her nails into Izzur's muscular chest, Pyrah hoped that she was breaking skin.

Izzur grunted, pulling back, an amused smile splitting his handsome face. It did not fool Pyrah. He was dangerous, and if he realised what she had done, her life would be forfeit.

"Rest first," Izzur said. "Then you'll be escorted to Artroth."

Pyrah nodded, allowing herself to be dragged inside. It was quiet in Luthur's halls. Thankfully, Laelyth and Rhodys were nowhere to be seen. Izzur led her past Luthur's rooms and to her own. He opened the door, and Pyrah stepped in.

Everything was as she had left it. Rhodys hadn't bothered to search her rooms.

When it became apparent that Izzur intended to stand outside her door, Pyrah stopped him with a simple touch of her hand. The great lump was blocking her escape route. If he was to collapse outside her door, she would have a conundrum. He needed to die in her rooms.

"We must come to an understanding," Pyrah said. She widened her eyes a little and blinked. The oaf probably thought she wanted to join forces with him to grant herself some semblance of safety.

Izzur cocked his head to the side. He took the bait and stepped into her room. "Your life has been spared. You obey me and your emperor."

"The emperor wants the young, doesn't he?" Gritting her teeth, she stepped closer into the Artrothian's personal space, pressing her body against his.

"Rest first," Izzur grunted. She could see him swallowing thickly. His dark eyes would not meet hers. "We can worry about consummation at a more appropriate time."

"What exactly did you offer my uncle?" Pyrah reached out, running one hand down the plane of Izzur's hard chest. "Am I destined to lose all my children?"

"I have been told that the first three of our offspring will belong to the emperor's service."

"*Three*?" Pyrah cried.

Something caught Izzur's eye, and he wandered across her room to pluck up one of Charyss' flower crowns. "Your eldest's handiwork, I presume. She's stronger than she lets others see. Obey me, and I may be able to find a way to convince Rhodys to spare your daughters. Under my wings they have a chance to live out their days."

Pyrah forced down hope that Izzur might be able to protect her children. He didn't know the enmity between her and Rhodys. Besides, the poison was already in his system. "Where has Rhodys taken them?"

"Somewhere safe," Izzur said. "We already have a human fort under our control."

"Where?"

"I wouldn't worry, my sweet. Your uncle has become frail. When he's ..." His fingers loosened, and the flower crown dropped uselessly to the floor.

"Rhodys will be emperor."

"He's the strongest son," Izzur said. "The most powerful inherits. When Rhodys takes power, he promised me that any children I sire with you will remain in our care. All I have to do is back his claim and fight for him."

"Do you believe him?"

"I don't have any reason not to." Izzur's brow furrowed. He sat heavily on the edge of Pyrah's bed, rubbing his temples.

"Are you in pain?" Pyrah asked. She couldn't help but let a smile touch her lips as she observed him struggling. "Shall I call for help?"

Izzur began coughing, wheezing and fighting for breath. Pyrah knew the moment realisation hit. He glared up at her, his eyes burning in fury. "You wretch."

It wouldn't be long now. Izzur's body was shutting down, and he didn't have the strength or the power to fight her or call for help. She turned her back on him, stripping from her ruined dress. She cared not for the male dragon's gaze upon her naked body. She searched for a linen shirt, leather leggings, boots and a short overcoat, uncaring of the Artrothian's plight.

"I would fly free," Pyrah said. Izzur's glassy eyes watched her. She could tell this was the first time in his life that he felt like prey. She was the predator. "I told you I was more like my mother."

"I will find you, Pyrah," Izzur gasped. He laughed, his chest compressing with exertion as he did so. "And you will pay."

"The poison was in the nail paints," Pyrah said. She stood over him and watched as her new husband slipped into unconsciousness.

Although the poison in his bloodstream would be diluted with the blood and the rain, Izzur would never open his human eyes again. It would take some time before he breathed his last sigh ... but she had to move quickly. Once his human heart perished, his dragon would be free. He would manifest, and he would be angry.

Pyrah whirled around, snatching up a leather pouch of gold she kept for special occasions. She also grabbed a bone comb, as vain as that might be, and a hidden dagger she kept in her room.

Without glancing at the expiring Izzur, Pyrah carefully opened her door and peered out into the hallway. It was early still. Rhodys was notorious when he was younger for enjoying sleeping the morning away. As powerful as dragons were, they could also be lazy beasts if not probably tamed by their human half.

Creeping through her own home like a criminal seemed truly bizarre, but she moved with as much haste as she dared. Soon enough, she reached the top of the stairs. The sun was rising. She had little time to make her way through the village unseen.

Fleeing down the stairs, Pyrah ran towards Elryk's hut, hoping to catch sight of him. She was worried that she had no hint of his whereabouts. If Rhodys had captured him, he would have let the whole village know. Rhodys couldn't help himself. Had she been mistaken about Elryk? Had he abandoned her too?

Pyrah burst through Elryk's front door. It was still dark inside, everything left the way it should be. The bed hadn't been slept in; the fire pit was cold. There was no sign of him anywhere. Impatiently, Pyrah tossed a few items to the side. She grabbed Elryk's favourite spear, dried fruits, salted meats and some fresh buns that Charyss must have made for him the day before. She stuffed the food and coins inside one of Elryk's hunting packs that had been left by the door.

Sensing the tendrils of panic setting in, Pyrah grabbed an empty canteen and a thicker cloak before leaving the hut through the back door.

Elryk's cheeky birds squawked at her as she went to stride past. Feeling sorry for them, she paused and opened their cages. Elryk had few friends in the village. Like her, he was an outcast, and she doubted he was friendly enough with the other hunters for them to take care of his animals. Wherever he was now, Elryk would not want his precious birds starving to death in their own cages.

Pyrah stepped foot into the cool of the forest. Not once did she look back to Wymeria or whisper a goodbye. She knew in her heart of hearts she would never be returning.

It was well past midday when Pyrah stopped for a rest. She had not heard Izzur's bellow of rage as his dragon emerged. She had heard rumours that when the human heart died, the dragon might manifest stunned, almost docile. She wasn't sure if death by poison was peaceful enough for such a phenomenon to take place.

Pyrah nestled down beside a tree, drawing her legs close to her body. Every fiber of her being ached. Now that the immediate danger had passed, her ability to ignore her body's injuries was impossible.

She closed her eyes for a moment, tilting her head back. "May the sun warm my scales ..." She drifted off before she finished reciting the dragon's prayer.

It was a rough hand on her shoulder that made Pyrah's eyes spring open. She jolted upright, terrified that Izzur had already found her. Her hand darted to her dagger, and an ugly snarl left her lips.

"Calm down!" A woman with a devilish smile and dark braids was leaning in so close to her face that their noses were touching.

"Nahilya!"

The healer laughed, prodding Pyrah's side. "You were snoring like a snapdragon."

"I most certainly was not." Her hand came to rest around her neck, fingers brushing over the rough texture of the snapdragon necklace. "How did you find me?"

A deep, booming laugh caught Pyrah's attention. Hyn's good eye watched her from the safety of the path. Pyrah's lips parted with a wordless cry of relief. Elryk stood further away, scowling down at her.

"Nix," Elryk said. He frowned at her, eyes raking over her battered body. A blue bird clung to his thick leather gauntlets with sharp talons. The creature flapped his wings, swinging upside down as he merrily cackled.

"Let's have a look at those wounds." Nahilya sidled closer, and Pyrah could feel the warmth of the other woman's power wash over her. She exhaled, feeling relief as her body knit itself back together.

Pyrah lifted her head. "Where have you been, Elryk?"

"More to the point, *sudunah*," Elryk replied, his teeth clenched, "what have you done?"

"Luthur was a problem, so I removed the obstacle."

Elryk crossed his arms against his chest. Nix squawked in protest and nipped him.

"He would have given my girls in marriage," Pyrah protested.

"Your husband did something stupid, so you killed him? In the *middle* of a summit?" Hyn asked. "Murder isn't a common way to make friends."

"You used to trust me," Elryk grumbled. A look of hurt crossed his face. "I'd protect those girls to the bitter end."

"What have *you* been doing?" Pyrah asked. "I was expecting to see you sooner."

Elryk shifted, rubbing his arms. "I was there when the girls and Torryn were taken. I knew I had to hide and formulate a plan."

"He found me in the forest," Nahilya said. She stood as her power finished the healing process.

"I also lay in wait," Hyn rumbled. "When we saw the female dragon take off with your children ..."

"Elryk decided it was best we follow to find out where they were being taken." Nahilya wandered a little way towards the stream to wash her hands. Something was wrong. If they knew where the girls were, why hadn't Elryk rescued them? Why had they come back for her?

Pyrah was sure she looked a sight. She could feel the dirt and sweat clinging to her skin. She jutted out her chin defiantly. "Excellent. Let's get my children."

She went to barge past the others, but Elryk's hand shot out to grab her. "Pyrah ..."

Damn his soft voice, speaking to her as if she were some animal that needed his gentle coaxing. She'd had enough of being treated like a dumb beast, tethered and subservient.

"What is it you have failed to tell me, brother of mine?"

"Chieftain Rygard, what do you know of him?" Hyn asked.

"He's one of Luthur's fiercest rivals," Pyrah answered. "A proud man with a substantial stone fort."

Pyrah had been envious of Rygard's fortress of stone. The village of Avhyl was the pride of southern Ramyr. From there, Rygard's family had ruled for generations. Years of accumulated wealth and soldiers gave the chieftain of Avhyl power over the south.

"He has sided with Rhodys," Elryk said. "They've the girls imprisoned behind stone walls."

"If he doesn't already, Rhodys will have a sizeable force of battle dragons with him." Hyn's good eye peered at her as if gauging her reaction. "Whatever Artroth is planning, they're serious about destroying what little we free dragons have."

"Were you seen?" Pyrah felt her temper fraying. Inside, her dragon was raging.

Hyn sniffed in indignation. "I am the greatest tracker in Ramyr. I wasn't seen by any Artrothian lizard."

Pyrah dug the toes of her boots into the dirt. "What do we do now?"

"Can't stay here." Nahilya sighed.

"They know where I live," Hyn said. He reached up, pointing at his missing eye. "I would hate to lose the other one and live forever in the dark."

"The Green Isle," Elryk suggested. "It's uninhabited. I've smuggled supplies into a cave system for the day we needed to flee. They'll be looking on the mainland for us."

Pyrah's shoulders drooped. "They'll be looking with greater urgency. I killed my second husband this morning."

Hyn barked with laughter, slapping his thigh. "Would've loved to have seen the bastard's face when he realised ..."

Pyrah looked down at her hands held loosely at her side. There was some small part of her that regretted her murderous actions. Both Luthur and Izzur died terrible deaths. She told herself that they deserved it.

Luthur was controlling and stupid in his greed. And Izzur? Izzur was loyal to Rhodys and the emperor. She flicked her gaze over to Elryk. If Elryk had a dragon, she knew she would be at the emperor's side, happily serving him as a princess, a dragon of royal blood.

In some unholy twist of fate, Elryk's emptiness had saved and doomed them.

"We'll be spotted in the air," Pyrah said. She stamped down her feelings of guilt deep within her soul so she wouldn't be forced to examine her flawed arguments.

"Not if we fly west and high. We can loop around," Hyn said. "Trust me."

Where Hyn had been, a large black bull dragon now stood. Uxhyn had changed, no longer a meek shield-fire. Pyrah knew he would fight to the death. He extended his claw and offered it to Nahilya and Elryk. "It's time to make plans for war."

Chapter Eleven

Rhodys

Wymeria

The art of meditation never failed to soothe Rhodys' inner chaos. As a child, his tutors showed him the beauty of a relaxed mind after he had done the duty of dispatching his traitor mother. As the future emperor, he needed to be stronger than his brothers and sisters. He was grateful for the harshness of his father. An emperor must demonstrate a willingness to make sacrifices for the good of Artroth. Executing his mother was evidence of this commitment to his people. Mercy and pity were weaknesses that could be exploited.

Yet tonight, meditation was difficult. He had left his weeping cousin on her knees in the mud while he returned to her feasting hall. Chieftain Luthur's carved wooden chair was in a prime position to enjoy the food and drink. With Pyrah's screams still fresh in his ears, Rhodys carefully studied the grandeur of what humankind had offered his cousin. It was woefully disappointing. How had Pyrah survived living like a cat among scampering rats?

Rhodys inhaled, closing his eyes. He held his breath and then slowly exhaled. His fingers danced along the naked blade on his lap. He breathed in ... and out ... and in ... His fingers halted on the cold steel. Why had he kept this prize, the blade that he used to butcher his lady mother? Surely his inability to rid himself of the dagger was a sign that he wanted to snatch back time. He wanted to hold his mother again ... to hear her laugh and tell him stories of the great dragons of old.

That dream had died when she turned her back on Artroth. On *him*. To this day he could not understand why she would commit treason. It still hurt. And Pyrah had seen it, had known he was tormented by his mother's last words.

"I love you, Rhoddie." He still heard her voice whispering to him in the hushed quiet. He both longed for her and loathed her.

"No! Go away, Mother. Haunt me no more." Rhodys groaned, slamming his fist on the table. The silver platters and goblets clattered with the impact.

Rhodys closed his heart to all thoughts of his gentle mother. Finding himself staring into the air, he took his dagger and carved a portion of what seemed to be a game bird. He dragged a plate closer, stomach rumbling with hunger. Eagerly, he added a portion of meat to his plate. He considered the aromatic stuffing, which seemed to be a combination of crushed nuts, lemons and lime, and gave himself a generous helping. He tore off a hunk of bread and poured a glass of wine.

"I thank you for your hospitality," Rhodys said, lifting the goblet up to salute Luthur's corpse. He drank deeply, savouring the tart bitterness of the wine. It had since gone warm, but warmth never bothered Rhodys. Pouring a second drink, he glanced back at the dead human. Luthur's skin now had a waxy pallor. His face was twisted in agony. Rhodys ran his tongue along his lips, letting himself feel the disappointment that he hadn't been able to slay the man himself. It was something else Pyrah had taken from him.

"You underestimated the might of dragons, Chieftain," Rhodys told the dead man. "Pyrah should have put a blade in your back before you put a babe in her belly."

It was a travesty that a human married a dragon. Worse was the resulting pollution of the bloodlines. Pyrah should have known better. The moment he saw the dark-haired slip of a girl, he knew it was his cousin's child. He felt little pleasure in knowing that his aunt, Latunya, would not be pleased in hearing she had human granddaughters.

Furthermore, his father, the great emperor, would be very angry with Pyrah for daring to birth not one but two vermin. Once she was returned to Artroth, Pyrah could not expect to see her mother or be allowed to raise any future children she had with Izzur. A fitting torment for a traitor of Artroth.

Dragonkind was slowly dying, and here she was raising two more miserable little mice. The line of dragons was sacred. If the bloodlines did not remain pure, their people would be doomed. Dragonkind could not afford to be weak.

Artrothian history clearly taught that when dragonkind was weak, humankind rose up against them. Humans had strong beliefs that the gifting, power and dominion of dragons belonged to them. They did not care for the future generations. When the humans came, the hatchlings died first.

Those too young to have reached their first manifestation during adolescence were the perfect murder victims for a mob of self-righteous humans. Greedy, self-serving rats. The lot of them.

Rhodys would burn his soul before he allowed any human to take a measure of control in Artroth. This was what Pyrah and her kind were doing. By allowing other pockets of a new population, they weakened Artroth's armour. Only united under the banner of the emperor could their people hope to endure for the millennia to come.

Artroth's downfall, of course, had been predicted many times. But seeing the future was notoriously difficult, and Rhodys hoped to avert the tragedy by uniting his people.

Rhodys poured himself another drink and eyed the door. He had sent Yirys with Pyrah's little rats to Rygard's fort to the east for safeguarding. To his remaining escort, Izzur, he had gifted Pyrah. He didn't expect Izzur to still be with her. Izzur liked a good fight, and Pyrah was a fighter ...

Rhodys let himself doze. Once his father had given the order to fly to Ramyr, he set off, not waiting for a larger escort. He flew against the wind, determined that the victory would be his and not one of his brothers. Father's dragon was ill with a strange malady. Once he died, Rhodys knew he was the one who would ascend the throne. As the son born with the most power, a winter's dragon, he knew his place. However, he still needed to prove himself to the citizens of Artroth. He was much younger than his brothers ... They had experience on him.

He needed to plan what to do with his siblings once he was emperor. How many of them would willingly bow to him? And how many of them would choose to die? The easiest course of action was to slaughter them all.

Rhodys closed his eyes, slipping back into a meditative state ...

Only to be rudely disturbed by a roar of fury. Fingers gripping on the chieftain's chair, Rhodys inhaled slowly, his nostrils flaring as he gritted his teeth. His mind groggily caught up with the events of last night. He must have slept. The light coming through the slatted windows suggested it was mid-morning.

Another roar punctured the air, and Rhodys barked back a sardonic laugh. It was the sound of an angry bull dragon. The only other dragon in Wymeria was Izzur. Pyrah must have done something naughty.

"What has Pyrah done?" Rhodys sent through his mental mind link with Izzur.

Izzur's irritation was palpable through the link. He could feel the rage bubbling in the other male dragon's blood. *"She killed my human heart!"*

Rhodys blinked, not quite sure whether he should curse or laugh at his companion's ill fortune. He had expected Pyrah to try something. As a child, she had always been mischievous and far too clever for her own good.

"Pyrah! She killed me! She escaped, and I am stuck."

Curses came to Rhodys' lips, and he jumped to his feet. He moved through the meeting hall, noticing that the humans had wisely abandoned the building. The ruckus Izzur made ensured that finding him was not difficult.

Rhodys paused outside the door of what he assumed were Pyrah's personal rooms. Izzur's face was pressed against the door frame. Killed within a confined space, his dragon did not have the room to move about freely. Seeing his faithful escort caught in such a predicament, Rhodys couldn't help but laugh.

Izzur rumbled and slammed his face against the door.

"You should have been more careful," Rhodys said. As miserable as Izzur was, Rhodys couldn't summon sympathy. "You should have suspected she was capable of violence."

Forgetting who he was talking to, Izzur growled again, saliva dripping from his fangs and his eyes rolling back. Rhodys decided to forgive the gaffe this time around. The dark red dragon was the closest he had to a friend, and he had been told that sudden deaths could greatly addle the mind of a dragon once they manifested from human flesh for the last time. It would take time for Izzur to accept that his humanity had been slain.

"What was she doing inside?" Rhodys crossed his arms against his chest and tapped his foot.

Izzur attempted to turn, only managing a few inches. "Fool that I am, I thought that she could do with a rest before we forced her to fly to Artroth."

"Ah, women ..." Rhodys remarked. "You do something kind, and they bite your hand."

"Didn't think you had a kind bone in your body," Izzur replied.

"Give me a moment to get clear of the building," Rhodys said, shaking his head. "Then demolish the building if you must."

Rhodys could hear Izzur swearing and cursing as he strode from the building. He had done a quick sweep of Pyrah's home the previous night and decided that the humans had nothing worthy for him to take.

He continued down the stairs, lifting his face to the golden sun. The storm he conjured had since passed over, and the warmth of the sun had dried up the evidence of his power.

He briefly thought to send a torrential downpour to join with the heat of the day but thought better of it. His power was depleted by the might he had already displayed.

Like the meeting house, the village seemed deserted. He could still sense humans hiding behind locked doors. Pathetic, really. A locked door had never stopped him from taking what he wanted.

He didn't need to tell Izzur he was clear of the building. Izzur's keen dragon hearing was waiting for the moment he could demolish Pyrah's room. The groaning of timbers was all the warning the citizens of Wymeria had before the dragon burst free.

Izzur lumbered out of his cage, scattering splinters of wood in his wake. A pair of woman's smallclothes swung from his horns.

"We should join Yirys at Rygard's fort," Izzur rumbled.

But Rhodys had sensed others' presence on the wind. He let the breeze wrap around him, telling him of an angry Artrothian general and a great lady looking for him. He strode out to stand in the middle of the road so that he was easily visible from the sky. The escort he left in Artroth had finally caught up with him.

"General Rivyr," Izzur rumbled unnecessarily as a large dragon with deep burgundy scales burst into the view. Rhodys grinned at Izzur's troubled expression. Rivyr, he knew, would have a few choice words to say to Izzur and his current predicament.

Beside his father's favourite general was his aunt, a frightening dragon of lilac scales. Latunya had gained a reputation for being merciless since she took part in the torture and execution of her husband.

Behind them flew a company of dragons. Scales of multi-coloured hues glimmered in the midday sun. Fresh dragons to join his venture was a welcome sight.

Rhodys glanced at Izzur, who had finally discovered the smallclothes on his horns and was shaking his head back and forth to dislodge them. He was unsuccessful. Pursing his lips, Rhodys did not offer to help and returned his gaze to the incoming dragons.

The moment his claws hit the ground, General Rivyr prowled forward. "You were supposed to wait for a proper escort, Prince."

Rhodys lifted his chin, ignoring the hot anger in his gut. Allowing the general to vex him would only give the older dragon proof that he needed to be managed. To put the general back into his place, Rhodys needed to be cold and calm. Once his father was dead, Rivyr would need to follow his commands. "This is my expedition. You're here to serve me."

"I'm a veteran with many years of experience, Your Highness." Rivyr did not sound impressed. His eyes caught sight of Izzur and his horn decoration, and he frowned. "One would think you would gladly listen to advice I could give you."

Rhodys growled from the back of his throat, watching as the other dragons landed where they could. Many circled to find a place outside of the village. Rivyr had brought more numbers into Ramyr than he had anticipated.

"I was hoping Commander Hael would come," Rhodys grumbled.

"My brother's place is beside the emperor," Rivyr said, his judgemental gaze still on Izzur and the smallclothes.

Latunya landed beside Rivyr, and she returned to her human form. She brushed back her dark hair, casting a critical glance about the meagre village. She strode forward, her heavy purple robes swishing against her ankles. Then she glared at Izzur, her lips curling in disgust.

"Must you display your soldiering depravity?"

Izzur tried to shake the smallclothes from his horns again. He lifted a claw to tear them from their perch, dipping his head. Golden eyes that simmered with anger stared unblinkingly at Latunya. Two columns of grey smoke curled from his flared nostrils. Izzur was known for his hot blood and had fought his way up the ranks from nothing. He was a proud dragon and had little patience for Latunya's clear dislike of the 'common' battle-dragons. "This was not how I expected my wedding night to go. I apologise, my lady, for the fragrant display of my wife's smallclothes."

Latunya was not impressed. She ignored Izzur and turned to Rhodys. "I suppose you gave him my daughter against my advice."

Rhodys inclined his head.

"Bring her to me." Latunya's demand was the moment Rhodys had been dreading.

"She escaped," Izzur ground out.

"Escaped?" Latunya raised an eyebrow. She had been against giving Pyrah to Izzur, claiming he wasn't bull dragon enough to claim her wayward daughter. Rhodys glanced at his guard, thinking that his aunt had been eerily right in her prediction. "How?"

"Seems she dosed me with a slow acting poison and ran ..." Izzur grumbled. "It took quite some time for my human heart to perish and raise the alarm."

"You're telling me she's had several hours to run." Rivyr frowned. The tone of his voice lowered to a dangerous purr. "This wouldn't have happened if you had a proper escort. Where's Yirys?"

"We have Pyrah's daughters," Rhodys said, thankful he had some good news to tell the general. "She's taken them to a safe location."

"And Laelyth?" Rhodys hated that the general was looking at him as if he had personally failed.

"She left sometime around midnight," Izzur said.

"You fool!" Rhodys spluttered. "Why didn't you stop her?"

Izzur's scaly lips parted, and he snarled at the latest rebuke. "She's the wife of Xavryn, a royal dragon. I don't have the lineage to command her to do anything. Besides, she's pregnant."

Rhodys groaned. He did not need his older brother siring an heir during this time. If Laelyth were still in Ramyr, he could do something about the inconvenience.

"And Elryk?" Latunya asked. "Please tell me you were able to slit his throat and any spawn he may—"

"He has no children," Rhodys assured her.

"Where is he?" Rivyr demanded.

"It seems he wasn't in Wymeria when we arrived," Izzur said, sending Rhodys a sidelong glance. Rhodys wordlessly agreed with Izzur. Sometimes it paid to be creative with the truth. "There's been no sign of him."

Latunya drummed her fingers along the side of her leg. "So both of my children, the reason we are here in this dragon-forsaken country, have evaded capture?"

Rhodys bit his lip to stop himself from saying anything unflattering to his aunt. She might have been a wife and mother to traitors, but she was still highly favoured by his father. After his mother died, Latunya became a fierce advocate for the family.

"What is it you suggest, Aunt?"

"Burn the village to the ground," Latunya said. "Kill the humans. Make an example of Wymeria."

A slow smile curved on Rhodys' face. Yes, a burning human village was the perfect thing to cheer him up.

CHAPTER TWELVE

Pyrah

THE GREEN ISLE

Boots discarded on the sand, Pyrah stood on the shoreline. In times of trouble, she came to the sea. This was the first time that communing with the waters did not soothe her soul. She stared at the far horizon, her toes resting in the soft foam of the water. After they had landed on the Green Isle, Hyn had pointed out the direction her daughters had been taken. She stood vigil on the shore, feeding her fury and fear.

As an Artrothian mother, it was her duty to protect her young. Her heart throbbed in her chest. The consequence of her failure could very well cost her daughters' lives. She had never been so far away from her children.

"This place is beautiful."

Pyrah huffed, hoping that if she failed to acknowledge the healer, Nahilya might leave her alone to wallow in her morose thoughts.

"When I was young, I wished that I might harness the power and beauty of the sun."

Pyrah lifted her face, basking in the last of the golden rays of the sun as it slowly dipped from view. Soon the moon and the stars would replace the fiery disc, and the world would be shrouded in darkness.

Dropping to a crouch, Pyrah dipped her fingers into the coolness of the water. A flick of her hand, and from the depths, a figure was created. It stood taller than any natural formed man, so she had to tilt her head back to stare into the sightless, watery eyes.

"Rhodys, you bastard," Pyrah snarled, and with a curt gesture, the watery statue sprayed into thousands of tiny droplets.

Having power over water was both useful and dangerous. But sometimes Pyrah wished for something more. Nahilya might want the power to harness the sun, but she desired to reach into her enemies' chest cavities and make their hearts burst. In the darkest part of her imagination, she twisted and tore Rhodys' vital organs so that her cousin might die screaming.

Pyrah turned to stomp up the beach, disregarding the healer's presence. Nahilya obviously wanted to bond. This wasn't a time for maidenly gossip.

"Impressive," Nahilya said, following her. Pyrah had to give her credit. The healer did not even as much as splutter as she destroyed water Rhodys. Nahilya lifted her arm and whistled. There was a flutter of wings overhead, and Elryk's proud bird perched on her arm. "You should save your feminine rage for the battlefield."

Pyrah paused to glare at Nahilya, whose expression was one of casual acceptance. She fished out a nut and offered it to Nix. The bird pressed his impressive hooked beak to the soft skin of Nahilya's cheek before clicking his tongue at her in a parody of a kiss. He cocked his head inquisitively to the side before reaching out to take the treat. His target acquired, Nix spread his wings, squawking as he flew into the cover of the trees.

"What do you want?" Pyrah asked.

Stepping forward, Nahilya drew herself closer so that she was no more than an arm's width away. "A fight is coming. I want you to know I stand with you."

"And Elryk."

"Yes, and Elryk," Nahilya confirmed with a nod of her head. She dipped and picked up Pyrah's boots, thrusting them into her hands. "But we are not talking about your brother right now. You need my skills; I'll stay by your side. I swear it."

"You have no idea what this feels like," Pyrah spat. Torqui's irritation and anger snaked up her spine.

"You're right," Nahilya agreed. "But as a healer, I have witnessed grief many times."

"I'm not grieving."

Nahilya simply hummed and took the crook of Pyrah's elbow. "Come, Hyn and Elryk have set up the cave. I've fished and gathered some food. Tonight, we should feast and plot."

Guilt twisted in Pyrah's belly. While her brother and Hyn had swept out the cave and Nahilya had foraged for food, she had spent hours standing on the beach imagining the multitude of painful ways she might kill Rhodys. It was deeply satisfying but not helpful. She let Nahilya drag her from the beach and into the shade.

"Hyn believes that standing alone on the beach might not be the wisest place to be," Nahilya said.

Pyrah nodded her head.

"Goodness, does the healer ever stop talking?" Torqui grumbled in her mind.

"He's worried that if Rhodys sends out patrols, you'll be spotted. I told him to leave you alone."

"I won't stand out in the open," Pyrah promised, her shoulders slumping. Hyn's concerns were valid. She had not been cunning.

"If it brings you comfort—"

"I can be with the river waters," Pyrah replied. She shrugged. "It's not the same, but I can still commune with it."

When they reached the cave, Elryk stared up at them. Concern was obvious in his steady green eyes. He was kneeling by a pot that had been among his treasures. Pyrah wished he had told her about his secret cave.

"Let me," Pyrah said. She gestured sharply, and the water began to bubble.

"I could have lit the fire myself," Elryk muttered. He opened his fist, and flames ignited from his outstretched palm.

"This way is quicker," Pyrah quipped.

"And safer." Nahilya took Elryk's hand in hers, leaned forward and blew out the flames. Pyrah spotted the small shiver that curled up her brother's spine at the feel of Nahilya's breath on his skin. She knew from experience that if Elryk didn't want his flames to be extinguished, it couldn't be done by simply blowing them out.

Leaning back on his heels, Elryk smiled up at her. It was forced. He might have forgiven her for killing Luthur in a careless manner, but he was anxious for her daughters.

Hyn sat hunched over on a felled log, descaling a fish. Suppressing a shudder at his scarred face, Pyrah moved further into the camp. Hyn's broad shoulders drooped further, his frame looking too big for the space he was occupying. He touched his slim knife blade to his cheek. "We're not going to get lucky next time Rhodys catches us."

"He did this to you?" Pyrah asked.

"Aye," Hyn muttered, returning to his fish. "I made the mistake of thinking it was possible the sprite could be reasoned with. Stupid to think he might take after his mother."

Elryk snorted humourlessly. "Now we're scar twins courtesy of Prince Rhodys."

Hyn didn't look up, but one corner of his lips quirked. "Better my eye than my life."

Returning his gaze back to his bubbling pot, Elryk began shucking shellfish that he had collected for their dinner. His fingers moved with deft efficiency.

"How did you get this collection of goods on the island?" Pyrah asked, gesturing uselessly to the cave and the odds and ends, which ranged from cooking pots, blankets, clothing and weapons.

"A boat," Elryk said simply, throwing a handful of sea creatures into the boiling water.

"You hate the ocean."

"I'm fine as long as I don't get too close to it."

"It's quite a comfy hideaway," Nahilya said. She rummaged around in Elryk's assortment of knives until she found one to her liking.

The Green Isle was the home to large orange fruit with long, soft spines. They were full of tangy juices that were bursting with flavour. Someone had gathered a basketful, and Pyrah felt a twinge of guilt that she had been of little help setting up camp. She exhaled. It was time to change that. Sitting beside Nahilya, she began to peel and slice the island fruits, imagining Rhodys' death over and over as she worked.

Sleep eluded Pyrah. She lay on her back, staring up at the roof of the cave. Where were her children now? Try as she might, she couldn't find the right words to whisper a prayer for their safety.

The deep rumble of Hyn's snores contrasted to the soft sighs of Nahilya as she slumbered peacefully in Elryk's arms. Feeling an ache of jealousy, she turned over and reprimanded herself. Elryk deserved to have some happiness in his life even if she was miserable.

Peering at her brother's relaxed face as he slept, she knew that Elryk was besotted with Nahilya. She had watched them both closely during their dinner. They had the easy relationship of a couple that had been together for some time. This was yet another thing that her twin felt he had to keep from her.

"You should sleep, Pyrah." Elryk's eyes opened a sliver. Pyrah wasn't surprised her scrutiny had roused her brother. They had shared a womb, and Elryk was keenly attuned to her thoughts and feelings. He knew her better than she knew herself.

"I can't sleep," Pyrah replied. Her voice caught, and suddenly, breathing was difficult. "Not when I know Rhodys is alive and has my children."

A dangerous gleam lit Elryk's eyes. Even in the dimness of the cave, Pyrah could imagine the great dragon her brother could have been. She envisaged him as a large bull dragon with scales of crimson and horns of silver. It seemed unfair that he, the better of the twins, should be denied his sacred birthright.

Pyrah choked back a sob and heard Elryk sigh as he rolled to his feet. She felt his strong arms pull her into his warm chest as he lay down beside her. She buried her nose into his shirt, fighting to control the tumultuous feelings ravishing her gut. It had been years since she took comfort from her brother like this.

"We'll get them back, I promise." Elryk's arms tightened around her.

Pyrah huffed, swallowing the need to scream her fury to the skies.

"I mean it, sister. I'll fight till the bitter end."

"I know," Pyrah said. Her fingers dug into Elryk's shirt. She couldn't imagine living life without her twin at her side. "That's what scares me."

A distant rumble interrupted their conversation. Thunderstorms along the coast of Ramyr were not rare, but something in the still, warm air sent a shiver of dread up Pyrah's spine. She lifted her head to listen to the Wind Song. Elryk did the same, although he could not hear it as well as her.

"That's not a natural storm," Elryk whispered. Pyrah could feel his heart thumping in excitement.

Both Hyn and Nahilya stirred.

"Rhodys is the Dragon of Winter Storms," Hyn grumbled.

"Why would he bother?" Nahilya asked. Her voice was slurred as she rubbed at her sleep-addled eyes. "It seems like a massive use of power."

"It is," Pyrah said. She sat and unwound Elryk's muscled arms around her middle. "It takes a great deal of power to hold and manipulate a storm."

Overhead thunder crashed, and the cave lit up with the flash of violet lightning.

"But why?"

"A show of strength," Elryk said.

"It'll also make tracking his movements harder." Hyn seemed amused. "I *like* a challenge."

"It will frighten the *vehyl* into submission. Such a show of force will tell them they are powerless against him." Pyrah knew she was right. It sounded like something a spoiled Artrothian prince would do.

Rain started to fall in great torrents. Pyrah closed her eyes. Her power hummed, and she could feel the seas being swept into a violent rage.

"We should still try to sleep," Elryk muttered. He lowered his voice and spoke in her ear. "Are you well recovered, *sudunah*?"

Pyrah nodded, and Elryk returned to Nahilya's side. She lay her head back down on the rocky floor and closed her eyes. Hours passed, and she could feel the drumming of the storm, a consistent barrage of Rhodys' power. Outside, the wind curled about, buffeting and tearing at the trees.

She listened, straining her ears to hear what the Ramyr wind had to say about Rhodys controlling her. She spoke of the sinking ships and the distressed call of a small *vehyl*. He was lost in the storm. Power flowed through him like an unstoppable river. He struggled beneath the waves, and the seabed trembled until he rested on a new patch of land in the middle of the ocean. He was cold and shivering ... having no strength to create a shelter from the rock with his power.

"Go to him," the wind whispered. *"Great Dragon Mother, go to the lost* vehyl.*"*

Pyrah rolled to her feet. As the lightning forked across the sky, she saw Hyn's stern face, his eyes watching her. She wondered what he sensed from the Wind Song.

"I must go."

"Pyrah ... you can't possibly go out in this weather." Bless him, Elryk was always the more sensible of the pair of them.

"I must."

Pyrah didn't allow for further argument. She stumbled to the cave entrance and manifested into her dragon. Unbothered by the stinging pricks of rain, she leapt into the storm. Wind Song called, and she would answer. Someone was out there. Knowledge that this stranger was going to change her life sent shockwaves of anticipation along her spine.

CHAPTER THIRTEEN

Torryn

THE STRONGHOLD

Shame washed over Torryn with every beat of his wings. Laelyth's command lost its power over him within a few short miles of Wymeria. The moment he felt the spell falter, he battled with conflicting emotions. There was a part of him that desperately wanted to return to Pyrah, but fear held him back. He was only one vulnerable, untrained dragon.

Torryn felt bile filling his mouth. Rhodys knew he was uneducated in the ways of dragons. For him to know this with certainty, someone had told him Torryn's secrets. And the only other dragon who knew his true origins was Ayrahylse. So he continued to fly until he could see the familiar sight of his mountain home.

His chest felt tight. Running was his only option if he wanted to survive the Artrothian invasion. Pyrah and the others could think the worst of him. They made it quite clear he didn't belong among them. They had abandoned him first.

"Why did you take me as a life-mate?" Torryn roared to the sky. When he first met Ayrahylse, he adored her. He would have given her anything. Why was it that with all her intimate knowledge of him, she refused to empathise with his fear of the enemy? Why betray him to Artroth? "It's over ..."

The tightness in Torryn's chest loosened a little. Breathing came easier as he accepted his days with Ayrahylse were done. She had made it clear that she would side with Artroth. Like many of dragonkind, his wife lusted over the power and prestige that the empire could give her. Siding with Artroth was not compatible with his survival. And he knew she would hand him over if it meant a little more power.

Torryn flew low over the lake and soared through his mountains. He would continue to his swamps. The humidity and the smell would stop Ayrahylse from venturing into those lands. A hunt was what he needed to clear his head, fill his belly and allow him to plan his next move.

Snapdragons were strange wingless monsters, with their dull, scaled hides and elongated snouts. They were full of proteins. One snapdragon could sustain him for a week.

Flying over the swamps, he saw a dozen of the creatures sun baking on the banks, their bellies pressed to the mud and mouths wide open. He circled their territory, determined to select the largest snapdragon he could carry off.

Dipping his wing, he flew lower, looking for a perfect target. It wasn't long before he spotted two gigantic males gliding under the sludge of the swamp. He took the time to observe them both and decided on the older of the pair. The hide of the creature was torn from a recent fight, and a bloody stump was all that remained of its front left leg.

He barrelled downwards, swooping towards the unsuspecting snapdragon. The impact of his dive broke the middle of the unfortunate creature's back with a resounding crack. In the next heartbeat, he was shooting upwards out of range of the second snapdragon, who had surged out of the water to bite his tail. Snapdragons had the nasty habit of launching their long reptilian bodies from the water to ensnare prey. With his tasty meal clutched in his front claws, Torryn laughed at the futility of his prey's threatening hisses as it lay limp in his claws.

Landing nearby, Torryn placed his prey on the ground and pierced its skull with one of his sharp talons. The creature stilled, and he considered his prize. His kill was aged and had lost a recent battle. In addition to his missing leg, the snapdragon had two festering wounds along its belly.

"Are you going to share your treat with an old woman?"

Torryn started, lifting up his snout to see that Jilearah had hobbled into the clearing. He couldn't be entirely sure how she survived in the swamps without becoming a snapdragon meal, but he had come to the conclusion it was some type of human magic. His nostrils flared, and he returned to his human form.

Jilearah might be an odd character, but she proved to be a good companion in times of loneliness. He would of course share with her, but only her.

"Why did you choose the mutilated prey when you could have had something better to fill your stomach?" Jilearah came closer, prodding his kill with her walking stick.

"He was injured and would die anyway," Torryn answered. He knelt by his prize, withdrawing his hunting blade, and sliced off portions of meat. "Killing the healthy one would be a waste."

"I know how much you like to please your mate, the self-proclaimed queen. She does not eat damaged prey."

"It's over," Torryn replied. "I am not returning home. I no longer have to worry about finding undamaged prey to please my life-mate."

"Over, you say?" Jilearah asked. "Good. About time you shook that parasite off. Been trying for years to get you to see reason. What sparked your decision?"

Torryn laid his blade down on his kill. He glanced up at the old woman, who grinned toothily back at him. "Artroth is coming. She'll choose them."

"Well, dear boy," Jilearah said, hobbling closer, "Artroth can't have you."

"I'm only part Artrothian," Torryn confessed. "My mother was a human who had an affair with one of them. Unfortunately, I was born with powers ..."

"Who's to say it was unfortunate?"

"Artroth now knows that I live," Torryn said. "I'll be hunted."

"It won't be that way forever."

Torryn sighed, running his hand along the tough hide of his kill.

"You are the spark; your son the flame."

Torryn snorted. Jilearah fancied herself a seer.

"After your last visit and your determination to ensure no child would sprout from your body, I looked into your future. I see a child. Many centuries from now. A small boy, his dragon trying to manifest. He's chained to Artroth, but you'll break those chains so he might break them for others. Under your gentle talons, his dragon will manifest for you. He will be flame and fury. A noble father to a nation. Upon his brow will sit a sovereignty that Artroth will lust after."

"A pretty dream."

Jilearah laughed at his unbelief. "Gahryk set events into motion to ensure you will have this son."

Torryn snarled at the mention of Gahryk's name. "You know of Gahryk?"

"It's unimportant." Jilearah waved away Torryn's agitation. "Do you know the difference between a hero and a villain, I wonder?"

"I highly suspect you are going to tell me," Torryn bit out.

"A hero understands self-sacrifice and will give up everything of themselves until they are ashes on the wind. They would burn for what they believe in. Villains believe they are the heroes. But when tribulation closes in, they reveal their true scales. They fight for themselves and for their desires. They'll sacrifice nothing. But all stories, all great stories, those that are worth telling, need someone like Gahryk. A visionary."

"A visionary?"

"A visionary does not lose sight of the greater good. Neither a hero's passion nor a villain's desires will get in their way."

Torryn scoffed.

"It's true, my dear. Laelyth will be the grandmother of the biggest threat Ramyr will ever face. She's also the great-grandmother of Ramyr's greatest hero." Jilearah chuckled. "She is both the doom bringer and the hope giver this land will need. By returning Laelyth to Artroth, Gahryk is ensuring the existence of the hero this country will need in its darkest hour."

Torryn remained unimpressed. "So we in the here and now will suffer in the hopes of something in the uncertain future."

"A little pain for Pyrah, the Green Lady, and it will be enough for her to begin a new race of dragon. The dragons of Ramyr are about to rise up. And you will help her." Jilearah lifted a bony finger and thrust it in Torryn's direction.

Torryn lowered his gaze, his shoulders slumping. "You speak of such grand schemes. The situation is hopeless."

"It's only hopeless when the hero gives up." Jilearah grasped a generous helping of snapdragon meat. "Spend a few days in the wild, and whatever you do, do not go to the lake. If I can spare you some pain, Great Father, I will."

It wasn't unusual for Torryn to spend a few days out in the wild hunting. He knew that if Ayrahylse were truly with Artroth, she would soon raise the alarm that he failed to come home. As much as he wanted to avoid the inevitability, it was time to leave his territory and never return.

In a moment of weakness and desperation, his mother had revealed his existence to his dragon father. Torryn had been condemned to spend the rest of his life running and hiding. He was only eight summers old when his mother's ship docked in Artroth. She sent word that she wanted to speak with his father.

Growing up on an all-female pirate ship, Torryn knew he was rapidly approaching the age where his mother would leave him ashore. As her family didn't want anything to do with him, Torryn knew that if his father would not have him, he would be abandoned.

Nothing prepared him for the excitement of seeing dragons flying overhead. Torryn stared up at the sky, craning his neck so that he nearly fell backwards on his rear end.

"This him?" A tall man with long dark hair, high cheekbones and a regal air stalked forward out of the milling crowds. His mother intercepted the stranger, and they spoke in hushed whispers. The stern, dark gaze of the tall man still haunted Torryn to this day. He could still remember the pressure of the man's fingertips gripping his chin. "There's nothing special about him. How do you know he's mine?"

"He has powers," his mother hissed. There was desperation and fear in her tone. He stood up taller; if his father didn't take him now, who knew where his mother would leave him. "Tell me what to do with him!"

"What do you do with any unwanted pup?" the man said, his hand flying to his blade. "Best get it over with."

Torryn didn't know what came over him. The ground beneath them trembled, cracks splitting the docks. Used to seeing Torryn's unpredictable power manifesting itself, his mother, in a rare show of maternal instinct, grabbed his arm and ran along the splintering decks. She hoisted him up the gangplank as Torryn's powers created havoc among the Artrothian docks. They sailed away and never returned.

It was his last voyage. From then he was left on his island home until the day he manifested and was forced to flee.

Manifestation for him should have been impossible. It was said that those with human ancestry polluted the dragon's bloodlines. He was supposed to be empty. But here he was with the hide of an Artrothian dragon. He often wondered in the dead of night what his father would think of his bastard-born *vehyl* son not only having power but having scales as well. He wasn't a fool enough to think that his father would rejoice. No, that wasn't the Artrothian way. He would kill him to hide the disgrace of him siring a *vehyl* child.

He stood, stretching his wings. Jilearah had warned him not to go back to his lake. But he would go one last time to say goodbye to the place that had given him both peace and joy. Without looking back, Torryn took to the sky.

It was in the air that he decided he wanted to look out for Neo and his carpenter father. He would like to see them and hear the child's laugh.

He soared over his home, and soon he was gliding over the lake. That was when he spotted them. His wings almost gave out, his mouth opening with a cry of shock. Neo was lying face down with his father in the water.

Tucking his wings close to his body, Torryn dove. His claws broke the surface as he fished both father and son from the lake. He settled them onto the pebble bank, shaking his head back and forth. The humans were bloated, their skin grey and their eyes staring unseeing into the Otherworld. They had been dead for some time.

"No!" Torryn cried. How could this have happened? He had been so careful. "No, merciful Otherworlds, no!"

"Get yourself together!"

"Ayrahylse!" Torryn gasped, blinking through the salty tears in his eyes. His wife's yellow scales swam in front of his vision. He backed away. He thought to flee without confrontation. "What are you doing here?"

"Did you think I was so dull that I could not figure out why you came to the lake?"

"What have you done?"

"I only did what needed to be done," Ayrahylse answered. She glanced down at the dead humans. "You didn't come home. There are consequences to disobeying Artroth, Torryn."

"*Disobeying* Artroth," Torryn parroted. His chest ached. Looking down into the innocent little face of Neo, he used a gentle talon to tilt the boy's face so that he might look upon him one more time. "You're a monster to attack and kill a child and his defenseless father."

Heavy thuds landed on the bank, interrupting Torryn's thoughts. He whirled around, finding himself under the scrutiny of three very large dragons. His hackles rose; they were strangers in his territory.

"Manifest into your human form," said a male dragon with scales of steel grey. He looked Torryn up and down with proud violet eyes. "Under the order of Emperor Cilvryn and Prince Rhodys, you are to be detained for examination."

"Get off my land." A snarl rippled on Torryn's lips. He lowered his head and charged. The grey male laughed and easily sidestepped him. Jaws grabbed his horns, wrenching his head around so that he stumbled off balance. A lithe female dragon with bright orange scales jumped on his back and dug in her claws.

Torryn screamed his rage into the sky. He was easily defeated by the two dragons. The third large male of burgundy approached, stalking him, dark amber eyes glinting. A growl ripped from Torryn's throat at the wordless threat of the bigger male.

"General Rivyr, what ..."

"Hold him still, Filgaryn, I want a good look at our catch."

Torryn bucked ferociously under the weight of the two dragons. He sent a pleading look to Ayrahylse, who refused to make eye contact.

"You're quite a remarkable size for a *kairn*. Who would have thought I would sire such a magnificent-looking creature?"

"*Kairn*? Sir?"

"He's a mongrel. I sired him on a *vehyl* pirate."

"He's a good provider," Ayrahylse said. Rivyr's eyes turned towards her, and she met his cool gaze with a raised eyebrow. "He's a prolific hunter. He's strong. His power carved out my palace."

One of the two dragons holding him down grunted in agreement.

Rivyr lowered his snout, his eyes narrowing so that he could peer into Torryn's face. "Control over your power and a self-taught hunter. Shows intelligence."

Torryn growled and lunged, nipping Rivyr on the nose. He was pleased that he tasted the sharp tang of dragon blood.

Unconcerned, General Rivyr stepped away. "Feisty. Good. Manifest back to your human self. You shall not return to your dragon state until you are given permission. You belong to me now. You shall serve the emperor."

When Torryn didn't return to his human state, he felt a wave of pressure from one of the dragons holding him down. He found himself returning to his human form, his body no longer in his control. He was forced to his feet to face the dragon that had sired him.

His captors had returned to their human forms, and Torryn took the split-second opportunity to punch the man on his right in the jaw. His fist exploded with pain while the man who was supposed to be holding him hollered. The female guard punched Torryn in the guts, and he doubled over.

Rivyr lifted his head and laughed. "A temper. Wonderful."

Torryn had never been so infuriated in his life.

Chapter Fourteen

Bryn

Aboard the Wyn-Tyn

Bryn lay listlessly in his hammock while the gentle swaying of the *Wyn-Tyn* lulled him into a stupor. Sliding his long, bony fingers into the pockets of his threadbare trousers, he knew his search was futile. His stomach clenched, and he swallowed back tears. Although he had prayed all night that he might find one pitiful coin, there was nothing left.

"Otherworlds," he croaked, trying in vain to stop the swell of the pain in his gut. He cursed again, resisting the urge to scream.

Bryn's lithe body still bore the bruises from the beating at the hands of sailors from a rival trading ship. They had laughed and mocked him when they robbed him of the entirety of his earnings. Earnings that could have given him the opportunity to escape to better prospects on dry land.

To the delight of the crew, he had stumbled up the gangplank dazed. For his tardiness, they had cut his rations for the voyage. It did not bother him as much as the captain thought. He was no stranger to hunger.

Being the youngest member of the crew, Bryn had little in common with the older men. While they were still in merry spirits, drinking and gambling, he fled down into the hull to seek his hammock.

Aboard the *Wyn-Tyn*, Bryn was the lowest of the low. To earn any stray coin, he had to work thrice as hard as any other crew member. He took the beatings dished out by the captain, hoping that one day he might earn his freedom.

"My whole life has been a disappointment," Bryn muttered.

That wasn't entirely true. Many years ago, his name wasn't the Artrothian word for the number four. He had a proper name, although he could no longer remember what it was. Life working for the Artrothian elites might have been harsh for the adults, but his mother kept him busy and out of the way. Bryn wished he could remember her face.

But Bryn's mother was murdered when he was still very young. His memory of that day was like looking through a fog. He could remember the sound of her choking on her own blood and the feel of her panicked hands trying to hold him.

His father, a great dragon of the western island of Artroth, had found him and rescued him from the labour camps. Bryn could still hear his cries as his father took his hand and dragged him away from his dead mother. He wailed when his father gave the order that she should be cast into a furnace to be burnt. There was no funeral, for who would mourn a human slave? At first Bryn was afraid of his draconic father, but fortunately, it was decided that he would be kept in secret.

Bryn was taken into a room littered with all sorts of curiosities and sat upon an oak table. Tears clouded his vision as his father etched an inked drawing into the crook of his elbow. It hurt, but he was too afraid to protest. The symbol drawn onto his brown skin was the number four, and this was how he received his new name.

"You must forget your mother, boy," his father said. "If the emperor's men capture you, you must not speak of her ... I'll keep you. I wish to study human behaviour. You must promise to behave yourself."

Cloistered away in his father's house was not a difficult life. He spent hours pondering the delights of his father's mechanical contraptions, his strange drawings and his macabre collection of preserved animals. There was something about Bryn that intrigued his father. Under his watchful gaze, Bryn was asked to build from all kinds of materials. It pleased his father to see his creativity, and his blood was often warm with the hum of contentment. But then his safe world was shattered.

Rumours circulated their island. His father's behaviour became increasingly erratic. In their last few days together, Bryn was ignored. At night he could hear his father pacing and rattling through his belongings.

The morning the emperor's soldiers came to their door, they found his father had fled into the night. Remembering the warning about not being seen, Bryn dived into the hiding spot he had been shown in case of emergencies. From behind the fake wall, he listened to the soldiers searching the house and harassing the servants.

Three days later, he crawled out from his sanctuary and into the quiet halls. Unsure what to do, he stole food from the kitchens and stowed away on the first ship leaving Artroth.

He had been paying his debt to the captain of the *Wyn-Tyn* ever since.

Once, when the captain was in a good mood, he told a fellow trader that he rescued Bryn at the tender age of five summers old. If the captain's guess was correct, he would be fifteen now. Ten years he had worked until he had blisters upon blisters on his fingers. And he had nothing to show for his decade of servitude.

Bryn closed his eyes to drown out the drone of the voices of the crew and prayed he might dream of the skies of Artroth.

Bryn tumbled out of the hammock as the ship lurched underneath him. His wrists twinged as he landed against the hardwood deck.

"Otherworlds!"

The ship heaved in the opposite direction, and his body rolled. Booming thunder rattled the timbers of the vessel. Scrambling, he grasped on to a low hanging rope. To his dismay, his feet were wet. In the dim lighting, he saw the shadows of the ship's rats scampering from their hiding places.

Not wanting to die below deck, he made his way towards the ladder. His hands shook as he stepped up onto the rungs. The ship thrashed about, and he smashed his head upon the ladder. Cursing, Bryn forced his trembling limbs to obey. He needed to get up onto the deck.

All around him the ship groaned. He could hear the screams of the crew as they battled the wind and the waves. During his time aboard the *Wyn-Tyn*, he had experienced plenty of storms. He had come to the grudging acceptance that he would likely die at sea. Now, facing this storm, he was reluctant to do so. He felt it in his bones; there was something sinister and unnatural about this storm.

The ship suddenly dipped and moaned as Bryn hurled himself to lie flat on the deck. Blinking the water from his eyes, he stared at the scene that greeted him. Most of the crew was already overboard. The captain was shouting orders at the sailors about him, but in their panic, no one was listening.

Thunder rumbled once more; purple and blue forks of lightning lit the sky.

Bryn choked back a surprised shout. In the moment the sky lit up, he saw two long tentacle arms embracing the ship. The sky exploded in vivid colours, and he watched the muscles of the tentacles ripple, constricting around the ship. The vessel creaked in protest.

A moan of despair left Bryn's lips. "Kraken."

The crew was abandoning ship, yelling curses and pleas for mercy to the sky.

Pushing himself to his feet, Bryn scrambled along the tilting deck. He could hear the *Wyn-Tyn* splintering under the pressure of the gigantic monster's grip.

The ship lurched, and Bryn fell to his knees. Determined to reach the port side, he stood and ran. His hands touched the rail. Drawing in a deep breath, he looked down into the cold, dark water.

Life for Bryn had been a misery, but he didn't want to die. He didn't want a tomb under the waves. He climbed onto the rail, closed his eyes and jumped.

The waves crashed around him. The screams of the men were muted as his head was submerged under the water. In desperation, he kicked his legs, and his arms flailed about. Darkness surrounded him, and he thought his lungs might burst.

Bryn prayed that drowning would be quick and painless. He wondered if no name bastards like himself had a place in the Otherworld, or would his soul be banished into silent darkness?

There was a dragon prayer his father had spoken over him when he put him to bed ... stars, moon and sky? Was there one for the sea?

Brave, Bryn told himself. *I can face my fate with courage.*

He loosened his lips and let the water rush in. Better to confront death than to fight the inevitable.

Something soft and pliable wrapped around his middle, and the water pulsed with an unnatural blue light. Bryn had expected darkness to take him. Maybe the strange light was the Otherworld beckoning him home.

He looked down. His body was encased with a long, flexible arm. He struggled, the will to live stronger than the desire to die. Suction caps stuck painfully to him, and he longed to scream.

The monster ... the kraken had him. He waited for the crushing pressure and the sound of his bones popping. Instead, he burst from the sea, the kraken waving him about high above the ship's wreckage.

Fear stole his breath. Writhing in horror, he shook his long hair out of his eyes. The tentacle arm began to dip, and the kraken brought its terrible face to the surface.

Bryn was confronted with a large orange eye that glowed in the moonlight. The creature brought him closer, turning him this way and that, inspecting him closely.

"Please ..." The word tumbled from Bryn's lips. Whether his plea was to let him live or kill him quickly, he wasn't sure.

The kraken twisted, face bobbing on the surface.

It shook him up and down until he was dizzy. The creature paused and looked at him again. *"Use your power, little monster."*

Bryn gaped like a fish that had been pulled from the water. Power. Had the kraken spoken to him?

Power ...

The waves trembled beneath Bryn and the kraken. His skin warmed, and he was cooking. Releasing him, the kraken dropped him back into the ocean. His body hit a wall of water, and he felt as if he were engulfed by flames.

A memory tickled his mind. When he was young, he used to play in the gardens, molding little cities from the earth. His talent for building had greatly pleased his father, and desperate to earn affection, he worked very hard on his little cities. So hard that the skin of his hands was often blistered from the burn of the power he held inside of him.

Bryn's eyes snapped open. Trembling and blind, he stretched out his hand and willed for dry land.

The sea gurgled in protest, and Bryn struggled to remain conscious. His body drifted as everything around him started to vibrate. He blinked against the crushing pain and the little black dots that danced in front of his vision. Then his hands were touching ground, which was growing around him and expanding at an alarming rate.

The waters were pushed back, and the ground continued to increase around him. He fell to his hands and knees, limbs shaking under the strain of growing his own island. A desperate, tired laugh slipped from his lips. His head bowed, and he let the stinging rain hit the bare skin of his back. He welcomed the pain; it meant he was still alive.

The skin of his hands grew warmer still. The burning power was looking for relief in the creation process. He poured everything of himself into his land and held back a sob.

There was no telling how long he was left to the battering elements before a great thump caused him to look up. He bit back a gasp of surprise. A colossal emerald dragon lowered her snout to stare at him.

"Please!" Bryn licked his lips. Would it be best to ask the beast to leave him alone or finish him? Most dragons were not like his father. Most would kill him if they knew of his powers.

"I won't eat you," said the green dragon. She spread her wings, and the rain peeled back like a curtain. "Let me give you shelter."

Wet hair obscured Bryn's face as he stared up at the dragon. She seemed unperturbed by his lack of trust and stepped forward. She lowered herself to the ground and nudged him next to the scales of her hide. Warmth seeped into his numb limbs, and a moan escaped his lips.

There was no way he could fight the dragon, so Bryn huddled against her. Content that he was protected from the elements and warm against her belly, he let his eyes close. If the dragon decided he was a worthy snack, it would be a quick death. The rhythm of his breathing became regular, and he dozed.

His body still shook with exhaustion, but Bryn let himself float in the pleasant haze of his semi-aware state. He sunk further into unconsciousness, and his body began to burn.

The dragon was growling at him, the low notes tugging at something inside of him. His lips parted of their own volition, and he answered the dragon's song in kind. Within him something struggled, willing to be heard and to communicate with the large green dragon. A strange darkness fell over him, and calm washed through his mind.

Heat pooled in his shoulder blades, and his skin rippled. His soft, tender flesh morphed as he cooked. He had never felt so powerful in all his miserable life.

Bryn welcomed the embrace of darkness.

CHAPTER FIFTEEN

Pyrah

THE BARREN ISLAND

The torrential rain ceased with the first rays of sunrise. Tucking her wings close to her body, Torqui took the opportunity to study her new hatchling in daylight. The scales along his back were a combination of dark brown and black. His belly scales were burnt orange and bronze, reminding her of dying coals in a fire.

Battling through the storm, listening to the promises of the Wind Song, Torqui had not expected to find an island that wasn't there a few days ago. She had landed to find a boy on the cusp of manhood who burned delightfully with power.

When she had fled Artroth, Torqui thought she would never be witness to a first manifestation. The event was sacred, only shared with an *aluel* or *lullah*.

Last night, huddled in the middle of a violent storm, was hardly the ideal first manifestation. The boy was fatigued and hungry, and his dragon body quivered at her side. But it was over, and Torqui found herself immensely pleased with her find.

"A son. A gift for the dragon mother, a balm to soothe your grief," the Wind Song whispered.

At first her boy looked up at her with fear. Exhaustion rolled off him, and along with it the searing heat of power he had used. He recoiled against her touch, even as she lowered herself down and curled around him to protect him from the weather. Her warmth lulled him to sleep.

A whimper of pain heralded the beginning of his change. Hands clawed at his brown skin, his back arching all the while he was unconscious. Torqui could only watch in wonder. Here was a boy who was not pure Artrothian, whose power was still searing her, and of all the impossibilities, he had a dragon that was struggling to manifest. She had always been taught that only those of a dragon mother and father could manifest. That was why it was important to keep the bloodlines strictly to dragons. The Artrothian Empire had always maintained that the existence of half-breeds and empty ones would be their ruin.

Lowering her snout, she calmed the struggling boy with a deep-throated dragon hum. It still came as a surprise when the unconscious *vehyl* boy answered the dragon call. Then he stilled and was quiet.

A sigh of relief escaped the boy's lips as a pair of dark, leathery wings burst from his shoulder blades. His skin rippled, scales covering his limbs, and his eyes opened and glowed with power. Where there had been a scrawny boy, a fully-fledged adolescent male dragon slumbered.

Keen to return to the camp and settle her new hatchling in a safer location, she nudged her dragon boy awake. He blinked, hissed and curled up into a tighter ball. She tried bribing him with flying, but he was uninterested.

"Hatchling, we must go," Torqui said. "I have somewhere safer. You can sleep there."

Common sense eventually won. He stretched and stared at her with tired, dejected eyes. Encouraged by his movement, she thought to get him on his feet. Torqui hoped that once he moved, he would perk up. He lurched to the shoreline obediently and unfurled his wings as he was instructed.

"Who are you?" he asked. "Do you have food? I'm starving."

"I heard young males are always hungry." Torqui studied the hopeful glint in the hatchling's eyes. His nostrils flared in the instinctual hope that there was a meal nearby. "I am Torqui, the Lady of the Sea ... and the Wind Song has called me to be your *lullah*."

"I don't mean to be rude, but I don't understand. My mother is dead. What did you do to me?"

"Dragons commune with the wind. Last night it brought me to you, and under my care you manifested. I am to be your *rshon lullah* ... your dragon mother, child."

The young dragon sat on his haunches and blinked.

"Can you tell me your dragon name?"

He cocked his head to the side, and a brief flicker of confusion warred in his tawny eyes. Most young instinctively knew the name of their dragons. These names were written on the very fabric of their souls. "Daerys ..."

"A fitting name," Torqui said. "I won't lie to you, young one. We're at war with Artroth. You must come with me."

"The Artrothians ... if they find me ..."

"They'll kill you." Torqui saw no point sweetening the lie. A hatchling who was overconfident with their protection was a dead hatchling in a time of war.

A shiver wound up Daerys' tail. His eyes darted upwards, searching the skies for enemy dragons.

"There are a few of us camped nearby," Torqui said. "Come, I'll take you to them, and you can rest in safety."

Although Daerys did not voice any complaints, Otherworlds, bless him, Torqui saw the signs of crashing fatigue. His scaled lips pursed together as he tried to coordinate his body. If he took flight, he would not have the strength to fly the distance to the Green Isle.

Daerys was not ready.

There was only one solution. Torqui commanded him to return to his human body, which he did with little fuss. He was too lean for her liking. Ensuring he rested and ate well would be her priority. The first manifestation was difficult for any dragon. Ill health, the effort to build an island from the sea, and being born anew was too much for him.

Torqui comforted herself that subsequent changes would become fluid and more natural, requiring less energy. Only time would tell if he had comparable stamina to a full-blooded dragon.

During the entire flight to the Green Isle, Daerys lay like a limp fish along her back. Even as she landed on the beach and bellowed for Uxhyn, he did not stir. She dragged his body to the shade, studying him as she waited. His long dark hair was brittle with a life spent at sea. He had a pleasant face, long dark lashes and a slight bend in his nose from a break. His clothes were atrocious, and she wondered if he was a salt-rat, a young unfortunate who had sold himself into servitude. Torqui would never understand the desperation for a hammock to sleep in and a hunk of bread.

"Look what the storm washed up," Hyn said, crashing out from the vegetation. He brushed a hand through his greying hair and studied Torqui's find.

"I need your help to get him to the camp," Torqui puffed.

"Might I take a look?"

Torqui nodded. "Yes, he's exhausted."

Hyn crouched down to look at Daerys' still body. Firm fingers ghosted over the boy's ribs, and Torqui winced as her hatchling cried out in pain. Dark, accusing eyes glared at Hyn, and then his head lolled to the side. The boy scrunched up his nose and held his breath.

"He needs a healer," Hyn grunted. "Broken ribs."

"He didn't complain."

Hyn looked up at her with a toothy grin. "Dragon sons will not complain to their *lullah* about broken bones. You'll find raising a dragon different from a human."

Gently, Hyn dug his hands under Daerys' knees and shoulders and lifted him. "He's on the light side. I'll carry him to the cave for you."

"He said he was starving."

Hyn barked with laughter. "Don't you remember what it was like to be a young dragon, always hungry? I'll go hunt for him."

"Thank you. That's kind."

"One of the curses of being a shield-fire dragon, I'm afraid," Hyn said as he trudged back to the cover of the trees. Torqui returned to her human form to follow on his heels.

"He's lost consciousness again," Hyn said.

Pyrah exhaled and glanced up through the canopy towards the blue sky. The wind was still, waiting for something to happen.

"Do you suppose there will be another storm tonight?" Pyrah asked.

"No." Hyn stepped through the winding path they had created that led to the cave. Despite his great, hulking size and his enormous feet, he moved stealthily, as fluid as water. "The effort to create and control a storm of that size is immense. Rhodys will be resting for the next few days."

"If we could only provoke him to a display like that and then take advantage."

Hyn stopped, glancing over his shoulder at her. "He's not the only dragon from Artroth we need to consider. Rhodys is a talented general, and he'll be well protected."

Thrusting her chin out, Pyrah pushed past Hyn. "I killed Izzur with little resistance."

"You killed only his human heart. Your new husband will not be pleased with you. Izzur was just the beginning." Hyn's whispered rebuke still reached her ears as she marched forwards. He remained quiet, saying no more on the matter.

She entered the clearing of their cave first. The harsh scraping sound of sharpening weapons greeted her. Elryk was busy sitting upon a large boulder, a gleaming sword across his lap. His emerald eyes narrowed at her sudden appearance, his lips pressing into a firm line.

"Flying into a storm is rarely a good idea."

Pyrah moved forward, smirking at Elryk's worried expression. "I can look after myself, *sudunyn*."

Elryk grunted, glancing over her shoulder. Pyrah hadn't realised how far behind Hyn lagged. "Hyn, what have you got?"

Pyrah's face lit up. "A mystery. The Wind Song brought me to him."

Hyn lowered Daerys onto a sleeping mat. He grabbed a second blanket and patted him dry, taking care to leave any broken bones alone. Pyrah watched him, a wave of affection taking her by surprise. It was rare to see a male Artrothian be so gentle with young that was not his own.

"His power is still stirring beneath his skin. We need to get him dry." Hyn's fingers tore Daerys' threadbare shirt from the boy's body. "What's this?"

"What?" Pyrah leaned over and peered down at whatever held Hyn's interest. It had been many years since she saw Artrothian markings, but there one was, tattooed on Daerys' skin.

Hyn rubbed his thumb over the rune. "A slaver's mark."

"It's the number four. I have heard of no Artrothian overlord who uses that symbol." Pyrah dismissed the thought. Her hatchling wasn't a slave.

Hyn grunted. "Artroth is a large empire which covers hundreds of islands. You don't know everything about our ancient race and our practices, Princess."

"He's a dragon. He manifested under my protection."

"That may be so," Hyn rumbled. He turned his dark eyes away from Daerys and stared up at her. "But he's a boy with a past. Keep that in mind."

"I'll hunt. He's going to need food." Elryk stirred from his reverie. She could see the familiar envy hidden in the way he held himself stiffly and the clench of his angular jaw. He jumped from the rock and snatched up his spear. "If you are his mother, that makes him my nephew. I swore to protect yours till the—"

"Bitter end." Hyn turned back to Daerys, whose eyes were fluttering open. A low moan escaped his lips.

"Water ... please."

Striding up behind Hyn and Daerys, Elryk bent and offered his own water canteen. His green eyes roved over Daerys' body as Hyn lifted the boy's head and pressed the lip of the canteen to his mouth. Wearily, Daerys stared back at Elryk over the rim, assessing whether Elryk posed a threat. It was the look of one who had become accustomed to being prey. That would have to change.

Nearby, Nix alighted on a branch, clicking his beak in agitation. At the sound, Daerys started. Pyrah grasped a piece of the island's fruit that she had cut up last night and held it out to the bird. He launched and landed on her outstretched arm. He grabbed the fruit and dropped to the ground beside Daerys' head. Prize in his talons, the parrot shredded it with his beak before inching forward to preen Daerys' hair.

"Stay here with him, Hyn," Elryk muttered as he spun on his heels. "He needs Nahilya and food."

"Elryk ..."

"Let him go," Hyn grunted. He shooed the pesky bird away and pressed the canteen to Daerys' lips again. "This would be hard for him to see a new dragon while he remains empty."

Teaching Daerys to fly was a harder task than Pyrah expected. After Nahilya fussed over him and two days of rest, she decided it was time that she got him into the skies where he belonged.

So, after breakfast, Pyrah led everyone down to the beach. As they walked, Daerys spoke of Artroth and his misfortune of becoming a salt-rat on a trading ship. Pyrah half listened to his words, vowing to reassess them later when they might be easier to digest. Her inner dragon did not like the knowledge that he was a salt-rat, uneducated and lowly. Young should be hardy, strong and resilient. But she knew if any dared attack Daerys, the dragon mother within her would not allow them to see the next dawn. She would die for her salt-rat.

When they set foot onto the sand and Pyrah gave Daerys the command to manifest into his dragon, the boy's pleasant demeanor changed. Refusing to look in her direction, he shook his head and balled his fists at his side.

Gritting her teeth, Pyrah repeated her instruction that he do as he was told. Infuriatingly, the boy looked towards Hyn to rescue him. Pyrah could not understand the young man's sudden aversion to manifesting into his dragon form.

Having more patience than Pyrah, Hyn grinned at Daerys and manifested into his gigantic black dragon. Uxhyn blew warm air at him playfully, which swept small grains of sand into Pyrah's hair and face. She scowled up at the black dragon, and he merely flashed his fangs at her.

"Come, hatchling, it's easy."

Daerys stared at him and then turned to Elryk.

"A downed dragon is a dead dragon," Elryk said. "Artroth is patrolling Ramyr's skies, and if they find you ..."

Exhaling noisily, Daerys squeezed his eyes shut and tensed his body. At first Pyrah thought it looked like he was experiencing uncomfortable stomach cramps ... then his form melted, and a young adolescent dragon took the human boy's place.

It was another argument to get Daerys to unfurl his wings. He stood on the beach looking uncomfortable and shy.

Dragons were not shy.

"I'm not made for flying," Daerys protested. He turned his snout to the sky and huffed. "I'm not supposed to even be a dragon."

Before Pyrah could snap again at her reluctant hatchling, Elryk sent her a look which clearly said, *Say nothing.* He clambered onto Daerys' back and patiently explained how it was possible for a large reptile to fly. He used his spear to show the young dragon how his tail could be used like a rudder. He spoke at length about how his wing movements would manipulate the air and keep him in the sky.

Having enough of his shyness, Pyrah manifested into Torqui and rammed him with her horns. Startled, Daerys took a few uncertain steps backwards. She rammed him again. His nostrils flared in fright.

"Come, get away from me," Torqui snapped. "Fly."

"Torqui, he doesn't understand our ways," Elryk said.

"He's about to learn." Uxhyn's booming laugh made the ground tremble beneath them.

She gave Daerys no choice. She hurried him along the beach until he launched himself into the air to move away from her onslaught. Reluctant hatchlings could be coerced to fly if given the proper motivation.

"Why?" Daerys cried.

"You're flying, aren't you? It's the Artrothian way."

"I am not Artrothian! I am not one of them."

Torqui huffed. "I am your dragon mother, and you, *mynrell*, will fly and fight every day, building your muscle strength and stamina. You were not born to be a crawling lizard on the ground."

Shortly after they arrived back at the cave, Hyn and Elryk left to hunt. Daerys watched the two men disappear with a strange look of jealousy on his face. Then he scowled, threw himself onto his blankets and went to sleep.

Pyrah knew she had been hard on him, but war was brewing. She let her eyes go to the little ball completely hidden by blankets. Flying was a fundamental skill he needed. Without it he would not survive. It was her job as *rshon lullah* to ensure her heir, her *mynrell*, had the necessary skills to live.

"Here, let me help you braid your hair into something more manageable." Taking Pyrah's long auburn hair in her fingers, Nahilya sat down beside her. The healer had in her possession the comb Pyrah took from her rooms. Content to wait to find out what the healer wanted to talk about, she sat in silence while Nahilya attacked her tangles. As a chieftain's wife, she had never worn her hair in braids.

"It's interesting that the Wind Song said he was the first Ramyr dragon," Nahilya said. Her gaze landed on the lump under the blankets. Pyrah's enhanced dragon hearing could hear his soft snores. Nahilya's fingers sectioned Pyrah's hair as she began to braid. "Born of an Artrothian *vehyl* servant and a dragon. He is Artrothian."

"Maybe being Ramyr is more than bloodlines."

Nahilya's fingers paused. "Maybe. It gives me hope that some dragon fathers are still hiding their illegal half-breeds."

Pyrah did her best to remain immobile. And failed. "What do you mean?"

"It's not uncommon among the minor dragon families," Nahilya said, tugging on Pyrah's hair. "Your father was a part of the royal clan. He was the exception to the rule getting Elryk out. Minor dragon families have been sending half-breed young away from Artroth's shores for generations."

"I don't understand."

"This land is called Ramyr by dragon folk ... It's Artrothian for ..."

"Safety."

Nahilya drew in a breath. When she spoke, she chose her words carefully. "It's up to us to defend her now. It seems the royal house wants to bring us all back into alignment."

"Uncle Cilvryn isn't the most even-tempered of dragons," Pyrah said. "Rhodys less so. They believe that every drop of dragon blood belongs to them."

"And I'm going to show them the error of their ways." Nahilya turned her eyes back to the slumbering Daerys. "He's a sweetie."

"He's almost a man," Pyrah replied.

Nahilya snorted. "He's young. You'll need patience as he learns to grow into his wings."

"I'll be a good *lullah*." Pyrah's promise was more for herself than Nahilya. Tears pricked her eyes as she thought of her two very human children. Here was a human boy able to manifest into a dragon. If she had been a better mother to her daughters, might their dragons have made themselves known? Charyss had a power, after all.

"You were already an excellent mother," Nahilya said. "Yes, you have your flaws, but you loved your girls, and you protected them from human greed."

"It wasn't enough." Closing her eyes, Pyrah could envision her girls before her. Ancient One's Talons, if she were granted a second chance, there would be a lot she would change.

"Charyss has power," Pyrah said. "She loved plants and healing. She was always running barefoot in the gardens, creating flower crowns."

"I know. Elryk is a very proud uncle," Nahilya replied. She finished the first braid and moved on to the next. "What was it like?"

"What?"

"Feeling a young dragon manifesting beside you?"

Pyrah breathed in a lungful of air. "It's the most amazing rush of power I have ever felt. It was a heady feeling, the moment of victory when he finally emerged, safe beside me."

"I have always dreamed of the feeling," Nahilya said.

"One day you might," Pyrah replied. "It's the same power when you deliver your newborn baby safely, and she's lying in your arms, all wrinkled and new. And you know that you've lost a piece of your heart to a defenseless little human."

Nahilya glanced towards the forest, the braid in her fingers forgotten. Without a word being spoken, Pyrah knew what the healer was wishing for in her heart of hearts. She licked her lips, preparing to tell her that her dearest desire was foolish in a time of war. She thought better of it and said nothing.

CHAPTER SIXTEEN

Torryn

THE STRONGHOLD

"Release him!"

Torryn groaned in relief, resting his head back against the cold stone of his cell as he stared up at General Rivyr. At the clipped command, the general's underlings scrambled forth and unlocked his shackles. Unsteady, Torryn stumbled, curling his fingers around his bruised wrists. It felt like an eternity since he had been let to hang against the wall, the stone scraping along the planes of his back.

The torches of the dungeons flickered, and the human form of his sire stalked forward. With his approach, his servants melted into the darkness of the cell. Raising his head, Torryn studied the harsh lines of Rivyr's square jaw and his dark, penetrating eyes. The general wore a thick cloak of royal blue wrapped around his broad shoulders. Two thick silver clasps of a dragon biting its tail pinned the material into place.

"Admiring the symbols of my ancient house?" General Rivyr's fingers ghosted over the dragon on his right shoulder. "Do you have a human name, boy?"

Torryn turned his eyes away from the glittering of the clasps and glared up at the general. "I am thirty-four summers old, hardly a boy."

The general grunted, crossing his arms against his chest. "Your human name?"

"Rori."

The general wrinkled his nose.

"Ha! You and me both."

"We'll keep to Torryn," the general decided. "Strip."

"No."

General Rivyr cocked his head to the side, seeming unsure if he heard correctly. "It wasn't a request, son."

The last word cut through like a knife. The gleam in Rivyr's eyes told him it was meant to wound him.

"I am not your son," Torryn snarled. "I survived without the interference of Artroth."

"Yet I find my blood under the rule of a self-made queen."

"I stay with my wife because I choose to."

"I doubt choice had anything to do with it. How long has that dragoness kept your emotions bent to her will?"

Torryn said nothing. Alone in the dark, he noticed his thoughts hadn't strayed far from the betrayal he felt at Ayrahylse's hands. He could still see the dead eyes of little Neo and his father. Pain and anger seared his heart at the mere thought of them. For the first few hours in his cell, he had screamed himself hoarse.

"Poor vulnerable dragon." Rivyr chuckled and shook his head. "The deaths on your claws are due to your nonexistent training, Ayrahylse deliberately lured and killed another dragon. Yet you let her slander your name, isolate you from your kind ... She stole from you."

"Ayrahylse would never ..." Torryn's words were a reflex. He knew deep down that Ayrahylse most certainly would destroy someone if it meant she achieved her own ends. She had been willing to give him up.

"My poor uneducated boy," Rivyr replied. "Now strip. Our healer will examine you."

Torryn stared, clenching his jaw.

Rivyr's hands took the collar of his shirt and ripped it from his body as if it were no more than a flimsy piece of parchment. Glaring, Torryn couldn't help but flinch at the power of his father's grip.

"Shall I tear your trousers from your body too, or shall you be a good boy and step out of them?"

Torryn snarled. His hands went to the waist of his pants and slipped them down his thighs. Refusing to be cowed, he straightened, staring into Rivyr's eyes in a challenge. He hated that he was forced to be obedient.

Pleased with his work, Rivyr turned away and spoke to the healer. "Examine him."

Torryn had no choice but to allow the healer, an older man with a stern expression, to touch him. He felt the warm rush of power flood his blood as the healer searched for any issues.

"Well?"

"His physique is above average of a male his age. Comparable to one conscripted into the emperor's army. He eats well in both human and dragon forms. Most definitely leans towards shield-fire rather than battle-fire. And he's been poisoned recently and recovered."

Torryn swallowed and squirmed under the weight of Rivyr's calculating gaze. He knew the emperor wanted to examine him closely to figure out what kind of anomaly he was. If he were to find out he had made himself willingly infertile, it might be enough to find himself impaled on a spear.

"It's called hunting to avoid responsibilities ..." Torryn snapped.

The healer sniffed.

"I enjoy hunting in human form. Any Ramyr hunter will tell you that the properties of a particular leaf are beneficial to the human body. It allows the hunter to stay still for long periods of time. Slows the heartrate, breathing and metabolism." It was a barefaced lie. "Couple it with one too many meads, and it can cause havoc on your insides. Most unpleasant and smelly, I assure you."

"You hunt in your human body?" The healer forgot his professionalism for a flicker of a moment, his lip curling at Torryn's casual mention of diarrhea.

"Obviously you have never felt the thrill of killing a snapdragon with your bare hands. Nothing like slaying another predator as big as a fisherman's hut and hauling his scaly hide onto the bank."

"Snapdragon?" The healer was certainly wary of his story.

"Certainly. Tender white meat. Full of protein. Satisfies my dragon for a week or more."

His story got the desired result and turned the Artrothians' thoughts away from his poisoning to Ramyr hunting practices.

Rivyr growled and called out to one of his minions standing in the hallway. Studying the man who was responsible for his conception, Torryn noticed the hard plane of worry on the general's face. The torches that lit up the cells under the Stronghold flickered. A smirk lifted Rivyr's lips as he caught Torryn observing him.

"Such a shame for a man to be imprisoned in the home he created," Rivyr said. He took the goblet full of a foul-smelling mixture from his lackey. Bemused, haughty eyes swept over Torryn's naked form. Rivyr's minion stepped forward, a neatly folded bundle of clothes slung over his arm. Torryn immediately recognised him as the Artrothian he punched in the face when he had been taken into custody.

"You will put these clothes on," Rivyr commanded. "This is Filgaryn. He's to be your jailer and companion."

"A pleasure, I am sure, Fil." Torryn relished the look of indignation that flashed across Filgaryn's face. Dragonkind were very particular about calling one another by their true names. They considered the use of monikers the height of disrespect. Even prisoners, the enemies of the emperor, were referred to by their true names. To have a name stripped from you was believed to be worse than execution.

"You're a prisoner here," Filgaryn rumbled. He tossed his long ebony hair over his shoulder. Fierce violet eyes bore into him. "You'll use my true name. To do otherwise is rude."

"Oh, I know." Torryn chuckled. "I do so love riling Artrothians."

Filgaryn snarled but restrained himself to look in the general's direction for instruction. Torryn was not fooled; he could see the man's clenched fists at his side. As he had predicted, he hit a nerve.

"Enough, Torryn. You will learn to be civil." Rivyr seemed unaffected by the tension.

"Says a man that would have willingly killed what he sired," Torryn replied. "I call that uncivilised."

Rivyr's eyebrows quirked as he regarded Torryn. "You're strong-willed, my son. I expected no less. But Filgaryn is my lieutenant, and you'll respect him."

Torryn flinched at the title of son. Using it stung, and from the gleam in Filgaryn's and Rivyr's eyes, they knew it made him uneasy. His mother, after she had kept a troublesome, unwanted son, never fully accepted him after his powers made themselves known.

"Dress now."

There was very little choice. It was cold in the dungeons anyway. With one eye on his father and his aide, he dressed, ready for whatever devious game they wanted to play with him. The healer regarded his old clothes, and scrunching his nose, gathered them, bowed and left without another word. Torryn bit his tongue and finished dressing.

"Drink."

Recoiling from the cup that Rivyr thrust under his nose, Torryn could only look at the herb mix. The dragon inside him was horrified. Something was wrong. "What is it?"

"Something that will allow you to be housed in more suitable quarters while you are properly reeducated," Rivyr said. "Drink."

Torryn eyed the cup speculatively. "No. Something is wrong."

"Your senses do you credit," Rivyr replied. "This mixture is one that Prince Rhodys pried from Pyrah's little daughters. Seems to stop a dragon temporarily from manifesting. You'll drink this every morning under Filgaryn's watch."

Torryn stepped back, shaking his head frantically. "No."

Filgaryn followed him until Torryn's shoulders were once more backed against the wall. With nowhere to go, Filgaryn grasped his short hair and wrenched his head back. The expression on the general's face didn't waver. He took a firm grip on Torryn's chin. From the corner of his eye, he watched the general's movements. The lip of the cup was brought to his mouth, and he was forced to swallow.

Torryn could not help but cry out in dismay as his mind lost the grip of his dragon self. He blinked rapidly, trying to keep that part of him conscious. A feeling of nausea crashed over him. His knees buckled, but the general's painful grip on his chin stopped him from collapsing.

"Listen to me well, son," Rivyr said. "You're a half-breed, and you'll obey."

"I am not your son," Torryn mumbled.

He heard Rivyr's soft snort as the darkness crashed over him. "You're more like me than you know."

Torryn slid down the dungeon wall, his father's retreating footsteps ringing in his ears.

"Take him to his rooms to rest."

Torryn opened his eyes to one of the humbler bedchambers in the Stronghold. He groaned softly and rolled off the straw pallet, thankful that at least he had been provided with blankets. His next task was to survey his surroundings, looking for potential escapes. The room was sparsely furnished, with a pallet and a small desk, one candle and a pile of books.

Closing his eyes, Torryn tried to summon his dragon, only to fail. Another quick check revealed that his power was also dampened. He bit down on his cheek, suppressing a roar of frustration. If there was a guard outside the door, he didn't want to give him the satisfaction of hearing his pain.

He sat hunched over on his pallet, rocking his body back and forth. He was tempted to stand and see what books he had been given. But knowing Artroth, it was nothing wholesome.

The door creaked opened, and Filgaryn sauntered into the room. The smirk on his face widened as he no doubt enjoyed the look of dejection on Torryn's face. He was carrying the cup of herbs with him. Without a word, he placed it firmly down on the table and gestured to it.

Torryn stared at him unblinkingly, and Filgaryn held his gaze. It was not a battle he was going to win. Slamming his hands down upon his thighs, Torryn growled as he stood. He stomped over to the desk and downed the herbs in one go.

Filgaryn winked at him and took the cup from Torryn's lax fingers. "Your power is quite remarkable."

Torryn snarled, baring his teeth, not worried if he looked more beast than man.

Filgaryn was not intimidated. "Why would a dragon like you hide behind the shadow of Ayrahylse?"

Torryn remained silent.

"She's a liar and a cheat." Filgaryn tapped his fingers on the cup and set it down on the side table.

"Lying has become a way of surviving."

"But you are no liar," Filgaryn grunted. "It's not the same. Tell me what happened to your child."

"He was not strong enough. He died."

"Did Ayrahylse tell you what is done to children with human heritage?" The smile on Filgaryn's lips didn't reach his eyes. "They are destroyed because it is believed that they will not manifest a dragon. It seems after centuries of assumptions, you've proven that theory false."

"Butchers, the lot of you."

"Did Ayrahylse tell you what she did?"

"She wouldn't ..." Torryn mumbled. "She was devastated. I was ..."

"He had no dragon. It is the Artrothian way."

"No." Time stood still, and Torryn felt his knees bend. He sat heavily on his pallet, looking up at Filgaryn in horror.

"So she didn't have the honour to be honest with her ever-loyal life-mate," Filgaryn said. "She hid away a husband of hers that was a half-breed. One that could build her a palace styled from the glory of Artroth. Your silence has protected a murderess."

"What is Ayrahylse to you?"

"She murdered my brother, her intended, in order to try to snag a more powerful dragon."

"She was attacked," Torryn snarled, shaking his head.

"She's a liar."

"What do you want?"

Filgaryn stepped further into the room. "I'm not saying we're allies, Sweet Talons, no, but if there were an opportunity, would you help me take care of Ayrahylse?"

Torryn grunted, looking down at his hands. "She killed our child?"

"I heard her talking to the general about a baby you sired. How she lured you away from your home, asking you to hunt for her. Once you were gone, she ended the boy," Filgaryn replied, studying his fingernails and looking bored with the conversation.

"How?" Torryn demanded. "How did she do it?"

"I don't think you need the details," Filgaryn said. Was it his imagination? Did his enemy's expression soften a touch? "The knowledge will only torment you."

"How?" Torryn bellowed. Tears pricked his eyes. The form of Filgaryn blurred as he stood abruptly, his fists clenching at his side. "How did she kill my son?"

"Suffocation," Filgaryn said. He lowered his voice. "I won't say anymore. You can't bring the *vehyl* babe back."

Grief welled inside Torryn's heart. It drew up its ugly head, and the reality of the betrayal crashed over him. His blood cooled. The pain came in waves, turning his world into a jumbled mess. He had tried to be a faithful husband, kind and loyal. But there was no looking past the truth.

Filgaryn turned, and as the door was about to open, Torryn spoke. "He might not have been empty."

"Pardon?"

"The babe ... It was weak, but I felt—I heard ..." Torryn murmured. His mind was screaming at him to be quiet, but the words continued to spill from his mouth. "You can't truly know if a *vehyl* is empty of dragon until they're about eight or nine. I've seen it before."

"There are more *vehyl* like you?" Filgaryn stopped by the door.

"I heard his dragon." Torryn wept into his hands. "It was weak, a little echo ... but it was there. I didn't tell Ayrahylse ... What have I done? This is my fault."

"Otherworlds ..."

Defeated, Torryn looked up into the lieutenant's face and knew he had spoken too much. There was no retracting his words; Filgaryn already knew the truth. He wasn't the only one who wasn't pure Artrothian who had a potential dragon. True, he hadn't found how to call a dragon forward from a young *vehyl*. He had tried occasionally, but the unmanifested dragons remained out of reach.

Satisfied, Filgaryn turned back to the door. "We could potentially get her for killing dragon young, excellent. The general will be very interested to hear this."

"You'd use my son's murder—"

"We'll use his memory to exact revenge if we have to," Filgaryn said. "It's too late to bring him back to the world of the living. But you can still fight for the deceased."

"I'll help you," Torryn vowed, his shoulders sagging. "If there is a way to harm Ayrahylse, I'll do it. But it won't stop me from trying to escape."

There was a flicker of amusement in Filgaryn's expression. "I expected no less."

The door closed, and Torryn could hear the soft exhale of Filgaryn on the other side. "And Torryn, it's not your fault."

"I knew you were mine the moment I laid eyes on you."

Emotionally exhausted, Torryn lifted his head from where he lay on his straw mattress. His mind was awhirl with the dreadful knowledge of who Ayrahylse was. His heart was heavy with regret.

General Rivyr seemed to fill the whole doorway. He observed Torryn in silence. The faint smell of healing herbs tickled Torryn's nostrils. It was with some surprise that he realised the general carried a bowl, strips of bandages and a towel draped from his muscled forearms.

"Sit up. Let's take a look."

Torryn obeyed, doing his best not to look in Rivyr's direction. His eyes felt itchy and raw. The skin of his knuckles was bloodied from where he had repeatedly punched the stone walls.

"If I had known you were unaware of your son's murder ... I would have spoken to you myself." Rivyr came and sat next to him on the bed, the action seeming too intimate. "It was not Filgaryn's place to ... never mind."

Torryn stole a quick look up at his father, and then his eyes darted back to his hands in his lap.

"Where did you bury him?" Rivyr asked. He plucked up one of Torryn's hands, turning it over to inspect the bruising.

Torryn said nothing and swallowed thickly. His throat was unbearably dry from his bout of screaming rage, followed by his heartbroken sobs. Rivyr had come to him prepared; no doubt the guards outside had complained about the noise. He refused to be embarrassed.

"I would pay my respects."

"*You?*" Torryn snarled. He jolted as the general busied himself with cleansing his wounds. "Why? His life would have been less than meaningless to you."

"He is my grandson," Rivyr replied. "We old dragon families have rites and ceremonies that date back before the emperor's family. A loss of a child ..."

"When I was a child, you drew a sword on me ... I remember. "

General Rivyr huffed, his head bowed to his task of cleaning Torryn's seeping wounds. "Do you remember what startled you into spilling out your power, Torryn?"

Torryn blinked. It was the sword, wasn't it, that had frightened him?

"I had three sons to protect," Rivyr said, sending Torryn a sideways glance. His eyes glinted as if he thought his words might convey more than what he was willing to say. "I did my duty and protected all of them that day ... even if ..."

"What?"

"Torryn." Rivyr lowered his voice. "Tell me, where did you bury your boy? I am highly attuned to the Wind Song. Let me see ... let me hear that your child has been properly cared for in the Otherworld."

"I took him to the highest mountain peak." Grief was a hideous beast. It reared its head, and Torryn felt another wave sweep over him.

"Beautifully appropriate." Humming, Rivyr began binding his hands. "I hear you have made friends with Filgaryn."

"Not how I would phrase it," Torryn replied. "The wall and I are better acquainted with one another."

"Filgaryn says you haven't touched the books. I was under the impression you enjoyed reading."

Torryn snorted.

"I watched over you, you know."

Torryn froze. The general's predatory eyes swept over him.

"I knew where you were, foolish boy. After the display of power at our first meeting, I admit I was curious. So I watched you grow from afar."

"You never handed me over to the emperor. Why?" For the life of him, Torryn could not understand why a general would not give him up to the slaughter. If the emperor found out that Rivyr was aware of his existence and did nothing …

"The emperor is not all knowing. When your power attacked Artroth's docks, I sensed our blood link. You fled with your mother, and I was satisfied you were no harm to me."

Crossing his arms against his chest, Torryn eyed the general, not believing a word that was spoken. "I can do damage now."

General Rivyr raised his eyebrows. "It's not particularly wise to threaten one's jailer. But never mind, I have your dragon under control until such time you can be trusted."

"You'll let me live?"

"Do you really think I would go to so much effort if you were to die anyway?"

"There's more to the story."

"You are a clever one," Rivyr remarked. He strode to the table and picked up one of the books, flipping through the pages. "Artroth is weakening. We are not as prolific at producing young as *vehyl*. And in a few centuries or maybe a few decades, our bloodlines will begin to diminish. When the emperor perishes, Artroth will be plunged in chaos."

"You want new dragon blood?"

"Our dominion over the world is waning. Your little slip that there are more unmanifested dragons in Ramyr is interesting. Tell me how you manifested on your own."

Torryn shifted his gaze away from the general. "I thought you were watching."

"I can't see all," Rivyr replied. "I see much. I saw you leave your island home; I saw you meeting with the old woman and drinking her potion. I know what you did to your body, Torryn, and I can protect you from the emperor's wrath. Can you do further harm by telling me what I want to know?"

Torryn sighed. No. Artroth already knew too much. He licked his chapped lips as he began his story. He was fifteen, struggling to find a way to survive among his mother's people. Lack of control over his powers meant that his reputation preceded him, and finding employment was not always an easy task. There came a day a group of bandits decided that a lone boy was an easy target and attacked him. He felt a blinding fear and burning rage as they sliced his sides open. Under his feet, the ground quaked with the force of his power. The earth opened up, swallowing the bandits and crushing them. With horrendous screams of his enemies ringing in his ears, his power continued to stream out of him. There was no escape. Peace only came when he collapsed, his power spent. When he woke many hours later, a magnificent mountain range stood in the place of the flat green fields. And he was a blue dragon.

"My power killed so many people that day, so I fled."

"Do you know why we take and stringently train our children at seven?"

"No."

"So they learn young how to master their power, so power doesn't dominate them. Some powers can be very dangerous if the wielder doesn't first understand themselves and their gifting. Can you tell me how old you were at the first sign of your power?"

Torryn shook his head. "No. I was always building and playing around in the dirt and rocks whenever we were on land. I always came home filthy."

"Good. A hatchling should be free to explore their world. A pristine hatchling is one that is not learning," Rivyr said. "I cannot wrap my head around how well you have been able to develop your gifting."

"I fought for everything I had," Torryn said.

"Through struggle we are strong," Rivyr replied. "Have you eaten?"

Torryn shook his head.

"I'll have food brought to you." Rivyr tsked and turned to leave.

"Wait. What's happened to Ayrahylse?"

"Your *wife* is with Prince Rhodys, trying to seduce him as we speak." The curl of the general's lip told Torryn that Filgaryn's assertion that he did not like Ayrahylse was true. "I will not step in your way if you and Filgaryn decide to act. Young Galvrayne, Ayrahylse's intended, who she murdered, was a promising student of mine. My heart still burns with rage."

CHAPTER SEVENTEEN

Pyrah

THE GREEN ISLE

Hidden in the shade of the surrounding vegetation, Pyrah observed her new hatchling. A quick glance told her that Daerys was alone, tending to a bubbling pot. He seemed blissfully unaware of her scrutiny. From the tantalising smell, he was preparing yet another seafood stew. He wriggled closer to the open fire, his dragon subconsciously inching closer to the heat of the flames. Wanting to understand him more, she continued to watch him. Born of human flesh and raised in poverty, he was different to her. And yet ... not so different.

Daerys still held himself like prey around her. When in her presence he was on guard. He clearly preferred the company of the parrot over dragons. The feathered fiend would happily sit on Daerys' shoulder and rearrange his hair. The clever creature had coaxed the boy into feeding him the tastiest pieces of his meal. Elryk had to put a stop to it. The bird needed to be able to fend for himself. If the worst should happen ...

When he was forced to interact with the more sentient of their group, Daerys kept close to Elryk and his eyes cast down. Instinct was driving him; his dragon was wary of other dragons and judged Elryk the best candidate to form an alliance with. She had heard rumours of similar behaviours exhibited by other vulnerable young when they were first adopted into another dragon clan. It wouldn't be long before his dragon's curiosity forced him to seek her out. Already his gaze watched her every move, and he hung off every word she said.

She had ceded to Elryk's assessment that Daerys needed some time to build up more strength before they headed back to the mainland. Even though he had no dragon of his own, her brother was by far the best judge of a new dragon's abilities. Knowing the absence of her daughters rankled her, Daerys worked hard so they could leave the island.

Pyrah could still see the pleased look on Daerys' face when Elryk said that he was almost strong enough to make the flight to the mainland. She couldn't help the unease in her belly. It would be his first longer flight; it would be challenging for him.

On the other hand, Daerys did not do well with learning to fight in his dragon form. Anytime either Uxhyn or Torqui showed any movement that could be taken for aggression, Daerys either submitted or tried to slink away. Her unease morphed into panic and fear for him. They were at war; he needed to learn how to challenge larger dragons than himself. He needed to fight.

"He's been mistreated," Uxhyn would rumble in her ear. "Patience, Green Lady."

Drawing in a deep breath and slowly exhaling, Pyrah knew she could no longer ignore the signs that Daerys' dragon may have been permanently damaged because of mistreatment. Hands covered in callouses, this boy knew hard work. He was shirtless, his ratty trousers rolled up to his knees. Along his sinewy back was a spiderweb of scars.

Faced with irrefutable proof of Daerys' lowly status, Pyrah felt her blood burn in fury. Her first instinct was to stomp forward and demand names. The dragon mother within her would see the annihilation of any who had mistreated the one the Wind Song had gifted her. In that moment, another thought occurred to her. She claimed for herself the title of dragon mother; this boy was her son.

Her burning fury was doused by this realisation. She stood entranced, staring at Daerys in wonder. The Wind Song had chosen *her*. The boy before her was no less than some miracle, a half-blooded child who had successfully manifested. Grudgingly, she had to admit Hyn's assumptions about Daerys' slavehood were correct. A natural born Artrothian would belittle his existence. Could Pyrah continue to align her thinking to that of her ancestors, or were some of those traditional beliefs destructive?

Pyrah dragged in a deep breath. Those responsible for Daerys' suffering were long gone. It would be best to allow her fledging some dignity, and so she would remain silent. What she had said to Nahilya was true: he would be rapidly growing into manhood. If opportunity for revenge ever rose, it would be Daerys' choice.

A quick glance around the camp told Pyrah that Daerys had been very busy replenishing their supply of firewood and water.

He was singing a sea shanty to himself. She had noticed the habit before but had never stopped to listen to the words. The song was about a monster from the deep, with eight long tentacles rising from the depths to rescue a drunken sailor.

"Do you suppose they rescue humans often?" Daerys asked. He remained crouched over the pot, his head bowed down.

"Who?" Pyrah replied, surprised that he had sensed her.

"The kraken. The monster of the deep."

"I'm the mistress of the sea," Pyrah said. "I've never sensed a kraken."

"I used to pray the monsters were real." Daerys finally stood, stretched and glanced over to where she was hiding.

"I thought a handsome boy like you would dream of the merfolk."

Daerys shook his head, his long hair whipping him in the face. "The kraken is far stronger. They've been known to wrap their tentacles around ships and take them to their watery graves."

"You've nothing to fear. There's no kraken."

"I don't fear the kraken," Daerys replied. "I've seen her with my own eyes."

"The sea is full of majesty and mystery, but there is no kraken. If there were, I would know. There are tidal pools on the south tip of the island where you might be lucky to find smaller creatures to satisfy your curiosity."

Daerys wrinkled his nose at her. She noticed for the first time the golden specks in his eyes and the dusting of freckles along the bridge of his nose. Other than their first meeting in the storm, Pyrah had not spoken to the lad other than to bark orders or force him to fly. His initial reluctance gnawed at her. Even now, she bristled at the way he recoiled from those with dragons. The show of deference and fear was not what she wanted from him.

Elryk and Nahilya would give anything to be able to manifest into a dragon, and Daerys, who was not born to be a dragon, wanted to squander his good fortune.

"What are you afraid of?" Pyrah stepped into the camp, hating the way Daerys flinched and turned away from her.

"I don't want to say."

"Why not? How can I help you if you won't talk to me?"

Daerys' brow furrowed, and then his worries began to spill from his lips. "What if I fail you? What if I am no good at being a dragon? How long before ..."

"Before what?"

"Before you abandon him." Elryk slipped silently into the camp. His expression was one of compassion as his gaze swept over Daerys.

Nix squawked happily and flew to his new human friend. Looking incredibly guilty, Daerys stared at the parrot, patting the blue and green feathers. He shuffled from side to side.

"Why would I abandon him?"

"We're at war," Daerys muttered. "If I am no use ..."

"*Sudunah*, Daerys was born on Artroth. What is our people's custom when one is found lacking?"

Daerys' eyes flicked over to Elryk and to the spear he was holding in his strong hands. Pyrah frowned and stepped further into the camp. "Sweet talons, do you think I would hurt you if I am disappointed?"

"Our mother was willing to give me up," Elryk said.

Pyrah ignored Elryk's input. "Is this why you whine like a reluctant child and refuse to spar properly?"

"What if I fail?" Daerys flushed, and he looked away from them.

"Daerys, what if you're magnificent?" Elryk countered.

"Uxhyn and Pyrah are magnificent. I'm just ..."

"A fledgling. You'll grow into your wings," Elryk said. "You're not yet a man or a grown dragon. For that, we need to bulk you up a bit. Feed you some good hearty meat, boy, and put some muscles on your skeleton."

It was dusk, and Daerys had disappeared. Pyrah was not concerned; she had chased the boy all over the island, and he had obviously slunk away to rest. After Elryk had his words with Daerys, Pyrah decided on another approach in training her hatchling. Putting aside that she was a grown dragon, Pyrah had manifested and pounced on Daerys.

Instead of directly confronting him, training him explicitly for battle, she goaded him into chasing and wrestling with her. The dragon instincts in Daerys responded beautifully. Young dragons were known to be playful. The lack of aggression put him at ease, and he was less inclined to immediately submit.

"Uxhyn will be pleased," Nahilya said. She sat next to Elryk, preparing another dinner of fish wound in long strands of kelp. "Do you think he'll be ready for battle when the time comes?"

"He needs to be," Elryk replied. "Where is he?"

"It's healthy for a young dragon to wander off on occasion and exert independence," Pyrah said. "There's nothing on the Green Isle that could harm him."

An angry bellow interrupted the still of the campsite. Pyrah bolted to her feet. She recognised the sound belonging to Uxhyn. The black dragon was furious; it was a roar of extreme irritation.

Pyrah manifested, grabbing Elryk and Nahilya about their waists. She bent her hind legs, her claws digging to the soft earth around their camp as she launched into the air.

"Daerys!" Dragons known to one another could communicate mind to mind. She breathed a sigh of relief, feeling a sullen hum from her hatchling. He did not yet have the skills to communicate back, but he was alive and well.

"Come get your boy," Uxhyn's voice rumbled, deep and foreboding in her mind. *"Before I peel the scales off his behind."*

"Torqui?" Nahilya ran her small hands down her neck.

"They're safe," Torqui replied. "Uxhyn is angry."

At the height she was flying, it did not take her long to spot two dragons arguing on the southernmost beach. She winced as Uxhyn smacked Daerys' long snout. The younger dragon yelped and snarled in response. Uxhyn smacked him a second time.

Torqui landed nearby, and Daerys had the sense to look suitably chastised. Her hatchling lowered his bronzed belly, shuffling so that he could distance himself from Uxhyn. He retreated to stand behind her, his scaled chin pressed submissively to the sand. The black dragon's nostrils flared in anger; he flashed his fangs at Daerys, a clear warning to behave himself.

"What have you done?" Torqui demanded, rounding onto Daerys. It took effort to rile a shield-fire. To see Uxhyn so angry, she knew Daerys had done something to warrant the black dragon's reaction.

Lifting his front clawed hand, Daerys rubbed at his eyes, which were watering. A snout smacking was a common enough chastisement for disobedient hatchlings. He would survive the embarrassment.

"I've done nothing, *Lullah*!" Daerys cried. "I came to the southern tip like you said."

Uxhyn growled. "You little cretin! Give me one good reason I shouldn't cut a switch for your human behind! Try me, boy, and you'll feel the sting of consequence."

Daerys rumbled, his scaly lips curling. He shuffled backwards, his tail carving a jagged line in the sand.

"Daerys?"

The young dragon's eyes swivelled to Torqui. He must have realised he was in a considerable amount of trouble; he lowered his snout to the sand and hunched his shoulders.

"Your boy was playing with a sea monster!" Uxhyn cried.

"It was the kraken," Daerys said.

"He let the damned beast have its slimy tentacles all over him, and when I told him to move away, the little wretch said no."

"Kraken isn't slimy."

"The kraken?" Torqui repeated.

"I told you she was real; you wouldn't listen to me." Daerys lifted his head in a moment of defiance.

"When an older and wiser dragon tells you to do something, hatchling," Uxhyn said, his voice rising to a boom, "you do it."

"She wouldn't hurt me."

"It's a sea monster … It had its tentacles wrapped around your belly. One little hug, and you'd be a very dead fledgling and a meal for a hungry monster."

"You're being dramatic," Daerys grumbled.

Uxhyn roared and prowled forward. Alarmed, Daerys scuttled away, kicking up sand in his haste to move out of Uxhyn's range. Although Uxhyn looked fierce with his missing eye and cracked horn, Torqui was quite confident that he would not harm her hatchling. She allowed Daerys to feel the panic and fear of a more powerful dragon skulking him. One way or another, he would learn how to join the dragon community.

"Daerys," Torqui growled, finally taking pity. Uxhyn moved away, his good eye glinting. "Go back to camp and stay there."

"But she had a nest …"

"That doesn't make it any better," Nahilya murmured.

"You're in disgrace," Elryk said, crossing his arms against his chest. "Do as you are told."

Daerys' scaly lips puckered into a frown. He snarled unhappily, and with one last glare at Uxhyn, he took off. Torqui watched him go, shaking her large triangular head. Not long ago, she had been hoping to see more of a fight in him. Now she wasn't so sure.

"Hatchlings," Uxhyn rumbled. "It's their curiosity that get 'em killed young."

"A kraken." Torqui sighed.

"With a nest," Nahilya added. "What news have you brought from the mainland?"

Uxhyn sighed, looking weary with the world. He manifested back into his human self and brushed his hand through matted grey hair. "Rhodys is taking control of more human settlements. Any of our kind he comes across are taken prisoner. And there's more ..."

"We're listening," Elryk said.

"Rumour is Rhodys is weeding out humans with powers. He's looking for half-breeds like Daerys."

"So Rhodys knows there's a chance for humans to manifest." Torqui sighed. Terror for her children blossomed in her chest. She snorted a plume of smoke, raising her head in the direction of the mainland.

"Charyss ..." Elryk groaned.

Torqui suppressed the pang of guilt at her child's name. There was so much she had failed to do. "She's a clever girl. She'll keep her power hidden."

Elryk was kind enough not to point out that Artroth already knew that Charyss had power.

"How did he find out about half-breeds manifesting?" Nahilya mused.

"Torryn," Hyn snarled. "He's a half-breed himself. He must have told Rhodys to save his own scales."

"Torryn, a half-breed?" The idea Torryn may have betrayed them sent shivers up Torqui's spine. What else might the father of lies have said to Rhodys? Did they have to pry secrets from her former lover's lips, or did he gladly share his knowledge?

"Aye, bastard son of some trader woman, or so the rumour goes," Uxhyn said. Torqui breathed a sigh of relief. Gossip didn't make Torryn a real half-breed. "I thought you were close at one time."

That was putting it mildly. Torqui returned to her human form and ran her fingers absently along her snapdragon necklace. During all their summer trysts, Torryn had never discussed his personal life. He had wanted to know about her and life in her uncle's court.

"We go to the mainland, and we find as many half-breeds for ourselves. If we can help them manifest, we can build an army to fight back." Elryk shifted his weight and looked over the ocean.

"You want to take the young into battle?" Pyrah's mind went immediately to her newest hatchling. Rhodys already had her daughters; she didn't want him to take her son as well.

"It's their battle, Pyrah. We have to use the resources that have been left for us."

"The humans are suffering too," Hyn said. "I'm sure we can get them to join us. There was a time when humans were almost willing to fight against their scaled masters."

Pyrah grinned. Now was the time for vengeance. She would worry about readying Daerys for war in the morning. "Tomorrow, we fly."

"The next hatchling is mine," Hyn said, stomping his way up the beach.

For a long moment, Pyrah watched his stiff form. Then, slowly, she turned her eyes out to the glistening ocean.

"A kraken ..."

Daerys had tried to tell her of the legendary monster of the deep, and she had failed to listen to him. Could it be that the seas held mysteries and wonders that even she wasn't privy to? Why had the creature chosen Daerys, a dragon of land?

"A nesting female," Elryk said, wincing as he too looked out over the ocean. "You'll have to keep a close eye on your hatchling."

CHAPTER EIGHTEEN

Rhodys

RYGARD'S FORT, AVHYL

Invading a colony of humans was a delicate affair. Rhodys stalked through the stone fort of Avhyl, half listening to the human lord who was its master. Chieftain Rygard had to trot in order to keep up with his long strides.

Rhodys did not slow for the *rokun*. He cast a critical gaze over Chieftain Rygard. The ravages of time had not been kind to him. Rygard moved stiffly on aching joints, grunting with the effort. His once dark hair was silver. Rings set with precious stones decorated stumpy fingers. He might have been a handsome man in his youth, but years of fighting and feasting made him somewhat less impressive than Luthur of Wymeria. Pyrah's husband at least had the sense to maintain discipline and keep his body in peak physical condition.

The speed at which Rygard accepted Artrothian forces also lessened Rhodys' estimation of his intelligence. Greed with the chieftains was key. Promises of gold, power and the backing of Artroth lured the simple-minded humans into alliances that in the end would lead to their destruction.

The humans simply believed that Rhodys was here to dismantle the influence of his dragon kin in Ramyr. Some even hailed him a hero, as many refugee dragons fled the moment they heard whispers of Artroth coming. They thought they understood him, that all he wanted was to kill his enemies and he would support humans in their grab for power.

Some in Artroth, namely his second eldest sister, Corinah, likened Rhodys to a leech. He didn't mind the comparison. He knew what both his allies and enemies had to offer him, and he took it.

Rygard had one of the most impressive forts in Ramyr, controlled a great deal of land and had the resources to feed Rhodys' army without them resorting to eating humans.

"Are you pleased with your accommodations, my prince?"

"They are satisfactory. Bring me anyone rumoured to have association with Artroth. I will test all personally." The discovery of Charyss' power had been intriguing, and Rhodys was keen to test those with any dragon blood. But what truly excited him was Torryn, a half-breed who was able to manifest into a healthy dragon.

Rhodys wasn't the only one interested in Torryn. General Rivyr had all but demanded to fly south to capture him. The general's request was the perfect excuse to have his father's lapdog removed from his presence, and so Rhodys readily agreed.

"Association with Artroth, Your Highness?"

Rhodys resisted the urge to snarl into the human's face. "Anyone rumoured to have dragon blood."

Rygard raised his eyebrow, as if Rhodys' command was amusing to him. Foolish humans didn't ever think to mask their thoughts and feelings. The man clicked his heels together and fled to do his bidding.

Rhodys turned to his newest recruit. "What exactly do you want?"

Sensual pink lips parted, and Rhodys raked his eyes down the slimming dress of silver and the soft tendrils of golden hair. Everything about Ayrahylse the Corrupt was manufactured to lure him in. She was one of the most attractive Artrothian women he had the pleasure of meeting. Her charm was her weapon. She slunk forward with the confidence of a hunter and caressed his arm with the lightest of touches. He felt the touch of her power trying to sway his emotions.

Ayrahylse might think that he was a spoiled prince and easy prey, but Rhodys was not easily controlled. He grew up among the snakes of his father's court. His status as a prince meant that he had the privilege of being trained on how to throw off certain powers.

"General Rivyr and Filgaryn have overrun my palace," Ayrahylse said. She leaned a little closer. "It is not a comfortable situation to be under the general's scrutiny. I thought to petition you to let me come under your command instead."

"I seem to remember you had something to do with Galvrayne's death," Rhodys said, watching as the skin on her pale cheeks flushed.

"It was an unfortunate misunderstanding," Ayrahylse answered. "The general will not drop the matter."

"I don't imagine he would," Rhodys remarked. Galvrayne's murder had been a turning point in Rivyr's illustrious career. He still burned for revenge. Pity that the object of his ire was so pretty. He grinned, imagining Ayrahylse drowning in a pool of her own blood. "What can you offer me?"

"You don't have to worry about waiting for Rivyr to begin torturing Torryn for information," Ayrahylse said. "Not when I can tell you his secrets in full."

"Are you sure Torryn was a half-blood?" Rhodys didn't see any point talking around the issue.

"I wedded and bedded him," she said, her voice a low purr. "I know exactly what Torryn was."

"Who sired him?"

Ayrahylse's smile was cruel. "One cannot know for sure. But you no doubt noticed his golden horns. There's one renowned clan that produces young with golden 'crowns' every few generations."

"Interesting it came through in a *kairn*," Rhodys muttered.

"Bastard he may be," Ayrahylse said, "but his power and control over the earth is unlike anything I have ever seen."

"He sprouted from an ancient line," Rhodys said.

"Our home, the Stronghold, is a marvellous show of his power. Perhaps, my prince, you would care to inspect it for yourself?"

"Rivyr already sent a report."

Ayrahylse stepped closer, pressing her warm body close to his. "There's nothing like seeing it in person. You could make a closer examination of your prisoner. My prince is wise. You may learn something that Rivyr and I have failed to find."

Rhodys felt his lips tug into a flicker of a smile, knowing Ayrahylse was resorting to flattery as bait. She was beautiful and dangerous enough for him to enjoy her for a time; he would of course discard her the moment she no longer fitted his plans. He had little desire to properly take a female dragon as a life-mate.

"Is that what you want, Ayrahylse?" Rhodys asked. "For me to tear apart your mate?"

"Your Highness is free to make his own decisions, and I bow to your infinite wisdom."

Rhodys snorted. "Sweet Talons, woman. What do you really want?"

Ayrahylse's lips curled into a smile, her eyes narrowing in mischief. Running a fingernail delicately up his arm, she leaned in closer. "To give myself to something fully; something better than Torryn."

"Is that so?" Rhodys loved the chase. Was there anything better than taking another dragon's mate while he was still alive? He leaned in closer, capturing Ayrahylse's perfect lips with his.

Lounging back on the bed of furs, Rhodys enjoyed the afterglow of knowing he had conquered another bull's mate. Ayrahylse's small body curled around him, warm and inviting. He ran his hand down her golden hair, and her doe-like eyes looked up at him.

Rhodys wasn't fooled by her languid movements or the shy smile parting her lips. Ayrahylse was a dangerous woman. She had already killed her first intended and betrayed her life-mate. Luckily, he was just as treacherous.

"That was a delightful respite, my prince."

Her nails lightly raked the planes of his chest. She wanted him to ask how he compared to the damned half-breed. But he wouldn't. Rhodys knew his worth.

Pouty lips pressed against the crook of his neck. "I only want to serve you, Prince Rhodys."

"Hmm." Rhodys doubted the truth of those words.

"Torryn has many uses for Artroth. His kind needs to be studied so that we might better understand our own limitations and potential." Teeth grazed Rhodys' burning skin. "But take his golden horns and talons and give them to me."

Rhodys laughed and considered her request. He sat up and swung his feet over the edge of the bed to search for his clothing. As he pulled his trousers over his hips, he turned back to her expectant expression. "Do you want his head as a trophy once my father is through with him?"

Ayrahylse smiled. "I wasn't aware that was an option."

Rhodys' lips parted. He wondered how one might incorporate a severed human head in decorating a chamber when the door to his own rooms banged open.

"Please tell me you weren't here entertaining while you should have been hunting those traitorous children of mine!"

There were two dragons that would dare barge into Rhodys' private chambers unannounced. The first was his father, the emperor, and the second was his aunt. Latunya swept imperiously into the room. She always managed to look like she was floating, no matter how furious she was. His aunt's assessing gaze took in Ayrahylse and dismissed her in the same heartbeat.

"I see I was correct in my assumption."

"Calm down, Aunt," Rhodys said. "Ayrahylse and I were discussing appropriate tactics in—"

"I very much doubt there was much conversation. Are you hoping to sire another *kairn*? She is still the life-mate of another dragon."

On the bed, Ayrahylse shifted uncomfortably. "Rhodys annulled my bond with Torryn. I'm free to be with whomever I please."

Latunya's cruel eyes speared Ayrahylse where the younger female had curled herself up in Rhodys' bed.

Still shirtless, Rhodys strode across the room to pour himself a glass of wine. He brought it to his lips. "True-born children are a liability at this stage. Having little bastards allows me options without being tied down to one bloodline."

Latunya did not look impressed. "She had a child with the half-breed."

"Torryn could be a valuable piece in the emperor's collection," Ayrahylse said. "Besides, you married the traitor Parlyn."

"Get out," Latunya snapped, waving her hand imperiously at the door.

"My prince ..." A momentary glimmer of confusion swept over Ayrahylse's face. She expected Rhodys to defend her. When it became apparent he wasn't going to say anything, Ayrahylse gathered her flimsy gown from the stone floor, bowed and fled.

Latunya watched on in amusement. "She's a murderess, you know. Our people will never accept her."

Rhodys lifted the goblet to his lips. Latunya was a ruthless battle-dragon and politician. There was a reason that the emperor kept her close to him after the betrayal of his wife. When Parlyn defected with the twins, instead of losing influence, she solidified her power with her wits and brutality.

"I plan to take this dragon forsaken land," Rhodys said. "I may need a woman who is as bloodthirsty as you, Aunt."

"A woman, not an empress. You think to offer her the crown and a place at your side but not deliver ..."

"It is an amusing pastime. Ayrahylse thinks to make herself my equal. I may have a hatchling or two with her ... but she's not the empress I'm looking for. You didn't come here to discuss my personal activities. What is it you want?"

"Pyrah and Elryk ..."

Rhodys sighed and rolled his eyes. "They'll surface."

Latunya growled. "I want them dead. They've sullied the royal bloodline. They must be stopped."

"A sentiment that Pyrah's new husband wholeheartedly agrees with," Rhodys said. He thought of Izzur, who spent most of his time prowling around the courtyards, muttering dark threats and curses upon Pyrah. "But my father wants your daughter alive."

Latunya's lips curled back into a snarl. She snatched up a goblet and poured herself a drink. Her nails clicked against the gold. "Parlyn has poisoned her. We need to get rid of her daughters ..."

"Not yet," Rhodys said. "Patience. They might be useful as bait."

Latunya drank deeply from her cup and slammed it down on the table. "What have you learned from them?"

"It is indeed true that Charyss holds a power but no dragon. The little fiend fancies herself an herbalist. The Ramyr have a tonic that doesn't allow an Artrothian dragon to manifest. Rivyr is using it on the half-blood up north with much success."

The light in Latunya's eyes showed she was intrigued. "And what of the half-breed brute?"

"Let's move Pyrah's daughters to a more secure location," Rhodys said. He turned to look out the window. "I've learned what I can from them ... Our imprisoned dragon in the northern mountains might hold more secrets that will become key to our invasion. I'll fly with our dragon forces to thoroughly examine him."

"Rivyr won't be pleased if Ayrahylse accompanies you," Latunya said. "He's a powerful man; best not upset him too much."

"The general needs to understand that I'll be emperor soon."

A ghost of a smile touched Latunya's lips. "A difficult thing for a bull dragon of his caliber. I'll make preparations."

CHAPTER NINETEEN

Pyrah

TAMARYN, WIDOW'S BAY

Over their humble dinner of cold fish, Daerys timidly suggested that they should look for others like him in Widow's Bay. He grudgingly admitted that this was where he had first entered Ramyr. This did not come as a surprise to Pyrah. The port towns that lined Widow's Bay were busy; ships from all over the known world docked there.

They landed a few miles west of their first village, Tamaryn. It was one of the largest and busiest ports in Widow's Bay. According to Hyn, it was also a favourite port of anyone fleeing Artroth.

Elryk and Nahilya leapt from Torqui's back. Holding out his arm, Elryk whistled to Nix, who had cheekily hitched a ride upon Daerys' head. The parrot clicked his beak, ruffling his feathers. Elryk repeated his command, and Nix obeyed, taking flight and grumpily landing on her brother's outstretched arm.

Grinning at the bird's antics, Daerys returned to his human form. Torqui did the same, moving forward to clutch her boy's elbow as he regained his equilibrium.

Having scouted ahead, Hyn was already waiting for them. The older man was leaning up against a tree, clutching a bunch of red wild berries. The skin on his fingers was already stained red.

"Here, boy," Hyn said, tossing half of his bunch to Daerys. "They're good for digestive health and energy."

Daerys stared down at the berries in his hands. After his stunt with the kraken, he had been avoiding Hyn. Young dragons needed to learn to temper their urges and listen to larger, more experienced dragons, so Pyrah had let Daerys' anxiousness take its course.

"Eat, hatchling," Hyn said. "You eat like a mouse. No dinner last night and nought for breakfast."

Pyrah felt a twinge of unease. Hyn would make a better foster parent than her. Last night she had been too preoccupied with her own thoughts to realise that Daerys had gone to bed with nothing in his stomach. As angry as Hyn was with her hatchling, he had noticed and was trying to get something into his body. Why would the Wing Song choose to bless her with a hatchling and not Hyn?

"You're a growing dragon. You cannot afford to go without meals," Pyrah said.

"Not hungry," Daerys muttered, toeing the ground.

Elryk clapped Daerys on the shoulder as he strode past. "Eat. It's a long walk to the town."

Rolling his eyes, Daerys brought the berries to his mouth and bit into them. He tossed one to Nix, who intercepted it midair.

"I think we were spotted overhead," Hyn said.

"What makes you say that?" A dribble of red ran down Daerys' chin. His dragon must have been ravenous as he shoved a few too many berries in his mouth. Self-conscious, he tried to wipe the juice from around his lips. "Are you using your tracking powers?"

"It's the power of observation." Glancing over his shoulder, Hyn smirked and pointed in the horizon. "Riders coming fast."

"The chieftain would have sent for them to investigate," Elryk said.

"Might as well rest here and wait for them." Nahilya roved her eyes over Daerys. For a young, untested dragon, it had been a long flight.

"I'm fine." Daerys rolled his shoulders for dramatic effect. "I can go on."

Hyn let his body drop to the ground, and the others did the same. Under the shade of the trees, they waited for the riders to approach. Even though they were in their human forms, the riders' horses could sense the dragons lurking under their skins. The animals baulked, and their riders halted at a safe distance.

"State your purpose, strangers."

The humans of Tamaryn must be nervous, Pyrah thought. There were at least a dozen men. Each of them carried weapons and wore thick leather armour. It was an endearing trait of humans, thinking that armour was enough to save them from the wrath of dragons. Steel breast plates allowed for quicker cooking, and leather added another arid stench to the smell of burning flesh. Some dragons enjoyed the aroma.

"We wish to speak to your chieftain." Elryk lifted his face, dropping Nahilya's hand and walking forward.

"I've heard of you, scar face," the lead rider replied. Both Hyn and Elryk glared. The speaker lowered his spear, and glowered in Elryk's direction. "You're Elryk of Wymeria ... Can't say I have heard of your sour friend. These are troubling times. You're to come with us."

Remembering who she was, Pyrah held her head up high as the chieftain's men marched her into the town of Tamaryn. She flicked her gaze to Elryk, who seemed well at ease, and then to Hyn. When the riders had threatened Elryk, they came to an unspoken agreement: let the humans think they were in control. During their march they could gather what information they could before acting.

Their cooperation meant that they weren't bound, but Pyrah could tell that Daerys was anxious. Her hatchling stayed close to her side, and he openly watched each of the riders.

"The townspeople are scared," Daerys whispered as they entered the main streets. Pyrah nodded. She had noticed the signs. Stares followed them, but no one dared to speak or call out. Children were hurried from the streets by their mothers; men's fingers itched to have their weapons in their hands.

"I'll take your slave to the appropriate quarters, lady." One of the chief's men laid a heavy hand on Daerys' shoulder. Pyrah was thankful that he had enough sense to keep his mouth shut.

"That is my son."

"He's a salt-rat, he is," another one of the fighting men said, licking his lips. "How do you think he'll go in the fighting rings? Not much to him. Reckon Bone would crush him in moments."

"Kindly unhand him," Pyrah said.

"Lady Pyrah, we all know you have no son," the first replied. "Unless Luthur whelped him on one of his own servants."

Loud laughter met Pyrah's ears. Before she could react, Hyn's fist struck the man square in the jaw. The man reeled backwards, landing heavily on the cobblestone street. Hyn loomed over him. "If Lady Pyrah says he's her son, then he's her son. Show some respect. This is dragon business, and I doubt you want to try a dragon."

The man who had been struck spat blood from his mouth. "Fine," he muttered. "Take him with you to the chieftain for all I care."

"Come here, boy." Hyn drew Daerys closer and draped his arm over his shoulders. "You're with me."

"I suppose I'm left to heal the human." Nahilya huffed, stooping by the man. She reached out her hand and healed the broken nose. When the newly healed man stood, Hyn growled, curling his lip.

They had no more difficulties from that point.

Word of their arrival must have reached the chieftain, for he met them at the uppermost step of his meeting hall. He welcomed them with a curt nod of his head before disappearing into the yawning mouth of his lodgings. His armed men ushered them up the stairs and inside.

At Hyn's side, Daerys stared in rapt fascination. So much so that Pyrah had to wonder how much time he had spent on dry land in the last decade.

The rectangular meeting house was at least thrice the size of the one in Wymeria. The walls were covered in thick tapestries showing scenes of ships and feasting halls. The fighting men of Tamaryn engaged in battle was a common theme in the artworks. She let herself feel a bubble of hope. If the people of this town were proud of their fighting prowess, it could only bode well for them.

"Your hospitality leaves something to be desired!" Elryk called out.

"The skies have been raining dragons," the chieftain replied. Without looking at them, he opened the doors to his meeting hall and stepped inside. "Come, we have much to discuss."

Pyrah eyed the chieftain of Tamaryn as they stepped into the meeting hall. He was at least a decade older than Luthur, with greying hair on his temples. His chair was carved with ships and sea monsters. The wall behind the chieftain was decorated with gleaming weapons.

"Why is it you pollute my hall with your slave? Take him away."

"If you would give us time, we could tell you our purpose and who this young man is ..." Nahilya said.

Pyrah knew these types of men. Politeness did not help. It was best to be direct.

"Chieftain. My name is Daerys. I faced the kraken and lived." Hyn grabbed Daerys' bicep to silence him. But Daerys hadn't finished. He raised his chin and looked the chieftain straight in the eye. "She judged me as worthy."

Slowly, the chieftain advanced, his stare never leaving Daerys' face. "Is what you say true, boy?"

"Yes," Daerys replied.

"A proud pup is what you are," the chieftain said. "You cannot possibly be human if the kraken spared you."

Uncertain, Daerys looked to Pyrah, then back to the chieftain. He stood taller, shoulders back and chest out. Pyrah felt a surge of pride. "I am a dragon."

"She recognised the monster within you. You're Artrothian then?"

Daerys flinched. "My father was a dragon."

"The dragons of Artroth are not our friends," the chieftain replied, turning his back on them. "They have made their low opinions of humans widely known. Forgive me, but surely you can see why I have little desire to consort with your kind."

"My mother was human," Daerys said. He stepped forward, and Pyrah reached out her hand to stay him.

The chieftain of Tamaryn paused and glanced over his shoulder at them. His gaze stopped on Pyrah. "Yet this dragon woman says she's your mother."

"Daerys manifested under my wings. I am his dragon mother. We have come to find out if you have potential dragons among you," Pyrah said.

Something dangerous gleamed in the chieftain's eye. She had sparked his interest. Humans held to the belief that dragons meant power.

"You said so yourself, chieftain," Elryk said. "Artroth is setting themselves up to be your enemy. Once they get a foothold, they'll take everything from you. The only way to stop the Artrothian threat is to meet it head-on."

"What would you have me do?"

"We either die handing ourselves over to Artroth or we die fighting them," Nahilya said. "I know I prefer to die fighting."

The chieftain rubbed his chin, spearing Daerys with an intense stare. "How will I know there's a hidden dragon in our midst?"

"Ask those who have a power to step forward," Pyrah said. "We know that this is a place where people with powers are known to integrate."

"With your permission, Lady Pyrah, my men will take your boy. They will scrub him, clothe him, and we will announce to the people that anyone hiding must come forward to train with your Daerys. I will send word to my outlying lands and other warlords who have not yet succumbed to Artroth. Meanwhile, the rest of you are my guests." The chieftain signalled to the side, and two of his men took hold of Daerys.

"*Lullah* Dragon ... I'd rather not."

"*Rshon Lullah*," Elryk corrected him. "It's a matter of respect to refer to your mother by her proper title."

Pyrah watched the intelligent gleam in the man's eyes as he studied her newly manifested hatchling. "I remember well the years when a boy is no longer a child but is not quite a man. My eldest son was a menace at his age. My second was a sullen little cretin. They grow out of it eventually."

"I doubt either of your sons ever deliberately approached a kraken," Hyn grunted.

"She wasn't hurting me," Daerys muttered. He tilted his head to meet Hyn's challenging gaze.

"Go, the chieftain is correct. We cannot hope to use you as an example to the people looking like this." Pyrah lifted her hand and dismissed Daerys.

Looking over his shoulder as he was led from the meeting hall, Daerys obeyed.

The chieftain of Tamaryn was so kind as to offer them lodgings in his own hall. Not wanting to worry about what trouble her new *mynrell* might find himself in, Pyrah demanded that he be housed in the rooms she was given. She ignored the spluttering protests of the chieftain of Tamaryn and repeated her request. He had no choice but to ensure Daerys was with a grown dragon.

She saw the look of greed and longing on the chieftain's face as Daerys was returned to the hall. Her son's skin had been scrubbed red, and his hair fell in soft waves. Daerys had been given a pair of leather boots and clean breeches, and a shirt and tunic. In fresh clothing, her fosterling looked respectable.

Humans coveted power. In that respect, they weren't different to dragons. If he could, Pyrah knew the chieftain would take Daerys for himself. Her hackles rose with the mere thought that a human believed he could take her hatchling.

Daerys seemed blissfully unaware of the chieftain's interest in him. He followed meekly as he was ushered to the top of the meeting hall steps. Bells were rung, and the people assembled to gawk at him while the chieftain paraded him as one might do with a prized hound.

The chieftain proclaimed any who exhibited powers must present themselves in the morning. The crowd murmured, shifting anxiously as their chieftain spoke of war with Artroth. Not all the *vehyl* were in favour of taking arms against Rhodys. Some of the prominent townsfolk began an argument with the chieftain.

As soon as it was polite, Daerys slunk away from the scrutiny. He moved away with hurried steps, nodding curtly to Pyrah.

It was late, and the humans continued to argue. She left, and Nahilya joined her retreat.

"How long have you known Hyn?" Pyrah asked.

Nahilya swept her long dark braid over her shoulder. "He was in Ramyr many years before me. He was the contact my family arranged. He's a good man."

"He is," Pyrah agreed. "Do you miss them, your family?"

Nahilya looked down at her hands. "There's not a day that goes by that I don't think about what might have been if I only had been strong enough."

Reaching over, Pyrah grasped Nahilya's hand. "I don't think having a dragon has anything to do with strength."

Nahilya had no reply.

"I'm looking forward to a mattress tonight." Pyrah winced. She wasn't good at conversing like Elryk. She had a habit of saying the wrong thing at the wrong time.

"Good night," Nahilya said. "Rest well."

Watching the healer's retreating back, Pyrah thought she should say something more. Instead, she voiced her own growing concerns. "Nahilya! If anything should happen to me, would you ... would you find my girls, keep them safe with Elryk?"

Nahilya turned, tilting her head to regard Pyrah solemnly. In the dark, her eyes glinted with suppressed fury. "I will personally punish any man or dragon that harms your daughters. This I swear to you."

"Do you think they're still alive?" Pyrah choked on the words.

"I believe it is so," Nahilya replied. "What about Daerys?"

"Should I fall in battle, it's my hope that Uxhyn would take him under his wing."

"Uxhyn is a shield-fire. He's the best of us. He'll protect the hatchling with his life," Nahilya said. She opened the door to her room and stepped out of view.

Pyrah closed her eyes, murmuring a nonsensical prayer, and entered the darkness of her chambers. It was past the time for her to slip into bed and surrender to sleep.

Cursing as she tripped over Daerys' boots, Pyrah glanced towards her slumbering son. He was burrowed under his blankets, sound asleep on his pallet. As he rolled over, Pyrah could hear the soft intake of breath as he sighed in sleepy contentment.

It was mid-morning when the first human approached the chieftain's house. She was only a small slip of a girl. Her skin was deep ochre, which indicated that some of her parentage was not from the bay area. Black ringlets formed a halo about her head. Her manner of dress was a pair of men's trousers, a shirt and a leather apron.

"The fletcher," the chieftain said in an undertone. "She appeared a few seasons ago. Mother was a trader gone rogue who ended up at the foul end of the law."

The girl tossed her head up, piercing the chieftain with a confident gaze. She might be dressed poorly, but she was not one who was easily intimidated. Pyrah immediately liked her. "You called for those with power, chieftain?"

"Melayah, I am not accustomed to handing out free food for entertainment."

Melayah's lips twitched. Looking venomously amused, she looked at the chieftain as if he were no more than a bothersome fly. Pyrah immediately liked this girl. An unnatural wind blasted through the room, rustling papers and disturbing tapestries on the wall. The power grew until it pushed the chieftain clean off his chair.

"I don't want your charity," Melayah replied, staring down at the chieftain crumpled on the ground. "My mother's mother was a dragon. I command the wind."

Hyn eagerly stood. "This one is mine."

Pyrah inclined her head. Hyn had told her he wanted the next hatchling. She had no desire to fight him over new dragons. Hyn strode over to the girl, grasped her wrist and ushered her out the door.

"Where are they going?" the chieftain asked.

Raising an eyebrow at the chieftain's clumsy attempts to get to his feet and appear unaffected, Pyrah shook her head at him. "The manifestation of a new dragon is a sacred moment. New dragon parents are aggressive."

By mid-afternoon, a new dragon of glimmering oranges took the skies. Pyrah stood on the steps of the meeting hall, feeling elation as she watched the new dragon and Uxhyn wheeling over the village. At her side, Daerys hopped from one foot to another. She marvelled at how only a few days ago, he had been worried about flying.

"Go on," Pyrah said. "Go play."

Daerys threw a derisive look over his shoulder, manifested and launched himself into the air. Under Uxhyn's watch, the two young dragons circled one another. Snout to snout they hovered, all the while studying one another.

"Earth and wind," Pyrah said aloud. "A son and a daughter."

"Yes," whispered the Wind Song. *"As it should be. A new race of dragons is emerging away from the corruption and greed of Artroth's shores."*

Encouraged by Melayah's success, three more humans came to the chieftain's house believing they too could be a dragon. Two of the three were correct. The third believed he could see the future, but Pyrah thought it was more due to the overindulgence of mead. By nightfall they had four new hatchlings to train.

Twenty-two dragons joined their ranks by the end of the week. Helping so many new dragons manifest was tiring work, so Elryk and Nahilya started to train the new ones. Although the pair of them were 'empty,' they were of dragonkind and could teach the new young ones everything they needed to know.

Pyrah knew they had scant time to prepare themselves. They moved their location every night, constantly hunting half-bloods that might have dragons. The lack of interest from Rhodys was a concern. She had heard rumours of him.

Two days after returning to the mainland, they heard the first tales of the burning of Wymeria. This was when she noticed a shift in Daerys.

He was the first dragon she assisted to manifest, and he was by far her favourite. Daerys preferred to stay in his dragon skin. In the cool of the evenings, he paced, clearly agitated.

Where he once ate like a mouse, he seemed to be ravenously hungry and ate like a grown bull dragon. Sometimes during the day, he seemed withdrawn and fatigued. There was no mistaking it. Daerys was growing at an alarming rate.

"Growing pains," Hyn huffed knowingly one night as Daerys disappeared once more from the campfire. He was whittling from a piece of firewood and didn't look up from his chore. "He's going to be a big boy when he's fully grown. Keep him well fed."

Hyn's words did little to comfort Pyrah.

"His new body is readjusting. He's sore and hungry. It's a natural process for adolescent male dragons." Nahilya touched her knee lightly.

Pyrah couldn't help feeling alarmed at this news. She had experienced some discomfort as she grew, but nothing like what Daerys was going through.

"He needs to rest," Elryk said.

"Aye, I'll go to him shortly," Hyn replied. "Who knows, he might end up larger than me."

Try as she might, Pyrah could not imagine Daerys a grown man or a large bull dragon. When she thought of him, all she could conjure up was the memory of her sinewy young hatchling.

As the first born among the new dragons, Daerys and Melayah were popular among their peers. While they travelled from the villages and saw the evidence of Rhodys' expanding influence, Daerys was single-minded about training. He was the first one up breaking his fast every morning. While the other young dragons snoozed, he went to the fields and relentlessly trained his human body.

The headstrong youth that he was, Daerys was adamant that he would master all the weapons. Although he trained hard, he still lacked the stamina for swinging a sword for any amount of time. But he was quite clever with a battle axe and enjoyed throwing knives.

Melayah would join him. Hyn often watched the pair from afar. His first born among his dragons was a fierce girl. Pyrah could well understand his pride in his hatchling.

While Pyrah could see that Daerys was thinking about every movement he made, Melayah moved like flowing water. She favoured the two short swords she had taken from her home in Tamaryn. Pyrah wondered if her pirate mother had been the one to teach her. Despite the chieftain of Tamaryn's disdain for her, Melayah seemed proud of her mother's legacy. She drew her tight curls away from her face with a scarf when she trained, and it took Pyrah a few days to realise it was an old ship's flag.

While Melayah embraced her troubled past, Daerys did his best to conceal his origins. He went to great lengths to never reveal his bare arms to the other soldiers in their camp. She had caught him a few times, hand clamped over his Artrothian tattoo, his eyes unfocussed in the distance. She wished she had the words to soothe his unease.

"They both have battle-fire," Hyn said one afternoon, creeping up on her.

"I would like to see more aggression in Daerys." Pyrah turned her attention to where her hatchling was rolling in the long grass. She could hear his laughter and the blades of grass wedging into his motley brown and black scales. "He's going to make himself itchy."

"Not all battle dragons are aggressive for the sake of aggression," Hyn replied.

Pyrah hummed. "My mother was."

"As was mine," Hyn replied. "It's such a shame to introduce him to battle and release his full potential."

"What is the point of our existence if we don't embrace our full potential? After battle he'll find fullness and contentment."

Hyn remained silent for a long time. Concerned, Pyrah turned to face him. He was standing stiffly, his eyes trained upon Melayah. She could sense the turmoil her friend was feeling under his mask of calm observation. The muscles of Hyn's jaw were clenched shut, and a small, angry vein throbbed in his neck.

"You don't believe that is true?" Pyrah asked. "There's no greater joy than fulfilling one's purpose. Daerys was created for war."

"I like to think his existence is for something more than that," Hyn said. "The hatchlings deserve more than battle and blood."

"I lived in the emperor's court, and I have known many dragons."

"You knew the affluent," Hyn rumbled. His shoulders slumped ever so slightly. "There was no greater misery than being a tracker for the emperor."

"Is that why you left?"

"I was used by the emperor's men in hunting the half-blooded children of the dragons of lower rank. I am responsible for so much death." Hyn bowed his head, looking down at his hands. He balled them into tight fists and let out a cry of frustration. Pyrah thought he might weep, but when he lifted his chin to look at her, he was calm. "There's so much blood on my hands. I can never hope to atone for what I have done."

"Hyn …"

"Empress Sussette's death will forever haunt me."

A thrill of horror snaked up Pyrah's spine. "Rhodys killed her. Not you."

"Rhodys was a child in an impossible situation. I do not condemn him for his mother's murder." Hyn scoffed and shifted his weight. His good eye bore into the orange form of Melayah. He seemed intent on watching the sparring young ones. "Sussette employed me to smuggle the children out of Artroth. It worked for a few seasons … until we were betrayed by my parents and led into a trap by Gahryk."

"Gahryk? What does he have to do with anything?"

"The all-seeing one allowed Cilvryn to slaughter Sussette while forcing me to flee. He told me that I must come here to do what I was destined to do. It was he that bullied me from Artroth's shores."

"So Aunt Sussette died …"

"For a time such as this," Hyn growled, rubbing his temple. A pained expression crossed his face. Behind his mask of calm acceptance, there was a well of guilt. "Gahryk confirmed this to me during your dragon summit. Sussette was of no use to him. She died so I could be at your table."

"It wasn't your fault."

"I blame the emperor and his polluted court." Hyn's lips twitched as Melayah tripped Daerys, who grabbed on to her, and they both tumbled to the ground. "Many years ago, we were a noble race that protected one another. Pride has hardened our hearts, and now it's the beginning of the end."

"Hyn …"

He turned to her, his face alight with fury. Pyrah wondered how it was that she had underestimated the power and force behind the gentle giant. How was it she had missed his strength behind his quiet demeanor? Shield-fire he may be, but she knew he could fight with the same ferocity as any of Rhodys' battle dragons. "If we are to attack Rhodys, this is the time. You have taught me much. Live valiantly, my friend."

"Hopefully I won't have to teach you to die honourably," Pyrah said, letting her gaze sweep over Daerys. Tomorrow the fight for their crumbling world would begin in earnest. Hyn was right. It was for their kind that they would take to the sky.

CHAPTER TWENTY

Torryn

THE STRONGHOLD

Boredom made Torryn reckless. He lay on the lumpy mattress of his bunk, staring up at the stone ceiling of his cell. When Filgaryn stepped into his prison, Torryn didn't acknowledge him but slowly crumbled a piece of parchment in his fist. The books from Artroth were expensive, and he had put them to good use, making balls to play with. He threw his toy up with one hand and neatly caught it in the other.

"Any news, Filly?"

Filgaryn made an impatient sound in the back of his throat and glanced in disgust at the desecrated books. Over the course of his captivity, he had become accustomed to Torryn's biting tongue. This time the general's lieutenant did not rise to the bait. For whatever twisted Artrothian reason, the general had forbidden Filgaryn from physically harming him.

"The general would not appreciate you destroying his property."

Filgaryn clunked a full cup of poison down. His mood was far from pleasant. It would be wise for Torryn to tread carefully, but he was feeling foolhardy.

Filgaryn crossed Torryn's meagre cell and kicked his foot. "Up and drink."

"What if I don't want to?" Torryn asked, glaring at the cup of liquid that subdued his dragon.

"Otherworlds!" Filgaryn snapped. "Must we go through this monotonous argument every morning?"

"Yes," Torryn drawled.

"You're testing my patience."

"Ha!" Torryn threw his parchment ball up, and before he could catch it, Filgaryn darted forward and snatched it from under his nose. "Give me my ball back."

Tilting his head to the side, Filgaryn carefully unwrapped the parchment while keeping his steely gaze on Torryn's snarling face.

"Fine, I'll make more."

"No, you will not. The general has so kindly given you books for your entertainment."

"If the general wishes to show me kindness, then he can let me go." Anger and frustration bubbled in Torryn's gut.

"If the general lets you go now, you'll die," Filgaryn said. "Artroth rules the skies here."

Growling, Torryn stood, sidestepped Filgaryn and picked up the first book off the table. Filgaryn tried to catch hold of him, but Torryn jumped out of the way, tearing a page as he did so. As Filgaryn roared in fury, Torryn scrunched the parchment into a ball and lobbed it at his jailer's head.

"You're testing me!" Filgaryn shouted.

A bubble of laughter rippled through Torryn's chest. "Good. I'm going mad locked up like this. Sweet Talons, I long to claw my way out, maybe chomp on somebody's wings ... go hunting, swimming, sunbathing, anything!"

Filgaryn blinked, bending slowly to pick up the wad of parchment. A look of puzzlement crossed his features. "You've got dragon madness even though you have human blood."

"If I don't get out soon, I'll ram my skull into the wall until it is like rotten vegetable pulp." For added effect, Torryn paced the length of his cell. "Bring me a candle so I can burn something ..."

"I'm not bringing you a candle."

"Then fight me!"

"Trust me, I would dearly love to fight you," Filgaryn said, cocking his head to the side. "But the general says you're not to be hurt."

Torryn lunged, his fist connecting with Filgaryn's perfect jaw. "Then we'll fight as men."

There was something wildly wonderful about having your enemy taken off guard. Using the element of surprise to his advantage, Torryn pinned Filgaryn to the ground.

He laughed wildly, seeing the flash of Filgaryn's dragon in his eyes. His jailer would get his revenge, but Torryn was past caring. He was living for the here and now.

He punched Filgaryn's jaw again, loving the way the other man's head hit the stone flooring with a dull thunk. Filgaryn spat blood in his face, and Torryn cackled.

When the door opened and Torryn was pulled back from Filgaryn, he cursed and swore, his fists still swinging. Held between two of his father's minions, Torryn continued laughing until tears ran down his cheeks.

Filgaryn stood, brushing his hair out of his eyes and straightening his clothes. The trickle of blood down his face sent a thrill down Torryn's spine.

"Don't hurt him," Filgaryn said, pinching his nose. Torryn hoped it was broken. "His dragon is going mad."

"It's not natural for a dragon to be subdued," the guard on Torryn's left muttered. His Artrothian accent was thick. "He needs to fly ... feel the Wind Song on his scales."

Weighed down by his circumstances, Torryn slumped.

"He's got fight in him still," Filgaryn said.

"He's too quiet now," the other said. "This evil tonic is hurting his dragon."

"Provoke his dragon sensibilities while I give him his medicine." Filgaryn picked up the cup from the table.

"This isn't right. The prisoner has a fever ..."

Torryn tried to wrench his face away as Filgaryn's fingers brushed over his forehead. The lieutenant huffed, grasped Torryn's chin and forced the mixture into Torryn's mouth.

"We've orders from Prince Rhodys," Filgaryn said. "Let the general know he's unwell."

"If he's asleep, he won't be tormented, sir."

Pursing his lips, Filgaryn looked down at Torryn, a shadow of pity flickering in his violet eyes. He nodded once. "Do it."

Torryn could feel the power of the man on his left thrumming through his blood. Before he could protest, a crashing wave of fatigue overwhelmed him. He swore as his body sagged and the will to fight was sapped out of him.

Dumped unceremoniously on his cot, Torryn could only mutter, "I'll kill myself if I am to stay here much longer."

The monotony of counting the stones of his cell forced Torryn's hand. He devoured the books and scrolls that the general left him. The vile herbs he was forced to take caused rolling nausea, which he had learned to tolerate. He took his annoyance and anger out on the books. The next time Filgaryn opened his cell door, he stepped into a pile of miniscule pieces of parchment that Torryn had painstakingly ripped.

"It's snowing," Torryn rasped. His throat ached so badly he was glad to see Filgaryn and the dreaded cup. Opening his clenched fist, he blew parchment at Filgaryn.

Raising an eyebrow, Filgaryn shook his head and thrust the cup under his nose. "Drink."

"Someone is in a foul mood."

The mixture didn't have the same smell as previous batches. Torryn glanced up into Filgaryn's face, which was expressionless. "Drink."

Of their own volition, Torryn's fingers curled around the mug, and he brought it to his lips. The liquid was cool and tasteless. He blinked. It was water.

Filgaryn shook his head, looking back to the door. He closed it softly and locked it behind him. "Artrothian water. It'll help you recover and take the edge off your fever."

"Why?" Torryn's relief was palpable.

"Rhodys has commanded that we keep you drugged. The general doesn't agree. It's … affecting your dragon. If you want water and not drugs, I highly recommend behaving yourself."

A sly smile curled on Torryn's face. "Where's the fun it that?"

"I mean it, Torryn," Filgaryn snapped. "This isn't a game. We cannot have an out-of-control prisoner."

Torryn snorted in disbelief. "I don't believe you."

"Your wife, that whore, is rumoured to be mated to Rhodys."

The mention of Ayrahylse was enough for a storm of emotions to sweep over Torryn. There was regret and sadness, along with rage and bone-crushing grief. He let the feelings wash over him. Then, taking in the fact she would give herself to Rhodys, he felt a strange and terrible numbness.

Torryn sunk to his cot, his hands clutching his head. "I hoped that this was a nightmare and I would wake to a world where this is a lie."

"Rhodys has annulled your marriage," Filgaryn said.

"Then I am free." Torryn exhaled and laughed in derision. There was a part of him that expected this news. "I was leaving her when you caught me."

"*Kairn* you may be, but she doesn't deserve you," Filgaryn said. "Will you kill her if I gave you a chance?"

"She murdered my son," Torryn rumbled. Was it his imagination? Did he feel the stirrings of his dragon deep within his belly?

Filgaryn's lips curled into a cruel smile. "A volatile prisoner may be given an opportunity to escape …"

"How very tragic." Torryn's eyes flashed. "When?"

"Not yet," Filgaryn said. "We have one chance at this and one only. Listen, and the signal will be clear. If I let you fly free, you'll never attack General Rivyr's family."

Torryn blinked. "You're awfully loyal to your general."

"You'll never attack the general's family."

"Unlike Artrothian swine, I have a conscience," Torryn snarled.

"Be ready. The general is working on permission to have you fly under strict supervision."

When Filgaryn said he might be able to fly under supervision, Torryn never imagined the indignity of the situation. A few days after their conversation, Filgaryn announced that Rhodys had given permission for him to be weaned off the herbs that kept his dragon prisoner. It seemed the prince wanted to thoroughly examine his half-breed prize.

"We've met," Torryn grumbled. "He's already seen my dragon."

"Whatever he does to you, behave," Filgaryn replied. "This is our one opportunity. You have three days to prepare for seeing your beloved."

After two days of drinking the Artrothian water, Torryn felt his dragon stirring beneath his skin. Now his body practically trembled with the excitement of being almost free.

On the third morning, Filgaryn entered his cell with three of his underlings. Torryn couldn't help feeling excitement fluttering around in his belly, even as the lieutenant looked at him impassively.

"On your knees. Hands on your head."

Torryn looked at him, dumbfounded.

Striding over to Torryn, Filgaryn swung his fist into his stomach. Air whooshed out of Torryn's lungs, and he doubled over. He tilted his head to stare up at Filgaryn, who glared down at him.

The lieutenant leaned over and whispered in his ear, "For the punch in the face."

"Bastard," Torryn croaked.

"I'm the true born son." Filgaryn raised an elegant eyebrow and looked him up and down. "Remember what we discussed."

Torryn snorted and decided it was probably best that he did not answer.

The lackeys forced Torryn to his knees. Helpless to do much about his situation, he allowed the indignity and lifted his hands to place them behind his head. His wrists were chained. Looking pleased, Filgaryn stalked out the door. The guards grabbed Torryn's upper arms and escorted him from his cell.

Wedged between two soldiers, Torryn was resolved to behave and do as he was told. He allowed them to maneuver him throughout the stone palace that he had built. The grand pillars of fighting dragons, eyes winking with precious gems, now made his stomach curdle. He trained his eyes away. One of the soldiers noticed.

"Aren't you proud of your home?"

"It was a wedding present," Torryn said. He glanced at Filgaryn to see if his jailer would give any indication of how he should answer. Filgaryn was pretending he wasn't listening. Even to his own ears, his voice sounded flat. "I built this for her ..."

General Rivyr joined them before they stepped into the golden rays of the sun. He nodded curtly to dismiss the soldiers and took Torryn's arms. "Be careful, my son."

But it wasn't to Torryn that the general was looking. It was Filgaryn. Torryn felt like a pail of cold water had been dumped over his head.

"We'll avenge Galvrayne, *Aluel*."

Torryn's stomach heaved, his eyes swivelling between Filgaryn and the general. They were father and son. That meant that Galvrayne was the general's son, Filgaryn's brother and Ayrahylse's victim. Why had the general not thought to reveal they were brothers? Nay, Torryn scoffed, *half-brothers*.

"Wait for when you're in the air before escaping, Torryn," the general said. "Today isn't the day to take our revenge for Galvrayne."

"I'm not doing it for you," Torryn snarled. "I'm doing this for me. For my son, not yours."

The general looked him over, his expression almost sad. "Yet you are my knife, *mynrell*. I swear no son of yours will come to harm at the talon of our clan."

Torryn lifted his chin, meeting Rivyr's hard gaze in clear challenge. "You know what I did to my body."

"There's more than one way for our kind to be a father. You have a future, Torryn. You both do ... without me."

"*Aluel*, please." Torryn hadn't thought Filgaryn as one to beg.

"You know, Filgaryn, the highest duty an *aluel* has. It is nature's way."

Torryn sniffed.

Rivyr embraced Filgaryn briefly and then turned his eyes towards Torryn. "I'll give you this gift. I found your child; his song still lingers in the mortal realm. You may have buried him nameless, but know this: his dragon name is Syrif. A dragon of music and dance. Now his soul sighs with the Wind Song on the peaks of this mountain. One day your soul will join his, and you'll know peace."

Torryn shifted uneasily, unsure what to do with this knowledge. For all he knew, it was a lie meant to placate him.

"You're not much different than me. You grieve for your son as I grieve for mine." The general's voice softened. "There's nothing worse than losing your child. If I could, I would take that pain from you."

"Rivyr!"

Torryn winced at Rhodys' harsh yells.

"Do what you have to do to survive. There's no shame in that." Rivyr's whispered command was soft, spoken with such urgency that Torryn thought the general might have truly cared. "I'm so sorry, Torryn, I am. I couldn't accept you as mine without losing you. Now it's too late."

Growling, Torryn wrenched himself against his bonds. There was a rage deep inside of him that longed to be free, to rip out the throat of the man who sired him. Empty apologies were only words. Artrothians wielded words as weapons; they used them to manipulate and subjugate.

The general's grip tightened, and he dragged Torryn out into the sun. Being so long underground, the brightness stunned him. He turned his face away from the glaring light, ignoring the raucous jeers of the Artrothians who had come to witness the half-breed.

He stood on the very outcrop of the home he had built. He glanced back at the carved pillars. Without Ayrahylse, without the illusion that he still had a hope for a family, this place was no longer his refuge.

The general kept pace, dragging Torryn until he was face-to-face with Rhodys. It wasn't the Artrothian prince that held his interest. It was the two women on either side of him. The first was an older lady dressed in heavy purple robes stitched with gold thread. Her long dark hair was pulled back into a severe bun. When Torryn was dragged out, she had been in the middle of a hushed argument with the Artrothian prince. On either side of this woman were two miserable little girls he recognised as Pyrah's daughters. The second woman was Ayrahylse. Her gown was of soft silk, light grey and held at the waist with a silver belt. Her hair cascaded down her shoulders in a golden waterfall.

She was as beautiful as Torryn remembered, but looking at her was like taking an axe to the stomach. The pain of her betrayal washed over him once more.

"Wife," Torryn growled. "I prefer the blue gown on you."

"So," the older woman said, glancing towards Ayrahylse, "this was your bull dragon."

Ayrahylse whipped her head around to stare at the other woman. "Prince Rhodys has freed me from our marriage, Lady Latunya."

"How convenient for you," Torryn replied. "I hear you are already warming his bed."

Ayrahylse had the grace to flush. Latunya, however, had already dismissed him from her mind. She turned back to Rhodys.

"I'll go and intercept Xavryn's spies," she said, clapping her hands at the two frightened children. "Back inside to your quarters."

Charyss' eyes swept over Torryn, but seeing that he was a prisoner, her eyes dulled. She took her sister's hand to escort her inside. Heart heavy, Torryn watched them go.

"When you find Xavryn's men, bring them to me," Rhodys said.

Latunya nodded and manifested into a lilac dragon. She nodded her triangular head in Torryn's direction. "Make sure the emperor's prize finds his way back safely inside."

Rhodys stepped forward, ignoring the light purple dragon as she took flight. His grey eyes peered into Torryn's face, looking for any signs of weakness. Torryn wouldn't give him the satisfaction.

"You have a brave tongue, slave."

Torryn tilted his head back and laughed. "A dragon like me isn't meant to be held captive. You might find yourself burned."

It took all of Torryn's resolve not to flinch when Rhodys brandished a dagger. Twirling his dagger, Rhodys took another step forward. With the point of the blade, the Artrothian prince lifted Torryn's chin so their gazes met.

Swallowing thickly, Torryn refused to break eye contact with Rhodys. The dagger was pressed into his skin, slicing his skin.

"You get your boldness from your dragon blood."

"I like to think my boldness is my own," Torryn replied.

"You'll be held down as you manifest, and you'll be leashed."

"Leashed?" Torryn snarled. "I'm no dog."

"Don't you wish to fly, Torryn, dear?" Ayrahylse asked. She smiled demurely at him. "I know how you like to commune with the wind. If you wish to do so, you'll submit."

"You are surrounded, lizard. Fighting is futile," Rivyr rumbled at his side. There was a hidden meaning in the low voice. A warning to behave and be patient.

Filgaryn was at his side. His palm was warm on Torryn's back. The familiar touch was enough to ignite his temper, but he reined himself in.

"Kneel, forehead touching the ground." Filgaryn placed his hand on Torryn's shoulder, expecting he would be obeyed.

Taking one last look at Ayrahylse's face, Torryn knelt. She regarded him coolly as if he were less than a fly and not the father of her first-born child.

"Please do what you must to survive." Rivyr's deep voice echoed in Torryn's mind. *"Let me protect you."*

Turning his head minutely, Torryn looked to the general. His father made no sign that they were communicating, but he caught Rhodys' narrowed eyes. Before he could rouse further suspicions, he leaned his torso down and pressed his forehead to the earth. It was awkward with his hands chained behind his back.

Filgaryn's hands ran down his arms. There was a light squeeze on one of his hands. "When your chains are unlocked, you'll not move. I'll position you. Do you understand, lizard?"

"Yes," Torryn grumbled.

The chains may not have been around his wrists for very long, but Torryn felt a keen sense of relief as they were removed. It took all of his discipline to remain bent in the degrading position. His dragon longed to rip free. But if Filgaryn had planned an escape, it wouldn't do to ruin it too early. Every fiber of his being rebelled at the thought of placing his trust in his apparent half-brother.

Filgaryn took Torryn's left hand and placed it flat on the ground. Torryn breathed in through his nose and out through his mouth.

"So, you can behave yourself?" Rhodys said, his voice dripping with disdain. "I can see your dragon practically begging you to rip my throat out."

"He is not unintelligent, my prince," the general said. "He knows when to obey orders."

Filgaryn took Torryn's right hand and placed it down beside him.

Forehead pressed to the ground in surrender, Torryn longed to look up as he heard the clanking of chains. He sensed a few soldiers moving in position around him. Filgaryn's knee dug into his back. Even though he suspected what was coming, nausea roiled through his gut. Filgaryn was holding a chain to loop around his neck.

Two soldiers approached, pressing the point of their spears into his side.

"When I give you the word, you will manifest," Filgaryn said. "If you attack our soldiers, we'll impale spears through your throat. Do you understand?"

Torryn groaned.

"I said, do you understand?"

"Understood," Torryn muttered.

"Good." Filgaryn's weight shifted on his back. "Raise your head."

Humiliated, Torryn did as he was told. Behind him, Filgaryn readied himself. "Manifest."

The blue and gold dragon that lived within him burst free, and chains were wrapped around his neck. Every instinct within his bones cried out for him to defend himself. It was unnatural for a dragon to prostrate himself before an enemy.

Lashing his tail out, Torryn struck two guards, and Filgaryn tumbled from his back. He felt flames of fury igniting in his belly and rounded onto Ayrahylse. She was the cause of all his misfortune. Nothing but her blood would satisfy him.

Ayrahylse, seeing the danger of a bull dragon determined to kill her, gathered her silken skirts and manifested. She pushed past two gawking guards and scrambled to take flight. Torryn spewed fire in her wake.

"Kill him!" Rhodys shrieked. "He cannot be controlled."

The points of the soldier's spears pressed into his neck, drawing blood. Torryn didn't care. He gathered fire in his belly again, rumbling. A slim warrior woman dashed forward, planting a spear into Torryn's foot. While he bellowed his rage, she pressed her hands to his side. Her power was like Ayrahylse's. Against his will, his mouth closed.

Teeth sunk into Torryn's neck, and he was driven into the ground.

"Get down! Stay down!" Filgaryn's voice in his mind was stern.

Torryn blinked, looking up at his half-brother's dragon. Filgaryn's violet eyes shone with a vicious gleam, but his teeth didn't grip him any more than necessary. The warrior woman's power washed over him again, and the decision was taken out of his hands. The fire in his belly was quenched, and Torryn collapsed like a helpless child.

Closing his eyes in defeat, he lay slumped under Filgaryn's weight. He had lived a free dragon. Now he would die a slave.

CHAPTER TWENTY-ONE

Pyrah

RYGARD'S FORT, AVHYL

Pyrah never had the misfortune of meeting Chieftain Rygard of Avhyl. From Elryk's accounts and the whispers she had gleaned from Luthur's fighting men, his success in amassing wealth made him lazy. Behind the strong walls of his stone fortress, a man could afford to be arrogant. Pride would be his undoing.

She was sitting around their campfire with Daerys at her side when Uxhyn returned from his latest scout. They set up their base camp fifty miles to the west of the fort. A long distance for a human army, but a swift flight for dragons.

Pyrah watched as Uxhyn moved through the throngs of their eager hatchlings, each one of them wanting to hear his report of the enemy. He returned to his human form and beckoned to Melayah with a crooked finger. The other young dragons grumbled as he passed them, but Hyn ignored them and lowered himself on the ground beside Daerys.

"It's getting late," Hyn said, clapping Daerys on the knee. All of Hyn's scouting was done at night. His black scales hid him from the sight of the enemy, and so he was able to gather intelligence unhindered. "You should both be resting."

"We wanted to hear what you had to say," Melayah said. She leaned forward, prodding the campfire with a long stick so that the flames crackled and grew. Pyrah raised her eyebrow at the way Daerys admired her in the glow of the flames.

"Keen, are you?" Hyn said. "Very well."

Leading up to their planned attack, Uxhyn frequently scouted their surrounding areas. Unfortunately, Rygard wasn't as dim-witted as Luthur liked to boast. A healthy dose of intelligence meant that the architecture of Rygard's fortress was not only impressive but was designed to defend against armies. Rygard had drawn the plans himself.

Avhyl had been selected for the natural defenses of the hills. To the east the fort overlooked the ocean, and on the west a flat field that stretched for miles. Tall turrets, which were manned day and night, were stationed in each corner and midpoint of the walls. Guards changed their posts at random intervals. Hyn also lamented the thickness of the walls, which would take significant time and power to topple.

"There're huge pots, six along each wall," Hyn said, shaking his head.

"It's for boiling oil, setting it aflame and tipping on top of the enemy below," Melayah replied.

"Seen it in port cities in the east," Daerys said. "I've never seen them in use."

"It's terrible." Melayah shivered, sheathing a long dagger in her belt. She wrinkled her nose. "I never want to hear the screams of cooking men ever again. And the smell ..."

The presence of such destructive weapons concerned Pyrah. Some of the chieftains of Widow's Bay had provided them with a human contingent. The chieftain of Tamaryn led them, but Pyrah was painfully aware that they were there on a voluntary basis. She had hoped for better numbers and despaired that at the first sign of the might of the Artrothian threat, they would leave. Elryk echoed her own concerns. The humans had made no oath of loyalty to her, and if the chieftain were spooked, they would all follow him.

"The presence of the humans is useful," Hyn said, scratching the stubble on his chin. "But if we can't get them through the city walls, I'm not sure what use they are to us."

The conversation continued around Pyrah; she spotted Elryk strolling with Nahilya and a few other human commanders. Never would she send her vulnerable human twin against boiling oil. She could only imagine his skin cooking and peeling from his bones ...

"Dropping humans from the sky is not a good idea," Daerys muttered.

Hyn's eyes swept over Daerys' thoughtful face, clearly showing his bemusement at the thought. "Shall we make wings for them from bedsheets and have them glide into the fort? We could call them Stealth Moths."

"I don't think that'll work," Daerys said, tilting his head with a frown. "The humans would splatter on the ground."

Melayah thumped Daerys' bicep. "Hyn wasn't being serious."

Daerys responded with a sheepish, lopsided grin. "We need to take Rygard's forces by surprise, take out the pots before they have a chance to boil anything. If we can make the walls safe, we can land. There's no reason to open up the city to our forces."

"It has the added benefit of having the city closed to escapes," Melayah said, fingering the pommel of one of her short swords.

"We have sixty hatchlings in our number now … This could be done." Hyn looked thoughtful. "Shall I get Elryk to divide them into teams?"

"Yes," Pyrah said, chewing her bottom lip. "The human chieftains can split their men among the dragons."

For many years, Rygard had been a fierce rival of Luthur's. But his wealth and his confidence in his own might had made him lazy. The appearance and the support of dragonkind made him more so.

Hyn timed their attack on Rygard's fort in Avhyl perfectly. The black dragon had watched from a safe distance as Rhodys took a host of dragons north, leaving the fort under the command of the chieftain.

Those with manifested dragons were blessed with a keener eyesight. While Rygard's men would find it difficult to spot approaching dragons in the night sky, they could see the details of their enemies at a great distance.

There was a certain thrill flying into a great fortified city to take it without toppling its walls. Come morning, Torqui was certain it would be hers. The only sound as they made their deadly approach was the beating of wings.

Elryk had drilled the young dragons so that they kept their wingbeats in time with one another. It would limit the wind displacement and keep the sound to a minimum. Dragons were large creatures, and while one or two might be able to stalk an enemy in relative silence, a group of dragons was hard to disguise. Torqui could only hope that Rygard's men were so unprepared that they wouldn't realise dragons were upon them until it was too late.

Torqui turned her head to the side. Daerys dutifully kept up with her, his eyes glowing like embers in his excitement. His youth shone through with the muscle twitches around his lips. How he longed to snarl and snap and make his presence known. A common enough trait for a hatchling.

Lying down over her neck, Elryk let his hands run down her scales in the way he knew she liked. With his body pressed close, she could feel his heartbeat. Before they left, he vowed to find her daughters, no matter the cost, and bring them back to her. She shivered, wondering how much her children would have changed in their time as prisoners of Rhodys. She had no news of them, and so she had to assume they were still alive. If they were dead, Rhodys wouldn't hesitate to torment her.

Hyn led the charge from the west and Torqui from the east. The first point of attack was the oil buckets. Then they would shake off their human cargo and destroy Avhyl.

"Daerys, take the southern team. Remember, never run, never surrender."

"I'll fly like the wind, Lullah. I'll make you proud."

Inside Torqui's mind, Daerys' voice was soft and calm. She felt his glance linger over her before he swerved to the side, taking the southern team with him. It had been decided that Daerys and Melayah would split from Torqui and Uxhyn to take out the oil pots on the adjacent sides. She would ensure to herd Daerys' team once they dealt with their biggest threat.

As Torqui predicted, Rygard's men were woefully unprepared for dragons. Rhodys had the unfortunate habit of thinking everyone quailed in fright in his mere presence. He assumed that she had been emotionally defeated and abandoned. It would not have occurred to him that she would have gathered human reinforcements. He ruled her out a threat, and as a consequence, she had been able to grow her following. After today, Rhodys would be on his guard. So it was best to hit him hard and fast.

By the time their dragons were spotted by the men on the walls, it was too late. Large brass bells pealed a warning to the citizens of Avhyl.

Humans ran along the walls like ants, spears held at the ready. Torqui was no fool. A well-aimed spear could quickly incapacitate a dragon. A downed dragon was a dead dragon. While not a particularly rare skill, Nahilya was their only healer. Tonight, she would be busy. Battles and skirmishes held risk and loss. That was the life of a battle-dragon.

Along the southern wall, she caught Daerys' shadow. The flickering of the torches made the orange scales of his underbelly glow. She could almost hear his rumble as he spewed fire along the ramparts. He didn't slow but showered the walls with flames.

Rygard might have intended to cook their human soldiers with oil. But dragons could roast humans in their mail shirts. The screams of the men were haunting, but Torqui held very little pity for them. They had sided with Rhodys, with Artroth, and for that, they would die. It did not matter whether by dragon fire or axe or noose they would perish.

There was a beauty to dying bathed in flames, Torqui mused, watching as two men jumped from the walls, their bodies consumed by dragon fire.

Torqui noticed with great glee the three small dragons landing upon the wall among the flames. Daerys' team consisted of young ones who had skills with forming and repelling fire. Her dear brother had worked them hard, showing them how to use their powers.

"Our Embers are in place," Torqui shouted, using Elryk's pet name for Daerys' team.

On her back, Elryk patted her scales. "Daerys did well."

Practicing spewing large amounts of flames was dangerous. Daerys had never been given the opportunity to throw so much fire in one breath. Elryk was right. Daerys did exceedingly well.

Chuckling, Torqui swooped from the sky. She gave very little attention to the armed men on the walls. Half of them were panicking over the fire, while the rest were busy with fending off angry hatchlings who were plucking them from the wall.

"Wife!" The bellow of the enemy dragon was so unexpected that Torqui faltered. Barrelling towards her, his claws extended, was a familiar dark red shadow. There had been a part of her that knew sooner or later she would have to confront Izzur.

Torqui startled backwards, feeling Elryk and Nahilya clinging on to her as Izzur collided with her. She felt the cut of his talons, the smell of blood on his scales and the rumbling that promised fire. Twisting her head around, she bit at his chin and neck.

Izzur fought like a mad dragon, without reason or thought for himself. He seemed completely consumed by his fury, which made him unpredictable and strong.

"You killed me!" Izzur roared. He slammed up against her side, releasing her so that she plummeted and hit the ground before she could collect her bearings. Thankfully, Elryk and Nahilya tumbled from her back, battered but otherwise unhurt. "I could have protected you."

"I am no damsel," Torqui replied, wheezing as she got to her feet.

Izzur was not in the mood to show mercy. He rammed into her again, teeth closing around her chest and driving her backwards. Torqui stumbled, praying that wherever he was, Daerys remained unaware of her situation. She didn't need a well-meaning hatchling getting in the way.

There was a roar behind her, a man's voice. It was enough of a distraction for Torqui to rally her wits. She shook her head, wrenching back from Izzur. But he held fast. She felt the vibrations of footsteps, and Elryk, sword brandished, charged the dark red dragon.

Izzur, blind with rage, did not immediately register Elryk as a threat. He increased the pressure of his bite on Torqui's chest. His scaled lips parted, showing his white teeth painted with her blood.

"Let my *sudunah* go!" Elryk screamed.

Pinned by Izzur's weight and might, Torqui watched helplessly as Elryk swung himself onto the dark dragon's back. Unlike most Artrothians, Elryk was practiced at clambering upon a dragon. He moved with speed and grace, uncaring that Izzur moved beneath him. The dark red dragon roared and thrashed from side to side to dislodge his human attacker.

Flames licked up the blade of Elryk's sword, and his power burned before pulsing blue. Elryk's face twisted in determination. He balanced himself upon his knees, ramming the blade into the base of Izzur's skull. Hot dragon blood bubbled and sizzled on the magic. Sweat dripped from Elryk's forehead, and still her brother held on as Izzur wailed.

Under the fire blade's power, Izzur spasmed. His lips parted, releasing Torqui. A slow blink, and he was looking at her, no more than a scared hatchling. His wings trembled, and he gasped, sighed and collapsed to the ground.

Although the fighting around Torqui was fierce, a strange hush fell over her world. She was aware of Nahilya's hands healing her, even as she fell into the glassy portals of Izzur's eyes, frozen in death. She saw what the empire made of their battle-dragons. Those who fought under Artroth's banner inevitably became twisted, broken and empty. The thought saddened her.

Snarling, Elryk yanked his sword back, extinguishing the flames licking his blade. He jumped lightly off the back of the dead dragon and nodded curtly.

"Thank you," Torqui murmured, stunned to find she still had a voice. There was a part of her that knew her brother was extraordinary. He didn't need a dragon to be strong. Elryk the Empty was marvellous the way he was born.

"Anything for my baby sister," Elryk replied, a smile touching his lips.

"Hush. You are a grand total of ten minutes older," Torqui rumbled. Her tail flicked. "The hatchlings have done a wonderful job at dismantling the oil buckets."

One was left. It was the one closest to her. Torqui lumbered over and leaned against the brackets holding the contraption up. The oil bucket swung haphazardly on its hinges before groaning and toppling to the ground below.

Swords flashing before them, Elryk and Nahilya guarded her flank. The humans of the fort had regrouped and were desperately trying to defend themselves against the dragons and humans of Torqui's force. Melayah's observation that the closed gates would mean escape was difficult had been accurate. A quick glance at the gate below confirmed to Torqui that it was being viciously guarded by half a dozen dragons and a small group of humans. Rygard's men couldn't escape, which left them either fighting to the death or hiding.

Elryk leapt forward, his sword flashing before him. Among the humans on the wall, he took the lead. He seemed single-mindedly determined to guard Torqui's back.

A shrill cry to Torqui's left startled her. An enemy, a small girl, dashed forward. The mail shirt she was wearing was much too large, and the helmet was loose. But still she sprinted forwards, her hands outstretched. Only a few paces away from one of Torqui's newest hatchlings, the girl child manifested into a tiny silver dragon.

Stunned, Torqui's hatchlings surrounding her baulked. They were not ready to harm another dragon. The small enemy dragon flapped her wings, and much to Torqui's shock, ice crystals formed on her wings.

Otherworlds! Torqui hated winter. She was a creature of heat and warmth. Cold made fighting and flying difficult. With a feral snarl, Torqui shook her wings so that the ice shards were flung into the fray.

The silver dragon rumbled, her sound high and shrill. And a muzzle made from ice crystallised over one of Torqui's hatchlings, who whimpered and clawed pitifully at her face.

Roaring in fury, Torqui lashed out. The enemy dragon backed away, rolling onto her back, belly up in fright. She snarled and lunged at the silver dragon, who had dared use her power against her own hatchling, only to find Elryk getting in the way of a deadly blow. Killing the silver dragon would be easy. She had been a fool to show herself to Torqui.

"No!" Elryk cried out, smacking Torqui's snout.

Torqui growled. Of all the humans, Elryk was the only one she would ever tolerate smacking her. From the defiant look on her brother's blood-spattered face, he knew that.

"She's a child," Elryk said.

"Enemy!" Torqui rumbled, feeling the need for blood and vengeance pumping through her veins. "She sided with Artroth."

"She's manifested young. She's a *child*!" Elryk repeated. "She can't be any older than Vallah."

Upon the wall, the silver dragon cowered. She had folded herself into a tiny ball, her long, slender tail tucked under her body. It was difficult to see where the child began and where she ended. Two frightened golden orbs watched Torqui.

"What's your name, sweetheart?" Elryk knelt in front of the enemy, and Torqui wanted to sick up.

"Tya," the silver dragon whispered. "I'm nine."

"Rhodys left her to die." Elryk shook his head. While the average age for manifestation was between eleven and fifteen, it did sometimes occur young. "She shouldn't be here."

"Izzur was here ... There could be others."

Elryk looked at Torqui, his lips thinning to an expression that seemed to be pitying. "Izzur was lusting for revenge. He was waiting for you."

"Fine," Torqui snarled. She knew it was true; she had seen the madness in his eyes. Dragons who gave into madness were often abandoned by their commanders. Dismissing thoughts of her second husband, Torqui rounded onto the cringing Tya. "Fly away, child. Fly away and never return to this place."

"But ... my home ..."

Torqui lunged, snapping and snarling.

In fright, Tya cried out, stumbling to her feet and flapping her wings. She was a clumsy flyer, nothing like the skill that Daerys was now showing. Rhodys had taught this hatchling nothing.

The fighting on the walls was fierce but short-lived. Having the advantage of dragonkind made the annihilation of Rygard's forces easy. Elryk was silent as he stalked beside Torqui, his sword unsheathed and dripping with blood. She sensed he was unhappy with her, but he didn't say anything.

Nahilya was out of the way, tending to the wounded, so she would not have to endure the healer's stare. She knew that with any disagreement between herself and her twin, the healer would always take Elryk's side, no matter if her empty brother was clearly in the wrong.

She stalked along the wider streets of Avhyl before finding Hyn and Melayah in their human forms.

Melayah looked around calmly at the destruction, a frown upon her face. Her curls were wet with blood and sweat. She nodded her greeting to Torqui.

"Great mother, Hyn needs Nahilya's healing hands."

Hyn was panting, one large hand pressed to his side. His lips turned into a nasty scowl, and with his missing eye, he looked truly fierce. But his body was shaking, and his greying hair was soaked with sweat. "It's a scratch."

Melayah snorted. "More than a scratch, old man."

"Ha! The cheek!" Hyn laughed, his chest heaving with pain. He groaned and leaned against the stone wall, his eyes fluttering closed.

Torqui swept her gaze over the city. Hyn needed a healer. The burden of ensuring the city of Avhyl was destroyed was on her shoulders. Nothing could be left behind for Rhodys to scavenge.

Elryk stepped forward and placed a hand on Hyn's shoulder. "I'll find Nahilya."

"Be quick about it," Hyn whispered between his clenched teeth. His eyes remained closed.

"Did you find Rygard?"

At Torqui's question, Hyn's head lolled forward. She hated seeing him in such terrible pain. "He's the one who speared me in the side."

"I ate him," Melayah added.

"Eating requires swallowing." Hyn rolled his good eye at her. "You bit him in half. That's a big difference, *mynrell*."

"He tasted funny."

"That's because humans aren't made for dragon consumption." He stared up at Torqui, his expression pained. "I doubt I could forgive myself for the things I did tonight."

"Harden your heart," Torqui said. No good came of coddling shield-fires. "Saving our kind comes at a cost."

"You should be proud of your boy," Hyn said. "No loss to his team."

Torqui nodded. "And your teams?"

"One of mine," Melayah admitted.

"Two in mine," Hyn said.

"Excellent," Torqui said. "Those are good numbers."

"Did you see any enemy dragons?" Hyn asked.

"Two," Torqui snapped. "Izzur is dead, and a small female. I sent her on her way. Elryk was against killing her."

"Ah." Hyn peeked at the wound under his hand. It came away with dark blood. "Elryk would have had a reason for that. He has good instincts."

"I was expecting more enemy soldiers."

"It seems one of Rygard's commanders has gathered his men, and they are holed up in the main meeting house." Daerys landed, flashing his teeth in Melayah's direction. He sauntered forward, looking proud of himself.

"Then why didn't you do anything about them?" Torqui snarled. "They could be gathering weapons and forming a counterattack as we speak."

"Most likely," Hyn muttered, trying to force himself into a stand.

"Foolish man, stay," Torqui commanded.

Hyn paused his movements, looked at up at her and nodded. He slumped back into his hunched position.

Daerys toed the ground. "I thought it better to look for your daughters."

"My daughters?" Torqui repeated. She breathed in. "Charyss and Vallah are not your concern. Not while you've left enemies alive, foolish lizard."

"But *Lullah* ..."

Her children weren't in Avhyl. The clashing sound of the battle had died down, and she could hear the sighing whispers of the Wind Song. Rhodys had already moved her daughters.

Lifting her snout, Torqui wondered how much Charyss had told Rhodys. She hoped her child had enough sense to keep as many of her secrets as possible. Once Rhodys believed he knew everything ... Charyss would be useless to him. Unless ...

Rhodys had a newly manifested dragon. Was it possible that he would do the same to Charyss? Force her dragon to come forward? But no, Charyss couldn't be a dragon, could she? She was much too tender and kind-hearted for one of her kind.

"My daughters are gone," Torqui snarled. Fury curled in her gut. "And here you are, wasting time ..."

"I only wanted to please you, *Lullah*." Daerys hung his head and tucked his wings close to his body, looking thoroughly like a chastised hatchling.

"You're being harsh, Torqui," Hyn grunted. "Your boy spent a good percentage of his life living as a human slave. Hatchlings require a good deal of patience."

"Wind Song gave him to me," Torqui muttered.

"Be a good *lullah* then." Hyn's eyes bore into her own.

Torqui could feel her lip curling. How dare the old man challenge her! She rounded onto Daerys, who was watching her wearily. She had been determined to forget what she knew about his past. Although he was no longer cowed by either Hyn or Elryk, her words had the power to cut him down. Shame she was not accustomed to feeling welled in her gut. She should be building him up, not tearing him down. Under her wings he was to rise to be a grown dragon of great power and command, and it was her duty to see that he reached his potential.

"What would you do, *mynrell*, if you had command?"

"Leave. Never come back to this place."

Torqui snorted, smoke curling from her nostrils, but she clamped her lips shut at Hyn's reproachful glare. The boy may have grown up on a vessel no better than a pirate ship, but war and slaughter were not something he was comfortable with. Hyn was right; he would do better under a softer hand. She shifted. Hyn would have been a better *aluel* for him. He was indefinitely patient and understanding.

"They're the enemy, Dae," Melayah said.

"What?" Daerys exclaimed, rounding on her. Torqui found herself wanting to shield him from what she knew had to happen next. "You don't mean to kill them all?"

"It is the way of war," Torqui said. "We cannot leave a scrap of resource, living or otherwise, for Rhodys to use against us. We must take advantage of every situation we can."

"There's no room for mercy?"

"Not today," Hyn said, groaning as he stretched out a leg.

Torqui nodded her regal head. "Come, show me. Let's end this battle."

The wind whispered in Torqui's ear as she followed Daerys through the township of Avhyl. She heard its warnings. Once she committed to what needed to be done, there would be no going back. No cleansing of her soul. She steeled herself. Already she had committed heinous acts murdering her husbands, eliminating Luthur and Izzur before they became a threat. And she knew she would do it all again.

At least she could spare Daerys the act ... for now.

Daerys led her directly to the meeting house. It was a large squat building. The heavy oaken doors were locked and barred. Torqui tried not to think about the number of men that could potentially be hiding in a place like this.

Swallowing, she knew Daerys wanted nothing more than to run away from the ugly truth of war. She couldn't allow him. He didn't have the luxury of time to learn about casualties and sacrifice. He was a battle-dragon, naturally athletic, a protector and defender. The time was now for him to develop the courage to face the hard decisions.

"Stay," Torqui commanded.

Daerys locked his legs. His wings were half-unfurled, catching the sighing wind. She didn't know how much of the Wind Song he was able to hear at this early stage of his dragonhood. She hoped he found some comfort with it caressing his wings.

"Yes, *Lullah*."

Stretching out her long neck, Torqui rumbled and breathed dragon fire onto the wooden door. Such was the heat from her flames that the metal hinges melted. She paused as the door burned, counting to ten, ignoring the shouts of alarm within.

A man dressed in a full mail shirt ran from out of the doorway.

Torqui inhaled again and exhaled, her flames licking up his legs before consuming him. The flames burst through the open doorway, and the building ignited.

She had heard it said that on Artroth some dragons enjoyed the symphony of noises humans made when they died bathed in flames. She could not count herself among that number. Still, she stood over the building, watching it burn to the ground.

By morning, Avhyl would be nothing but ash; a place that was now useless in Rhodys' campaign against her.

When the screams died down, she nudged the very still Daerys and turned away. "Come, *mynrell*. It's over."

CHAPTER TWENTY-TWO

Torryn

THE STRONGHOLD

When death did not come with the stabbing of spears or the might of the dragons holding him, Torryn cracked one eye open. Filgaryn rumbled a warning sound, shifting slightly. The hot fury in Torryn's gut seared as he caught Ayrahylse watching him from the safety of a high perch. He scraped his chin along the rocky ground. His rage simmered to fear as he stared into her mocking eyes. His once life-mate was enjoying his shame and humiliation.

"Be still," Filgaryn said in Torryn's mind. He was sure his half-brother could feel the tremor in his body. *"I've got you."*

General Rivyr, still in his human skin, walked right in front of Torryn's nose. It was a foolhardy decision on his behalf. It didn't take a dragon long to spew fire, and human bodies weren't as flame resistant as a dragon's hide. Torryn's nostrils flared.

"There's no need for your fear, my prince," General Rivyr said, a hint of challenge in his voice. "He's like any other Artrothian. He needs to know he's been dominated."

Rhodys' face flushed at the general's implication. He pursed his lips tightly, clearly displeased.

The general ignored Rhodys in favour of turning towards Torryn and running a gloved hand down the scales of his cheek. "Hush now, you'll accept the chains and Prince Rhodys as your new master. He's a magnificent creature, my prince. No different really than a frightened mount."

Rhodys laughed. The sound was unmistakably cruel. "Ayrahylse has requested his golden horns and talons be harvested for her personal decorating."

Rivyr's eyes flashed, and he turned away from Rhodys. Torryn caught the way his hands clenched at his side. A snarl escaped his throat while his eyes sought Ayrahylse, who preened.

Rhodys' attention was solely on Rivyr so that he did not notice that some of the other dragons had also recoiled in both disgust and horror. They exchanged glances, tails swishing and smoke curling from nostrils.

"Does that upset you, General?" Rhodys asked.

"You'd defile a dragon body like a common *vehyl*?" Rivyr replied.

"He is a half-breed," Rhodys said. His cruel grey eyes didn't leave Rivyr's face. "What does it matter if I rip open his belly and pull out his intestines or take out his fangs one by one ..."

"Gut him if you must. But the disrespect of dragon corpses is too far," Rivyr rumbled. "It's utterly macabre and bizarre."

"Stay still ..." Filgaryn warned, even as Torryn felt a rising wave of panic and apprehension. "Aluel *will get you out, I promise."*

It took every ounce of Torryn's willpower to allow the general to touch him once more without growling. He heard dragon Filgaryn breathe a soft sigh of relief.

"Now are you going to be a good boy and let Rhodys' soldiers bind you?"

Torryn's eyes glared incredulously at the general and shifted to Rhodys. "Yes," he muttered in defeat.

The soldiers inched forward, wrapping him in chains and ropes. Torryn hated himself, staying so still and meek. General Rivyr, he noticed, hadn't removed his hand from his scales.

"Spread your wings."

"Take it steady. We're not your enemy." Clear as a bell, Filgaryn's voice filtered through Torryn's mind. Shivering, Torryn spread his wings. It had been so long since he had taken to the skies. It felt like an age had passed since he last communed with the Wind Song.

Filgaryn moved to stand beside him. There was something in the lieutenant's face that did not, for once, show disinterested boredom or hatred. It was understanding and possibly grudging respect.

Three soldier dragons took to the sky first.

Torryn raised his snout, observing them, his heart soaring with the possibility of freedom. He barely noticed the nod of goodbye the general gave Filgaryn.

Gripping the chain in his teeth, Filgaryn urged Torryn into the sky.

From the ground, Torryn could hear Rhodys crowing. "Fly, little dog! Fly!"

The soldiers came to fly closer to them, each taking a dragging chain. Heart thumping wildly in his chest, Torryn watched them in growing trepidation. Did they mean to rip him apart using the chains?

"Each of the soldiers have lost family members or want to hide someone they love from Artroth. They're with us," Filgaryn's voice said. *"Be ready to fly for your life."*

At Filgaryn's words, the soldiers pulled on the chains. Torryn gasped in shock; his bounds became taut across his body. Breathing was difficult.

"Ayrahylse ... where is she? She must die." Not caring if the soldiers around them heard, Torryn's mind shouted into the void.

The soldier on the left, jaws full of chains, looked at him almost pityingly. *"Not today ... We can't both pursue her and survive Rhodys."*

"Trust me, Torryn!" Filgaryn grabbed ahold of the nearest chain and yanked. Bellowing at the sharp pain, Torryn took a heartbeat to notice the chains had snapped and were plummeting to the ground below. An outraged roar from the ground told him that their spectators were immensely unhappy with this development.

"Take your brother and fly."

Torryn didn't quite understand how he knew, but the soldier dragon who spoke seemed to be much older than him. She had dark brown orbs full of sorrow. Her posture seemed to be one of beaten down submission.

"Virrow—"

"He's exhausted ... and they come ..." Virrow looked defeated. *"Let me do this for Nahilya. She is my only living granddaughter."*

Twisting his head around, Torryn saw that Virrow was right. Rhodys had gathered a dozen battle-dragons, and they were charging forwards. Saliva dripped from the prince's fangs.

"Traitors!"

Torryn's attention flicked from Rhodys to his home. Ayrahylse had landed and was content watching the proceedings. General Rivyr had thrown off two dragons who were trying to hold him back. He manifested into his burgundy form and burst into the skies to pursue Rhodys.

"Leave my sons alone!" Rivyr bellowed in fury. The speed at which he speared through the sky was frightening.

"Sons?" Torryn muttered, even as Virrow nudged him, urging him to fly away. He couldn't stop staring, transfixed in horror as Rivyr barrelled through the lines of battle dragons and into the unsuspecting Rhodys. Sharp fangs latched onto the prince's neck.

One of his amber eyes rested on Torryn. *"Flee."*

"Ythryr may forgive me yet," Virrow said. She glanced at the battle dragons that had aligned themselves with Filgaryn and Rivyr. "For the general."

"Why?" Torryn turned towards Filgaryn as their escort burst forward to help the general with Rhodys.

"We have to go," Filgaryn said. But he didn't move.

Rivyr was still clinging to Rhodys, his teeth pinning the prince under him. It was clear the general's intention was not to kill Rhodys, only to stop him pursuing Filgaryn and Torryn. Battle-dragons loyal to Rhodys converged upon Rivyr in a confusing flurry of teeth, scales and wings.

Virrow and her band of rebels joined the fray. Torryn's stomach leapt with excitement as Rivyr clawed himself free. Blood ran down his flanks; scales had been torn from his face.

"I am at peace with my decision," the general's voice said in Torryn's mind. *"Freedom is the only gift I can give you."*

Excitement turned to a wave of nausea, knowing that no matter how hard he fought, General Rivyr and those who helped him would not survive the melee. The general would not abandon his post, nor would he harm the emperor's son. When he attacked Rhodys, he did so willingly, knowing that death awaited him.

"Why?" Torryn sighed to the wind. "Why?"

The steady beat of Torryn's wings stuttered as an ominous crack heralded a scream of pain from the general. Beside him, Filgaryn moaned softly, his head swaying side to side. A disgusted cry caught in Torryn's throat when a dark red wing was bent and torn from his father's spine. Rivyr tilted his head, his throat exposed, teeth sunk into the vulnerable flesh. Even at the distance between them, Torryn fancied he saw tears of pain track down Rivyr's face.

"Virrow!" Filgaryn yelled. Torn in half, the older dragon's body dropped from the sky like a stone.

The fighting around Rivyr paused for the barest second. Then Rhodys lurched forward, and a second wing was ripped from Rivyr's back. Scratched, bloody and dying, Rivyr locked his gaze on Torryn, then Filgaryn.

This time there were no words. Only a sense of the emotions that the general felt. Fierce pride and another emotion that Torryn didn't understand mingled. His mouth filled with bile as he felt the hope and longing that Rivyr held for his eldest son. The wind whipped around Torryn, whispering promises in his ear. Galvrayne was close, waiting to greet his father into the Otherworld.

Filgaryn's wings stuttered, and Torryn wondered if he too could feel the spirit of his elder brother nearby.

Rhodys clawed at the burgundy scales of Rivyr's chest. He thrust his fist into Rivyr, and Filgaryn screamed.

"Torryn!" Rivyr's voice cried, his body contorting and jerking. *"I'll find your hatchling. I'll hold him safe in—"*

Talons covered in thick black blood withdrew, and within his clutched claw, Rhodys held the general's beating heart. Rivyr's body slumped and was dropped to the ground.

In his mighty fist, Rhodys crushed the general's heart.

Filgaryn's wings quivered in the wind. He startled, coming back to reality. Those that sided with them would not hold back Rhodys' forces for much longer. He snapped at Torryn's side, no words necessary.

Torryn turned with Filgaryn and let him lead him from the Stronghold. Aware that Rivyr had injured Rhodys enough that the prince would not be able to keep up with them, Torryn forced his body to comply. The lingering effects of the herbs left him feeling fatigued and lightheaded. But he ignored the signs and obediently followed Filgaryn as they flew in confusing circles. Rhodys might be forced to land to tend to his injuries, but it wouldn't stop battle-dragons being sent to hunt them.

It wasn't until Torryn's eyes started to droop and he almost fell out of the sky that Filgaryn came to fly closer to him. Large, powerful grey wings guided him back into a better flying position.

"You're fatigued," Filgaryn said, worry etched over his face. "And hurt."

"I'm fine."

"You're falling asleep in the air." Filgaryn's nostrils flared, scenting the area. "Where are you taking us? Is there somewhere safe for you to rest nearby?"

"I was following …" Torryn blinked, feeling a fool for thinking Filgaryn was flying them in deliberate circles to confuse Rhodys' battle-dragons. He was a foreigner and had expected Torryn to naturally take the lead. Torryn had been too dazed to realise what the grey dragon's expectations were. He swallowed. "The swamps are nearby."

Torryn landed in a heap on the edge of his hunting grounds. Every muscle in his body screamed with exhaustion, and he ignored Filgaryn as the grey dragon took in the twisted trees that provided camouflage from the sky. The Artrothian wrinkled his nose.

"The dangers of what is lurking in the water and the smell keep most curious humans away," Torryn murmured. He curled his tail around his snout. It was a deadly mistake to return to a human form; snapdragons were notoriously opportunistic creatures. He had escaped from Artroth, and he had no desire to be eaten by a crawling reptile.

Filgaryn's claws found purchase on a nearby tree as he murmured to himself. The grey dragon drew in three deep breaths as if to compose himself, and then he snarled, swiping at the tree. The ground of the swamp was soft, and the tree toppled easily under Filgaryn's frustration.

Torryn felt he should say something. He shivered, mind warring with how he ought to feel about what happened with Rivyr. He had been a prisoner, kept in isolation and drugged. Then, at times, the general had been considerate of his needs. He glared down at his knuckles, skin warming at the memory of the general's touch as he tended to his self-inflicted wounds. Of Rivyr going to his poor dead son.

"Were you and the general close?"

Filgaryn turned to regard him with a withering stare. "He was my father, *elt aluel*."

"I …" He wasn't good at finding the right words to say in difficult circumstances.

"Father and I discussed the escape plan at length," Filgaryn said. "I knew this was coming. It's just …"

Not sure what he could do, Torryn nodded, feeling a sharp pang of sympathy for Filgaryn.

"Did the chains hurt you when we broke free?" Filgaryn asked. "You were struggling in the sky …"

"The drugs," Torryn replied, lifting his snout, hating to admit that he felt strained. But like it or not, his destiny was tied to Filgaryn, and it would be best to be honest about his condition. "I still feel sick from them."

Filgaryn had the grace to wince. He approached and blew hot air over Torryn's wounds. His scales itched as they fused together. "Many soldiers know the rudimentary basics of healing."

"Thank you," Torryn mumbled, feeling inadequate now that he was free.

Filgaryn hummed and stretched his wings, returning to his human form. "You rest, and I'll hunt. Which way are the legendary snapdragons?"

Torryn stared at him and burst into laughter. "You're not hunting a snapdragon in your human form."

"Did you not tell *Aluel* that you hunted the snap lizards in your human body? He said they'll satisfy a dragon for a week. We need to eat well if we are going to be on the run."

Torryn tilted his horned head back and laughed. "Manifest back into your dragon, dimwit, before *you* get eaten. I was hoping I could convince an Artrothian to come out hunting to these parts and get themselves killed."

Filgaryn's face flushed, and his jaw dropped. "You dared lie to an Artrothian general?"

Dragons were natural hunters, so Filgaryn didn't need extensive instructions from Torryn on how to hunt snapdragons. He hadn't been gone as long as Torryn was expecting when he returned with a kill. Torryn thought he would return gloating, but Filgaryn nodded in appreciation at the firewood Torryn had collected, then stepped back to contemplate his prize.

"I'll cook it," Filgaryn said. He glanced around nervously before returning to his human form. He paused again, staring at the dead snapdragon, chewing on his bottom lip. "The *vehyl* body has more physical demands than your dragon. A hot meal will do you good."

Torryn finally returned to his human self. Without a word to Filgaryn, he stretched out his hand, feeling the earth's essence hum around them. He closed his eyes and let the ground shift around them, creating a safe fort from any predators who thought them to be a tasty meal.

"Likewise, it's best we are able to sleep in our human bodies," Torryn said. "That way we'll conserve more energy."

"You've done this before," Filgaryn remarked. "Camped out in the wilds as a man."

"I liked the challenge. And sometimes I needed ..." Torryn nodded and crouched down beside the Artrothian. He held out his hand for the hunting knife, and after a heartbeat, the warm handle of the blade was pressed into his palm. "The belly meat is the best part. I'll show you how to carve up one of these beasties."

Filgaryn nodded, a curtain of long hair covering his face. He made only perfunctory comments as Torryn explained the best way to portion a snapdragon. When the slabs of meat were cut, Filgaryn swiftly stood and built a campfire. He returned to dragon form to spark the fire before becoming a man once more.

"Did you teach yourself to hunt and prepare snapdragons?"

"Yes," Torryn said tightly, not sure where this was going.

Filgaryn nodded, grabbing the portions of meat and skewering them to cook over the fire. "Father did say you were clever."

"Why didn't you tell me you were my brother?"

Filgaryn's stern gaze lifted from the fire. It was so much like the general that Torryn had to wonder why he hadn't seen their relation earlier.

"Half-brother," Filgaryn said. "And you were already antagonistic."

"I didn't ask to be born like this."

"Like what?"

"Defective. I would have preferred to be completely human."

"Humans are inherently inferior," Filgaryn spluttered. "Father died for you to have the full blessing of being dragonkind."

"I didn't ask him to," Torryn snapped. "He imprisoned me in my own home!"

"Would you have preferred to have been sent straight to the emperor, little brother?" Filgaryn retorted. "You have no understanding of what a dragon like Cilvryn does to prisoners. When he could no longer shield your existence, *Aluel* kept you from a fate worse than death."

Torryn's vision ran red. All he could see before him was the light dimming in the general's amber eyes, the blood oozing out of his wounds and his heart pulled from his chest cavity. His father paid the price to allow him to be free, and the thought left Torryn feeling confused and angry. Since meeting his father for the first time, he had hated the arrogant dragon. Why had he formed an escape plan? What was Torryn to him? Nothing. A mistake that he begat on a pirate woman. A son a mother didn't want ...

"Why?" Torryn choked out. "Why would he do this?"

Filgaryn stared into the fire, his brow furrowing. "What's the one thing that dragons hoard?"

Torryn shrugged. "I'm hardly a real dragon to ask."

"Heirs and bloodlines ... The emperor has already ignored my father's pleas to punish the murderer of my eldest brother, Galvrayne. Now the pompous fool who sits on the Artrothian throne thinks he can take our children from us. He thinks that he can balance out his waning power with amassing other dragons' bloodlines. The emperor has already said he would take my daughters if I were to sire any."

"Daughters?"

Filgaryn's sidelong glance was knowing as he looked at Torryn. "In Artroth it is believed that strong female dragons are sign of a powerful bloodline. Taking our sons is unbearable ... Taking daughters unthinkable."

Torryn blinked past the pain of his longing. He did not have long with his son before he died. He could not imagine giving up his child to the emperor. His father had uttered a dragon name that belonged to his son. Had they been words to soothe and manipulate him?

"He believed in death he could protect his grandsons, your sons."

"I can't have children, and he knew it."

"I beg your pardon?" Filgaryn looked affronted. "Our father was strong in the Sight. He saw your children."

"I took a poison from a medicine woman to ensure I would never sire a child."

"Why? Of all the ridiculous ... Why?" Filgaryn let the question die on his lips.

"Fear," Torryn said. "Ayrahylse was becoming dangerous ... I didn't want to have a child with her to be handed over to the emperor. I thought she wouldn't go to the nest of another bull dragon."

Filgaryn snorted. "Better without her."

"I don't think I'll ever forgive myself for being so blind." Torryn felt a stab of rage. He stood and stepped away from the fire. His feet took him towards the door of their hut, but Filgaryn stopped him with a simple hand gesture.

"Keep the dagger with you. Don't go far; I don't want to rescue you from a snapdragon."

Torryn looked down at the hunting knife. He knew without a shadow of a doubt it was an ancient Artrothian weapon. "I cannot."

"It was Galvrayne's. If you ever have a chance, plunge it into Ayrahylse's chest." Through Filgaryn's steady stare, Torryn could see his dragon stirring. "Let's find you a new mate. That'll cheer you up."

That night Torryn dreamed of the docks of Artroth.

He was a small boy again, clutching on to his mother's hand. She took him to the market square. He was thrust to stand before a tall stranger, a man with long dark hair and huge dragon wings.

"Your father," his mother's voice said. Torryn knew that she no longer wanted him aboard her ship. He was eight. Much too old for an all-female crew.

"How do you know he's mine?"

"I can't control his power."

Torryn blinked. He hadn't meant to be naughty. He wanted to stay with his mother. Tears pricked in his eyes, but he was much too old for those as well.

Above his head, two dragons clashed, snarling and roaring. He felt a spike of fear, and before he could crush his emotions, it bubbled out. His power streamed from him. The ground quaked, and the man looked up in horror.

"What are you doing bringing a child with such a strong power into the middle of the viper's nest?" the man cried. "Run, boy, run. Don't stop."

Torryn was rooted to the spot. The man's brows knotted together, and his tone lowered. He shuddered as a voice cut through into his mind. "Run, my son. I can't protect you."

The sound of a sword being unsheathed had him reeling back in horror. He stumbled backwards and fled. The man's voice had changed. "There's only one thing to do with a pup like that: drown him."

He ran alongside his mother up the gangplank while his earth moving power went wild.

"Run!" cried a voice within his mind. "Run, don't stop. Don't come back."

When they were out to sea, he was sent to bed without supper. He could hear the arguments up on the deck. Tears he had been fighting fell. He knew when they reached their home port, his mother would give him up. He had no doubt in his mind she would choose the sea over him.

Rolling over, he had the sense he wasn't alone. The man from the docks was standing over him. He wiped at his tears, smearing them all over his face. "I'm sorry."

"Don't," the man said. "Ythryr, bless you, child."

CHAPTER TWENTY-THREE

Torryn

THE SWAMP

Torryn woke to Filgaryn shaking his shoulder. He blinked, mourning the loss of the gentle sway of a vessel at sea. His mind reached out, trying to remember that last voyage with his mother, but the memory of his night imaginations was already fading. All that was left was a vague recollection of a man's voice.

"It's dark," Torryn murmured into his arm. He grimaced at the drool on his sleeve. He hadn't slept this well in days, which was odd because he witnessed General Rivyr's murder yesterday.

"We should go. It's a few hours before first light."

"Fine." Torryn rolled onto his back and stared up into his brother's pinched face. In the grey light of approaching dawn, he could see the uncertainty and fear in Filgaryn. His brother's attention was on the thick earthen door that Torryn had erected to block other predators from entering while they slept.

"I'm surprised you didn't slit my throat in my sleep."

"I was tempted," Filgaryn replied. He sounded tired. "I thought to use your hard skull to knock down the stone door you erected."

Groaning, Torryn thumped his brother's side and heard the satisfying gasp.

"There've been rumours of Pyrah, daughter of Latunya, building a resistance army."

"Pyrah is like a spark on dry kindling," Torryn replied, getting to his feet. He gestured to the stone door, and it crumbled under the influence of his power. "She's dangerous. I'd advise caution before joining her. She's not fond of me."

"She'll be less fond of me; I can assure you." There was a sardonic light in Filgaryn's eye, an ember of humour.

"Oh?"

"I'll tell you the tale when I'm more so inclined." Breathing in deeply, Filgaryn stepped out into the swamp. "Let's say I was a younger son with many older male cousins. I made up for their solemnness."

"Don't tell me you bullied Elryk the Empty?"

Filgaryn snorted. "No. I was more determined to rub shoulders with larger dragons than me. Elryk was too young to harass."

"Where do you suggest we go?" Torryn followed Filgaryn out in the cold of the clearing. The swamp was fine for hunting, but he never enjoyed sleeping here. It was much too dangerous and wet.

Filgaryn raised his eyebrow at him, and Torryn wondered how he had missed the similarities between the general and his half-brother. Was it deliberate, he wondered, the general giving Filgaryn custody over him? Could he be expected to work with his half-brother? While he lived an unhappy existence, afraid of his own power and running and hiding, Filgaryn was born of a dragon. A general. Filgaryn was born knowing what he was. Torryn knew from his brief encounter with his father in Artroth that he grew up in a wealthy family.

"You're the local," Filgaryn replied. "Take us somewhere remote."

"There are mountains to the south. The peaks are higher. The mountain deer are plentiful, and the ocean is close for fishing."

"Fresh water?"

"Nearby."

"And the humans?"

Torryn shifted, refusing to meet Filgaryn's eyes. "They're afraid of these mountains."

Filgaryn raised an elegant eyebrow as he studied Torryn's face. "Why?"

"They're said to be the home of a demon prince." Torryn felt a fresh wave of shame and despair flood over him. His skin prickled with the embarrassment of his catastrophic mistake. "They call the place Levly Peak."

"*Lizard Peak*?" Tilting his head back, Filgaryn laughed. "You rose the mountains from the earth a second time?"

"It was an accident."

"I would have dearly liked to have seen the *vehyl's* faces. Very well, it is time to take me to your mountain."

Torryn could honestly say he was many things. One thing he was not was unprepared. While the other known dragons tended to stay in their own territories, he had explored the lay of the land.

He knew that his reputation as the dragon of deceit made him vulnerable, prone to rumours and betrayal. So under the guise of hunting, he had scouted the natural cave systems of the mountains that he had grown from the ground. When he found potential places, he used his power to carve out dens, which were large enough for half a dozen dragons.

Among the rock and earth, Torryn was at home. He loved the cool mountain air when it caressed his hot scales, and the sighs of the Wind Song.

"Welcome home, king of the mountain."

Torryn blew hot air in Filgaryn's direction, snarling as his brother banked to land. He followed the pure Artrothian dragon down onto the mountain side.

Ayrahylse may have fancied herself the queen among the *vehyl*, but Torryn was master of the land and sky. He let the air ripple over his wings, watching as Filgaryn prowled along the dragon den, sniffing. Biting down a sigh of impatience, he swooped to land beside his brother.

"This den is not empty."

Torryn lifted his snout and scented the air. His lips curled back in annoyance. He could smell her; a dragon sleeping in his safe den.

"Steady," Filgaryn said. "We don't know what's in the cave. Do you recognise the scent?"

"No," Torryn replied tersely. "You?"

"I do not," Filgaryn confirmed. "Stay behind me ..."

Ignoring Filgaryn's command, Torryn stepped around him, slapping him with his tail as he did so. He prowled forward. The muscles of his forelegs were taut, prepared for battle. Filgaryn growled and followed him inside.

The caves resounded with a soft, rumbling purr, and Torryn crept closer, sure to keep his belly close the ground and back legs ready to spring into attack.

"Who's there?" The voice sounded very young.

"The master of this den," Torryn replied. "Who are you?"

"I'm no one."

Behind him, Filgaryn scoffed.

Torryn ignored him. "We both know that's not true. Give me a name, or I'll light this cave up."

"Tya." The voice became shrill with terror.

"Enough!" Filgaryn snapped. He pushed past, his narrowed eyes gleaming in the dark. "It's a small hatchling. Don't you know what this means?"

Torryn grunted and followed Filgaryn's lead.

In the far corner of the cave was a small silver dragon. She pressed her hindquarters into the rock of the cave, her wide golden eyes watching them fearfully. Torryn immediately felt a sense of shame for how he had responded to her presence.

Filgaryn rumbled a low, soothing note, but it did very little to calm the small dragon.

"I'm Filgaryn, and this blustering hide of hot air is my *sudunyn*, Torryn. We're the sons of Rivyr Spymaster. Who is your family, little one?"

The small silver dragon sniffed. "I am Tya. I belong to no one."

"Can you tell us what happened?"

"A dragon sent for all humans with any powers. They took us to Prince Rhodys, and he forced a dragon out of me. But I was too small to fly away with him, so they left me with the mad one. Then the great she-dragon came and burned down the walls of Avhyl, but I couldn't fight her. She wanted to kill me, but a man with hair the colour of fire told her she was naughty ... She told me to fly away and not to come back. I didn't know where else to go."

"It's going to be okay," Filgaryn said, taking a small step towards her. When Tya recoiled, he stepped back. "Manifest back into a human, little one. You're using energy staying in your dragon body."

Tya looked at him, eyes full of misery. "But I'm cold and hungry."

"Torryn is a great hunter. He'll go and bring you back something good to eat. My side is warm."

The expression of doubt was still on Tya's face as she regarded the pair.

Filgaryn smiled at her. Somehow on his dragon lips, it didn't seem to be menacing. He made a gesture with his claws and blew. A globe of light shone between his deadly talons. Winking, he reached up and hung the light seemingly in midair.

"At home we call this dragon lantern."

Torryn knew he looked like an idiot, staring up at the globe, seething with the memory of how long he had to beg Ayrahylse to share this piece of Artrothian genius with him. She had enjoyed making him beg.

"Stay here, Tya. I would have a word with my brother." Filgaryn nudged him, and Torryn reluctantly left the cave and went back into the light of day. "Do you know what this means?"

"I gave Rhodys too much information, and now he is using it to create more enemies and build his army."

Filgaryn rolled his eyes. "Salvation of our kind. If we can multiply our numbers through coaxing dragonkind out of human skin ... we might not be as doomed as the emperor has feared."

"She's very small."

"Aye," Filgaryn said with a sage nod. "She's young for her first manifestation. Prepubescent. I'll look after her. We don't want to hand her back to Rhodys."

"No, I guess not." Torryn stared at Filgaryn in speculation. "I thought that you would find her lacking. Inferior."

"It's true that we can't expect the same power from a—" Filgaryn stopped, looking Torryn up and down as if a thought suddenly occurred to him. He shook his head. "Never mind. I'll be her *aluel*."

Torryn frowned.

"You're not ready," Filgaryn said. "You have more to learn about our kind. How can you be expected to look after a hatchling?"

Unfurling his wings, Torryn didn't bother looking at his half-brother. He had no idea of what to think of his 'family' now. "Very well, I'll find something for your hatchling to eat."

Torryn returned to the cave to find Filgaryn in dragon form tightly wrapped around a sleeping girl. She couldn't have been more than ten summers old. Long strands of dirty strawberry blonde hair stuck to her forehead. In her sleep, she was drooling.

One lazy dragon eye opened. "What?"

Torryn shook his head, dropping the two harts he had captured. He licked the blood from his teeth. "Nothing."

Filgaryn snorted in disbelief. "It's not nothing."

Torryn tilted his head, staring at Filgaryn and the girl. "I never expected someone like you …" He gestured hopelessly with his claw. "Could …"

"Could what?"

"Could bother to look after a small one."

Lips peeling back, Filgaryn snarled at him. "And when you say someone like me, you mean …"

"Artrothian."

"It wasn't always like this," Filgaryn said. "Once, before the great divide between *vehyl* and dragon, we ruled our own families and clans, separate from humankind. Our world changed when humankind grew greedy. They came to our shores thinking to hunt our children and plunder our sanctuaries. They prized the horns and teeth of killed dragons. Parts of our young one's bodies were used as jewellery. Our battle-dragons rose with the fires of retribution. After the war against the hunters was over, dragonkind didn't stop their vendetta. Humans, proven to be weaker and inferior, were enslaved to the budding Artrothian empire."

Torryn snorted. Small streams of smoke curled from his nostrils. "You speak of something that happened goodness knows how many millennia ago."

"All legends have a base of truth. I've been to the Nests of Ayr-Rouhella and have seen the skeletons of the unmanifested dragons that humankind invaded our islands to kill."

"Unmanifested dragons?"

"Little children who did not have a dragon form. In our long forgotten past, dragon parents did not have need to rigorously guard their nests," Filgaryn replied. "Humans favoured taking teeth, shoulder blades and fingers."

Torryn thought he was going to be sick. "Why those bones?"

"The hunters took the teeth, wings and claws before they could come into being. There is good reason that our kind hate humans. There are hundreds, maybe thousands of child skeletons in the caves of Ayr-Rouhella. The winds on that island still weep to this day for our lost hatchlings," Filgaryn said. He glanced down at the sleeping child, who hummed in her sleep and nuzzled the warm scales of his belly. "One day when the white dragon rises, the wars will cease."

"He'll be of Ramyr. He'll have no love for Artroth," Torryn replied. "He's a story."

Filgaryn shifted. Under the dragon lantern, his steel-grey scales looked like armour. His violet eyes narrowed. "I don't believe that to be true. Father foresaw his coming. Gahryk the All-Knowing too. When so many with the Sight see the same thing … There's more for the emperors of Artroth to worry about than our crumbling bloodlines. If they keep punishing dragonkind, the white dragon will fly against them."

"One dragon to take down the emperor."

"He's a symbol of what is to come. The place marker in history. A dragon born on the feast day of high winter."

"And you think he's out there somewhere?"

"His time has not yet come. Like it or not, we need each other if we are going to survive."

The small girl murmured and rolled over. Torryn felt a pang of jealousy that his brother had taken the hatchling for himself, but he knew he was right to do so. They were in a time of war and great danger. Filgaryn was military trained, understood Artroth and was better equipped to keep her safe, while he was still learning about his enemy.

"The she-dragon, Pyrah, what can you tell me about her?"

"I thought you knew of her in Artroth."

"That was a long time ago, Torryn. She was a child when she left. She's a woman now."

"She's thirty-two summers, has two daughters with the chieftain of Wymeria, Luthur, who is no longer of the natural world. As far as I could tell, the children showed no signs of dragons. Elryk lived nearby, and he dotes on the girls. He's loyal to his sister, fiercely protective. While Pyrah can be unpredictable, Elryk is known to be more reasonable." Torryn licked his lips at the long-lost memory of Pyrah's searing kiss.

"Yes, Elryk was always the more amiable of the twins," Filgaryn said.

"The she-dragon is in trouble." Tya yawned, rubbing her eyes with her small fists. She blinked lazily up at Torryn and sneered at his kill. Pointing a small, delicate finger at the buck, she said, "I can't eat raw meat."

Filgaryn hummed, the sound reverberating around the cave. He pointed his snout at the kill and breathed dragon fire over it.

"*Rshon mahthyt*!" Torryn yelped, jumping back from the stream of fire. "That's a bit extreme."

"Dragon dung? You Ramyr have an interesting way of swearing." Filgaryn shrugged. "It's cooked, is it not, brother?"

Pressing his lips together, Torryn manifested back into his human body. Filgaryn followed suit. He knelt by the kill, unsheathing a dagger. He sliced a neat slither of meat off the first hart, humming as he did so.

"Ramyr certainly has beautiful prey creatures." Filgaryn ran his hand through the ruined fur of the deer.

"If you had given me time, I could have skinned them and saved the pelts."

Filgaryn dipped his head in acknowledgement. "Feeding the little one is more important. We can kill for pelts later. We won't be here long."

It hadn't escaped Torryn's notice that he didn't know what powers Filgaryn possessed. Did his brother have some sense that danger was approaching? He himself felt nothing. But could he rightfully trust his own instincts after his own life-mate, his *ketur*, had betrayed him so deeply?

Looking away from the sight of his kills, he moved a little further into the dark so Filgaryn might not read his expression. He had made so many terrible mistakes, and others' lives had been forfeited for them. He couldn't rely on either his man or his dragon.

"Torryn, you must eat."

"I eat when I am hungry."

"No," Filgaryn snarled. "You'll eat when the Artrothian tells you to."

"This isn't Artroth, and I'm not your slave."

"No, I'm the experienced battle-dragon." Filgaryn was unable to hide the bite of his tone. "Bull dragons of our size require a lot of energy and need to eat more in times of high stress. Eat, brother. We are flying for our lives."

Torryn had no answer for him.

"Fine. If you faint while flying, I won't go back for you."

"I wouldn't ask you to," Torryn snarled. "I didn't ask for your help or for any of this. Did it cross your *superior* Artrothian mind that I might not want your help?"

Tya grabbed the forgotten sliver of meat, clutching it to her chest. She darted further into the cave with a furtive glance at the pair of them. Her teeth were biting her lips so hard that a small bead of blood stained them.

"You're an arrogant fool," Filgaryn replied. "You wouldn't have survived Cilvryn's court. If *Aluel* hadn't rescued you ..."

"I was a prisoner," Torryn snapped. "I've no father."

"Beyond a little humiliation, were you beaten, starved or tortured? No, none of father's dragons touched you. Sweet talons, he tended to your wounds, searched for your child to ensure he was properly respected in death. You might not have the wits to see it, but he was a good *aluel* to you. He traded *his* life for yours ... There's no higher duty for an *aluel* in Artroth."

Torryn's shoulders dropped. He pushed past Filgaryn and commenced dividing the crispy carcass with the discarded knife. "I'm sorry for your loss."

"I don't expect you to mourn him," Filgaryn answered. "But you shouldn't disrespect him."

Torryn had no words in which to make a reply. He bent his head and continued to carve the kill. The hot juices ran over his fingertips. Aware that Filgaryn was behind him, he ensured his movements were swift and sure.

"Did I somehow dishonour my child? Ayrahylse didn't tell me what to do with the body."

"No," Filgaryn replied. "You did well. All that was left for me and *Aluel* was to add our own prayers for Syrif."

Torryn looked sharply up at Filgaryn.

"I'm your brother," Filgaryn said. "Artrothians don't do halves, and that makes me Syrif's uncle. I'll not utter any more half-brother jibes. I'm sorry, Torryn."

Torryn shook his head. How could Artrothian society have such a complex understanding of family and yet treat lacking members of their clans so horrendously? It confused him how parents could sacrifice their own children. Then his human mother had abandoned him. Were humans that different to dragonkind? His head twinged.

"He saw Galvrayne in you," Filgaryn said. "When he saw that his lost son took Ayrahylse as a life-mate, he was very angry. But he couldn't do anything, couldn't warn you. Ironically, she killed Galvrayne because he was a shield-fire. He was powerful but not the dragon she wanted. Then she made her den with his younger brother ...”

"Another shield-fire; a half-bred beast." Pausing in his task, Torryn glared down at his fingers. "Must you remind me of my failings at every turn? Do you know how much I hate myself for falling for Ayrahylse's tricks?"

"Hate is such a strong word," Tya said, brushing strands of hair away from her face. The fat of her dinner stuck to her fingers, and she wiped it through her hair. Torryn could sense Filgaryn's frustrated disgust at the very human behaviour, so he intervened. If Syrif was Filgaryn's nephew, did that mean in Artrothian custom Tya was his niece?

"You need a bath, little human."

Tya tilted her chin. "I had one two weeks ago."

"Exactly," Filgaryn muttered.

"You two aren't clean."

"We'll bathe as well," Torryn said. "We've been running for our lives."

"So have I," Tya said. "We better be careful the green lady dragon doesn't come."

Torryn exchanged a glance with Filgaryn. "If Pyrah is about, I'll handle her."

CHAPTER TWENTY-FOUR

Rhodys

THE STRONGHOLD

The search for General Rivyr's rat-faced son and the prisoner came up empty. In the days following the general's surprise defection and the daring escape from custody, tongues began to wag. Rhodys heard talk that their undertaking was not supported by the emperor. Doubts were whispered in the dark halls of Ayrahylse's stone palace.

Rhodys retreated to a room that ironically looked like a royal audience chamber. Globes of light hung between pillars of twisting dragons, their glow lighting up the precious stones of blue, amber and green. Ayrahylse lounged on a throne, her golden hair unbound to frame her pretty face. The gown she wore was silver and sheer so that he could see the shapely curves of her thighs underneath the skirts. He bristled at her audacity to take the title of queen and look down at him and the spacious chamber like a benevolent ruler.

Pink lips curved into a coy smile as she spotted him. She moved to sit upright, long, elegant fingers slipping the thin straps of her dress back in place.

"No sign of Torryn?" Ayrahylse asked. She clicked her fingers, and two small figures scampered out of the dim lighting.

"None." Rhodys continued striding forward. He glanced down at the girls Ayrahylse had taken to serve her. He felt another flare of annoyance. Pyrah's daughters, Charyss and Vallah, might have little use left in them, but he hadn't given Ayrahylse permission to have them. They were his bait.

"My prince?" Charyss approached him, wincing as he looked down at her. "Wine?"

"Is it poisoned?"

Dragons had better hearing than their human counterparts, so he caught the soft mutter of the younger child. "Not this time."

Ayrahylse stirred and stood on sandaled feet, the material of her dress falling like sheets of rain. As Vallah approached with a platter of fresh fruits, roasted nuts and cold cuts of meat, Ayrahylse grabbed the child's dark, dirty hair. She shook the girl roughly and pushed her to the ground.

Charyss turned her face towards her sister's abuser, small lips parting in a wordless cry. Dropping the goblet at Rhodys' feet, she ran to her sister's aid. Wine splashed over the stone floors, and the goblet rolled away.

"Leave her alone!" Charyss cried. Her small hands clawed at Ayrahylse's fingers.

Entertained by the spat, Rhodys looked on. Charyss was strong in her anger, and her blunt nails scratched Ayrahylse's skin.

"You little ..." Ayrahylse slapped Charyss across the face, and the sound echoed through the cavernous chamber.

"Enough!" Rhodys stepped out of the wine puddle and strode up to Ayrahylse's abandoned throne and sat. He looked imperiously down at Charyss, who clutched her reddening cheeks with the palm of her small hand. Sniffling, Pyrah's eldest daughter refused to let the tears welling in her eyes fall. "Vallah, go back to your cage. Ayrahylse, leave me ... Charyss, clean the mess up!"

"My prince!" Ayrahylse pouted and batted her eyelashes. "Could I not relieve your stress?"

Rhodys snorted and waved Ayrahylse out of his presence. She stared at him, contemplating whether she should argue. Luckily for her, she decided not to test Rhodys' patience and swept out of the room. Pyrah's daughters shared an uneasy glance.

"Your cage, little mouse!" Rhodys' nostrils flared.

After dipping into a clumsy curtsy, Vallah slipped through the dark pillars and disappeared. On her knees before him, Charyss cocked her head to the side to listen to her sister's footsteps. She took one steadying breath and crawled to the wine to mop it up with the hem of her dress.

Rhodys stared at her bowed head as she worked in silence. Unlike her sister, who was wild and untamable, Charyss had a certain air that she maintained. She had fastidiously braided and bound her long dark hair to eliminate matting. Yellow flowers were woven throughout the strands. If she were sired by a dragon, she might have been stronger and grown into a woman worthy of Artroth.

"More wine, my prince?"

Rhodys blinked, bringing himself back to the present. Charyss stood before him, her slim hands clasped. He shook his head and gestured that she should leave him to his thoughts. His delay in reporting Rivyr's death to the emperor would soon raise questions about his silence. Sending word of his apparent failure in subduing Ramyr needed to happen soon.

"What do you plan on doing to my mother?" Charyss paused by one of the columns. She had spoken so softly that Rhodys almost didn't catch her words.

"That is for Emperor Cilvryn to ultimately decide," Rhodys said. He shook his head, wondering why he was giving this information to an insignificant mortal. "She killed Izzur, one of my talented fighting men."

Charyss' eyes glinted. But when she spoke, her voice was hard. "If he tried to take her by force, then he deserved everything he got."

Rhodys barked with laughter. "And your father, child, did he deserve such a terrible end at the hands of your mother?"

Charyss flinched back, her pale cheeks reddening. "We don't—"

"Prince Rhodys!"

Suppressing a moan, Rhodys stood as his aunt Latunya entered the chamber. On her heels were two of his brother Xavryn's guards. He had been expecting her to return to box his ears for his miscalculation and the escape of a prisoner. When he had commanded her to bring Xavryn's spies to him, he hadn't expected that Rivyr would be dead from his own claws. What he said from here would have to be guarded.

"We have been hearing disturbing reports, Prince Rhodys, in regards to your valiant efforts to bring Princess Pyrah home."

Rhodys recognized the guard who spoke as Mairtyr, one of Xavryn's closest allies and friend. If his brother was willing to send him to Ramyr, then something had to have happened to make his brother suspicious. He learnt from his mistakes as a rash youth and took his time in answering.

"Pyrah is prone to violence," Rhodys said. He shrugged, as if allowing his cousin free reign had been a part of his plan. "She was bound to fight back."

Charyss forgot herself and snorted humourlessly, and for the first time, Xavryn's guards and Latunya noticed her. Time among his men had hardened the little mouse a little, and she raised her chin. "My mother isn't the only one you have to watch out for."

Rhodys glared at her, then raised his gaze to settle on Latunya. He felt his aunt study her human grandchild. There was one trick that Charyss was good for.

"Charyss, go get your *special* spiced wine," Rhodys said. "The one you served me on our first meeting. It seems we have much to discuss."

Charyss' eyes widened, and she bolted from the rooms. He hoped that the child understood his implication. With Rhodys clearly not wanting to come to heated words, Mairtyr visibly relaxed. His brother's favourite was a shield-fire but had worked himself up through the ranks with his cunning and war strategy. The second guard Rhodys did not know.

"Is Pyrah a problem?" Mairtyr asked.

"My daughter was always potentially a problem," Latunya replied.

"Laelyth did describe in great detail Pyrah's reputation in Ramyr," the unnamed guard said, nodding her head sagely. "But what concerns me most is the talk around your own men about Rivyr."

"May his soul find peace in the Otherworld." It took all of Rhodys' effort to part his lips and murmur those words.

Mairtyr raised his eyebrows, meeting Rhodys' challenging gaze. "We heard it was you who ripped him to pieces ..."

"Careful." Latunya reached out with her mind. She did so cautiously. Mairtyr was already staring at her crossly. He sensed her warning she was broadcasting into Rhodys' mind. He might not have been able to discern what was said, but it was enough they were communicating behind his back. *"They were both highly favoured by Rivyr and Hael."*

"Rivyr had been poisoned," Rhodys said at length. "The Ramyr are famed for their terrible herbs and roots. He went mad in the end, drove Filgaryn off ... and it would have been me and half a dozen others dead if we did not defend ourselves."

"Mad?" the female guard asked.

The soft pitter-patter of footfalls heralded Charyss' return. She held a large tray awkwardly with two full cups.

"Only two?" Mairtyr eyed the tray, licking his lips. Rhodys knew he had a weakness for fine wines.

"I feared I might drop four," Charyss replied. She coyly approached the guards and served them both and curtsied.

"Charyss has a special flare with her spiced wine," Rhodys said. "Please don't wait for me. Drink ..."

Rhodys preened inwardly as the guards drank. He turned his gaze to Latunya, who did not look impressed. A smirk blossomed on his lips.

"Whatever the circumstances around General Rivyr's death, your reputation has taken a battering," Mairtyr said. He looked down at the wine, his brow furrowing, and glanced at his companion. "It has a rather bitter aftertaste, doesn't it?"

His companion grunted and drained her cup. "Your brother is questioning your loyalty, my prince."

Tilting his head back, Rhodys laughed. "Charyss, my dear, why don't you tell our visitors about your wine."

Charyss looked up at him in horror. She backed away, shaking her head.

"You've been drugged," Rhodys told Xavryn's spies. "You won't be able to manifest, which makes killing you and your dragon easier."

Springing from the throne, Rhodys' body shifted forms. Wings burst from his shoulder blades, and he barely had time to register the shock on Mairtyr's face as his jaws crunched over his body. The unknown woman turned to run. He sensed that she was trying to manifest and was failing.

His giant claws loomed over the top of her retreating head. Bones shattered as he crushed her underfoot. He turned around, looking for the newly manifested dragons of the deceased guards.

"They can't," Charyss mumbled. She was huddled by a column, her thin, spindly legs drawn up to her chest. Peeking around the fingers covering her eyes, she was crying from fright. "The drugs will stop them manifesting even in death."

"You've made a mess," Latunya said. "Was that necessary?"

Rhodys leered down at his aunt, his dragon heart still pumping with the excitement of spilled blood. "My father is weakening, and we can't afford for Xavryn's spies to return back to him."

Latunya shook her head, as if he were a child who was giving his tutor incorrect answer after incorrect answer. "But here, where your men might see the bodies? They're losing faith in you."

Rhodys turned his back on his aunt. "Then I will have to earn it back."

Latunya swept across the floor. She bent and picked up Mairtyr's discarded sword. The Artrothian steel gleamed under the lights as his aunt brought it close to inspect. Running her finger along the blade, she said, "Now, I say it's time to send my daughter a message she can't ignore."

CHAPTER TWENTY-FIVE

Pyrah

LEVLY PEAK

By the time Pyrah and her armies left Avhyl behind them, the fortified town was nothing but a smoldering warning for Rhodys and all of Artroth. The message was clear. Mercy wasn't a thought that Pyrah would entertain. She would burn each settlement that sided with her cousin.

They left the ruins of the city in favour of the mountains. Here they could regroup and decide their next course of action. While Rhodys had studied and trained for war from the tender age of seven, most in Pyrah's faction had no experience outside of small skirmishes. What they lacked in military prowess they would make up for with determination, passion and fire.

They made their base camp at the foot of the mountains, which was covered with the pleasant shade of trees. The woods here were plentiful with prey, and their army would not be in want for food. The moment they were settled, Elryk and Nahilya set out with some of the hatchlings to organise a hunt and collection of fresh water.

Nahilya had looked to Pyrah as if to check if she wanted to join their hunt. But Elryk whispered something soft into the healer's ear. Pyrah watched with no small amount of jealousy as Nahilya smiled at her brother as if the sun rose and set with him.

Elryk was planning on hunting for more than food, Pyrah knew. She shook her head; she would allow her brother some precious time alone with his lover. They were at war, and the promise of tomorrow was not a guarantee. In the coming battles, one or both of them might lose their lives. Let them have what little joy the world had to offer them.

Angry that she felt envious of her brother when he only deserved goodness, Pyrah turned away from the pair.

Once Elryk and Nahilya disappeared, she manifested into her dragon form to fly over the mountains. She needed some time alone to gather her thoughts and steel herself for the future. For some of their hatchlings, the brutality and necessity of destroying the enemy was too much. Uxhyn was with them. Otherworlds bless his giant heart, he had the patience to cajole and comfort them.

The mountain air was crisp and deliciously cool against her scales. She scouted the area, taking note of places to hide if it became necessary to move their camp quickly.

Flying from Avhyl, they had spotted a large glassy lake. She wheeled around and headed in its direction. Lakes meant fresh water, and with the number of hatchlings and humans they had in their midst, it was an invaluable resource.

She skimmed around the lake and was shocked to hear human voices. The humans had been told to stay away from the lake until Uxhyn could confirm it was safe. Water was a tempting place to be and a potential place for the enemy to set traps.

Beating her wings, she flew a little higher so that she might spy on who they were and assess whether they were harmless or a threat. All threats needed to be dealt with swiftly.

She was able to track them easily enough. The first man had the longhair favoured by Artrothian men. He was speaking lazily with another male. In the next heartbeat, she recognised the short tight curls and his brown skin.

Torryn.

Sucking in a breath, she watched him for a moment longer. He was in the water, washing his torso, trousers still on. His eyes were trained upon a child who was clambering around the rocks.

What was Torryn the Deceiver doing with an Artrothian and a small child?

Stretching out her neck, she scented the air and felt a zing of apprehension realising both the other man and the child had dragons within them. She wheeled around, biting her lips to stop the angry rumbling from bubbling up her throat.

It was Torryn who raised his head to the sky. He lifted his hand in a clear gesture to show that he knew she was there. Cursing, Torqui dove and landed upon the bank, scattering the pebbles under the force of her dragon body. She wouldn't have it said that she was afraid of Torryn.

The other man stood, regarding her with clear amusement, while the child shrieked and hid behind him. Torryn waded out from the shadows to greet her.

"I see you haven't changed too much," the long-haired Artrothian said, tilting his head up to look at her. He tugged the child closer to his body. "Tya, it's alright. She won't hurt you."

"Filgaryn," Torqui rumbled. Then she manifested back into her human to show him she was unafraid of his presence. She rounded onto the cringing child, surprised Filgaryn would bring her into Ramyr when war was inevitable. "Trust you to be irresponsible enough to bring a youngster to battle. Does your mate know?"

"We found Tya hiding from you and Rhodys in the caves. Filgaryn has taken her under his wing," Torryn said. Pyrah turned to study his face. Since she last saw him, he seemed to have aged. His eyes held a haunted light. "We've heard stories about you, Green Lady."

"All nasty, I hope?" Pyrah asked. She paused to look at the girl again. "Tya? Rhodys' hatchling? I told you to leave."

Lifting a steadying hand to the child's arm, Filgaryn raised an eyebrow. "Is that any way to speak to a child?"

"You're in more danger than you know," the small girl said.

"Are you threatening me?" Pyrah took a step forward, but Filgaryn intercepted her.

"No," the girl said. She tilted her head to the side. "Rhodys is already considering how and when to kill your daughters."

"Hush, child," Filgaryn murmured.

"Aren't you Charyss' mother?" Tya asked. "She has upset Rhodys. Her time is running out."

Pyrah stepped forward, cursing her heart for feeling a fluttering of hope. "You've seen my daughters?"

"Yes," Tya said. "I was their maidservant before I was given the dragon. But they have no dragon and therefore no worth in Rhodys' eyes."

Pyrah closed her eyes, recalling her daughters' faces, their smiles and soft hair. Charyss' love of flowers and healing had grown with her. And Vallah. She missed her youngest's bravado and wicked tongue. As each new day dawned, she had to fight not to think of them. Some mornings it was hard to move out of bed as waves of doubt and dread overwhelmed her.

"Why are you in these mountains, Torryn, with him?"

"We told you already, we're hiding," Torryn replied.

"You expect me to believe that?"

Torryn shrugged. "Believe what you will, Pyrah. You've always thought the worst of me."

"That wasn't always true," Pyrah snapped. "I loved you before you betrayed me."

"Oh," Filgaryn exclaimed, raising his perfect eyebrows. "Now the truth comes out."

"You took my heart, Pyrah, then tossed me aside to marry Luthur," Torryn snarled. "Was I supposed to wait and live my life alone because you were too wrapped in the idea of being someone important?"

"I married Luthur for Elryk ..."

"And not because my status wasn't good enough for you?" Torryn's tone held a clear challenge. "I was willing to fight for us—for Elryk as well, dammit! And you left me, bidding me to live a loveless life. When Ayrahylse showed interest in me ... why should have I denied her? I'm not yours to command."

Filgaryn laughed, ignoring Torryn spearing him with a dirty look. Face twisting in anger and hurt, he stomped up the bank. He stopped before her, so close that their noses were almost touching. Dark eyes glinted, and pain swept over his expression. His hair was still wet. Pyrah longed to reach out and brush away the water droplets caught in his hair. The memory of swimming with him, his body entwined with hers, surfaced against her will. She still remembered the taste of salt on his lips and skin.

"Well, you'll be glad to know I have sworn off female dragons. First you, then Ayrahylse ... The pain of love is not worth it."

"I was waiting for you," Pyrah said.

"I was willing to do battle for you," Torryn replied. "And you played me for a fool."

"You're a proven liar with little control over your own power."

Filgaryn shook his head. "Princess, he built an entire palace in the side of a mountain. A palace with detailed carvings of our kind, jewels and many rooms. Torryn, you'll find, has more control over his power than even Rhodys."

Pyrah opened her mouth to argue, and when no rebuttal was forthcoming, clinked her jaw shut.

Torryn swept his eyes over her once more, and she couldn't help but wonder if he liked what he saw. But then he stepped past her. "Goodbye, Pyrah."

"Let us hide in peace," Filgaryn said. He stood and gestured for Tya to follow the trail into the trees. "Go on. The she-dragon is full of hot air. She'll not bite."

Tya gathered the tattered remains of her clothes and skirted past Pyrah.

"Stay away from my armies," Pyrah demanded, determined to remain a little in control.

Torryn glared, his chest heaving. The expression on his face changed from fury to hunger. He turned and strode towards the small girl. He took the child's hand and tugged her further under the cover of the trees.

"The last we knew, Rhodys has made his camp in my home. Your girls were with him," Torryn said. "And Nahilya ... if she is with you, it is possible I have news for her."

For his part, Filgaryn smirked over his shoulder at her. The trickster of Artroth was amused. When he reached Torryn, he clapped him on the back. There was a teasing note in his face when he spoke. "Your dragon wants her, brother."

Filgaryn's keen eyes swept over her, and she knew the words were for her as well.

Pyrah lay on her back, staring up into the night's sky. She inhaled deeply, drawing in the sweet smell of the forests. Hands on her belly, she held her breath and then exhaled.

Otherworlds. She had lain on the cold, hard ground for hours, meditating, and all she could see in her mind was Torryn. In the dark she could still feel the strong lingering touches of her former lover and the warmth of his body. From the moment she had dismissed Torryn, her dragon had wanted him and him alone. Her dragon had been angry when she refused his invitation to fly away with him.

She was a princess of Artroth; she shouldn't have to spend her days running from civilization and live a cloistered life hidden away. She was born to live her life in the sun. Oh, she had used the excuse that she was protecting Elryk, that she was forced to marry Luthur. But she had deceived herself.

Torryn had managed to live undetected from Artroth for many years. He could have kept Elryk safe.

The accusation that she married Luthur because she wanted to be important rang true. A young Pyrah would have never mated herself to an obscure dragon. He had worked with stone. A tradesman, not even a chieftain's fighting man. His foolishness would have been the better fate for her. Torryn had made something of himself. He had married well ... Had it been fair to expect him to wait for her?

She endured the nights spent with Luthur by imagining she was with Torryn.

It was undeniable. She was still in love with him.

So she lay alone on her pallet, remembering with regret the days when she was young and so sure of herself. The sound of wings disturbing the air above snapped her from her half-awake state. They had a curfew on the dragons in camp; no one in the sky after dark. She rolled to her feet and stepped closer to the dwindling remains of their campfire.

Lifting her chin to the sky, she saw a black shadow. It was a large dragon, not one of their hatchlings. She dismissed it as either Filgaryn or Torryn trying to frighten her away from the mountains, but something seemed off.

The shadow swooped, laughing as he dropped a bundle. "A gift from Prince Rhodys!"

The mysterious package dropped and bounced on the earth with a soft thump. Pyrah approached cautiously. Anything that Rhodys sent was not something she wanted.

"Up!" Elryk yelled somewhere behind her in the dark. "Wits about you!"

A few feet away from the bundle, Pyrah stopped. She tilted her head to the sky. The large male dragon had disappeared from view. But that did not mean he wasn't lurking in the darkness.

The hum and activity of the camp stirring behind her seemed to come from another plane. She stared at the ground, hardly daring to move. At her side, her fingers itched. She knew that she must look. Dread curled in her belly, which was closely followed by fear. She knew that she didn't want to know what Rhodys thought might be a good gift for her.

"Pyrah?" Nahilya touched her elbow. "Do you want to look together?"

Pyrah did, not knowing why she was so reluctant. She was frozen in place. The package hadn't exploded. She was being a coward. Touching Nahilya's hand lightly, she shook her head.

"Pyrah?"

"No," Pyrah murmured, forcing her lips to move and form coherent words. "Thank you, Nahilya, I can look."

Stumbling, she took the few halting steps towards the parcel. It was a canvas bag. There seemed nothing particularly special about it. She reached out her hand, hating the way her fingers trembled on the drawstrings. Her hands came away sticky and warm. Bile rose in her throat as she lifted her fingers to her face to see that they were covered in blood. Phantom claws gripped at her belly, constricting her insides so it was difficult to breathe.

Tipping the bag, the first thing she saw was bloodied flowers. She stared down at the delicate yellow petals. She jiggled the bag, and something heavy rolled onto the dewy grass. Pyrah sucked in air until she thought her lungs would burst.

The wailing screams of a woman, high and animalistic, reverberated in her ears. Her hand flew to her belly, and she was shocked to realise the cries were coming from within her. There was no control over her voice; her soul was howling.

The warmth of Nahilya's power flooded her fingers. She looked up into the eyes of the healer. She was speaking, but in her distress, Pyrah couldn't hear the sounds of her words. Clasping Pyrah's hands tightly, Nahilya attempted to draw her close.

Pyrah clutched her stomach, doubling over in grief. She muffled her screams as she rested her forehead against Nahilya's shoulders. The healer's grip tightened on her. She could feel her tears mingling with her own.

"*Lullah!*"

Through a curtain of salty tears, she looked up. Daerys was running towards her.

"My child!" Pyrah screamed, pulling away from Nahilya. Her mind was beginning to make sense of what she saw. "My poor, innocent child!"

Charyss' eyes stared up at her, dull and lifeless, frozen forever in the horror of her last moments. Her mouth was twisted in terror. Bright yellow flowers adorned her soft, dark hair.

"My little one! My baby."

Daerys reached her, staring down at Charyss' head. His mouth was slightly ajar as he gaped like a fish. "Mother," he whispered. "Tell me what to do."

Pyrah wanted the sight of Charyss taken away and yet wanted her eyes to never leave her daughter's face. It made little sense, but she feared that if she looked away, her firstborn would be lost for eternity. Confronted with her child's mortality, she felt a stirring of guilt as her troubled thoughts turned to Vallah. She glanced back into the sky, searching the darkness, wondering if Rhodys would be sending a second head from the skies.

When her children were born, she had prepared herself for the fact their lives would be short. They were condemned as mere humans. She was afraid and convinced herself they were less Artrothian. To make herself feel better about her helplessness, Pyrah told herself she couldn't understand them. She was afraid to love them without abandon, knowing all too soon, she'd be grieving their loss.

Charyss' life had been cut short, and now her heart burned with rage and pain she never thought she could experience. She hadn't loved them any less than if they had been dragonborn. No. She had denied her feelings, ignored her maternal instincts out of fear, leaving Elryk to take up the slack. And now she would never be able to express to her eldest daughter how much she meant to her.

"*E vydel el taldyn!*" Pyrah cried, pressing her forehead into the dirt and sobbing. "*E vydel el taldyn. Elt rshon desn tollah hy el!*"

"I love you fiercely." Pyrah's shoulders shook as she cried out with the force of the dragon mother inside of her. "I love you fiercely. My dragon heart beats for you!"

Strong hands gripped her, pressing her body into a warm chest. Pyrah's heart continued to burn, her stomach roiling with nausea. The ground beneath her felt unstable; it was moving. She screamed and she cried as the arms tightened around her.

Breathing in, she recognised her brother's dragonless scent. He smelt of home, of quiet strength and the forest. Her fingers clutched on to his sleeves. He had been more of a father to her children than Luthur. Through the bond they shared, she felt his grief relentlessly buffeting his own heart.

"Hyn, can you please take Charyss somewhere else?"

"No!" Pyrah cried. "No. Don't take my baby! Don't take her away!"

Elryk's arms tightened. "Hush, *sudunah*, Hyn can look after her until you are ready to say goodbye."

The fight left Pyrah's body, and she sagged in Elryk's arms.

"I'll fly after him!" Daerys said. "I'll fly after the one who hurt my mother."

"No!" Pyrah croaked. She lifted her head in the midst of her grief to take in the concerned face of the one the Wind Song had given her. She shivered. Charyss' fate had been sealed. Excited by the twist of fate at having a new dragon son to herself, she had ignored what the wind had whispered. Daerys was the balm to her grief. She couldn't let anything happen to him.

"Is there anything I can do, *Lullah*?"

Pyrah shook her head. In Artroth it was traditional to burn the dead. She couldn't bear to place poor Charyss' head in the flames. She turned her head away and vomited.

Elryk rubbed soothing circles on her back, his palms warm and grounding. "Go, collect some wildflowers. Stay close to the camp."

"Yes, sir."

"Flowers?" Pyrah felt a wave of confusion. Flowers were an impractical item for Daerys to collect. What use were they?

Head bowed, she listened to the soft footfalls of Daerys as he left her side.

"The task will keep Daerys busy and safe," Nahilya whispered in her ear. "He needs to feel he can help his *lullah*."

Pyrah closed her eyes, wishing to shut away the reality of the situation, and fell into a still and silent blackness. In her brother's arms, she calmed.

And then the ground shook, and the camp erupted with screams.

Chapter Twenty-Six

Daerys

Levly Peak

Daerys was no stranger to death. Living on the high seas for the majority of his life, he had seen sailors taken by sickness, fighting, infection and drowning. The sound of Pyrah crying out in the draconic language sent chills up his spine. It had been many years since he heard it spoken, and he had still understood her words of anguish. He knew that he would only see pain and horror imprinted on the little girl's face. But try as he might, he could not look away from the head. He had been relieved when Elryk dismissed him from Pyrah's side.

Melayah joined him, grasping his hand in hers. Her fingers trembled, and he was comforted to know that she was disturbed by the scene as well.

"She might have grown to be my sister." Daerys lifted his chin, blinking back tears for Pyrah, and took in the shifting stances and the hushed buzz of whispers. Unease was spreading quickly; hands were laid on weapons, and some were already heading for the cover of trees.

Daerys caught sight of two members of his 'Ember' crew. He raised his hand to hail them. They stood together, arms crossed against their chests, looking a little too relaxed. Their lips quirked into smirks as they watched at a distance Pyrah's grief.

Hearing their laugh, he paused mid-step. The sound curdled his stomach while his mind raced to confirm what his heart was already telling him. Melayah felt his burning rage, and her fingers dug into his palm. Come morning, there would be bruises.

"Traitors!" Daerys cried. Several heads looked up at him.

Sensing they were being watched, the Embers locked their gazes with him. Their elated expressions fell, but it was too late. Several other members of the camp were coming to the same conclusion as Daerys.

"Stay there!" Daerys barked, lurching forward, intent on cornering them.

The pair ignored Daerys' order, manifested and took flight. Determined to catch them, Daerys growled and rippled into his dragon form.

"Stay!" Melayah yelled. She shifted fluidly, cutting him off. Many of the other dragons nearby were doing the same thing. "Mother dragon needs you."

"Melayah!" Daerys called.

"I'll get 'em!" a young sandy male hatchling cried. "I'll rip out their throats!"

Daerys stood, his wings unfurling, one eye on Pyrah's weeping form and the other on escaping Embers. The sky lit up with fire ... The Embers swerved, and the shadow of a very large navy dragon dove through the pursuing dragons. The sandy male's tail was shorn from his body, and he fell screaming to the ground.

Melayah jerked out of the way as a crimson dragon even larger than the navy passed her.

A few heartbeats later, the camp was full of screams, fire and manifesting dragons. Daerys charged through the fleeing hatchlings, bellowing for Pyrah and Uxhyn. He kept his vision forward while enemy dragons swarmed the skies above. Melayah was right. His job was to protect Pyrah.

All around him, their foe swooped, grabbing humans and tearing them apart. Young dragons still grounded did not stand a chance. Daerys' eyes flicked upwards; any dragon that had taken flight needed to fly through a gauntlet of larger dragons. Wings, teeth and scales fell from the sky. His heart thumped in his chest, and he bellowed once more for Pyrah.

His cries were answered by another female dragon with flashing bronze scales. She eyed him with some interest. "Aren't you a pretty little morsel?"

Daerys hissed at her.

"You're nice and strong. Rhodys will welcome you, young one. No need to die out here."

Spreading his wings, Daerys spewed fire at her. The female dragon nimbly dodged the flames, laughing. She pumped her wings, keeping her place with ease.

"Now, now. Play nice."

The female dragon surged forward, and she toppled him with her weight. Daerys was pinned under sharp claws that held him down, piercing the scales on his shoulders. The female brought her head down to whisper, "Prince Rhodys requires some prisoners to examine. Stay down."

Not wanting to be subdued, Daerys roared and lashed out with his tail, which connected to the enemy dragon's back legs. She snarled, biting her teeth into Daerys' neck. The points of her fangs only grazed his scales, but her grip was strong enough for her to hold his head down.

"Lullah!"

"Free yourself and fly!" Torqui's voice, full of anger and might, cut through Daerys' mind. She was out there somewhere, waiting for him to break free.

Daerys knew that if taken prisoner he would soon be killed, or worse, used against Torqui. He could not physically move without causing himself an injury.

Gathering his power, he felt the ground beneath him quake. The dragon holding him snorted in shock as the ground opened beneath them. She spread her wings and took off. Daerys, ready for the effects of his power, lurched to the side, hoping to skim along the ground to find an escape.

Above the fight, the sky trembled with thunder. Rain hammered down in heavy droplets. He had heard Torqui and Uxhyn discussing Prince Rhodys' great power over storms. Lightning flashed, illuminating the sky, and Daerys felt his stomach drop at the number of enemies.

Gasping, he dove for the cover of trees. If he could use his scales to blend in, he might be able to find Torqui in the chaos. His shoulder and neck stung where he had been pierced, but he raised his snout to the sky, desperate to catch sight of Torqui.

He spotted Uxhyn and Melayah fighting the large female that had him captured. To their left he spotted one of the Embers who had betrayed them looking on.

Daerys shot into the sky, lowered his head and smashed into the Ember's side. The betrayer cried out in alarm as he was jolted off balance. Claws raked down Daerys' face, but he lunged again. He bit down on the sinewy muscles of the Ember's neck. Flapping his wings, he used all his strength to disable his enemy.

Around them the air reverberated; a streak of purple lightning forked across the sky. Out of Daerys' peripheral vision, he saw the silhouette of a dragon. He had no time to react. He dropped the Ember and dove. The large dragon chased him. Before Daerys could reach the ground, he summoned his power. A tower of dirt and rock formed a barrier between himself and this dragon.

He could hear the rumbling laugh. "Well done. You'll make a fine addition to my collection."

"Lullah!"

Daerys sped along the ground. The malevolent dragon swerved around the obstacle.

Ahead of him there was a roar and a blur of dark grey. Daerys tumbled to the ground, his claws raking the earth. A blue streak tore past him as well. Two large male dragons intercepted the dragon pursuing him. Daerys stumbled to his feet and slipped into the shadows.

"Lullah!"

His heart hammered in his chest. There was no answer from Torqui. She wouldn't abandon him, would she?

Exhausted, he crept along the shadows, glancing at the devastation. Tattered parts of dragons and humans lay on the ground. The grass was smoking. Their numbers were depleted; the survivors disappeared into the forest.

By the fire he caught sight of Elryk and Nahilya fighting back-to-back. It seemed the dragons had also brought with them human forces. Nearby he spotted a sword.

Manifesting into his human form, Daerys darted forward and grabbed the blade. He flexed his fingers along the handle. His shoulder and neck ached with his injury, but he ran to aid Elryk and Nahilya.

Elryk was fighting valiantly, and Daerys found himself wishing to be like him. The one who they said was empty of a dragon looked calm and relaxed as he engaged enemy after enemy.

Yelling, Daerys joined the fray, his blade clashing against the sword of an enemy soldier. Daerys' opponent was a similar age to him, but Daerys was better versed with the weapon. In the span of three movements, the opposing soldier made a mistake, and Daerys struck.

He tried not to think about how it felt to have his blade impale his enemy, or the look of shocked confusion that crossed the other boy's face. As the boy sunk to his knees, the light fading in his eyes, Daerys pulled his blade back. The sword came free with a wet sound.

He swallowed. Bile stung his throat.

"Keep fighting. Sword up," Elryk shouted. His left hand was wreathed in flames.

Daerys of course knew of Elryk's affinity for fire, but it was still a shock to see him wielding his power. Uncontrolled flames could be devastating for both them and the enemy.

"DAERYS!" Elryk screamed.

Daerys blinked, spinning on his heel in time to block the attack of another enemy soldier. He parried the next two blows, dancing out of range of his foe.

Where was Torqui?

"Daerys, take Nahilya and fly."

"No!" Nahilya cried.

Daerys kicked at his opponent's shin, tripping him. He thrust his blade through the man's throat, ignoring the way he gurgled and spasmed under his weapon. He flicked his gaze up into Elryk's pinched expression.

Elryk nodded at him, gesturing curtly with his free hand. A curtain of fire burst from the ground. Heat seared Daerys' cheeks. He looked up at the brewing storm, wondering how long Elryk could hold his flames before Rhodys extinguished them.

Elryk's face twisted in fierce concentration. He swung his sword and decapitated the next enemy. "Daerys. Obey. I'll hold them off."

"I'm not leaving you!" Nahilya shouted.

Elryk grabbed the healer's upper arm, pulling her close. His lips descended on hers, and he kissed her. "Go now."

Daerys' body lurched, his chest bursting with an abrupt pain. Stunned by the blow, his eyes flicked downwards. His lips parted, but no sound escaped his lungs. An arrow was lodged in his ribs. Drawing breath was difficult. Slowly, he lifted his hand to the wound. Spots of light danced in front of his eyes, and blood coated his fingers. He was vaguely aware of falling to his knees.

"Stay with me! Stay with me!" Nahilya grabbed Daerys' arm, her fingers pinching his skin.

"Get him out!" Elryk yelled.

There was the beating rush of wings. The dark shadow of a dragon drifted above him. Long, nimble claws curled around his aching body. His mind fuzzy with pain, Daerys slipped into the embrace of darkness, hoping his torment would not be prolonged. He prayed that his death torn asunder by dragon claws would not be too painful.

CHAPTER TWENTY-SEVEN

Pyrah

LEVLY PEAK

Torqui was screaming, her battle cry echoing the pain and hurt that she felt to the very core of her being. She flew through the enemy lines, twisting wings, stripping scales and slashing throats in a crazed frenzy. Her emerald scales and claws were sticky with dragon blood, and yet she thirsted for more. Her dearest Charyss was dead, and she had witnessed first Yirys, then Rhodys attack her son. The more who met their grisly ends at her claws, the safer her hatchlings would be.

For once she was thankful for her harsh upbringing. She was an unstoppable flame that could not be extinguished. All around her, Rhodys' power of lightning and thunder crashed. It only served to fuel her temper.

Rage bubbled and boiled in her blood. Her eyesight was red in her rage. There was no room for fear. Everything she was she poured into killing those before her. It wasn't until her mouth was full of hot blood and she found herself above the fighting that she came back to conscious awareness.

She shook her head in confusion. She had lost herself to the bloodlust. She had little memory of the fight.

Exhausted, she tried to reach out to Daerys and found a strange darkness. She called out for him, bellowing his name, hoping above all hopes that he might be able to answer her over the din of battle. There was no reply. She screamed for him, searching the battlefield below. The ground was slick with blood ... The remains of young dragons and human soldiers were scattered over the ground.

"Have we lost something, dear one?"

Torqui froze, lifting her gaze to look upon a lilac female dragon that she had once known well. She blinked, half wishing and half fearing that the dragon before her was a trick. *"Lullah ..."*

"What have you become, my daughter?" The words were spoken gently, but under the tone was a threatening purr. Torqui tensed, waiting for the attack.

"My son," Torqui murmured, internally chiding herself for speaking. Her head swayed side to side, hoping to catch a glimpse of Daerys. "My son is down there somewhere."

"Such a shame."

Torqui hissed at the insincerity in her mother's tone. "What do you want?"

"This is a precursor," Latunya said, sweeping a taloned claw over the battlefield. "Surrender and hand over Elryk, and you might find mercy."

"Mercy?" Torqui tasted the word over her tongue. She glanced over to her mother. Dare she hope ... "Is there any mercy for Elryk?"

The expression on Latunya's face never shifted, and Torqui felt ill to her stomach. When she had given birth to Charyss and then Vallah, she had hoped that her mother still had some tender feelings for her son. Elryk was her flesh and her blood. A child she had reared, a boy she had high hopes for.

"Elryk is a good man," Torqui said, her voice cracking. Her eyes glanced over the Artrothian forces that were gathering above the onslaught, their job complete. Her army had been obliterated ... She had nothing left. "He is strong, kind and loyal. You should be proud of him."

Still nothing from her mother, and Torqui's heart broke for Elryk.

"And what of my second-born daughter?" Torqui was afraid of the answer. A sob caught in her throat. "Is Vallah alive?"

Rhodys rose to join Latunya. Seeing them, her mother and cousin side by side, brought bile to Torqui's throat. A snarl rumbled in Rhodys' belly as he studied her blood-spattered scales.

"Ythryr the Blessed, curse you both," Torqui whispered.

Rhodys laughed at her, turning his attention to Latunya. "Our escaped rats are here. Filgaryn and Torryn were spotted during the battle."

A flutter of hope lifted Torqui's spirit a notch.

Latunya raised her eyebrows.

Yawning widely, displaying rows upon rows of teeth, Rhodys inched closer towards Torqui. "The emperor is desperate for female dragons to return home, so this is your last chance."

Torqui shook her head.

"I'll give you a week to surrender. Bring with you Elryk and that delightful young male hatchling ... the one of black and brown speckles and belly of bronze," Rhodys said.

"You're not having Daerys!" Torqui snapped.

"Daerys." Rhodys hissed the name between his blood-soaked teeth. "He's a powerful little one ... Bring him into my fold, and I'll consider letting Vallah go. Fail, and I'll send her to you in smaller pieces than Charyss."

Torqui opened her mouth, her mind awhirl with the impossible situation. How could she, a mother dragon, choose between the child of her body and the boy she had rescued? She loved them both fiercely in her own way.

"One week, cousin ..." Rhodys nodded and turned his back on her.

Latunya swept her imperious gaze over Torqui one last time, her scaled lips drawing into a tight line.

Torqui watched the Artrothian force glide away, tears in her eyes ... afraid that when she landed, she would find Daerys, or worse, not find him. Alone, with only the Wind Song to caress her scales, she could hear the sounds of the dead and dying below.

It was over, and it was time that she faced the facts.

The moment her claws touched the ground, the chieftain of Tamaryn approached her. He was gravely injured, his skin a clammy grey. Large hands clasped at his open wounds, and Torqui knew he would soon be dead.

"We can't endure this madness," the chieftain said. He fell to his knees with a low moan of pain. "Humans aren't made for this type of battle. I'm sending my men home. Find another way to defeat your kind."

Torqui nodded, her eyes misting over, wanting nothing more than to curl up into a little ball and hide away from the world. She could already see that the humans who survived had slunk away ... All that was left was carnage.

"Peace go with you," Torqui murmured. It took everything within her to utter those words. She considered it might have been wrong for them to conscript a human army against Rhodys.

Without a backwards glance at the chieftain, she drifted through the camp, rumbling for Daerys and Elryk, even though her brother could not answer her. Her wanderings were aimless until she happened upon a black lump.

Dark, twisted wings ... a body that no longer breathed. Torqui returned to her human form, racing forward through the slaughter. No ... it couldn't be ...

Melayah was already there, on her knees, weeping. The girl's curled hair was thick with the dust and blood of battle. The skin of her face and neck was covered with her tears and sweat.

"Uxhyn," Pyrah said with a breath. "Not you."

Over the time that they had built their armies, she had become used to the presence of the large black dragon. He had been reserved but ultimately a kind and loyal friend.

Reaching out with a trembling hand, Pyrah pressed her palm to his scales. They were cold. "Rest now. You have atoned."

"He fell from the sky," Melayah whispered, scrubbing her face with her fist. "He's gone."

Pyrah leaned forward, pressing her face against Uxhyn's still body. "May the sun kiss your scales; the stars bless and guide you. May the rainstorm help you grow, and the moon give you her light in your darkest hour. Farewell; I am privileged indeed to call you friend."

"What was that?"

"The dragon's prayer," Pyrah whispered. "My father taught it to me when I was very young."

"We can't leave him here. Like this. All alone," Melayah said, her voice catching in her throat.

"We have no choice," Pyrah replied. "We can't take him with us."

Melayah nodded, brushing some of her dark curls away from her face. She was a strong girl, Pyrah reflected. She would do what was necessary. Uxhyn could be proud of his hatchling. "I got some of our forces into the forest."

"Did you see Daerys?"

"I lost sight of him." Melayah winced. "I'm sorry ... I lost him ... once Uxhyn ..."

"It's okay," Pyrah whispered. She drew the girl close to her side and patted her hair. "Battles are chaos. I lost sight of Dae too, and I'm his mother."

Sniffing, Melayah tilted back on her heels, looking over Uxhyn's still form. "It was the Embers. I saw them moments before the attack. They were ready to leave."

"Rhodys won't accept them. It's the Artrothian way."

"I want them dead," Melayah snarled. "And Rhodys is after young dragons ..."

Pyrah shook her head. "Artrothians never take in a traitor. If the foolish hatchlings think they can go to my cousin for safety, he'll kill them."

Closing her eyes against her threatening tears, Melayah drew in a deep breath. "I want to be the one."

"Pardon?"

"To kill the Embers. I want to hunt and to kill them myself."

Pyrah turned her gaze back to Uxhyn's bulky frame. The Embers had been his hatchlings. It was a terrible betrayal. One did not attack their *aluel*. And that was what they had done by betraying them to Rhodys. They were responsible for all the death and destruction.

Standing back, Pyrah sighed into the darkness.

"I have a hatchling. Elryk said he was very important to you."

A thrill of dread and hope wound through Pyrah's blood. She knew the voice even though it had been years since hearing it like this.

"Torryn? You have Daerys?"

"Yes, we have a young bull dragon of browns, blacks and oranges. We've brought him into our den high in the mountains. He was gravely wounded."

"Wounded?"

"Arrow. Nahilya was able to heal him. He's sleeping now."

"Pyrah?"

Starting, Pyrah turned towards Melayah's inquiring face.

"If you ever had any love for me, keep him safe. I have an important task."

Pyrah could feel the shiver of curiosity through her link with Torryn. *"Filgaryn is watching over him like a snapdragon watches a buck."*

Pyrah wiped her hands on her trousers and stood.

"Come, Melayah, it's time to hunt."

In the end, the Embers were sly enough to stay away from Rhodys and his dragons. Torqui and Melayah tracked them to the opposite face of the mountain range. They had made their nest on the lower regions, believing that they would be safe from the wrath of mother-dragon.

It was not so.

Her child was dead, Daerys injured and Uxhyn slain. Their numbers had taken a heavy toll. A toll that they could not afford when it came to Rhodys and his quest to subdue the land.

It was conceivable they thought they might find favour on the winning side. Those with human blood always assumed they could buy favour.

As the sun began to rise, Torqui led Melayah towards the Embers' hideout. She entered first. The smaller dragon stalked the Embers, watching their breaths as they slumbered on. She was a creature of beauty, her muscles stretched taut moments before she sprung onto the first one.

Melayah pounced and he was gone, never to wake again. A mercy. The next wasn't so fortunate.

The sound of Melayah's jaws crunching around his companion woke him. He sat up, wide-eyed and staring. Torqui knew he saw his death. Part of him was resigned, but the other part wanted to fight. A true battle-dragon. A shame he chose the wrong side.

His pale lips parted in a wordless cry as Melayah bit him in half. A quick but bloody death.

"There were three Embers in Daerys' team," Torqui murmured.

"Tyme was killed on the battlefield," Melayah replied, her voice taking on little emotion as she stared down at the warm corpses. "I didn't see him conspiring with these two. We must think of him as innocent."

It struck Torqui then that she didn't know each of her hatchlings well. She didn't recall the names of the two that had betrayed her. It was wrong. So very wrong that she didn't have time to learn and know each of the new dragons before she took them to war.

She was resolved to do better next time. Starting with Melayah.

"Come," Torqui said. She led the younger dragon to the lakeside where she had met Filgaryn and Torryn only a few short hours ago. Then she had been confident of her place and role in the world. Now she wasn't so sure.

Together they watched the sun rise in the sky through the canopy of trees.

Melayah lifted her snout to the sky and wept. Torqui let her, standing by her side, a silent witness to the terrible tragedy that Artroth had brought to their shores.

In life there was time to celebrate and there was time to mourn. Best pour their hearts out now. Let them roar their grief to the sky.

Chapter Twenty-Eight

Daerys

Levly Peak

Daerys groaned, licking dry, chapped lips. He was adrift in a fog of confusion. From the depths of his consciousness, he felt the phantom sting of teeth tearing at his scales. The winds of battle still caressed his skin as he fought to open his eyes.

"Here, drink this." Strong arms lifted him to a sit. A wave of dizziness caught Daerys off guard, and his head lolled forward. Hands lifted his chin, and a cup was brought to his lips. Cool water mixed with his blood. Daerys gulped, longing for the fresh water to cool his burning throat. He choked. "Easy, slowly now."

"I was hurt," Daerys croaked. His human hand lifted to his chest, and he blearily opened his eyes. He expected his fingers to touch the shaft of an arrow. It was gone.

The stranger, a man with long dark hair and violet eyes, took the cup away. Daerys shivered, feeling the power coiling about him. "Healer Nahilya took care of the arrow. But best take it easy until you feel better."

Daerys tried to stand, only to find the stranger pushing him down.

"Hush, you're safe here."

"Are you the blue dragon or the grey?" Daerys muttered. He had a vague memory of two large dragons intercepting the enemy that had been on his tail. "Who are you?"

"I'm Filgaryn. I am the grey," the stranger said. He turned and gestured, and a small girl came to stand beside him. "This is Tya, my *mynrell*, and the blue dragon is Torryn."

"Daerys ..."

"I know," Filgaryn said. "Torryn has gone to scout out somewhere safer to hide. Elryk and Nahilya are looking for survivors."

"Melayah ..." Groaning, Daerys closed his eyes against the throbbing pain in his head. "Pyrah? The green dragon, Torqui?"

"I don't like her," Tya said. "She's scary."

"She's not so bad. She's my mother."

"I thought so," Filgaryn said. "She has something she must attend to and will come for you as soon as she can."

"Must she?" Tya grumbled.

"It wasn't at all like I thought it would be," Daerys said. "War."

"It never is," Filgaryn replied. "Any man or dragon when first confronted with the fury of the battlefield says the same thing."

"I thought I could be a good soldier," Daerys said. "Now I doubt ..."

"Doubt has no place on the battlefield." Filgaryn moved away so that all Daerys could see was his back.

"Are you Artrothian?"

Filgaryn's posture stiffened.

"I was born in Artroth. Spent the first few years of my life hiding in cupboards and secret passages ... Yet I miss those days. Life was a game, and Father and I were winning," Daerys said. "Until one day, we lost."

"You were born in Artroth? What can you tell me about your life?"

"Nothing of value. I can't even remember my proper name. I must have had one once, before Father marked me." Daerys rolled up his sleeve, revealing the ink on his skin. "He named me Bryn."

"It means 'four'." Filgaryn turned his face away. He seemed uncomfortable with the tattoo.

"Father's face has faded into memory; I can no longer recall the sound of his voice. The more I chase the memories, the more I lose."

Filgaryn hummed, looking thoughtful. "Every time you spread your wings and fly ... he rises with you."

"Pretty words," Daerys said. "Words to comfort a child."

"I have to believe they are true," Filgaryn replied. "Otherwise, I've nothing left."

"I hear the Otherworld is a beautiful place," Tya added helpfully. "The day you step over that threshold, you'll find everything you lost in the mortal world. That's what my mama taught me."

Daerys drew his knees up to his chest, and this time Filgaryn didn't stop him. "Do you think we really have a chance? To defeat Rhodys?"

"Death is merely a doorway into the Otherworld. There is nothing to fear. Enemies cannot touch you once you reach the immortal lands. So if I am destined to give up my life to allow others to live free, then I will do so with joy."

Pulling himself to his feet, Daerys stumbled towards the entrance of the cave. The sun was rising, a golden orb in the sky.

"Lullah?"

"I am coming." Pyrah's voice entered his mind, a melody of hope. Daerys felt a wave of relief sweep over him. *"I'm on my way."*

The moment young Tya caught sight of Torqui and retreated, Daerys rushed to the cave entrance to greet the green dragon. Torqui landed with a heavy thump. Her wings remained outstretched, and the muscles along her spine were still taut. There was something terribly wrong.

Melayah landed to the side, her wings tucked in close to her body, and her head was downcast. She shuffled to the side and avoided Daerys' gaze.

"Melayah, what's wrong?" Daerys stepped from the cave and into the open.

Melayah shrunk back, shaking her head.

The hard expression on Torqui's face softened, and she beckoned Daerys closer with her claws. Unafraid, Daerys obeyed. The green dragon lowered her snout and snuffled him. She raised her head a moment later, piercing Filgaryn with an amber eye.

Melayah stood behind, rigid, her eyes staring straight ahead. Stepping past the emerald dragon, Daerys reached out to her. "Where's Uxhyn?"

"Gone," Melayah croaked.

"Gone? What do you mean gone?"

"Daerys," Filgaryn said, the timbre of his voice dropping softly, "he's left the mortal realm."

Heat rushed to Daerys' cheeks, and he felt like a pathetic fool. He turned his head to look at Melayah carefully, the way her forelegs hunched over, the droop of her wings. She looked forlorn. As if the weight of all Ramyr was on her shoulders.

"I am very sorry to hear of his demise, young friend."

Torqui lashed out with fang and claw. There must have been some part of Filgaryn that was expecting her reaction. He backed away; his hand was outstretched to push the curious Tya out of the way. He manifested into his grey form, and the small girl took cover underneath his belly.

Filgaryn's stern, violet eyes pierced Torqui, his lips curling back. There was something between the two, Daerys could tell. In truth he didn't understand Torqui's apparent dislike of Filgaryn. He quite liked the grey dragon.

Swaying his head to the side, the grey dragon studied Melayah and ignored the rumbling coming from Torqui. He stepped past the green dragon and nudged poor Melayah with his snout.

"Take time to mourn," he said. "Soon you'll find that the sun will rise once more. Uxhyn would want you to continue to grow and live without him."

"You have my thanks for looking after my hatchling, trickster. It surprises me that you are mature enough to be trusted." Torqui still held herself stiffly as she stepped between Daerys and Filgaryn.

"I've no desire to hurt the boy." Filgaryn grinned at her, flashing his perfectly white teeth. "When you left Artroth, I was a boy. Now I am a man. Fear not; I have not taught your hatchling any of my tricks."

"What tricks?" Tya tilted her head and regarded Filgaryn curiously.

"Filgaryn the Unseen can make himself invisible. He has the nasty habit of stalking the unwary."

Filgaryn barked with laughter. "I was young and wild. If one is foolish enough not to be diligent, then one deserves to have the scales scared out of them."

"You behaved like a child," Torqui snarled.

"I *was* a child. I recall a little girl of the sea swamping Prince Rhodys with waves. I, at least, didn't play dangerous games."

"You picked on the weak."

"And the strong ... There was one time I snuck up on my great-great grandsire. Another time I caught my legendary uncle, Commander Hael, off guard ... I was the bane of my *aluel's* existence." Filgaryn's voice halted. He swept his dark eyes over Torqui and turned away. "That was until Ythryr the Blessed taught me a lesson."

"Ythryr? He's a tale told to the young and feeble." Torqui looked as though she thought Filgaryn's story was questionable.

"Ythryr, the Father of the Beginning, still stalks the nests of Ayr-Rouhella. I've seen him. Touched his gleaming white scales."

"Who is Ythryr?"

"The Great Father, also referred to as the first and greatest of the dragon emperors. He died many millennia ago." Torqui made a chuffing noise, and small plumes of smoke curled from her flared nostrils.

"If he is dead, then how has Filgaryn seen him?" Daerys asked. Torqui was right. Filgaryn's claim was unbelievable.

"His soul calls out to the lost ones and waits for the return of glory to dragonkind." Filgaryn looked away, his expression smoothing over.

"Do you suppose this Ythryr will come?" A flutter of traitorous hope tickled Daerys' belly. "Or is he for Artroth?"

"No. If Ythryr truly existed, he is in spirit, bound to the land and skies he once ruled." Torqui studied Filgaryn speculatively. "Why would he show himself to you?"

"As a son of his bloodline, he came to me when I humbled myself and sought his ancient wisdom." Filgaryn grinned at her, flashing his sharp teeth.

"How long will you work alongside Torryn before you dump him?" Torqui glared at the Artrothian so fiercely that Daerys thought it a miracle he didn't burst into flames.

"Torryn is *elt sudunyn*. I have no intention of dumping him; that's more in line with your philosophy."

Torqui bristled. "Be careful with Torryn. He is the dragon of deception."

Lifting his head to the sky, Filgaryn laughed and lumbered further out into the mountain's sunlight, still chuckling to himself.

"What is it you find so funny that you mock me so?"

"Torqui, dear Green Lady, Ayrahylse's deception was clever. Use a few truths to paint a bleak picture and isolate her mate, who didn't have the connections to defend himself."

"You said Torryn had great control, when no one has seen any evidence—"

"Are you under the assumption that Torryn owes you an explanation?" Filgaryn snapped.

"We were attached for a time."

"Before you tore his heart asunder and he flew into Ayrahylse's trap. Torryn is an earth mover … His power has permeated this land. The soil whispers of the great blue dragon with golden horns. If you had the wits to listen, you could hear the spirit of this land is tied to him."

Torqui huffed. The Artrothian seemed to have successfully silenced her, and Daerys was keen to meet Torryn.

"I'll lead you to Torryn, and we'll find the empty ones." Filgaryn didn't even deign to look in Torqui's direction.

Torryn met them in the sky. Daerys could only gape in wonder at the azure scales and the golden horns on the elder male's head. Along the blue dragon's back, he carried Elryk and Nahilya. Curled up between his shoulder blades, Nix, Elryk's parrot, enjoyed the free ride. Wind ruffled his feathers as he clicked his beak and preened himself.

Behind Torryn flew four other hatchlings. From what Daerys could decipher, the human toll had been high, and they lost the armies that they had amassed.

The Artrothian attack had been devastating. Out of nearly sixty young dragons, only six of them survived. And for him it had been a close call.

Filgaryn was also disappointed by the numbers, he could tell, even though the grey dragon said nothing.

Torryn led them north along the coastline, and when they reached a point, he turned his body to fly in an easterly direction. They followed a large bay, its waters unnaturally clear. While they flew overhead, Daerys fancied he could almost see the bottom of the water.

"Stonethaw," Torryn said as he swooped down.

Daerys could have cheered to see these mountains. His wings felt stiff as the blue dragon led them down to where the mountains met the sea. He lifted his face, inhaling the salt of the sea and the fresh mountain air. This would be a good place for a dragon to make their den.

CHAPTER TWENTY-NINE

Pyrah

STONETHAW RANGE

Bitter disappointment hung over the camp. Pyrah was torn between wanting to tear her human flesh from her bones and flying into the sun. Would it not be better for her to be burnt to a cinder?

Her eyes slid to Daerys, who seemed quite taken with Filgaryn. They sat together, Tya wedged between them, while they quietly taught the child the Artrothian language. Some Ramyr words were similar when it came to dragonkind, but for a child who had grown up a *vehyl*, she was sure there were plenty of concepts Tya didn't understand.

Filgaryn spoke with a heavier accent. His *r*'s were rolled, the emphasis of his words noticeably different to the dialects known to the humans in Ramyr. Daerys, on the other hand, seemed to remember his native-born language but had lost his accent. A shame, really. The cadence of his speech held the lowborn drawl of a salt-rat.

Filgaryn, to his credit, did not comment on Daerys' valiant attempts to mimic his speech. The young one seemed frustrated, realising for the first time that he had lost a part of his heritage.

The surviving hatchlings, three female, one male, huddled in their own corner of the cave. Eyes full of doubt and suspicion, they watched Filgaryn and Tya. The four of them had all been Uxhyn's young. When they left the cave to mourn the black dragon, Pyrah had not expected them to return. They said very little, but they remained.

"What happens when you die?" Tya asked, pressing herself against Filgaryn's leg.

Heart heavy, Pyrah leaned up against the cave wall. Her fingers scrambled for purchase, only to find herself stumbling. The cave was thick with tension as the question remained unanswered.

Elryk huffed, stood and swept from the cave.

"The Otherworld is a place of peace. There is no more pain, no more tears," Pyrah replied. She looked to her hands, which she clasped in front of her to stop them from shaking. She dearly wished she could believe her own words.

"Do you suppose the dead still love us?" Tya asked.

"Yes," Nahilya replied. "I hold to that truth."

Pyrah wondered who the reclusive healer had lost. When they had reunited in the air, Nahilya seemed withdrawn, and Elryk was quietly attentive and concerned. If she knew Nahilya better, she might have enquired. Perhaps she was cheating herself by remaining so aloof.

"If the Otherworld is so lovely, why is it that people are so sad when someone dies? Shouldn't we be happy for them?"

Curse Tya and her questions.

"Because we cannot follow our loved ones there. In this mortal life, we are weaker. We doubt and stumble in the dark. What we must hold to is this: suffering is not forever." Filgaryn ran his hand down Tya's strawberry blonde hair. His gaze softened, but his tortured expression remained.

"Do you think Uxhyn suffered?" asked the young male of the survivors.

Melayah turned to her nest-mates. "No," she answered shortly. "He was dead before he hit the ground."

Uxhyn's hatchlings shifted, casting nervous glances among themselves.

"Let's hope if we die, we go quick," one of the girls said. She lifted a shaking hand to push away a mass of bright red curls.

Elryk returned to the group, a leather satchel in his hands. He halted by Nix, who was hanging upside down from the roof of the cave. Pyrah had never appreciated how strong the bird's talons were. Her brother scratched his finger along the feathers of his neck.

"How did he survive?" Filgaryn asked.

"He was in the trees," Elryk answered. "I've trained my birds to stay hidden and quiet during skirmishes."

"The satchel ..." Pyrah belatedly wondered where Elryk had found the bag. It was not one he had in his possession before the attack. He collapsed beside Filgaryn and fished out two bottles.

"We should drink."

Filgaryn looked at the bottles, uncertainty written over his features. "We should keep a clear mind."

Melayah stood from where she was leaning up against the cave wall. Stomping over, she snatched the bottle, unsheathed a dagger from around her waist and removed the cork with a swift movement of her blade. "Give us this night to forget. Dawn will break with new problems."

After grabbing another bottle from Elryk's satchel, Filgaryn used his teeth to open it. "Very well then."

"Hail to the fires of retribution!" Melayah proffered her bottle up in a mock salute and drank deeply. She gasped and swallowed the dark liquid.

"Never run. Never surrender." Elryk chuckled and shook his head. "It's strong mead."

Filgaryn mirrored Melayah's actions and took a big drink. He smacked his lips and passed the bottle to Elryk. In Artroth, a pure dragon would never share a drink or a meal with someone whose existence was considered inferior to his own. Elryk's eyes widened in shock, but he accepted it and drank.

Pyrah stepped forward cautiously, keeping her face in a careful mask as Tya flinched back from her. She couldn't blame the child for being wary of her. Their meeting had been on the battlefield, and her threats had been dire. After her behaviour, which Elryk was admittedly right to chastise her for, she could not expect Tya to want to be in her presence.

She plucked the bottle from Elryk's loose fingers after he had a drink and brought it to her lips. Her brother was right. The liquid burned on the way down. But being one of dragonkind, she liked it when alcohol burned her throat. She did not fall easily prey to drunkenness.

How she wished she might sink into a stupor. She might be able to close her eyes without thinking about the terrible expression on Charyss' face. The moment of her daughter's death would be with her to her dying day.

"*Lullah?*" Bless him, Daerys looked up at her with his dark, knowing eyes. Pyrah cursed. Charyss was gone and Vallah's fate uncertain. It was for Daerys that she must fight, and Melayah.

Melayah had returned to her place by the cave's entrance. The girl blinked up at her, pushing her voluminous curls from her face. During the afternoon, she had sneaked away, washing her face and her clothes. Slightly damp, her clothes clung to her. Pyrah had noticed Daerys' interested gaze and rebuked him with a sharp gesture. "Can I get you anything, dragon mother?"

Pyrah shook her head, lifting a hand in defeat. She swallowed a mouthful of bile, with the unbidden thought that Charyss' head had been lost in the battle. She would not be able to pray over her child's body or pay her proper respects. "I need some air."

No one stopped her as she dashed from the cave. The cool breeze of the evening caressed her flushed skin as she started a frantic clamber down the mountainside. She slipped, and sliding along the loose rocks, she cut her hand.

The sting of the cut Pyrah could ignore, but the pain in her gut she could not. She leaned over and threw up the contents of her stomach, half lying on the rocks, retching long after she had expelled all food and drink. There she lay, letting the hot tears of grief drip down her nose.

She had not been the most attentive or understanding of mothers. Maybe it was her pure Artrothian blood that made it impossible for her to understand the complexities of humanity and explained her inabilities as a mother. Elryk ... Elryk had been her daughters' strength. He had been the parent when both she and Luthur failed them.

Surely now she understood that she was cursed. Woe to her. Only to know the depth of her love for her daughters when their lives were stolen from them. Who would greet dearest Charyss in the Otherworld? Would Luthur discover a devotion for his daughter that he didn't know in life? Perhaps his mother? Would her child find any solace and comfort in death?

Lifting her face to feel the soft fingers of the wind, Pyrah manifested into her dragon form. Unfurling her wings, she leapt into the sky. In times of trouble, there was only one place where she could find the illusion of peace. Water.

The waters nestled between the Stonethaw Range and the wide inlet were protected. It was a serene place, perfect for a moment of quiet reflection. She murmured an old prayer for her lost daughter, sweeping her eyes across the rugged edges of the mountain to the silver stars, and then finally to the still, crystal waters.

Returning to her human form, her fingers fumbled on the fastenings on her tunic and leggings. She stripped herself of her clothing until all she wore was the golden snapdragon necklace that Torryn had gifted her in her youth. Her fingers ran along the small spines of the creature's back. It was a fancy piece to keep with her, but it reminded her of a time when she still had an ember of hope for her future. Now, after losing both Uxhyn and Charyss, that hope was fading.

She strode towards the inlet, uncaring of her nakedness. As the water lapped around her thighs, she trailed her fingers along the surface. Her power curled around her fingertips, warming the skin on her palm. The water welcomed her home.

"Oh, Vallah," Pyrah whispered. She swallowed back a lump that was lodged in her throat. If only she could hold on to the hope that her feisty youngest child might survive, maybe she could manifest it into being. Deep down, buried under her own confident mask, she knew she would not survive the death of another child. Her heart had been broken; pieces of her soul were scattered to the winds. She clenched her fists and bit back a wild cry of fury. This wasn't time to give up on life. This was a time to fight.

"Do you suppose it's wise to be out here alone?"

Pyrah stilled her limbs and kept her expression carefully neutral, pretending she had not been caught unaware of her surroundings.

On the rocky bank, Torryn, in all his bestial charm, stood observing her. As a princess of Artroth, she had seen many magnificent bull dragons. None looked quite as handsome as him.

"Filgaryn said you were brothers." Her statement came out more interrogatory than she would have liked. "General Rivyr was your father."

"He sired me. That's true." As Torryn cocked his head to the side, his golden horns gleamed in the moonlight. She knew that Filgaryn spoke the truth of their relation. If she was honest with herself, she knew the moment she met him many years ago during a midnight swim.

Artroth was a cluster of islands, and it was said that many centuries ago, the islands were ruled by different draconic families. General Rivyr was rumoured to be directly descended from Ythryr, the great king of the western islands of Artroth. His family was famed for the golden horns that occurred within their young every few generations. She wondered if Torryn knew the tale.

"Your mother?"

Torryn tilted his head to the side. He was a large dragon, and yet he made each of his movements seem graceful. He was born for dragon scales. "A human sailor. She wouldn't interest you."

"I suppose that explains your respect for the ocean." A thought occurred to Pyrah. "Why didn't you tell me you were a half-breed?"

"I didn't trust you," Torryn replied. The simplicity of the statement hurt. Worse, Pyrah knew that he had been right to keep the truth from her. "And in the end, was I not right? You took my heart, whispered pretty little promises, and married another man."

"I married a human," Pyrah said, bristling. "You married a *dragon*. After Luthur was dead, we would have been free to be together."

Torryn's brow furrowed, and she watched as he melted into his human body. "I didn't want to be alone for my human life. You had children, a brother, and a village. I had nothing. I was alone." Torryn's voice wavered with emotion. "Then I met Ayrahylse, and she loved me for a time. But I was a fool. I jumped at the opportunity even as I burned. *E birelle'n ion tryth garah.* I felt an all-consuming burn for you. And you *left* me."

Pyrah stood and waded out into the shallows, drawing the water to herself to wrap around her body. The liquid gown caressed her burning skin and shimmered in the moonlight. She didn't do it for modesty's sake. No. The water was clear, but she could see Torryn's rising interest in his dark eyes. He had always been so easily captivated by her power. Willing her feet to keep moving forwards, she gathered her courage. If she stopped, she would lose her nerve. Tonight, she was going to take what she wanted.

She still ached for Torryn. Even after not laying eyes on him for many years, she burned with the pain of missing him. He had been the other half of her soul, the more understanding, level-headed one with a sense of reason. What would life have been like if she had run away with him?

Torryn shifted his weight, his eyes never leaving her face. She felt him suck in a breath as she reached to cup his cheek with her palm. He shifted again, his hands hanging loosely at his side. When she reached him, she wrapped her hands around his neck and stretched out to touch her lips to his. Torryn slowly let out a small shuddering breath, his hands coming to rest, featherlight, on her waist. Upon the touch of his fingertips, her water dress cascaded down her body. She took his slight movements as permission and stepped closer so that her breasts pressed up against his chest.

Knowing that Torryn was close to giving in, she ran her tongue along his lips, seeking entry. His mouth opened with a moan, and she felt the moment his stiff muscles loosened and he relaxed under her touch. His strong arms snaked around her, drawing her closer against his body. He kissed her back with the ferociousness that spoke of the bull dragon within him.

"You make me come undone, woman," Torryn gasped. His lips trailed down her slender neck and along her collarbone.

"Good," Pyrah replied. If Torryn weren't holding her up, she was sure her knees would have buckled. "The water is beautiful. I'll make the swim worth your while."

"Are you sure?"

"My husband is dead, and Ayrahylse is a traitor. And if we don't indulge ourselves tonight ... tomorrow, we might die. If we are to go to our deaths, I would know the taste of you."

There was still a hint of weariness in Torryn's eyes. "I'm a shield-fire. Once you give yourself to me ... my dragon will be loyal to you and you alone. He'll pine for you like a helpless little hatchling."

"Good," Pyrah whispered. She nipped at him, grazing her teeth along his warm skin, pleased when he shivered in pleasure. "Burn for me. Let me bring you to your knees."

"There's something you ought to know," Torryn said suddenly. The haze of the pleasure left his eyes as he stepped away.

"Torryn," Pyrah groaned.

"I have no hope of having my own nest."

Pyrah cocked her head. That wasn't the confession she was expecting.

"I took a poison," Torryn said. "I'm infertile. I will sire no child."

Winding her fingers through Torryn's short curls, she tugged him forward. "We're at war. This isn't the time for repopulating dragonkind the natural way. Now, out of your pants and come for a swim."

"We should return."

Pyrah hummed, running her fingers over the warm skin of Torryn's chest. Even under the greying dawn sky, his dragon still warmed her with desire. The taste of him lingered on her lips.

"A few more moments."

A soft exhale, and Torryn rolled onto his side; his hand snaked down her spine to rest on her lower back. He looked at peace, his eyes closed and his facial muscles relaxed.

"Do you want to be found like this?"

Lifting her head, Pyrah smoothed her fingers to his shoulders and looked down at him. His eyes opened in a sliver. She shuddered at the intensity of his gaze. "I am not ashamed."

"Hmmm ... Good." Torryn's voice was a low, rumbling purr. Under his skin, she felt his magnificent dragon move. She bit down a sly grin, feeling how content the blue dragon was.

"Was your mother truly human?"

"Are you ashamed to be with me now?"

"No," Pyrah said. She caressed his cheeks and leant up to press her lips to his. "Before Daerys, I never thought a dragon could manifest from one with human blood. I am glad I am wrong."

Torryn's lips twitched. "So very wrong."

"You'll be reminding me for years to come."

Surging forward, Torryn rolled her onto her back so that he was up above her. His lips claimed hers before his teeth nipped down her throat, grazing her skin until she trembled with a tingling warmth. "I'll be reminding you for centuries that you, Princess Pyrah, were in fact wrong."

Never had Pyrah ached so for a man. She grinned up at him and arched her back in invitation.

Torryn rolled to his feet, laughing at her disappointed look. "Sometimes the anticipation makes the lovemaking all the sweeter."

Pyrah's fingers curled around a stone, and half sitting up, she flung it at him. It sailed through the air and missed. Torryn laughed again as he fumbled with his pants.

"Filgaryn is looking for us." She admired his lean hunter's form as he thrust his shirt over his head. "Aren't you going to get dressed?"

"Let him see," Pyrah said, raising her eyebrow.

Torryn's brow furrowed at her. His dark eyes stared at the golden snapdragon necklace that was sitting flush against her skin, only a few finger spaces from her breasts.

"You kept my gift. Why?"

"I was never ashamed of what we had," Pyrah said. "There were many nights I wished that you'd come and dispose of Luthur and save me from a lackluster marriage. But I see I made a choice to be with him over you ..."

"I wish I fought for you," Torryn replied. His eyes flicked towards her, and she looked into the depth of his. Blessed by her dragon heritage, she could see the flecks of golds, oranges and yellows in his brown eyes. "I wish I wasn't deceived."

Torryn turned his back to her, lifting his head to the sky. Dawn was fast approaching. The golden rays of the sun would light the world, and with it, increasing the danger if Rhodys and his dragons were out searching for them.

Great blue leathery wings sprouted from his back. His body contorted and blurred for a heartbeat until his dragon form emerged. Claws dug into the pebbles, back legs bent, and he was airborne with the whoosh of his wings.

Pyrah's hair whipped around her; the air was disturbed by Torryn's gigantic wings. She raised her head to the sky and watched him disappear on the horizon. He was right. It was time to face reality once more. Last night was a welcome reprieve. She hoped that once this nastiness was over, he would view her as more than a distraction.

She had spent many long nights denying that she loved him still. When he moved on without her, she had been unbearably jealous and angry. Luthur had thought her merely infatuated with him. No. It was something more. For years, she had burned for him. He had been her all-consuming fire.

"I am not ashamed," Pyrah whispered to herself. Wetting her lips with her tongue, she looked forward to hunting him down for their next tryst.

CHAPTER THIRTY

Torryn

STONETHAW RANGE

Still giddy from his night spent with Pyrah, Torryn landed on the side of the mountain. He stumbled, sending a spray of rocks flying as his claws dug into the earth. A rumbling laugh escaped his throat at his own clumsiness. He steadied himself and lumbered towards the cave.

The instant Torryn entered, Filgaryn speared him with a stern gaze. His brother was in his dragon skin, curled around Tya. His lips twitched into a smug grin, and he watched as Filgaryn's nostrils flared.

"Don't you look well rested, *sudunyn*." From Filgaryn's low sardonic drawl, his brother was aware of what he had been up to. The sound of the grey dragon's voice was enough to wake Tya, who stretched and patted Filgaryn's warm scales.

"I had a lovely evening," Torryn replied.

"Did you? You're looking entirely too pleased with yourself." Nahilya, the empty healer, eyed him suspiciously and extracted herself from Elryk's arms. She rolled over onto her back, bringing her hand to her head. "I'm never drinking again."

Beside the healer, Elryk was still asleep, his mouth slightly ajar as he snored. His red hair fanned about his face. Torryn wondered what he might say if he knew he had taken his sister to his bed last night.

Pyrah's *mynrell*, Daerys, was curled up with the other hatchling. The other four hatchlings, the survivors, were already up … He had caught sight of them conversing a little way from the cave. At least two of them had hangovers.

Torryn exhaled and returned to his human body. He turned, grinning at the sound of claws hitting the ground, expecting Pyrah, but was disappointed when he came face to face with Gahryk. A low rumble wove up his throat, and he felt his fists clench at his side.

When he had heard no tale of Gahryk assisting Artroth, Torryn assumed that the other dragon had simply gone to ground. He heard that the Artrothians still had a healthy respect for Gahryk, and seeing the way Filgaryn eyed him wearily, Torryn believed those tales. Jilearah, the old woman seer, had told him he was neither hero nor villain but a visionary. Whatever Gahryk's vision might be, he couldn't agree with his methods.

"That's the difference between you and me, Torryn," Gahryk said. "You don't have the stomach for what must be done."

"What is it you want?" Filgaryn snarled, curling his body around Tya.

"General Rivyr dead? Good, it's all happening as it should." Gahryk's flippant remark raised Filgaryn's hackles. His brother stood, snarling, his wide nostrils flaring. "Come now. Sacrifice happens in war."

"I wonder, if the outcome you want requires your sacrifice, would you give up your life?" Nahilya's hands shook Elryk awake.

Gahryk tilted his head to stare at her, as if the healer had said something deeply amusing. "The outcome I want does not require my life, my dear."

"A pity," Melayah muttered. The young dragons had since stirred. "Hyn warned me about you."

"Hyn warned you about a great deal of many things," Gahryk said. "But not all of those things would cause you harm."

"I asked you what do you want?" Filgaryn snapped. The very muscles along his brother's scaled back were testimony of how angry and frustrated he was. "You only come when it benefits you."

"Incorrect assumption, son of General Rivyr. I'm fighting for the vision of dragonkind in the millennia yet to come."

"And it doesn't help us here in the now," Elryk snapped, drawing himself upright. "Tell me, could you have prevented Charyss' or Uxhyn's death?"

"Yes."

Such a simple statement.

Elryk roared in fury, lunging the distance between himself and the seer. He raised his fist and punched Gahryk on the nose. There was something magnificent about watching a man attacking a dragon.

"She was a child," Elryk yelled. "An innocent child."

"A child, yes," Gahryk agreed. "Innocent, no. She knew the formulas in which to trap dragons in their human bodies, and now Artroth has this information. The consequences of her weakness will echo for all of dragonkind for centuries."

Torryn shivered in horror at the mention of the herbs that had been forced upon him during his imprisonment. He shared a significant look with Filgaryn. The mere thought of his time confined to his human flesh, unable to manifest, brought with it a wave of horror.

"And so, you let her die," Elryk finished.

"You loved her well," Gahryk said. "There was no escape for her once she divulged that information to Rhodys. Even the Wind Song warned Pyrah and sent her a son."

Elryk turned away from Gahryk, his shoulders shaking in what Torryn could only assume was repressed anger. From where they had lain the night before, Nahilya watched on.

"I brought you a gift," Gahryk said.

"I don't want anything from you," Elryk snarled.

"I think you might want this one," Gahryk replied. He tucked his wings closer into his body, revealing the form of a sleeping child. The girl's dark hair was a mass of knots, her face dirty and tear-streaked. "You'd be very proud of her. After her sister was taken, she escaped, and I plucked her from the wilderness to bring her to you."

Elryk, still facing away, seemed unmoved.

Torryn watched as the girl stirred, bringing her small fists to her eyes and rubbing. Her knuckles were bruised and bloodied. She sat up on the dragon's back, looking around the cave. She was lost and confused.

"Vallah?"

Pyrah had returned.

"Vallah?" Running into the cave, Pyrah halted by Gahryk's side. She lifted her arms up at the child and beckoned to her.

"Mama!"

Elryk had turned to watch the scene, his face slack and his mouth forming a little 'o' of shock. He seemed frozen on the spot, staring wide-eyed at the young girl as if he hardly dared to believe his eyes.

Slipping from the back of the dragon, the little girl landed into Pyrah's arms. Pyrah smoothed the matted mess of hair back before clutching the child to her chest.

"My girl!"

The return of Pyrah's daughter was an emotional moment. After those who knew young Vallah welcomed her back into their fold, Gahryk quite succinctly dismissed the younger dragons from the cave and set up a war council.

It was clear to Torryn that Filgaryn had some dealings with the seer before. From his reaction to the old dragon, his brother had little reason to trust him.

Once she ensured her daughter would be safe with Daerys and Melayah, Pyrah sat next to Torryn and wove their fingers together. At his questioning gaze, she tilted her head to the side and smiled at him. Her fingers tightened.

Elryk, still annoyed by Gahryk's presence, grimaced, turned his face away and said nothing.

"You do know, Pyrah, daughter of Latunya, that you'll have no young with Torryn?"

Pyrah lifted her chin and met Gahryk's gaze. "Torryn already told me, all-knowing one. You cannot poison him against me."

"Did he now?" Gahryk raised his eyebrow and stared at Torryn, who wanted to squirm in the uncomfortable silence that followed.

"Why are you here?" Torryn was sure that if Filgaryn had to ask one more time, his brother might erupt into flames. He had heard from his mother that this phenomenon happened when Artrothian dragons became extremely vexed. When he was small, she had threatened to leave him with his mysterious dragon father. His mother had been sure that his naughtiness would result in his father bursting into flames.

Gahryk was unconcerned with Filgaryn's anger. "You know some of my plans."

"What I know is that you nudged Father into accidentally overhearing Ayrahylse giving Rhodys information about Torryn. From there you asked Father to break Torryn out of captivity and give his life to do so."

"Yes," Gahryk murmured. "How unexpected that he got you out of captivity too."

"One can only assume that you want Torryn for something."

Gahryk hummed. "I'm not the one who wants Torryn."

Pyrah pulled her hand away from Torryn's as if she had been burned. Torryn could feel a growl rumbling in his throat but contained it.

Patience, Torryn told himself. *When dealing with Gahryk, one needs patience.* He eventually would speak of what he meant to. But first, there was always a period of frustration.

"The emperor is weak," Gahryk continued.

Torryn leaned forward, resting his chin on his forearms. "We've heard he is unwell."

"Indeed." Gahryk laughed. "So very unfortunate that someone in his court was easily convinced to poison him. At this stage, the emperor's healers are flummoxed. They will be until he suddenly expires in a season or two."

Torryn couldn't help but wonder what type of dragon was reckless enough to risk getting caught poisoning the emperor.

"As we Artrothians know, the strongest heir of the emperor will ascend the throne."

"Rhodys," Pyrah snarled.

"Yes, but unfortunately, he is not well-loved and is hated more than his brutal father. His brothers are many years his senior and have stable personalities, which could see Artroth flourish."

"We don't want Artroth to flourish," Torryn rumbled. "Nor do we want Rhodys as an emperor."

"The lovely Laelyth is the wife of his eldest brother. She is already with child ... Now, the ushering of a new emperor is always tenuous for vulnerable nieces and nephews. I think you'll find Rhodys' brothers will resist his rule ... and Rhodys knows this."

"Tell us plainly. Is Rhodys to be emperor? What have you seen?" Elryk leaned forward, an intense light in his green eyes. Torryn shivered at the strength of the hatred within the empty one's gaze.

"I've seen many things ... Rhodys is not emperor ... Xavryn, the husband of Laelyth, will take the crown. He is not a kind man, but he has no interest in Ramyr for the time being. The start of his rule will be an upheaval, and he'll be busy keeping himself on the throne and the dragons of Artroth in check."

Pyrah sighed, brushing her hands through her hair. "So there's nothing we can do until the emperor is dead."

"You'll rebuild searching the western coast of Ramyr. Go, build an army, and when the time is ripe, the emperor will die. Rhodys' attention will be torn between Xavryn and keeping his foothold in Ramyr. It is then you'll strike."

"How will we know when this happens?"

Gahryk smiled and laughed. "Your little Daerys will bring you news from a most unexpected source."

After Gahryk left, Filgaryn exited the cave. Elryk's curious parrot, Nix, fluttered noisily after him. Instead of joining Elryk's discussion, Torryn followed Filgaryn, hoping that his brother might share his insights. It came a shock to him to realise that he trusted his wily half-brother.

He found Filgaryn standing with his back to the cave. Nix perched upon his dark head like a large feathered crown. The Artrothian dragon seemed unbothered by his bird companion as he stared up into the sky. Their young dragons were flying, wheeling about and sparring.

"Is Gahryk reliable?"

Arms crossed against his chest, Filgaryn ground his teeth. He shook the blue parrot from his head, and Nix squawked at the indignity and joined the young dragons in their practice flight. "We've no choice. The nerve of him to expect Father to lay his life down … while he remains on the sidelines."

"I guess that makes your father … a hero."

Filgaryn turned his head, staring at Torryn with large incredulous eyes. "You're changing your mind about him."

Torryn snorted, booting a large rock so that it careened down the mountain. "I met a human seer that told me heroes would give everything of themselves to be burned until there is nothing left to give. Not a bad way to go out if I'm honest."

Filgaryn cleared his throat, looking away. "He cared, you know. Father never wanted you to suffer. In his own Artrothian way, he cared."

The thought made Torryn uncomfortable. "So, we fly west then?"

"West."

"I don't trust Gahryk."

"Wise, I would say," Filgaryn replied. "Gahryk has no love for Artroth and will see the empire destroyed ... only ... he's not concerned with preserving our numbers. It doesn't matter to him how many lives are lost. Look at the child, Charyss."

"It wasn't lost on me that he believes we won't see victory over Artroth for many centuries. I wonder ... why do we fight?"

"I suppose it's Gahryk's definition of victory that matters here. I've to believe there's freedom out there for the likes of you and me, and we don't have to wait. If we're destined to fall, let's burn brightly."

"Do you have any family ... a mate back in Artroth?" Torryn felt a flicker of shame he didn't ask earlier. In helping him, Filgaryn would be banished from Artroth's shores.

"Our great-great grandsire is still alive. He'll not be pleased to learn about *Aluel. Aluel* has a brother with whom he shared a strong kinship bond. Why uncle didn't come ... He should have been here with us." Filgaryn's shoulders drooped. A moment later, he stood tall, a sly smile touching his lips. "Let's not leave it to Xavryn ... Let's make things difficult for Rhodys now."

"What do you mean?"

"There are many clans that are discontented in Artroth. All a blaze needs is a spark ... If we can get a rebellion brewing on home soil ... oh, it's perfect."

Without bothering to look at him, Filgaryn took to the sky. On the ground, Torryn was left dumbfounded by his brother's jittery actions. Filgaryn had thought of something, but he didn't want to trust Torryn with the details. That much was perfectly obvious.

"What am I supposed to do?"

"Wait for my return."*

It was dark when Filgaryn returned. Everyone had retired for the evening, and Torryn kept vigil outside of their cave. He waited in the dark, still silence of the night, searching the skies for his brother.

Filgaryn landed heavily, a gasp of pain bursting from his scaly lips. Torryn strode out to his brother's black shadow. As he approached, he could see that scales had been torn from Filgaryn's flank and his teeth were coated in blood. But there was a distinct air of smugness about him.

"Are you going to tell me?" Torryn pressed his human hands against his brother's ribs. Filgaryn seemed to bask in his own personal victory and ignored Torryn's ministrations.

"Curious little lizard." Filgaryn laughed. His violet eyes shone with a vicious mirth, and Torryn did not feel the sting of the Artrothian insult. "It took some convincing ... but we have a healer on the inside that is more than willing to quicken the emperor's death. And a female dragon angry and willing to undermine Rhodys' authority. She won't join us though. If she ever gets another opportunity, she'll kill me in a heartbeat."

Torryn shook his head. "Do I even want to know?"

"The ladies love me. Can't you tell?" Filgaryn's lips turned up into a smile as he manifested into his human form and hobbled towards the cave. Torryn noticed he cradled his arm against his chest. Whatever he did had been dangerous and cost him.

"How did you convince them to betray Artroth?"

"Father's healer ... the one that examined you," Filgaryn said. "Old family friend ... hates Rhodys. Now hates him more than ever after what the prince did to *Aluel*."

"I see."

"Ask Pyrah, your lover, about Yirys. Lovely woman. She was one of Rhodys' favourites until Ayrahylse. Nothing quite like a scorned woman ... She has a child from Rhodys, did you know? He plans to put the boy aside in favour of any Ayrahylse has with him."

Torryn blinked. He didn't know how he felt about his wife having a child with Rhodys. Not when a child had been denied to him. He felt envy, a sharp twist of the guts and pain. "Rhodys plans to replace his child?"

"Barbaric, I know. Unnatural for dragonkind to kill their own young," Filgaryn said. Torryn swallowed thickly and flinched, and Filgaryn sent him a sympathetic glance.

"Rhodys thinks Yirys is unaware that her little son is in danger from his own father. His battle-fire is untamed. Her best hope for her child is to rebel against Rhodys and back his older brother. In the past, new emperors haven't harmed the nieces and nephews of loyal parents."

"Artrothians make no sense. I thought they needed new blood for dragonkind to flourish." Torryn didn't mention the hypocrisy that it was barbaric to kill a pure dragon child, but a half-breed like him or empty like Elryk … that was perfectly acceptable.

"It is. But no one wants a young one to grow up to be a threat," Filgaryn replied. "This practice has been our downfall. Ythryr has cautioned us for centuries."

"Who's Ythryr? Never mind … I still don't understand."

"Ythryr, the first great dragon king. He was white of scale, crowned with golden horns, and was mighty among our kind. He rose up when the humans came to hunt our young."

Golden horns? Torryn blinked.

Filgaryn gave him a meaningful look. "We are the youngest of great Ythryr's bloodline. Word of our father's death at the hands of Rhodys will upset many in Artroth."

"Why would Rhodys kill off the young of his brothers?"

"Dragons are long lived, not immortal," Filgaryn said. "Rhodys plans for bloodshed. Would you leave a child alive whose parent you plan to unjustly murder?"

Torryn remained silent.

"I didn't think so."

CHAPTER THIRTY-ONE

Pyrah

TRADER'S BAY, LORLYN

Even along the western shores of Ramyr, news had spread of the dragons fighting the southern regions. With each ship that docked along Trader's Bay, the stories became wilder. Lorlyn, a beautiful town nestled in the northernmost reaches of the bay, was on high alert. Traders, pirates and merchants mingled, whispering about the Artrothian threat.

Walking the muddy streets of Lorlyn, they heard rumours of a fort destroyed and of battling young dragons killed by more powerful overlords. Pyrah could see the alarm on Torryn's face when he heard stories of humans taken as slaves, and in some cases, food.

In Artroth, it was an accepted practice that in times of war, the troops might eat humans to survive. Filgaryn strode ahead, his chin raised high as *vehyl* scattered before him. His long hair and stature gave him away as Artrothian.

Torryn took a few steps, lunging forward to catch his elbow. "Tell me it isn't true," he said. "Tell me you haven't eaten *vehyl*."

For a long moment, Filgaryn stared at his brother, assessing Torryn's gaze. Without breaking eye contact, he released his brother's grasp on his elbow. "Torryn, sometimes during war, hard choices are made."

"You've eaten *vehyl*."

Beside Pyrah, Daerys and Melayah exchanged wary glances.

"Not I. I grew up wealthy. Do you think a dragon would eat humans if there were any other choice?"

"Ramyr is plentiful with wild game."

Filgaryn inclined his head. "That is true. But anything we catch belongs to the royal dragons first. Guess which dragons eat last?"

"And you condone this practice?" Torryn demanded.

"It's all I have ever known. All that any Artrothian dragon has known ..."

"We need to be careful how we approach the *vehyl* in any case," Pyrah said, stepping between the two brothers. "Let's find somewhere more comfortable for the night."

Lorlyn was not a large settlement. But what it had were plenty of inns and taverns for the crews of the incoming ships. It was not difficult to find a comfortable inn close to the docks where she could breathe in the salt breeze. Nahilya stepped into the establishment first and bribed the owner for rooms. The poor fellow had a terrible back, and she relieved his pain. Thankful for the relief, he gave them several rooms for their use for three nights.

"We don't want to stay longer than that in any one place," Elryk commented. He allowed Nahilya to tug him from the tavern and toward the merchant stalls. Supplies were needed, and Nahilya had the knack of using her gifting to pay for items. This meant they could hoard their coins.

Pyrah dismissed telling Elryk about her encounter with their mother. Vallah had been returned to her, and she was unsure if the week of ceasefire still stood. Telling Elryk would only cause unnecessary pain.

Tugging her daughter up the stairs, Pyrah requested water to be drawn for a bath. The innkeeper wrinkled his nose at Vallah. Terrified, her daughter clutched her pants, pressing her frail body unbearably close.

"Lightly scented soap, a comb and a pair of shears would also be welcomed," Pyrah said. "When my son returns, fetch him whatever meat he desires. He's a growing dragon."

"Yes, my lady," the innkeeper replied.

Pyrah turned, sauntering the rest of the way to her rooms for the next few nights. She liked the deference from the human.

She sat Vallah on the bed, and while they watched the ragged serving boy fill the iron tub, Pyrah started to unbind and untangle her daughter's hair.

"When was the last time this mop of yours was brushed, my darling?"

"His royal highness, the great Prince Rhodys, was disgusted by me ... I thought if I was dirty, he was less likely to hurt me."

"Do not call that man by any honorific title," Pyrah said. Her tone must have been biting, as Vallah flinched and the servant looked up from his task. "Rhodys does not deserve your submission."

"Rhodys deserves a hot poker up his ..."

"That's enough!" Running her hand through Vallah's hair, Pyrah did her best not to wince at the grime. She could only imagine what her cousin and mother had put her babies through.

Vallah sniffled and ran her sleeve along her nose. "Charyss wasn't afraid of him. She called him a flatulent bully."

"I'm sorry ..." Pyrah choked back her insufficient words and grief.

Nervous, the servant left the room with a nod of his head. Pyrah knew the boy did not want to overhear the rest of the conversation.

"You'd be proud of her," Vallah said. Pyrah felt her daughter breathe in deeply. "She was brave."

"I am proud," Pyrah said. She dropped a kiss on her daughter's brow. She squeezed her eyes shut and let an errant tear fall. "Of both of you."

Ignoring Vallah's protests, Pyrah stood, blinking back her sorrow, and stripped the child. She helped Vallah into the tub and told herself it was steam wetting her face and not tears. Her hands washed her child without thinking, rubbing in the soap and scrubbing her tender skin. The attempt to wash Vallah's hair was a disaster. Pyrah tried to brush out the tangles, but after snapping the comb in half she had to admit defeat. Vallah's hair was matted with dirt, blood and lice.

Exhaling, Pyrah took up the shears and a fistful of Vallah's hair. The child wriggled and protested at the treatment, but she hushed her and did her best to ignore the tears. Strand after strand of Vallah's dark hair hit the floor until finally, she was left with a tuft on the top of her head.

Pyrah ran her hand through the soft hair on Vallah's scalp and kissed her daughter's cheeks. "Hush now, my darling. It's hair. It'll grow back."

"But it was my hair," Vallah cried. She reached out with a shaking hand to touch her head. "It's gone."

"Yes," Pyrah said. She picked up the shears again and grasped at her braids. At Vallah's stunned cry, she cut off a large section and let it fall to the ground. Her daughter stared down at it, wide-eyed. "Would you like to help Mama?"

A grin curled on Vallah's face. Pyrah knew that her daughter enjoyed playing with anything sharp. "Really?"

Pyrah nodded and handed Vallah the shears.

Chunk by chunk, Pyrah's hair, her pride, joined Vallah's on the floor. When her daughter had almost completed the task, she took the shears back and tidied up the rest of her hair. The others would be wondering about them.

Pyrah stood and offered her hand to Vallah. "Come now, can you help Mama be brave and face the others with my new haircut?"

Small fingers grasped at her palm. "I miss Charyss."

Swallowing, Pyrah tugged Vallah closer. "Me too, darling. Me too."

They left the room together and descended the stairs. Pyrah was surprised to see Filgaryn and Tya in the shared guest area. Filgaryn's posture stiffened; he was waiting for her. He gestured to Tya to stay behind.

"You've cut your hair," he said as he approached the bottom of the stairs.

Pyrah surveyed his incredulous gaze. Artrothian dragons were proud of long hair; her new severe haircut would be a shock to him. "It'll grow."

"Indeed." It seemed that the unthinking Filgaryn she had known in her youth had matured. His eyes swept over Vallah, and Pyrah knew that he understood her decision.

"I don't like it," Vallah pouted.

Gently, Filgaryn took Vallah's hand and pressed a heavy gold coin into her palm. He curled her fingers around his gift and said, "Ask Tya to take you to the market and find a lovely scarf for yourself and your mother."

Vallah looked up at him, her eyes misting over at the unexpected gift. "Go, child," Pyrah said, watching as her daughter clasped the coin to her chest. "Filgaryn wants to speak with me."

She watched as her daughter scampered off, taking Tya's hand. The two girls could be good friends, and she owed it to Vallah to try and get along with Filgaryn.

"Thank you."

"She's been through enough. It's a small gift." Filgaryn shrugged his shoulders, still looking unsure of himself.

"You wished to speak with me?"

"Yes, Torryn and Elryk have made some discreet inquiries. We should be expecting any *vehyl* with powers and potential dragons to arrive in the morning."

"I don't like that we don't have the opportunity to bond with each new dragon. It seems ... unnatural."

"It's unnatural for a dragon to be born of a human," Filgaryn muttered. "But I digress. We are at war, and we must take whatever advantages we can. Once this war is over, we can take the new dragons into the mountain ranges and create dragon clans ... but for now we are fighting for survival."

Pyrah could only describe the number of humans from Lorlyn as disappointing. Out of the five, they could only coax three dragons to manifest to join their group. But along with these humans, the people of Lorlyn offered two old ships and a smattering of humans to support their draconic army.

They stayed in Lorlyn for two days before moving to the next town off the western coast.

At each human settlement, they loaded supplies and men onto their ships before moving on. Understandably, none of the settlements wanted any evidence of them left behind, so they didn't linger.

Within a fortnight they built their dragon numbers back to twenty new hatchlings.

Daerys spent most of his time flying between the ships and Pyrah. She also had the sneaking suspicion he was teaching himself to swim in his dragon body and playing in the waves. He took longer than she expected, and the sea salt clung to his scales. She let him have his adolescent dragon fun. She had been denied that freedom, and Filgaryn said it was good for young ones to explore their physical boundaries without the interference of an overzealous *lullab*.

When Daerys returned one evening to their oceanside camp covered in sand and looking very sheepish, Tya asked the question everyone wanted answered. "What have you been up to?"

Daerys shrugged his shoulders.

"You've done something," Melayah said, leaning over and plucking seaweed from his dark hair. She lifted her hand to try and dust him off, but the sand clung to him.

"He tried to build a fort from sand for me to play with," Vallah announced, skipping into the camp. She tugged on her blue scarf over her ears. "It was a disaster. He got buried."

Daerys jumped at Torryn's booming laugh. "Sand is not a construction tool. Your power is designed for hardy materials, not shifting sand."

Daerys inserted his small finger into his ear and waggled it about. "The night Pyrah found me, I built an island. Where do you suppose the earth came from?"

"There are rocks and solid material under the waves, Daerys," Pyrah replied.

"Wait! Did he say he built an island?" Torryn looked incredulous. "The amount of power for an unmanifested dragon ... I'd like to see it for myself."

"I was very sick afterwards," Daerys said.

"I'd imagine so," Filgaryn said. "But back to the discussion at hand. We need a safe place to hide the ships and our armies."

"What about the Green Isle?" Daerys suggested.

"It would be like a small slice of home," Elryk said. His eyes slid over to Daerys. On his knee, Nix roosted, his head tucked neatly behind his wing. "And Torryn can visit your island."

"What will you call it?" Vallah asked.

"Pardon?"

"The island. What will you call it?"

"The ship I was on was the *Wyn-Tyn*. I guess it is as good as any other name."

"Do we have any other earth movers among our new recruits?" Torryn called all the hatchlings 'recruits' as if his dragon heart could not bear to get close to any of them. Filgaryn and Pyrah had been left with the task of calling out any dragons.

"Grief," Filgaryn had muttered when Pyrah had resolved to confront her lover about his reluctance. "He's not ready. No good would come from pushing him."

Pyrah shook her head. "You and Daerys are the only ones."

"Another large dragon island would be viable for our new recruits," Torryn said. "We could attack Artroth out at sea where they would be less ready."

"Sea battles are risky," Filgaryn replied.

"War is full of risk." Torryn didn't turn his gaze towards his brother but kept his eyes on his knees. "If we are to have victory, we need to risk it all."

"And the ships?" Daerys asked.

Pyrah moved forward. "I am the mistress of the sea. I can move our ships quickly to wherever we need. The idea of a new island is intriguing. Where would you suggest we place it?"

Melayah cleared her throat. "I can draw a decent map. My mother taught me the coastlines."

Filgaryn called for parchment and ink. In the flickering candlelight, Melayah painstakingly drew what she knew of the coast, the islands and anything else of note. From her memory Pyrah told the younger woman where Daerys had created his island.

When Melayah's masterpiece was complete, Filgaryn stood over it, considering everything carefully. Finally, he placed a finger into a piece of ocean. "Here and here ... We should grow these islands after Rhodys leaves Ramyr if we can coax him away. That way he'll be more surprised on his return."

"I didn't think that Artroth knew too much of the lay of the land of Ramyr." Melayah chewed the bottom of her lip. "Does the timing matter?"

"Timing is always critical in battle, young friend," Filgaryn said. "Rhodys might be arrogant enough not to worry about where critical land masses are, but he is still a dragon of great renown. A royalborn dragon."

"Listen, both of you." It was the first time that Elryk joined the conversation. Now his voice spoke in earnest as he addressed both Melayah and Daerys. "Do not engage a royal battle dragon or a seasoned dragon directly."

"I can't make any promises," Daerys muttered. "War is chaos. We'll all do things to survive."

Torryn was waiting for her in the dark. He seemed to prefer keeping their status quiet. Pyrah didn't know why he bothered; she was sure that everyone in the camp knew that they were a mated pair. She allowed Torryn's need for privacy and let him sneak around trying to get her attention. He had always enjoyed the hunt.

His large, warm hands grasped at her waist and tugged. There was a slight rumbling purr before he crashed his lips against hers, pulling her flush against the hard planes of his body.

Tonight, he said nothing but pressed himself against her, drinking up her presence as if he feared that he would not be able to hold on to her.

"Torryn ..."

He deepened the kiss, capturing whatever words she was going to utter from her mouth. Pyrah smiled against his lips at his surprised grunt as he ran his hand over her scalp. She shivered as his fingers ran along the short tuft of hair.

Finally, he pulled away, pressing his forehead gently against hers. He was gasping like a sailor that had been underwater too long.

"Come fly with me, ketur."

CHAPTER THIRTY-TWO

Daerys

THE GREEN ISLE

For the first time in his life, Daerys felt the sweetness of returning to a place he had called home. Perhaps it was because he spent so many years nameless and alone that the emotion was so strong. Never had he felt the sense he physically belonged in the world.

Landing on the beach, his dragon heart was beating with excitement. He lifted his snout to smell the salt air and hear the waves pounding the shoreline. The Green Isle was as beautiful and wild as the last time he saw it.

He turned to look at Melayah, who was studying the craggy rock pools nearby. She tilted her head, deep in thought. "The rock pools might have some creatures for dinner. Something different," she said, swiping her tight curls from her forehead. "Something interesting."

Filgaryn clapped her on the back as he manifested back into his human form and strode forward. "Take Tya and Vallah and teach them how to source their own food."

"What do you plan to do?" Melayah snapped, a hint of challenge in her tone. She scowled at Filgaryn's back.

The pure Artrothian dragon had a habit of barking orders. Daerys could only assume it came from his strict upbringing. He was a decorated soldier, and he was used to being obeyed. Filgaryn's imperious mannerisms were a reflex, a part of who he was at his core.

"I'm on sentry duty," Filgaryn replied. He kept striding away. He didn't even look back at them. "We've not heard from the Artrothian camp in days, and we need a battle dragon in the air."

Fingers intertwined with Torryn, Pyrah nodded her agreement. Daerys narrowed his eyes in suspicion as Filgaryn's gaze swept over Torryn, who tugged Pyrah closer to him. He caught the slight roll of the eyes and the wry downturn of the Artrothian's lips. While he didn't approve of the match, Filgaryn said nothing.

Daerys turned to observe Pyrah. When he looked closely, he could see the lines of fatigue on her face. Filgaryn would know what his mother had not dared utter. The constant strain on her powers had weakened her. She needed time to rest.

They had moved along the coastline quickly, and the ships they gathered were helped along by Pyrah's powers of the sea. She guarded their vessels from the tempest and pushed them along at an unnatural speed so they could keep up with the dragons.

"Do you think it safe, brother, if I were to take Daerys and show him how to make a mountain fortress for our dragons to take cover?"

Daerys frowned. The large blue dragon's thoughtful question surprised him. While not unfriendly, Torryn kept a respectful distance. He knew from what he remembered of his father's teachings that dragons didn't like their vulnerable young in the presence of larger dragons.

Filgaryn nodded and was the first one to turn to the expectant army of young dragons watching at a distance. Many of them kept to their reptilian forms. Others wandered up and down the beach, kicking the loose sand. A shiver ran up Daerys' spine. Everyone was feeling the nerves with the certainty the fight for their lives was quickly approaching. "A place for us to take shelter would be welcome. I'll fly far enough out that I'll be able to signal danger and give time for you to find safety."

"I can also show some younglings how fire can carve out a dragon home," Elryk said. His mother's twin didn't often showcase his power, and Daerys was curious to see what an empty one was capable of.

"Thank you," Pyrah murmured. She glanced sidelong at Torryn. Elryk's powers were unnecessary for creating a dragon home.

Daerys thought Torryn might argue, but he inclined his head and clapped Filgaryn on the back. "Stay safe, *sudunyn*. Come, Daerys, I will show you how to find the most suitable place to build mountains. Nahilya, keep everyone on the beach until it is safe."

Daerys had to jog into the tree line to catch up with Torryn as he disappeared. While he strode ahead, Torryn lectured him about the dangers of building from the earth and how it was imperative that he listen to the earth when his power stirred.

"The earth is like the Wind Song," Torryn said. "Just as the wind can speak to you … the land has her own language which you and I are a part of. When we build, we infuse the earth with our power. It becomes one with us."

Daerys blinked. "I haven't heard the earth speak."

Torryn paused and looked back at him, a solemn glint in his eye. "You are young. Unlike manipulating storms or turning invisible like my Otherworld-forsaken brother, we shape something that will last forever. We give our souls to the earth … And in return, the land gives us hers. Ramyr will be bound to you always. Here …"

"Here?"

"Yes," Torryn said, stopping and kneeling on the ground. "Palms on the dirt and listen."

Daerys couldn't help but raise his eyebrows, but he did as he was told. *Listen*, Torryn had said as if the command was helpful. How did one listen to dirt?

"What is dirt?"

"Muck."

Torryn snorted. "A simplistic answer. Earth is the foundation of all. It's to be respected."

"Respect the earth," Daerys muttered, closing his eyes. "Respect the earth … respect …"

Warm hands covered his own. The ground beneath them trembled. "Let me introduce you …"

No sooner had Torryn spoken than Daerys felt the full potential of his power for the first time. When he had created the island in the middle of the ocean, it had been under panic and fear. He made no room to hear the wonder of the power that was manifesting through him. The island of Wyn-Tyn was formed under the crucible of terror. In the moments that one believed their own death was imminent, the impossible was made possible. The ground opening during the battle again was driven by terror.

With Torryn partnering him, Daerys felt a tugging and longing. He belonged to something far greater than his own needs. The earth held secrets, might and majesty, and she sang out to him.

Before them, mighty cliffsides formed and grew while everything around them trembled. Lifting his head to the sky, Daerys laughed, feeling the power flowing through him. He briefly wondered what the others back on the beach might have felt and decided he did not care.

His body trembled under the exertion until Torryn seemed pleased with their cliff faces.

"A mighty dragon home we shall build for Torqui ..."

Daerys wiped the sweat off his brow, grinning. "You're like a love-struck hatchling. Shall I call you Pa next?"

Torryn scoffed and punched his arm. He waved his hand in the air, and from the simple gesture, the side of the mountain quaked and like liquid, reformed its shape. "We can take Elryk up there to form the cave, and every dragon home needs a good hefty ledge to land on."

"Why did you agree to let Elryk build the cave?"

"Every man wants to feel useful." Torryn looked down at him and smiled sadly. "Elryk holds a great and terrible power."

"He is very useful," Daerys said. "For one who doesn't have a dragon, he's the best at teaching new hatchlings how to fly. He seems to understand flight. How does a great man like Elryk be flightless and a *kairn* like me have a dragon?"

"We're not mongrels," Torryn growled, his fists bunching to the sides.

"You didn't see the squalor I lived in."

"Life can be cruel," Torryn said. "But what you went through ... I've faith that something great will come out of your trials."

"What good could—"

"I heard you made friends with an octopus."

Torqui flew Elryk to the new mountains not long after. She gave Daerys an approving nod as Elryk slipped from her back and strode towards the cave.

Heat radiated off Elryk's open palms as he spread his arms. Tendrils of fire flicked between his fingers, first burning red, then to an eerie blue, then powerful silver. The red-haired man's face was flush with sweat and fierce joy. His eyes fluttered closed, and Daerys had the distinct impression that Elryk wanted to crow to the skies. Whatever he had been expecting from the empty one was not this. He hadn't expected full, untamable power.

A few of their newest recruits, an orange and a yellow, both landed, and Elryk's eyes snapped open. His fists clenched, and he grinned.

Looking apprehensive, the young dragons hovered above. They were two young female dragons. Cousins, if he remembered correctly. Two of his mother's turns.

"The hottest flame is the best for melting rock," Elryk said. "Observe."

"We may want to step away," Torqui said in an undertone. "Elryk can get carried away."

Elryk flashed a brilliant smile at his sister. "If only I were born with a dragon, *sudunah*, I'd have melted Rhodys' face clean off as a child."

Everyone retreated to a safe distance, and Elryk swung onto the back of a yellow dragon. He called upon his power. At first, he formed a small finger of flame and let it ebb and flow around him. From his position, he instructed the young dragons to form their own fireballs between their sharp claws. Then he encouraged them to force more power so that their fire turned blue. Neither managed the strange silver flame. But Elryk didn't seem to mind.

When everyone was ready, the flame was directed at the rock. At first, the rock melted away slowly, dripping as if it were molten liquid. As the surrounding area became soft, the streams of rock became a river and puddled to the ground. Unlike water, the liquid was thick and slow moving. As it seeped away from the source of power, it cooled, and its outpouring slowed.

Elryk ignored the extra liquid. His face was upturned to the sky, eyes closed, revelling in his power. The trio didn't stop until a smooth cutout large enough for half a dozen dragons was made into the side of the mountain. Daerys could only stare at the unnatural surface and the river of rock slowly cooling beneath them.

Above their heads, Nix flew overhead, squawking his approval. His eyes closed, Elryk cried out in victory. His long auburn braids were slick with the sweat of his exertion. When he reopened his eyes, Daerys almost stepped back at the power radiating off the empty one. His parrot landed on his outstretched arm, and Elryk laughed. "Not all dragons have scales."

"That is one way to create a dragon home," Torryn said. He turned and crooked a finger at Daerys. "Let's fly to your little island, and I'll show you how you can make a home with earth powers."

Where the Green Isle was lush and teeming with sea life, Wyn-Tyn was sparse and flat. Its only remotely interesting feature was small tufts of grass.

"The Green Isle is as old as time. Your island is what, a few weeks old?" Torryn said. "It'll take years, possibly centuries, before it will look something like other islands."

"Centuries?"

"How very fortunate you are a dragon and will hopefully live to see the day." Torryn bent down, pressing his palm against the hard, unforgiving rock. "This land, Daerys, is blessed by your power. What a wonderful creation for your first try."

"It's ugly," Daerys muttered.

"Comparison is an *ugly* enemy." Tilting his head up, Torryn smiled at him. "It's a foundation. The beginning."

Embarrassed, Daerys toed the ground. "Where do we start?"

"If we want to trap Rhodys, we need formations that can hide an army of dragons. We don't need mighty mountains."

Daerys was thankful for this news. Building mountains had been hard work, and watching Elryk, he knew that creating a space for dragons within the rock was difficult too. His island purpose wasn't to be a sanctuary for dragons to make their homes. Wyn-Tyn was a military venture. A plain and practical land mass, a base for strategy and surprising the enemy. Daerys felt a surge of pride at that thought.

Torryn had him practice forming bumps that grew into hills. The blue dragon then showed him how to carve out caves large enough to hide dragons. He explained how to make the systems so they would be safe and not inadvertently crush a dragon who took cover.

Their practice took most of the afternoon. When the cool of the evening was close, Daerys promised Torryn he wouldn't linger to rest for long, and the blue dragon left to seek Filgaryn.

Daerys wandered towards the shore and stepped his toes into the white foam frothing on the beach. He loved the ocean. He might be a dragon of land, but sea salt ran in his veins. Was his preference his adoptive mother's doing or the life he had spent as a salt-rat?

Lifting his face to the dying heat of the sun, Daerys closed his eyes and breathed in deeply. For a long moment, he stood still, enjoying the quiet solitude.

"Little monster, why don't you come in?"

Daerys knew that voice. It was the voice that haunted his dreams. He had longed to hear her again. Her strange, otherworldly appearance made him curious. Likewise, he knew she was eager to learn more about him.

"The water is pleasant. Come play with me, child of wind."

Grinning, Daerys manifested and leapt into the air. He flew low over the tumbling, churning waves, looking for the kraken.

He didn't have to go far before three of the sea monster's tentacles erupted from the water. She caught him around his middle, her suction pads clinging to his scales. She was a thoughtful creature and did not bring her long, flexible arms to touch his wings. Uxhyn's fear of her was unnecessary. Oh, how he wished that he could have introduced Uxhyn to the kraken. He was sure the gentle giant would have come to love her power, strength and grace.

Holding his breath, Daerys was ready for the moment the kraken pulled him under the water. He kept his eyes open to peer at the giant, glowing eyes, which observed him with interest. Beneath the waves, she released him, and he used his strong limbs and wings to swim around her.

"You're tired."

One of the kraken's tentacles swept under Daerys' underbelly, and she lifted him to the surface. Legs either side of the soft limb, he let the kraken support him in a float.

"Such an unusual creature you are," the kraken said. *"You have such beautiful scales, and your fins help you fly. Your spirit hums with power."*

"Do krakens have powers?"

"Curious little fire-bringer," the kraken cooed. *"I thought you would never ask."*

The kraken's normally grey's skin pulsated, and Daerys caught sight of glowing blue rings of light. *"I am a witch of the ocean. There are many things I see."*

"I remember the blue light from the night the ship sank."

"Like calls to like," said the kraken.

"Did you sink the ship ... for me?"

"Power calls to power," replied the kraken. *"I bring you news."*

"News?"

"Yes. There is another scaled great one who rules a cluster of large islands ... You've been waiting for his death."

"The emperor of Artroth. He's dead?"

"It is as you say."

"Do you know for sure?"

"I see things. You winged ones aren't the only beings with power," the kraken replied. Her tone was clipped. *"The invading dragons have flown to meet the new emperor in battle. The dragon of storms seeks the crown for himself. His brother is screaming betrayal."*

"I have to go back with this news," Daerys said.

The kraken gave his tail a playful little tug. *"Yes, you'll come visit me again soon?"*

"I promise."

Daerys stood, using the considerable width of the kraken's tentacle as a platform. He shook water droplets from his wings and looked back down at the kraken, feeling a tight knot of regret.

"Go now," the kraken said. *"It's dinnertime for you."*

"I never asked you your name."

"Tavia will suffice." The kraken lowered her tentacle so that Daerys' claws got wet, and he was forced to bend his knees and leap into the sky. *"When pursued, fly low over water."*

Wings pumping up and down, Daerys had never been so keen to deliver a message. It was happening. The emperor was dead. Maybe Filgaryn had seen something on his scouting mission.

By the time his claws hit the beach on the Green Isle, everyone was waiting for him. The first thing he noticed was that Filgaryn had returned and was looking grim. He was standing with Pyrah, Elryk and Torryn in a tight circle.

"I have a message!" Daerys called. "Rhodys has gone home to Artroth. The emperor is dead."

Filgaryn's gaze hardened. He looked Daerys over. "It's here. The beginning of the end."

CHAPTER THIRTY-THREE

Pyrah

RHODYS' CAMP, GARROWMYTH

Pyrah felt a thrill of victory when she heard of her uncle's death. Through the bond she shared with Elryk, she knew he felt a savage sense of satisfaction. When they were young, too young for it to be known he was empty, he had been favoured by the emperor. His flaming red hair and his proclivity for setting things on fire had endeared him to Emperor Cilvryn.

The emperor's favour was a two-edged sword. Although Rhodys was his father's favourite, he saw the emperor's interest in Elryk as a threat. Children of dragons were raised to be resilient. Fully aware of the antagonism between Elryk and Rhodys, Cilvryn turned a blind eye. Emperor Cilvryn told their father that he should rejoice in Rhodys' hatred of Elryk, for the constant competition would give him a strong son.

Pyrah cast a sideways glance at Elryk and the three scars that ran down his face. Was letting a child get away with maiming another truly the way to have a strong son? Rhodys had little discipline, and she suspected he had grown to be mad.

"Garrowmyth," Elryk said, testing the town's name on his tongue. They stood side by side, overlooking the Ramyr town Rhodys had chosen for his camp. The smooth planes of his face gave no indication of what he was thinking. His hands rested on the pommel of his sword; his green eyes were fixed upon the town.

"What can you tell us about Garrowmyth?"

Elryk shrugged. "Town of mercenaries, from what I have heard. They kill their chieftains every few seasons."

"Rhodys had some earth movers," Torryn said. "I can see he's had some extra stone walls erected around the city."

It was with some pride Pyrah noted Rhodys' dragons hadn't the finesse of Torryn's or Daerys' creations.

Nahilya touched Elryk's shoulder. She stepped closer, and his expression softened. "Do you think it is true?" Nahilya asked. "Do you really think that Rhodys has returned to Artroth with all of the dragons under his command?"

"I may have had issues with Filgaryn in my youth. But one could always count on his trustworthiness," Elryk replied.

Beside Pyrah, Filgaryn shifted, his eyes sliding over to Nahilya and Elryk, looking amused that they still spoke of him as if he weren't there. "Rhodys cannot lose Artroth to his brothers. To do so would lead to his exile or worse."

"Do you think Xavryn will spare Rhodys?" Pyrah could not help the hint of hope seeping into her tone. Maybe Rhodys' older brother would become a kinslayer and save them the trouble. Xavryn was a harsh personality to be sure, but he adhered to a strict code. Before Rhodys, he had been the one everyone assumed would ascend the throne. While their father, Emperor Cilvryn, was alive, Xavryn had been very careful to remain aloof but polite to his much younger brother. If he wanted the throne, he would need to wait for Rhodys to make the first mistake, to take the first blood.

"Rhodys may give him very little choice," Filgaryn replied. "Rhodys doesn't plan on sparing any of his *sudunyn* or *sudunah*. It is no secret among his forces that his nieces and nephews are also in danger."

"Do you think Xavryn knows of the dangers Rhodys presents?" Pyrah asked.

A feral grin spread across Filgaryn's face. "Laelyth's mind powers are extensive. She was Xavryn's spy in Rhodys' camp. She left before Rhodys could detain or kill her. She also has some ability to read minds ... Rhodys wouldn't be able to keep secrets from her. Couple that with the fact that I bribed a loyal healer to help the emperor into the grave and implicate Rhodys ... Xavryn will see this as grounds to take the throne. Where Rhodys is rash, he is wily and patient."

"I didn't think Rhodys would have been so foolish to leave Ayrahylse here alone." Nahilya looked contemplative. "She didn't seem much like a battle-dragon."

"He may fear that Ayrahylse won't be accepted in Artroth," Torryn answered. He grimaced, fingering the bone handle of a hunting knife at his waist. It was a curiosity. The knife was ancient Artrothian. "She's a murderer."

While Artrothians accepted death in battle as a natural consequence of war, the act of murdering a dragon in the emperor's service was high treason. High-ranking dragons didn't always have the luxury of choosing a mate. Ayrahylse should have been content with being matched with Galvrayne. From what Pyrah could remember, he had the reputation of being disciplined and wasn't unkind. It was said it was difficult to get Galvrayne in a temper.

Elryk's flames crackled around his fingers, flickering from orange to blue. "Let's finish a war."

"Take Daerys and crumble the northern facing walls," Filgaryn said, turning to his brother. He manifested into his dragon form and turned to look at Daerys. "May the winds of battle treat you fairly, my young friend. Tya, when this begins, I want you to take Vallah and hide until one of us calls for you."

"But *Aluel*—"

"No!"

"I'll speak with you after the battle," Daerys said. With a dip of his triangular head, he gave Tya a little affectionate nudge. When they had arrived in Garrowmyth, he had opted to stay in his dragon form. Pyrah regarded him, taking in his somber expression. Torryn had assured her that he would look after him as if he were his own, and she trusted him.

"Yes, you will," Filgaryn agreed. "Melayah, cover Elryk and Nahilya."

Pyrah wasn't sure when Filgaryn had become their general. She flashed him an irritated glance, which he returned coolly, a smile tugging on his lips. Among their number, he had been the one to live in Artroth as a dragon. He trained, fought and bled in their ranks. She knew his experience was invaluable and so decided to keep her mouth shut.

"Daerys, fly fierce, *elt mynrell*. Vallah, *Lullah* will be back soon."

"I won't disappoint, *Lullah*." Daerys spread his wings and was gone.

Torryn rumbled, his scaly lips twitching, and he followed. "*E vydel el taldyn.*"

"I love you fiercely," Pyrah repeated, her eye on the blue dot that was her lover.

The ground beneath Torqui's clawed feet quaked as the walls of Garrowmyth came down under the influence of Daerys' and Torryn's power. She could feel searing heat of Elryk's flames against her scales as he melted the stone of another portion of the wall. The slow-moving, gooey mass was too hot for the enemy humans to cross.

Before the burning anger of the dragons, the human garrison left behind by Rhodys did not stand a chance. It occurred to Torqui that the human numbers were much lower than she had expected. In fact, they met very little resistance. She checked on her left-hand side; Melayah was shadowing Nahilya and Elryk. She manipulated winds to buffer the human enemies back so Nahilya and Elryk could advance without being hindered.

Content that their humans were safe and Daerys was under the watchful eye of Torryn, Torqui unfurled her wings and bellowed. Her nostrils flared at the arid smell of smoke on the wind. She wheeled about, nostrils flaring. Blessed with the eyesight of dragonkind, she caught the flash of flickering flames in the sky. The drifting shadows of a bronze and yellow dragon rose on the air currents.

They had plotted to meet Rhodys' forces on the land. Confident in their own strength, they had anticipated that Ayrahylse would not engage them in battle and would be within the city walls. They had also assumed that Rhodys would have left her alone. Clearly, this was untrue. Torqui recognised the shiny bronze scales of Yirys.

"Ships under attack!"

Against a pair of snarling dragons, their ships and humans would not prevail. Torqui wheeled around to meet them, feeling the ripple of acknowledgements of the others as she hastened towards their hapless humans. She didn't worry about stealth. She could not conceal her approach.

Spotting her, Ayrahylse soared upwards, and Yirys rumbled a threat. It was apparent that Ayrahylse would use the bronze dragon to shield her from any attack. Torryn's once life-mate lifted her head, eyes narrowing on Torqui. Her nostrils flared as if she could scent Torryn on her. Torqui hoped she could feel it and know that she now had a claim on her discarded husband. Torryn, the magnificent bull dragon that he was, did not crumble, but moved past the treachery of Ayrahylse.

Yirys swayed her head back and forth, her mouth slack and her tongue lolling. Torqui could see from the awkward angle that the bronze dragon was favouring her right-hand side. She was already injured.

"Where's your prince?" Torqui bellowed, a smirk spreading across her face as she guessed at Rhodys' real intention, even if Ayrahylse had not divined it. Even as a child, her cousin had a habit of breaking toys and moving on to the next object that caught his attention.

"Stay back. I'll deal with her!" Yirys snarled, one eye on Ayrahylse as she charged forward, her talons outstretched. Torqui let her come, meeting her in a clash of claws and scales. She sunk her teeth into the bronze dragon, who wrenched her head away.

"If I let you take me ... protect my baby."

Yirys' words sent a bolt of horror up Torqui's spine. An Artrothian dragon offering their life during battle to protect their young certainly wasn't unheard of. No one knew where the ancient practice had come from, but dragons had their own name for it.

"Tieryn-myn?" Torqui asked. *"You wish to die at my claws for your child?"*

"Tieryn-myn, yes, death for young," Yirys repeated. The tone of her voice was calm and resigned. *"Rhodys abandoned me here with Ayrahylse, who he is no longer interested in. He's growing dangerous. My son is hidden on the beach. Please, he is in danger."*

Torqui considered her options. Once she accepted Yirys' suicide at her hands, she was honour bound to protect her enemy's young and ensure their survival. *Tieryn-myn* was never a practice to take lightly. To break the sacred pact was to be cursed. What if Yirys' son was a full-sized adult?

"Please." There was a hint of desperation in Yirys' voice. No dragon offered themselves up without a cause. *"I took your children to safety."*

"Charyss is dead."

"And I am sorry about that. More than you'll ever know."

Torqui scoffed.

"Ruryk is only a baby ... please." Yirys bared her neck, twisting around so that it was difficult for anyone on the ground to see what was happening. Torqui swayed her head to the side. Ayrahylse was already fleeing. *Coward.*

"A mother's love knows no bounds," Yirys said. *"I know I don't have to tell you that."*

"Why give me your child?"

"I am one injured dragon. How long do you think I can battle you all before I fall?" Yirys replied. *"This way my death has meaning."*

Torqui struck without warning, her teeth puncturing the soft skin of the bronze dragon's neck. The coppery tang of blood coated her tongue, and Yirys gave a gasping sigh. Wrenching her head around, she finished the job, ripping out Yirys' throat. The bronze dragon plummeted from the sky and entered the water with a splash.

Torqui didn't watch the impact. She turned her snout to their ships. Flying over them, Torqui listened as the voices of men were raised in alarm. She let her shadow pass over them and then bellowed, "Abandon ship."

One by one the humans jumped overboard. Humans, when drowning, could panic and for such little creatures, they had a habit of hindering their own rescues.

Unwilling to get so close to panicking humans, she called upon her power. The feeling of it ebbed and flowed within her veins. She let the waters carry the humans to shore.

"Still," she called. "Let the sea bring you home."

The pale, terrified eyes of the humans below looked up at her. Many in disbelief.

"I can rescue you all if you remain still. Lie on your backs. The waters will help you."

She wheeled about, watching the first of the humans ride the sea into the beach. Those who were panicking calmed watching as others were able to make it to safety. She stayed out upon the ocean until she brought all the thrashing humans home.

She landed on the beach and lay her belly on the warm sand, watching their ships sink to the bottom of the ocean. She had chosen a length of beach away from the rescued humans as she wanted to be left alone after the events of that day.

The sand was glorious. She closed her eyes.

"You killed my mama!"

Her dragon eyes snapped open, and she lifted her head. A small boy, his dark curls in a tangle, raced towards her with a knife in his hand. His face was streaked with tears, and sand coated his legs. He couldn't be more than seven years old.

In warning, Torqui lifted her tail and thumped it down. "Enough!"

The child stared up at her, his mouth agape and tears running down his cheeks unchecked.

"Ruryk, son of Yirys, I presume?"

"Yes." The boy lifted his chin defiantly. "I'm going to kill you."

"You don't say," Torqui rumbled, manifesting into her human form. "Shall I make it easier?"

"I'm going to stick you with my dagger."

"Come on, then."

The boy stood frozen, looking at her with his too large brown eyes. Pyrah beckoned him with her fingers, and the child continued to stare at her.

"Do not torment the boy so," Torryn said from behind her. Pyrah turned. She had not heard his approach. He stood with Daerys at his shoulder. Filgaryn materialised from nothingness; the air around him shimmered with his ability. She felt relief wash over her, seeing that they were all unharmed.

"It looks like most of the humans had already fled Garrowmyth when Rhodys left," Daerys said. "Their garrison was woefully depleted. They didn't want a fight."

"Let it be a lesson, that taking something because you are more powerful doesn't foster loyalty with your underlings," Torryn replied.

"She killed my mother!" the boy screeched, stomping his foot.

"Ruryk, son of Yirys," Pyrah said, pinching the bridge of her nose. "Lord knows which male dragon sired the whelp."

Torryn's brow furrowed, and he turned to look at Filgaryn.

"Yirys incited the right of *tieryn-myn*."

Torryn shifted his weight. There was a flicker of surprise in his deep brown eyes. "She must have feared that his father could not or would not protect him."

"It leaves us in a rather delicate position. Do you have any idea who his father might be, Filgaryn?" Pyrah noticed that Filgaryn did not seem surprised by the turn of events. Perhaps the right of *tieryn-myn* was more common among the battle dragons.

"No," Filgaryn replied. "But in Yirys surrendering her life to you, you have promised to look after her young and protect him with your life."

Pyrah sighed, wishing she could kick at the sand. Yirys had made a poor choice of a mother. She did not want another child. She wanted Charyss. She would grow to resent the boy.

Lowering himself on his knees, Torryn held out a large hand to the boy. "If Pyrah feels she cannot, I can take him under wing. Does not dragon law state that if Pyrah is unwilling that I, as her *ketur*, might protect the child as an appropriate alternative?"

"It is as you say, *sudunyn*." The expression on Filgaryn's face didn't waver. Did anything surprise him? He stepped past Torryn where he knelt on the sand and approached the child, who darted back a few steps. "Do not be afraid, Ruryk. Have you started your battle education in Artroth?"

The child nodded, brushing his hands through his matted hair, leaving a trail of sand. "I started instruction last year."

"Then you understand that your mother has been defeated in battle. It was an honourable death."

"She's gone!" the child wailed.

"Yes. And we remain."

"I want to go to Artroth."

"Child," Filgaryn rumbled. "Your mother entrusted you to us. Artroth abandoned you here with two female dragons."

"Your mother was already injured," Pyrah said, not unkindly.

"*Lullah* fought with *Aluel* … He hurt her. I got scared, and I hid." Ruryk blinked back more tears and wiped his red nose with his arm.

"You have no reason to be. Your mother invoked *tieryn-myn* for you. We cannot harm you. This is Torryn, my brother. He will make a good *aluel* for you." Filgaryn kept his hand outstretched in invitation.

"But what of my *aluel?*"

"I would very much like to know who Yirys mated with," Pyrah grumbled.

"I do not know the child." Filgaryn shook his head, taking Ruryk's hand and drawing him along the beach. As they passed Pyrah, the child dug in his heels, but Filgaryn tugged and stumbled after him. Filgaryn firmly led the boy to Torryn and placed his little hand in his brother's. "He'd be a dragon of little consequence."

"That's not true," Ruryk snarled. "My father is a mighty battle dragon!"

Pyrah opened her mouth to protest. Torryn shook his head, his chest rumbling with laughter. "Oh, the pride of youth. All sons think their fathers are important."

"Fine," Pyrah said. "Take him to the creche of our young, and then we need to prepare for Rhodys' return."

As Torryn and Filgaryn guided the boy along the beach, Pyrah watched them.

"I can't help but think we're making a mistake," Daerys said.

"Yirys invoked an important oath. As much as I would love to end her line, we must keep the child safe," Pyrah said and turned towards her son. "Go, take Melayah and gather our men from the beaches. I'd like to speak with them."

CHAPTER THIRTY-FOUR

Torryn

RHODYS' CAMP, GARROWMYTH

Torryn felt very little guilt about lying to Pyrah about the identity of the child. From the moment Ruryk spoke, he had known whose child he was. Filgaryn was determined the child's identity should remain secret between them, and Torryn agreed. There was enough resentment for Artroth among their numbers without adding the child's parentage into the mix.

Ruryk followed him up the beach, sniffling. He squeezed the child's hand. There was little he could do to ease the boy's grief. One could only assume that if he knew it was Pyrah who killed his mother, he had seen too much of the battle.

"I know that you both know who my father is," Ruryk said. He turned his dark eyes up at Torryn and then to Filgaryn, who was shadowing him. "When he comes back ..."

"Are you his true-born son?" Filgaryn's voice was more challenging than Torryn would have liked, but he didn't interrupt. "Is your mother his *ketur*?"

"No. I am *kairn*." Ruryk lifted his chin and puffed out his chest. "When my father is emperor, that'll change."

"Rhodys will not protect a *kairn*," Torryn replied. "He left you with your injured mother alone and unprotected."

"He left his mate," Ruryk snapped.

"Ayrahylse was *my* wife. Your *aluel* is looking for the strongest bloodline to build himself an army of sons and daughters. Your life means nothing to him."

Ruryk bit back a gasp, his footsteps faltering.

Behind them, Filgaryn sighed. "It may be a harsh truth, my young friend, but it is best you forget who your father was."

"*Lullah* would never ask me to do such a thing ..."

"Child," Torryn said, lowering his voice. "She knew she had no choice. She was found on the wrong side of the war. And she knew things about Rhodys that no little one should."

"I have fire power!" Ruryk exclaimed. Small tendrils of flames flicked up his fingers. Impressive for a young one but not a threat to a grown dragon. "I could grow to be a strong son that is useful for the advancement of Artroth."

Torryn huffed. He did not understand the worship of one's sire. He certainly never had a father figure to fawn over. There would be little he could say to dissuade Ruryk from the notion that Rhodys was a great and powerful dragon.

"The only way to convince an Artrothian boy otherwise is to demonstrate your power. Children are ridiculously easy to manipulate." Filgaryn's quiet confidence radiated through his mind.

"What do you suggest?"

"It's time to build our island strongholds to trap Rhodys when he returns. Take the boy with you."

"Stop talking in your minds," Ruryk said. "It's rude."

Two days later, Torryn did exactly what Filgaryn had suggested and took Ruryk upon his back to fly over the ocean. Daerys flew beside them, glancing nervously at the boy.

"I know you lied to Pyrah," the young dragon said.

Torryn stiffened, hardly daring to look over at Daerys.

"I am guessing you have a good reason for it."

"Sometimes, Daerys, it's better for people to be unaware of the truth," Torryn said. "Ruryk is no more to blame for his father's misdeeds than you are."

"Yeah!" Ruryk shouted into the wind.

"You know who my father is?"

"The dragon that kept you as a little one was not your *aluel*. He kept you as a curiosity. When he inevitably became bored with you, he would have sold you back into the slave market." Torryn regretted his words as he spoke them. From his peripheral vision, he could see Daerys' eyes mist over.

"That's not true."

"You know it is, Daerys," Torryn said, lowering his voice. "Your slave master was playing *aluel* while it suited him."

"No."

"You were his fourth slave-child. It's written in ink on your human skin. The Artrothian number four."

"No ..."

"Artrothians who collect human young often kill the mothers when they separate the child ..." Torryn hated himself a little more with each truth he uttered. He could see the pain he was causing Pyrah's *mynrell*.

"My father didn't ..." Daerys choked on his own words. His eyes were glassy orbs. Torryn suspected he was recalling memories that he had buried deep. When Daerys spoke again, his voice was filled with pain that only came from finally understanding. "The auction house ..."

"Now, I'll keep your confidence if you'll keep ours." Torryn hated that he was hurting Daerys, but he knew in his heart of hearts Pyrah must never know the truth. He had already lost one life-mate. He didn't think he could bear to lose another mate he had a deep love and respect for.

Daerys lagged behind and didn't bother to make any further conversation.

"He's upset," Ruryk said from the place where he perched on Torryn's shoulder.

Daerys' sullen countenance didn't improve; he stubbornly kept his silence. Now in the middle of Addryn Sea were two new large land masses. Caverns, some connected with tunnels, dotted the islands. Here their armies could hide while they waited for their Artrothian foes. It took a day to build the additional islands.

Torryn growled in frustration. The young dragon's poor attitude tarnished his moment of preening under his adopted *mynrell's* approval. With a wave of his hand, Torryn sent Ruryk to go play among the cave systems and watched as Daerys' expression crumbled.

"I did not mean to hurt you. Your adoptive Artrothian father ..."

"I don't want to talk about *him*." Rolling his eyes skywards, Daerys rounded onto Torryn. "Do me a favour, and don't lie to me."

"Dae ..."

"Forget it," Daerys snarled. "I'm a salt-rat. I'll remain quiet and passive. You won."

"This isn't about winning."

Daerys didn't reply. Torryn could see the stubborn set of the boy's chin. "Your *lullah* will land soon with the rest of the hatchlings. Make sure you greet her properly."

Daerys' back stiffened at the mention of Torqui. "Of course, sir."

The moment Torqui's claws hit the dust of the new island, she noticed Daerys' sour mood. The boy's greeting was half-hearted, and he moved away from her and Melayah as quickly as he could.

Torqui moved towards Torryn, her head swaying hypnotically as she winked suggestively at him. She manifested into her human form, and Torryn reached to draw her closer. He kissed her deeply, running his hand over the soft strands of hair on her head.

"Has Daerys given you much grief?"

"He's been perfectly fine," Torryn replied.

He must have answered a little too quickly, as Pyrah raised her eyebrows and looked pointedly to Daerys. Torryn tilted his head to observe the young man as he assisted Filgaryn to split up the other dragons and assign them a cavern to stay.

"Really? He's behaving like a hatchling that has been on the end of a snout smacking."

"Sometimes boys Daerys' age need to sulk, Pyrah," Torryn replied. He glanced back to Daerys and decided that if he didn't change his attitude soon, a sound smack on the snout might be in order. "Let him be."

"I won't have him fly into battle like this." Pyrah swept past Torryn, calling out Daerys' name.

The young dragon lifted his head, wearily regarding her as she approached. His eyes slid over to Torryn, and he shifted.

"What has gotten into you?" Pyrah demanded.

Daerys shrugged and looked away. "Nothing, *Lullah*."

"Get your head sorted," Pyrah snapped. "Poor attitudes can get yourself or someone else killed."

"I'm sorry, Mother." Daerys had the grace to bow his head, looking contrite.

"Get something to eat and go for a sleep."

"Yes, Mother."

"You're fifteen, Daerys, I should be able to count on you to look after yourself. We're at war—"

A shriek interrupted Pyrah's lecture. Torryn watched as Pyrah cursed under her breath as she spied both Tya and Vallah in the shallows, evidently getting into some kind of mischief. She turned on her heel to move along the beach to see what type of trouble the pair was up to.

Daerys looked up at him, obviously expecting another tongue lashing.

"Ruryk called this island Dunnharrow. What about Gyptuum for the second island? It means 'lizard mine' in some of the languages in the far north." Daerys' glare hardened, and Torryn sighed in exasperation. "What more do you want from me? I've apologised."

Filgaryn narrowed his eyes in suspicion. "What did you do?" he asked.

"We gave him some hard truths," Ruryk said, bounding up to stand with Torryn. He nodded curtly. "He didn't like being put in his place. Dirty slave. Now he's having a tantrum, filthy pig."

"That's enough," Torryn rumbled. He watched as Daerys flushed scarlet, his fists at his sides. "Apologise."

Curling his lip, Daerys stomped away. "I don't want apologies from any of you."

"Apologies," Ruryk replied, rolling his eyes and looking wholly unrepentant. He smirked at Daerys' back. "Mangy dog."

Rapping his knuckles along Ruryk's head, Filgaryn glared down at the child. "No more of that talk. Speak in that manner again, and I'll wash your mouth out with salty water."

"You can't!"

Filgaryn raised an eyebrow. "Try me. If you are protected by my brother, that makes me uncle."

Ruryk pouted while Torryn changed the subject. "What have the humans decided?"

"Many of them have infiltrated coastal towns. They are gathering weapons and supplies if the worst should happen. With how flammable their ships are, they aren't keen on joining any battle. They'll fight other humans but no dragons." Filgaryn paused, turning his eyes towards Pyrah. "Go spend the night with your *ketur*. I'll help Daerys sort himself out."

Filgaryn's offer surprised Torryn.

"I feel it on the wind, *sudunyn*. The end is coming."

Brushing his hands along his pants, Torryn nodded to his brother, gave Ruryk one last stern glance and moved across the beach to where Pyrah was still scolding two hatchlings. He stood to the side and let her finish before taking her hand and tugging her towards one of the caves that was far enough away from the camp.

"Daerys ..."

"Let a young man have space," Torryn rumbled.

He coaxed Pyrah inside, and with a simple gesture, sealed the entrance. He had taught Daerys the importance of leaving spaces for fresh air to enter the underground systems. They could breathe comfortably even though the doorway was blocked.

The cave was plunged into darkness. Pyrah took advantage and pressed the length of her body against him. He wrapped his arms around her, pressing her even closer to him. His lips found hers, and his hands ran down her waist to her hips.

Pyrah tugged at his shirt, her fingers running up his sides to caress his chest.

"You make me burn, woman," Torryn groaned.

"This is hardly a comfortable place to sleep."

Torryn's lips sought hers again and then ran down the side of her neck, relishing the soft sighs and moans that escaped her throat. He smiled against her skin, breathing in the smell of salt and battle. His teeth raked lightly over her vulnerable neck, and she shivered under him.

"I'm not intending to sleep tonight."

Pyrah's hands were on his chest again. She pushed at him so that he stumbled, and she laughed. "If that's so, then I'm in charge tonight."

Again, Pyrah pushed him, and Torryn let himself 'fall'. His eyes were becoming accustomed to the dark. Pyrah was shrugging off her battle worn clothes. He could almost see the raised eyebrow and unspoken command. He obediently followed her lead.

"Good boy," she purred, straddling his hips. She languidly slid down, pressing her full length against him. "Let me make you mine."

CHAPTER THIRTY-FIVE

Rhodys

Off the Artrothian Coast

Rhodys looked over the turquoise waters of his homeland. Along the horizon he could see the islands that made the great Artrothian Empire. The warm summer breeze lazily slid over his scales, and he took a moment to breathe in the fragrant smells of summer.

When he had received Xavryn's message, a large packet sealed with thick red wax, Rhodys knew what news he would find inside. He could barely contain his excitement as his fingers shook, breaking the seal. Xavryn had sent no less than six heavily armoured guards.

Xavryn's words were perfunctory at best. The emperor was dead. Rhodys was to return home under the escort that Emperor Xavryn had provided him with. He tasted blood as he bit his lips to stave off his cry of frustration.

"What is it, Rhodys?" Latunya had stayed by his side. And Rhodys could not help but notice the suspicious glares of Xavryn's men as they beheld her.

"Xavryn has already been proclaimed emperor," Rhodys said, folding the parchment. He swallowed, half to hide his bitter disappointment and half to quench the bubbling feeling of fear in his belly.

"Prince Rhodys, the council greatly desires your presence to explain in full the circumstances of General Rivyr's death." The man in charge of his apparent bodyguard turned cold eyes on Rhodys. "Emperor Xavryn wishes to hear your side before he lays down a charge of murder."

"Murder!" Latunya cried. She lifted her head proudly, tossing her dark hair over her shoulders.

"One of your own healers returned to Artroth speaking of General Rivyr's violent death at Prince Rhodys' claws. Does the prince deny that he killed the general?" There was a steely challenge to the man's tone.

"I don't deny that I killed the fiend," Rhodys cried. He picked up his goblet and threw it across the stone chamber, narrowly missing the assembled men. The charge was a serious one, but he wasn't afraid of being convicted. He was a prince of Artroth.

"The lady Latunya's ability to properly provide counsel has also been called into question."

"How dare you?" Rhodys leapt from the throne-like chair, eyes flashing and ready to fight.

"Rhodys ..." Latunya laid a comforting hand on his arm. Her sly smile was enough to make Rhodys shiver. "Best we fly directly to Artroth. General Rivyr's family was well-loved, and they deserve a proper explanation of what that terrible half-breed did."

Rhodys understood. If he wanted to take the crown of Artroth from Xavryn's greedy clutches, it was best not to delay the conflict. The more time Xavryn had to prepare for his return, the more difficult the battle.

Xavryn had severely underestimated him. Fly now, and they very well might find his brother completely unprepared.

Reputation in tatters, and with Xavryn making a successful power grab for the crown back home, Rhodys was left with very little choice. After selecting a few hand chosen dragons to overwhelm, slaughter and discard Xavryn's men, Rhodys took flight for home in the dead of night. He could stay in Ramyr and crush Pyrah's band, take a new territory and give his brother enough time to establish his reign, or he could challenge Xavryn. The dragons in his command were becoming restless. His support was waning daily. He needed to act before his supporters realised Xavryn had been named the new emperor.

Yirys had tried to stop him. They argued, and during it her whelp, the one he had sired, ran off. He told her to leave him. But she betrayed him and stayed behind to look for the child.

And now on the far horizon, Rhodys realised he was wrong in assuming that Xavryn would be ill-prepared to meet him in a fight. Before they could reach the land, they were intercepted by a large company of battle-dragons. Leading them were Xavryn and no less than seven of their siblings at his side. Corinah, his bloodthirsty sister, flew on Xavryn's right-hand side. Fiercely loyal to Xavryn, she posed a great danger to him. She was aggressive and had very little love for him.

"Give Xavryn what he wants!" Latunya howled into the wind.

Rhodys would not concede defeat. "Stay with our horde. I'll see if Xavryn will talk."

Alone, Rhodys drifted forward on the air current. Xavryn, the fool that he was, broke from his own ranks to speak with him, his shimmering silver scales glinting in the midday sun. If his elder brother thought he was willing to parlay, Xavryn would be disappointed.

"Stop this foolishness, little brother."

Xavryn's words stung like a whip. Over two decades older than Rhodys, he had always remained aloof and uninterested. Rhodys bristled at the clear dismissal of his power. His brother was blind. He was no mere hatchling to be commanded. He was the rightful emperor, the strongest of Cilvryn's sons.

"You dare take the crown?" Rhodys snarled through his teeth, jaw clenching as his talons itched to rip out his brother's throat. For as long as he could remember, he had dreamed of killing him. "I was not home when the vote was made."

"You've made serious miscalculations in Ramyr," Xavryn said. "General Rivyr's—"

"Rivyr was a fool and a coward!" Rhodys howled. "He attacked me."

"You sound like a child." Cocking his head to the side, Xavryn surveyed Rhodys as if he were nothing more than an inexperienced hatchling. "Indeed, this is not the tale I heard. Commander Hael was quite upset."

"If Commander Hael wanted victory, he should have done as he was bid and joined my company in Ramyr. He could have controlled his traitorous brother."

"Perhaps the difficulty with Rivyr is that he was loyal to Artroth and not to you." Xavryn shook his head sadly and tutted. "The commander's place is on home soil, where our father, Emperor Cilvryn, asked him to stay. That you tried to overrule *Aluel* was yet another grave failing. *Aluel* failed to discipline you. Well, I won't make the same mistake."

"Step aside," Rhodys growled, snapping his jaws. "The crown is mine. I am Winter's Dragon, the most powerful of father's children. I inherit. If you surrender now, I will spare you and our siblings from my wrath."

Xavryn blinked his amber eyes slowly, a snarl quivering on his lips, which broke his stoic countenance. "Little brother, land and submit yourself to me, and I'll spare your life and that of your dragons. Fight me, and I will banish your company."

"You cannot."

Flashing his long, pointed fangs, Xavryn rumbled. "I have already signed the order. Laelyth returned from Ramyr and told me all the whisperings of your unhinged mind. I long suspected that in killing our mother as a child, you were permanently damaged. Your behaviour during this campaign—killing Rivyr, taking your bastard hatchling with you, bedding Ayrahylse the murderess—is all the evidence I needed."

"I did what I had to!"

"And Laelyth tells me of the plans you have on slaughtering all your siblings and their children to solidify your claim." Xavryn snorted, turning his long, sinewy neck to look back at their sisters. "Our *sudunah* are angry, little brother, that you would like to raise a talon to your nieces and nephews. They'll never support you."

"Aunt Latunya ..."

"Latunya favours you because you were young when she lost her own hatchlings. Your mind was still malleable ..." Xavryn licked his lips with a long, lizard-like tongue.

Rhodys lashed out. Infuriatingly, Xavryn banked slightly and ducked out of the way.

"What will it be, brother?" Xavryn asked. "Return home a prisoner or leave forever?"

Rhodys' lips peeled back into an ugly leer. "I choose *war*."

CHAPTER THIRTY-SIX

Daerys

DUNNHARROW

Daerys rolled his eyes at Pyrah and Torryn's retreating backs. Unable to stop himself observing them, he could feel his blood warming. Anger and something that felt suspiciously like fear competed for dominance in his gut. Pyrah had interjected herself in his life. She was *his* family. Not Torryn's. Yet she was with him, and he was once again left in the cold. He was alone.

"Come fishing with me." Filgaryn emerged from the dark, wrapping his strong arm around Daerys' shoulder and turning him so he could no longer see Pyrah and Torryn. He glared up at the older man, taking in the aristocratic features and the confidence that he would never possess. He glanced down at the fading tattoo mark on his forearm. If only he had been born to a different mother ...

"Is it true?" Daerys choked. He ducked his head so that strands of his hair could cover his face and his expression might stay hidden from Filgaryn. "Do I mean nothing?"

Filgaryn tugged him closer. "You're not nothing, Daerys."

"He never loved me. He wasn't my pa, he was my owner." Daerys swallowed, shaking his head so the tears of outrage he had been holding the last days would not fall and betray him. "You knew. All along you *knew*. In that cave that night, you said nothing ..."

"I had no desire to awaken any memories of the auction houses if you had forgotten them."

"I remember now. He ordered his men to slit her throat and burn the body." Daerys hated the way his voice cracked.

"Torryn should never have said those things to you. Dragons will do and say terrible things to protect their *mynrell* ..." Filgaryn said.

Daerys sniffed.

"Dragonkind have a different way of thinking about family. *Mynrell* means many things: son, daughter, hatchling, adopted child, fosterling ... As Torryn will protect Ruryk, Pyrah will protect you."

"She has an alliance with Torryn now."

Filgaryn chuckled, sweeping his hand through his long black hair. His eyes were alight with mirth as he looked down at Daerys. "They're joined as lovers, yes. Just wait until you discover the joy of the newness of a life-mate. That being said, she will protect her young over her mate. That's the way dragons are."

Daerys stumbled as Filgaryn nudged him. He opened his mouth to give the older dragon a piece of his mind when he spotted Melayah walking towards them. In the moonlight, she looked striking. In Lorlyn he had pilfered a yellow scarf to gift her. Elryk caught him in the act and took a birch switch to his rear end. The punishment was worth it to present it to her. Tonight, her spiral curls were held in place by the scarf. In the shadows her eyes gleamed with the promise of mischief.

Filgaryn winked and shoved Daerys, who stumbled forward, his lips twitching into a lopsided grin. He only had eyes for Melayah, and therefore didn't notice when Filgaryn disappeared into the dark.

"Are you well, Daerys? You seemed pretty upset when we arrived."

Daerys said the first thing that came to his mind. "Do you want to go for a swim?"

"A swim?" Melayah looked at him as if he had grown two heads. "We don't know what is in the water."

Sitting on the ground, Daerys shucked off his boots and pulled his tunic and shirt over his head. "They say I'm a mighty dragon. I'll protect you."

"More like you'll expect me to save your scaly hide."

Daerys hummed in response and stood to wade into the water. He trailed his fingers through the coolness of the ocean, his eyes on the vast horizon. He didn't think Melayah would join him. But a moment later, he caught the sound of water sloshing.

"Do you want to meet the kraken, Queen Tavia?"

"You want to call the sea monster?"

"We have dragons within us. That makes us monsters too," Daerys said. He stared at her until she succumbed.

"Alright, how do we find the kraken?"

"Swim, I guess," Daerys replied, shrugging his shoulders. "I'll see if I can contact her."

Reasonably confident that Melayah would be right behind him, Daerys swam out into open water. She had lived much of her childhood out on the ocean too; she had a healthy respect for the ways of the sea. As they entered the deep waters, Daerys reached out, trying to communicate with the kraken.

"Sea queen, sea witch!" Treading water, Daerys looked about, hoping to catch a ripple or a hint that the kraken was nearby. He glanced over to Melayah, who was also treading water, crystal droplets hanging from her curls. "Tavia!"

"Is she near?" Melayah asked, her eyes darting around the surface of the water.

"This is foolish," Daerys muttered. "It's dark ... I can't see anything."

"Or you could be patient."

Daerys' lips tugged into a smile as he felt the very tip of the kraken's tentacle wrap around his ankle.

"Hold your breath."

There was barely time to follow the kraken's instruction before he was yanked under the water. The movement of the kraken's jerk was abrupt, and his hands flew out in shock. Above his head he could hear Melayah screaming, and he had to purse his lips to stop his laughter. Strong grey tentacles wrapped around his middle, dragging him closer to the large orange orb of the kraken.

"You've brought me a friend this time. How delightful."

"Her name is Melayah."

Through the connection he had with the kraken, Daerys felt her amusement. *"Ready?"*

The flexible arm that held him thrust him upward and into the sky. Daerys hollered with laughter as his body launched and then landed into the water with a splash. He broke to the surface, flicking his head side to side, still laughing.

"She's going to kill you!" Melayah was screaming.

"Nonsense," Daerys choked. "We were playing."

The kraken allowed her face to bob to the surface and observed Melayah. *"I wanted to see if you could change into your flying form mid-throw."*

Chuckling, Daerys swam towards the kraken. "Let's have another go?"

"Daerys!"

The tentacle snaked around him again, and he gently rubbed the slippery skin. Underneath his fingertips, he could feel her muscles rippling with her power. Unlike many sailor myths he had heard, her skin was not slimy.

"Ready?"

Once more Daerys was flung into the air. Instead of remaining in his human form, he manifested and attempted to hover. The change was too quick, however, and he fell with a splash before he could correct himself.

The kraken stretched out a spare arm towards Melayah, letting it float nearby. *"Would you like a go, little friend?"*

Melayah stared at the sea creature, blinking the water drops from her eyelashes. She nodded jerkily, as if she couldn't quite believe what she was about to do. Almost reverently, the kraken curled her tentacle around Melayah and drew her close.

"Look up," the kraken said.

Both Melayah and Daerys turned their eyes to the sky. The shadow of a large unknown dragon tore through the skies. Daerys shrunk back, but Melayah manifested and took chase. He only dithered for a moment longer. He surged out of the sea, the saltwater pouring off him. The kraken's farewell was lost.

"Filgaryn!" Daerys screamed, hoping beyond hope that they would hear him before Melayah caught the stranger. Or the stranger caught them. *"Torryn ... Pyrah!"*

The large dragon was a light green male with black horns and talons. Melayah made no secret of their pursuit, and he turned his head to regard them. He hovered in place, and his amber eyes looked over them curiously.

"Get me Filgaryn," the green dragon said, and when Daerys didn't immediately obey, he barked, "Now, boy."

Melayah growled, lips peeling back to reveal her fangs.

"You don't have time ..." Urgency coloured the stranger's tone, and Daerys took a second to consider if he was safe or a threat. He had already called Filgaryn and the others. All he needed to do was to wait the other dragon out and he would be grossly outnumbered. Interestingly, the stranger did not look at all perturbed.

"What are you doing here?" Filgaryn had arrived. Close behind him were Torryn and Torqui.

"Is that any way to greet a friend?" the green dragon said, rounding onto Filgaryn. He blinked at Torryn, a sly grin splitting his face. "Good to see you well."

"Balyin served under our father as a healer," Filgaryn said, shifting his gaze towards Torryn. "You've met."

"What do you want?"

Balyin speared Daerys and Melayah with a contemptuous look, then returned his gaze towards Filgaryn. "Rest assured I'm here because of the love I had for your father, uncle and grandsire. At your request, I eased Emperor Cilvryn into the grave, thus luring Rhodys back home to ensure he has the crown."

Daerys swallowed. It sounded as if Filgaryn had something to do with the emperor's death. He noticed that Torqui likewise was eyeing Filgaryn with a frown. Whatever he had been up to, he hadn't conveyed the plan to her.

"As you anticipated, Rhodys and his siblings clashed. Unfortunately, the snake is not dead. He is returning and is upon you."

"Daerys ..." Filgaryn said. His eyes did not move from the healer's face as he spoke. "Take Melayah, inform Elryk and get the others into position."

"Yes, sir," Daerys murmured. As one, both he and Melayah tucked their wings into a dive and skimmed over the island.

Elryk and Nahilya were on the beach waiting for them.

"Enemy incoming!" Daerys cried. At the sound of his voice, hatchlings scurried to their position.

"Daerys, land!" Elryk cried, hailing him with his spear. "I'm flying with you."

Daerys did as he was told. Spear in hand, Elryk used Daerys' foreleg to climb onto his back. Elryk leaned down from his perch, fingers outstretched to his lover.

"Never run. Never surrender."

Nahilya's dark eyes narrowed. She strode forward and grasped his elbow. "What are you doing?"

"Protecting my family," Elryk replied. His voice was gruff with an emotion that Daerys could not pinpoint. "As long as Rhodys is alive, we'll never be free."

"Fine," Nahilya replied. "I'll fly with one of the newly manifested dragons with healing powers."

It was Elryk's turn to look unhappy. "Very well. Get Ruryk, Vallah and Tya to safety for me. Stay out of trouble."

"I will if you will."

Spreading his wings, Daerys took to the air, thankful for the comforting weight of Elryk on his back and Melayah at his side. On the far horizon, he could see the rapidly disappearing green of the Artrothian healer. Filgaryn had let him go.

"Get into your positions!" Elryk cried down at the hatchlings on the beach. There wasn't any time to organise their ranks into the practiced lines. All around Daerys the other hatchlings manifested and took flight, many of them scrambling to fall behind either Torqui, Filgaryn or Torryn.

Breathing in the fresh salt air, Daerys looked into the horizon to take in the horrible mass of dragons under Rhodys' command. He had hoped with the infighting of Rhodys and his brothers that there would have been fewer of them.

"Let them come to us," Torryn roared. "Conserve your energy."

Obediently, Daerys stilled his wings and hovered. "They seem so much larger than me."

Elryk stroked his scales. The feel of human hands never failed to be comforting. "Stay calm; fly smart."

Daerys swallowed another mouthful of bile. Elryk was right. Faced with Rhodys and his snarling battle dragons, this was not the time to panic. He sneaked a look at Torqui, who was content to hold them in position and wait for Rhodys' response.

Rhodys flew at the head of his army, whipping his head to and fro. His eyes burned with a feral light, and Daerys felt himself shuddering at the sound of his mighty roar. Evidence of a fierce fight between the royal brothers was all too apparent. Some of the scales of Rhodys' hide were torn. One of his horns was missing, and his posture was stiff.

Prince Rhodys was the embodiment of a nightmare. The skies darkened around him, and from nowhere, thunder boomed.

Without waiting for his own forces, Rhodys lunged forward, tucking his wings in and barrelling with a cry of rage. In a bid to keep up with their leader, the Artrothian dragons beat their wings. They seemed to be scrambling to form ranks ... They were fatigued. Many of them had visible injuries.

"Steady," Elryk murmured, running his hands down the scales of his neck. "Rhodys enjoys a little pain. His wounds will not slow him."

Two of their dragons failed to keep pace. They surged forward, meeting Rhodys' teeth and claws. Larger and more experienced, Rhodys swiped out with his talons and sliced the young dragons' throats. Black dragon blood spurted as their wings stopped beating and they fell.

"Otherworlds," Melayah murmured. Daerys shot her a concerned glance. He was glad he wasn't the only one feeling ill.

"Eyes forward."

Before any more of their inexperienced fighters could find themselves in Rhodys' deadly clutches, Torryn surged headlong into the fray with a burst of speed. The two dragons met with a thunderous boom. Daerys charged into a pair of dragons coming up close behind Rhodys.

Melayah was right behind him, along with three other small dragons who seemed nervous in taking a large dragon alone. That was the strategy they had been taught. Pick a target and collectively take them down, then move on to the next victim.

Target selected, they pounced. Their intended victim, a large black dragon, bellowed in rage. Daerys took the thin membrane of his wing and bent it. On his back, Elryk roared and thrust his spear through the soft tissue of one of the dragon's glowing blue eyes.

The black dragon screamed in fury. Writhing but unable to keep himself in the air, he fell into the ocean. Plumes of salt water crashed around him.

At his side, Melayah crowed. She turned her attention to the black dragon's companion, a red female who had two of their dragons clinging to her back with their claws. She was snapping at the younger dragons, twisting around, trying to dislodge them. While the red was distracted, Melayah tore out her throat. Severely injured, she was easy prey as Melayah summoned her wind power to push her down into the churning waves.

Daerys had a great love and respect for the sea. He loved the swirling pools of turquoise, cobalt and teals. Now the water below him ran dark, and the wind smelt of death and battle.

Daerys had seen sharks before, but never had he seen so many. Half a dozen gigantic grey shadows surged through the water, tearing the flesh of any of their fallen. Soon the sea churned with the sharks' feeding frenzy.

To get away from the hatchlings chasing him, one of the enemy dove and flew low under the battle. He was so intent on escaping the dragons in the air, he wasn't watching what was happening below. The turquoise waters churned underneath him until a wave rose from nowhere. Daerys cried out in shock as the wall of water tossed him into the ocean. Seeing the danger, the enemy dragon shot into the air. But the sharks were faster.

Spearing through the water, a shark leapt into the air, its teeth hitting the rump of the dragon. The dragon bellowed as he was forced back under the waves. From underneath him another shark barrelled up from the deep. The blue water was stained black with dragon blood. The enemy did not rise from the waters.

In all of his years sailing the world, Daerys had never seen anything quite like it.

On Daerys' back, Elryk laughed, forming a fireball in his hands. Daerys could feel the heat of the flames along his spines. "Torqui has brought along some of her pets to battle!"

Elryk released the fireball into a passing enemy dragon. She too fell screaming, her wings consumed by the flames.

Filgaryn flew among his once companions like a mad beast. Behind him he left a trail of destruction. He was frankly amazing, diving between the enemy who had no hope in touching him.

Torqui and Torryn worked as a team, killing as many foes as Filgaryn.

"Daerys, watch where you are flying!" Elryk screamed as Daerys had to jerk out of the way to avoid the claws of an enemy.

"Sorry!" Daerys yelled back with a laugh. He tucked his wings in and tumbled down. He spotted something in the water and swore.

Daerys had overhead Filgaryn counselling Torryn, saying that pure Artrothian children could be quite inventive when they decided to misbehave. Ruryk's good behaviour had been suspicious.

Now Daerys could see the wisdom in Filgaryn's words. He had no idea how the boy did it, but Ruryk, too young for his first manifestation, had fashioned himself a raft and was paddling out into the ocean towards the battle.

Daerys had a strong dislike of the boy. Ruryk was a true son of Artroth, proud and vicious. After Daerys complained about Ruryk, Filgaryn had soundly berated him. The elder dragon was right. He was almost a man, and Ruryk was a child who had grown up believing he was better than everyone else. Ruryk was Torryn's chosen son, and Torryn was Torqui's *ketur*.

"Otherworlds, grant me a firm birch switch!" Elryk had spotted the little boat. Against his will, Daerys' rump felt a twinge of sympathy for Ruryk.

Tucking his wings close to his body, Daerys spiralled into a tight dive. The force of his descent pushed the rickety boat under the waves. Ruryk squealed.

"You're lucky I'm the one who spotted you!" Daerys yelled.

Ruryk screamed obscenities in reply: that his father needed him, that he was a true-born Artrothian and one day he would be a prince among dragons. At first Daerys thought Ruryk was crying over Torryn ... but it dawned on him. His father was Artrothian. Had he spotted his father flying into battle? Daerys' stomach soured. He disliked the rising envy he was feeling. What would it be like to have a father you loved so much you would row a boat onto the ocean to join him in battle?

Elryk was not entertaining the tantrum. He shuffled forward along Daerys' back and grasped on to the wriggling boy. Daerys released him, and Elryk hefted him to sit before him.

"What do you think you are doing?" Elryk cried even as Ruryk continued his tirade of abuse. "Fly straight, Dae!"

There was a scuffle on his back. And a searing pain at the base of his left wing. Roaring in agony, Daerys plummeted before he could right himself.

"What have you done?" Elryk yelled. "You stabbed him, you little wretch!"

Human hands, warm and comforting, pressed against his scales. Daerys could feel the blade digging into his joint. Gritting his teeth, he attempted to steady himself. Black dots danced before his eyes. He was going to die over the ocean.

"Nahilya! Nahilya!"

Seconds later two enemies were on his tail, and he realised they were corralling him to trap him.

Before he could react, he felt teeth in his side. Elryk bellowed and thrust his spear at the silver dragon on their left. Ready for the attack, the silver dragon rolled out of the way, and an orange dragon on their right clamped her jaws around Daerys' neck.

Black spots danced in front of Daerys' eyes. He could hear Elryk's yells and feel the man's boots standing on his neck. The spear came crashing down on the dragon's face again and again and again until he was released. Daerys dragged in a deep breath, only to be sideswiped by the silver dragon.

Clutching the now pale Ruryk, Elryk fell from Daerys' back into the water. Thankfully he was flying low, as the kraken had advised. But the waters were infested with sharks ...

Daerys didn't waste any time. He turned and blew fire into the soft eyes of the silver dragon, turned his tail and dove after Elryk and Ruryk.

Grasping one human in each foreclaw, Daerys lifted them both into the air once more. The red-haired man looked deathly pale. He had dropped his spear, but otherwise he seemed unhurt. Ruryk, he was pleased to see, was vomiting.

"Cousin!" Rhodys' voice sounded nearby.

Adrenaline pumped its way through Daerys' blood.

Elryk flinched. "Go!"

Still stunned from the frenzy of the last attack, Daerys attempted to fly upwards. But a crashing weight hit him in the middle of his back. He plummeted back into the waves; there was no time to suck in a breath of air.

By some miracle he wriggled his way out of the clutches of the claws holding him. He pushed his head up through the waves, gasping.

"Elryk!" He wasn't afraid for himself. He could defend himself against sharks. But Elryk. Elryk was human.

The enemy dragon burst from the waves not far away. The skies opened, and heavy, cold droplets of rain pelted down. Lightning forked across the sky, illuminating it with blues and purples. Thunder boomed overhead. Daerys thought even the air quaked in the wake of Rhodys' power.

"Help. Lost Elryk!"

Nearby, Ruryk surfaced, coughing and spluttering. *"Aluel. Aluel!"*

There wasn't time to register Ruryk's words. One of their own, a speckled red and black, swooped, grabbed the child and was gone.

"Filgaryn! I don't know what to do!" Even as he projected these thoughts forward, he knew it was too late. Rhodys was grinning at him and lifted his front foreleg. Hanging limp, still breathing, was a pale Elryk.

Body trembling, Elryk looked up into the face of his cousin and enemy. His fingers scrabbled with his own sleeve as Rhodys continued to observe him with malicious delight.

With an inhuman yell, Elryk threw something. A long dagger hit Rhody's gleaming amber eye and buried itself to the hilt.

Rhodys lifted his head and laughed. There was a hysterical twinge to it. "I'll take my leave, cousin. Knowing I have lived valiantly and died with honour."

All thought fled Daerys' mind. His scream lodged firmly in his throat as Rhodys squeezed the life out of Elryk. Bones crunched, and Elryk's body shook. But the red-haired man stared Rhodys in the face and didn't utter a sound.

A cry of grief tore through the skies. At first Daerys thought it was Torqui, but it was into Nahilya's wide eyes he looked.

"Get out!" Daerys screamed. The shock of Elryk's death wore off, and he snapped back into the brutal reality of the battle. He burst from the waters. He needed to get to the little dragon healer that Nahilya was riding first. For Elryk's sake, he had to protect her. Just a little further ...

Behind him, a roar of rage made Daerys' insides clench. He sensed the waters parting as the larger battle-dragon pursued him. A sob caught in his throat; he knew he was no match for Rhodys.

Below, the waters surged and gurgled. Powerful grey tentacles erupted from the bloody waters. The kraken. She caught Rhodys around the middle, crushing his scream of fury.

Shocked and exhausted, Daerys turned his head, staring into Rhodys' angry eyes as the kraken squeezed him. The sound of splintering dragon bones and air escaping a tortured body would never leave Daerys. Rhodys twisted and slumped. His head hung loose from his broken neck.

The rain petered to a stop; the lightning disappeared. The kraken waved a cheeky tentacle at him before she dragged Rhodys' limp body under the water. Daerys hovered over the place where he had last seen his foe. No bubbles, no ripples, only an eerie silence.

Long moments passed; he was aware of the other dragons. The sound of their arrival was muted. His wings beat in a stuttered rhythm as he struggled to stay airborne. He continued to stare down at the waters, panting in exhaustion. His mind could not respond to the horrible sounds of Torqui's unquenchable grief, of Torryn trying to comfort her.

Melayah was at his side, nudging him to keep him propped up.

"Get him to shore." Filgaryn's voice came from far away. "Keep out of the shark-infested waters ... I don't know if Torqui can control her grief long enough to keep our dragons safe from the monsters of the deep."

"No." The word fell from Daerys' lips. "No, it cannot be."

"Dae ..." A sharp intake of breath. Melayah nudged him again. "Oh, look."

And Daerys did look. A long grey arm floated to the surface and uncurled. Lying on a bed of soft suction cups was Elryk, his long auburn hair fanned out around him. His eyes were closed. His chest did not move. Dead.

To his dying day, he would never forget Torqui's fresh screams for her twin. His own screams joined with his *lullah's*, snapping him out of his daze. He turned his head to look to Nahilya. She was gasping for air, her hand on her belly, but she didn't seem to make a sound.

"Are you happy?" Torqui screamed at an enemy dragon of lilac scales. "Are you happy, *Lullah*? He's gone. The other half of my soul is gone ... your son. The boy you raised to be a warrior ... he's gone."

Wings fluttering in the gentle breeze, Daerys crept forward. But Filgaryn nudged him back. "Let Torqui have this one, Dae."

The lilac dragon, who Torqui's words of anguish revealed to be her mother, looked dispassionately at the still form of Elryk. "He was empty. It had to be done."

"Does your heart not burn with grief for him?" Torqui screamed. Daerys had not been aware that dragons could cry, but tears streamed from Torqui's eyes. "Have you no compassion for the son you birthed?"

"I am glad he is dead." The lilac dragon looked around; she cocked her head to the side. The Artrothians were all but lost. "Aren't you going to kill me? I shall not stop until I kill all you hold dear."

Torqui stared at her mother. Daerys wondered if she hoped that she might eventually win her mother over.

"Stay here ..." Filgaryn rumbled. Daerys knew he was moving forward to challenge and finish Torqui's mother so she wouldn't have to. But the kraken beat him to it.

Tavia, who most were ignoring, cradled Elryk closer. With a free tentacle, she lashed out, swiping the purple dragon from the air. Daerys winced, hearing bones crunch. Torqui's mother didn't have time to scream before the weight of the kraken dragged her under.

Under the water, sharks circled, and then as one, attacked in a frenzy. The body of the purple dragon was lost under a curtain of blood.

"About time she was silent," the kraken grumbled. *"She was giving me a terrible headache."*

"Get to shore," Filgaryn said. "Torryn and I will finish the Artrothian scum."

With their prince dead and their wings in tatters, the remaining Artrothians did not last long against Filgaryn's assault. The battle was won, yet Daerys only felt defeat.

CHAPTER THIRTY-SEVEN

Pyrah

DUNNHARROW

While Nahilya wept openly, Torqui was left feeling numb and dizzy. Confronted with her twin's death, she pressed Elryk's cooling body to her chest. She remembered the old children's tale that spoke of a dragon's heart having enough strength to beat for another. Elryk remained lifeless and still. It was a story.

He was gone. Truly gone. Her twin, Elryk the Empty, was dead. She felt a stirring of shame that she knelt upon the soft sand, unable to help her injured *mynrell*. Filgaryn stepped in, urging Melayah to get Daerys to land on the beach. Silent, her adopted son now lay only meters from the incoming tide, sand clinging to his scales. A trickle of dragon blood ran down his side, and yet she couldn't force her feet to go over to him. The beach of Dunnharrow was littered with exhausted hatchlings. And she felt helpless.

Unable to stay with Daerys, Melayah nudged her brooding son further up the sand. She lifted her head and nodded curtly. She understood. Melayah was returning to the skies to help Filgaryn with the unenviable task of flying back over the waves to usher in the injured and lame. Then they would turn their attention to checking the dead for survivors.

Wandering to the shoreline, Torqui dipped her claws into the cool water. She admonished the sharks, and the moment she made her presence known, the creatures of the deep dispersed. Tilting her tear-streaked face to the sky, she reached out to the kraken. Daerys' sea witch friend had disappeared beneath the waves the moment she had finished cradling her poor dead twin to the beach.

She wasn't surprised to find Torryn, his luminous eyes full of understanding, at her side.

"It's not your fault."

Torqui nodded and looked along the beach again. Daerys was still collapsed on the sand, and guilt gnawed at her belly. He seemed dazed; she shouldn't have left him alone. Her chosen one's scales bore the obvious signs of a violent battle.

"It's not his fault," Torryn rumbled. "He fought hard."

Torqui turned her snout to observe Nahilya, who stumbled along the beach. The healer had cried herself hoarse, but as her tears dried, she walked among the injured, her gait determined to carry on. She felt a sense of shame watching her brother's lover moving between the young when there was only one young dragon she truly cared deeply for.

"Rhodys was a skilled opponent. A royalborn. We couldn't have expected a different outcome," Torqui said. She manifested back into her human form and called out Daerys' name.

The young dragon lifted his head in her direction, huffed and looked away.

"He doesn't want a healer." Torryn seemed uneasy. "He's still mad at me."

"Stubborn male fool," Pyrah said. She clenched her teeth, but determined to be a good mother to him, continued, "Get Nahilya."

She stomped along the beach until she was by Daerys' side. Torryn ignored her command and followed.

Daerys blinked pain-addled eyes at her as she lifted her palm to stroke his scales. "Show me your human form so I can assess how badly hurt you are, *elt mynrell*."

"I hurt," Daerys croaked. His eyes turned to Torryn, and his frown deepened. "I've been stabbed."

"Let me have a look." Torryn moved forward, and Daerys flinched.

"You have your own son to deal with." Daerys didn't seem to be too pleased to have Torryn so close.

"I heard you fished him out of the ocean. You have my thanks." Torryn's gentle hands paused over the dagger. "Who did this?"

"I think you know. And you know why." Daerys glowered. He glanced over to Pyrah, looking abashed.

"I'm sorry, Dae. I'll sort this out." Torryn stood, brushing sand from his trousers. "I'll get Nahilya."

Pyrah watched Torryn striding up the beach. He moved swiftly, with the gait of a predator. Daerys closed his eyes like one whose life energy had been drained from his body.

"Ruryk?"

Daerys' eyes snapped open. "How did you know?"

"Male dragons are not as subtle as they think. One, I've undressed Torryn enough times to recognise that Artrothian dagger as the one he carries. Two, Torryn and you have had an argument, which I suspect was about him lying to me about Ruryk's parentage."

"I'll not ask you to choose between him and me. I understand—"

"*Mynrell*, I am not choosing sides ..."

"I'll not live in the same den as Ruryk. I'll not do it."

"I know." Pyrah brushed the sand from Daerys' scales. "You are of age to ... I can help you establish your own den. Close to your *lullah*, of course."

"You will?" Daerys swallowed thickly, turning his gaze away to stare at Vallah and Tya, who both sat huddled together, weeping for Elryk. "I deserve to hurt."

"No," Pyrah murmured. "You fought hard."

"It wasn't *enough*. I wasn't enough." Daerys' voice sounded tortured. "It should have been me."

Nahilya approached, calling out Pyrah's name, and tears starting running down Daerys' face. As sobs started to overtake him, he apologised to the healer over and over. His words tumbled over each other, a torrent of regret and guilt. Always gentle, Nahilya hushed him, running her hands along his scales. Seated so close to the healer, Pyrah felt the brush of the magic washing over her heir. She felt a strong pulse, and then Daerys sucked in a lungful of air and immediately lost consciousness.

"It's best he sleep," Nahilya said. She pulled the knife out and closed the gaping wound. Pyrah noticed that the healer refused to look at her. "I'll check on him when he is awake. Torryn is dealing with the perpetrator."

Pyrah turned, grasping Nahilya's wrist, a burning question on her lips. "Did Elryk know?"

"What?"

"Did he know about the child?" Pyrah had never been so sure of an answer in all her life.

Nahilya shifted her weight, sighed and refused to meet her gaze. "No. I didn't want him to worry. I know we're at war ... but I wanted this child."

"I'll swear I'll be a good aunt, just as Elryk is ..." Breath caught in Pyrah's throat. She swallowed thickly, aware her voice cracked. For the first time in a long time, her display of deep emotion did not shame her. "... was a good uncle to my girls."

Nahilya's eyes never left the horizon. "We need to say goodbye to the dead. To honour them appropriately."

Confident that their sad little band was safe, both Torryn and Filgaryn flew to nearby land to collect wood for the funeral pyres. Along the beach they collected what they could of their dead and spent the next day building the pyres.

Wherever possible, the dead were honoured with fire in Artroth, and Pyrah had never given thought of the practice. Elryk had never spoken of his preferences, and she had never thought to be without her twin.

Filgaryn was in favour of the pyres. "Elryk had an affinity for fire. It seems suitable."

Pyrah could hardly speak. She glanced towards Vallah, who shoved her fists into her eyes to try and stop herself from crying again. Poor child. Pyrah regretted the hand she had in her father's death. Her daughter had been captured and imprisoned, her sister killed and then her dear uncle lost to battle. She was coming to her eleventh year in the world, and she had lost so much.

"His body will burn, and his ashes will mingle with the Wind Song." Filgaryn was trying to be comforting in the only way he knew how.

Nahilya flinched. "Any joy I might feel in this life turns to ashes in my mouth."

"Elryk's son will be a source of great joy for you," Torryn said. He took Nahilya's arm and led her towards the lead pyre where they had laid Elryk. He looked devastatingly handsome, his red hair gleaming in the sun. He looked to be merely asleep. Nahilya's steps halted before her lover as she dragged in a shaking breath. "Your son will grow old and will know the impossible white dragon."

"You've seen this?" Nahilya asked.

"My visions and dreams are by no means strong. But of this I am confident," Torryn replied. "Elryk's son will see the final collapse of Artroth."

The pyres were lit by those who wielded fire. Many of them stayed on the beach until the fires burned themselves out, the bodies of their deceased consumed by the flames.

"*Araae helphelwyn. Terini gorthorawyn,*" Filgaryn said.

"Live valiantly. Die honourably?" Daerys asked.

Filgaryn laid a hand upon his shoulder. Despite himself, the Artrothian seemed moved. "Yes. They are the words spoken after battle to honour those who gave their lives. I ... I did not know what else to say."

"Who do you suppose will meet an empty one in the Otherworld?" Pyrah asked. She regretted the question the moment the words left her mouth. No one had the heart to answer her.

"There's one Artrothian I am keen to see," Torryn rumbled, turning his back. "Time to find my once wife."

"Indeed, you'll find Ayrahylse back in her northern lair." How the ancient one, Gahryk, had been able to fly into their camp and stand among them without anyone sensing him, Pyrah didn't know.

"What are you doing here?" Filgaryn's lips twisted into a snarl.

"Handing you the last enemy." Gahryk shrugged as if the answer was obvious.

There was a furious flapping of wings and angry squawking. Nix flew into view. Elryk had left him on the Green Isle, safe away from battle, but it seemed that the feathered creature had come looking for his master. He flew closer, diving at Gahryk. His screeches were deafening to those standing around.

Nahilya lifted her arm. "Nix. Come."

Grudgingly, the blue bird landed on her forearm. He glared around those assembled, clicking his beak and puffing up his feathers. His head tilted as he surveyed his master's burning pyre. Nahilya stroked the bird's feathers, nattering to him. Pyrah had to wonder how much one of Elryk's birds could understand. Did he know his master was dead?

"Give us one reason we should trust you," Nahilya said, tearing her attention from Nix. "You let Laelyth betray us ... You've not helped at all."

"I am neither for or against you," Gahryk said. "I look for the dawn when the Artroth we know is no more. They're destined to failure."

"And what about those living in the now, Gahryk?" Pyrah hissed.

"Very good question, my dear," Gahryk replied. "What of your husband? Could you not have worked around him instead of murdering him for his stupidity? But I digress. You wouldn't have mated with Torryn if your husband were alive."

"What of Elryk? Could he not be saved?"

Gahryk looked Nahilya up and down. "He has sired his son. He has done what was required for him to do to ensure Artroth's demise."

"Charyss?"

"The child had nothing further to contribute."

Pyrah roared in fury, Torryn catching her about her waist. She would have dearly loved to scratch out Gahryk's mocking eyes. "I'll never understand you, Gahryk."

"I don't expect you to," Gahryk replied. "You're much too heroic. You'd gladly give your life ... Me, all that matters is that Artroth is destroyed, and I'm around to see it. Once it is done, I will give up the ghost."

"When will this be?" Filgaryn asked.

Gahryk laughed. "Not for another few thousand years."

"Be gone," Pyrah said. "Next time I see your smug, weaselly little face, I will kill you."

"This, dear Pyrah, is goodbye," Gahryk said, dipping into a low bow. "We'll never see each other again."

He unfurled his wings and turned his back. At the sound of Pyrah's gasping sobs for her daughter and her brother, he turned to look at her. Through the haze of her tears, she thought she could see the expression soften on Gahryk's face.

"She's at peace, Pyrah."

Torryn's arms tightened around her middle, and little Vallah burrowed her way into her arms.

"I'm not the monster you think I am. Charyss, Vallah or Daerys, you were destined to lose one of your children. The beheading was the kindest fate."

"Liar."

"She stands in a little garden made of flowers. Elryk is with her. She is safe. She is home."

Pyrah's knees hit the ground. She thought she had finished mourning for her lost child. She thought she had cried all her tears, and yet another wave of grief engulfed her.

"Do you not know who you are?" Pyrah wished she could silence Gahryk. "You are mother-dragon. *Lullah-Rshon*. The mother to all dragons of Ramyr. Torryn is *Aluel-Rshon* ... Your hearts were broken for a cause."

"I would give up everything to have my daughter back and tell her how sorry I am," Pyrah cried.

The disturbance of the air as Gahryk took flight played with the strands of Pyrah's hair. She swallowed, looking up into Daerys' eyes, and held up her hand for her son to pull her to her feet.

"Is all this necessary?" Daerys watched, concern evident on his face, as Torryn took Ayrahylse in his strong grip. The oldest of their group had flown to Torryn's Stronghold to find her. Nahilya and the children stayed in a quiet clearing near a lake that Torryn had been fond of. Grieving and exhausted, the healer did not have any desire to see the final revenge meted out.

Pyrah said nothing but laid a comforting hand on Daerys' shoulder. She too turned to watch the spectacle that was Torryn and his once life-mate. Ayrahylse had been exactly where Gahryk had told them to look, alone near the Stronghold. She knew that she would always remember the look of horror blossoming on the blonde woman's face.

Filgaryn was speaking, but Pyrah let the words wash over her. Instead she watched Ayrahylse's calm façade crumble. Torryn didn't speak, his Artrothian blade already bared and winking in the midday sun.

She hoped that this moment of revenge would be healing for him.

"You must forgive me, Torryn, beloved one." Ayrahylse struggled, trying to manifest, but Filgaryn was quick. The brothers exchanged a glance with one another, and Filgaryn took a fistful of Ayrahylse's golden hair and wrenched her head backwards.

"Torryn, please."

Uncaring for his once life-mate's pleas, Torryn fumbled with a bottle of tonic. Ayrahylse had betrayed him, and he had suffered under the influence of the cursed herbs. It was only just that she should sample a portion of Torryn's misery in her last moments. Tears ran down Ayrahylse's pale face as she was forced to swallow. "Please I can't feel my dragon."

"Just think, wife," Torryn replied. He took the crown of steel and diamond from her head and threw it to the side. "I might have let you live for Syrif's sake, but your son and his dragon are dead."

"Galvrayne, my *sudunyn*, my nest mate, is likewise dead at your hands," Filgaryn said. "You gave your life-mate to the enemy and gave of yourself to Prince Rhodys. For these crimes, we sentence you to die."

"Please ..."

Torryn swallowed thickly, his fingers dancing along the edge of the blade in his hand. Glancing towards him, Filgaryn paused, searching his brother's face that they were both in agreement.

"It's your justice to take, brother," Filgaryn said gruffly.

"Goodbye, Ayrahylse." The dagger plunged into Ayrahylse's chest, and she jerked. Torryn caught her reflexively and lowered her to the ground. Eyes wide, she panted for breath, but no sound was able to be emitted from her lungs. Her lips trembled.

"My child was a dragon?" Ayrahylse, in her terror, lost control of her thoughts. She broadcast her last silent question to the group.

"You killed our hours-old baby boy," Torryn said out aloud. His shoulders slumped, Ayrahylse still cradled in his arms. "It didn't matter to me if he had a dragon or not."

Pyrah shivered. Melayah took her hand and squeezed. How terrible to realise that you had been the one to cut off your dreams. What would Ayrahylse and Torryn's child have been like? She could imagine his dark eyes, tight black curls and dimpled cheeks. She could have loved that child for Torryn, brought him into her own nest.

"Ketur?" Pyrah reached out and felt Torryn's own hurt mirroring her own. He knew what it was like to lose a child. It was a different grief to her own, but no less real or painful. His fingers loosened on his blade as the light in Ayrahylse's eyes went dim.

"Let her go. It's over," Filgaryn said, coming up behind Torryn and taking the dagger from his slack fingers. "The tonic prevented her dragon from manifesting. She's gone."

Torryn's gaze did not shift.

"It's over, brother," Filgaryn said. "You're truly free."

"Well, I must say, that was quite a show." Their group startled and looked around. A large black dragon with a crown of golden horns sat perched on an outcrop. His front forearms were crossed over one another lazily as he yawned widely. "I suspect in the history annals to come, the Artrothian traitor will be but an obscure figure in history, one whose memory would fade in time. Forgotten ..."

Daerys growled and manifested into his dragon to confront him. He must have felt Pyrah's spike of fear regarding this large bull dragon. Before Pyrah could cry out in warning, Daerys lunged, closing the distance between him and the stranger. The black dragon laughed, reached out and pushed him away with little effort.

"Uncle!" Filgaryn cried, his countenance brightening while Daerys tumbled to the ground. "Blessed Talons, I'm glad to see you!"

The black dragon stretched out his snout and pushed Daerys to his feet. "There we go, young one. What have we learned?"

Daerys blinked up at him, hunched and growled again.

"Your blood is still boiling over with battle. Even still, one must always take the time to stop and think," the black dragon said sagely.

Smarting from the embarrassment, Daerys bared his teeth. Pyrah manifested into her emerald dragoness form, prowling forward. Torryn and Melayah mirrored her actions. Only Filgaryn remained human, standing vulnerable and unafraid of his uncle.

"I, Commander Hael, come with a message from the new emperor of Artroth, *His Imperial Majesty Xavryn.*"

Torqui had never heard anyone speak an emperor's name with such loathing sarcasm. She had heard stories of him in her youth, the brother of General Rivyr, famed for his ability of stealth. Enemies would not know about the commander's presence until he made himself known to them.

"Is this where my brother died?" The black dragon looked over the mountain range, tilting his head so that his golden horns reflected the sunlight. "His death song is both beautiful and ... horrific."

"What are you doing here?"

"Is this him?" Hael looked Torryn over. "The *kairn* son my *sudunyn* gave his life for?"

"This is Torryn, Uncle." Filgaryn slapped Torryn's foreleg.

The black dragon blinked, nostrils flaring. "A fine specimen if I ever did see one."

"What are you doing near my home?" Torryn growled, curling his lip to flash his fangs at the intruder. Pyrah and Torryn had spoken about this. Her *ketur* had a strong desire to return to his mountains, to his lake, and settle down in peace. Considering she had no special connection to Wymeria, she had agreed. These mountains were a perfect place for other young dragons to make their dens. She could keep Daerys and Melayah close, watch them both grow into adulthood.

"I have a message from Emperor Xavryn. Stay within sight of your land, and you'll have nothing to fear." Commander Hael was unconcerned with Torryn's show of aggression.

Torqui scoffed.

"You are right to be suspicious. The emperor is too busy keeping his own people under control. He still views your bloodline as his property ... There will come a day Artroth returns to your shores," Hael said.

"And why would the emperor send you to us?" Torqui snarled.

"The elders of our ancient bloodline have left Artroth. The new emperor is too afraid to chase after them." Hael yawned lazily. "First my brother's eldest son is murdered and his traitorous mate makes a deal with an Artrothian prince. Then my brother, a beloved general, is ripped to pieces in defense of his surviving sons ..."

"I broke a prisoner free," Filgaryn said. He looked pointedly to Torryn and then back to his uncle.

"That wasn't the story I weaved for the emperor," Hael replied. "Sending your father's loyal healer was a stroke of genius. He told the emperor that you flew after the prisoner and were pursued by Rhodys, and that the prince intended to kill you both. This was not a threat that Rivyr could accept. Being a good father, he went to your aid, and Rhodys murdered him."

"So ..." Torqui could see something akin to a blossoming hope on Filgaryn's face.

"The elders of our bloodline told the emperor that Rivyr died doing the highest duty of an *aluel*. A sacred duty of protecting one's own nest, given by the great Ythryr himself. Our people are discontent, and the emperor had little choice. Either I serve him or I find what remains of my blood and keep them out of Artroth's borders ..."

"We're banished?" Filgaryn asked.

"Is that a bad thing?" Daerys muttered.

"Indeed, it was the best outcome we could wish for, young one," Commander Hael said. He snorted, smoke curling from his snout. "I believe the emperor hoped I would go and lead his men to great-grandfather. Our elders have no wish to be found; they want peace. So, I came for you, nephew. You're all I have left now."

"There's Torryn," Filgaryn pointed out. "And Tya."

The black dragon blinked and bowed his crowned head low to Torqui. "It is a terrible thing to lose a twin, Princess. Rivyr was a whole twenty minutes younger than me. We squabbled something shocking as hatchlings. But as adults ... I'd do anything for Rivyr." Commander Hael stretched out his wings and exhaled noisily. "I guess this is home now."

"Don't expect to bark orders and expect me to do your bidding. These are my mountain ranges," Torryn snapped.

"You have Rivyr's temper. Excellent," Commander Hael said fondly. "The issue you would be facing now, nephew Torryn, is that Ramyr now has a population of dragons. And if rumour is true, dragons are hatching from human souls. You're going to need dragons with a little more knowledge to handle the challenges that come with a new race being birthed."

Torryn blew hot air out of his nostrils.

"I wouldn't dream of living in the same territory as either of my nephews. Dragons of power need to spread out. This is a courtesy to let you know I fully intend to find myself a nice home."

"Your wisdom and experience are appreciated," Torqui said.

With that being said, the black dragon spread his wings and took off, flying south. For a long while, Torryn watched him leave and then sighed and retreated to the quiet of the caverns. "What now?"

"I would like to fly south and make my home there," Filgaryn said. "I can watch the coastlines for any threats."

"Filly ..."

"Don't call me Filly." There was no heat in Filgaryn's response. He pressed his forehead against Torryn's in a rare show of brotherly affection. "You need to build your nest. And I need to build mine. This isn't farewell. I'll bring Tya back and visit from time to time."

"Until we meet again," Pyrah said, letting her dragon body melt away. She smoothed down her skirts. Torryn's dragon melted away, his fingers found hers and squeezed.

"Keep a tight rein on Ruryk," Filgaryn warned. He handed Torryn the Artrothian dagger before manifesting into his dragon form. "He's young, and he'll keep your hands full."

Torryn's face hardened. "I'll raise him right."

Pyrah shifted her gaze to Daerys. Even after a serious discussion with Torryn that had ended with them both yelling at each other in the defense of their hatchlings, she didn't feel completely at ease. She won the argument that Daerys didn't have to learn to live with the boy who stabbed him, and Torryn agreed they would both share the responsibility for Ruryk. Ruryk, for his part, needed to learn to tolerate the new breed of dragon.

Filgaryn seemed to sense their unease with their troublesome ward. He spread his wings out wide and bowed. "I'll be close by for the next few days. We still need to ensure that Nahilya's new home is comfortable and secure for her."

Nahilya did not wish to make her home among the cold rock of the mountain. So Torryn and Filgaryn had been busy designing a new home for her close to Torryn's lake. Filgaryn had even been hunting so Nahilya had stocks of food for herself and skins for blankets and clothing come winter. Pyrah worried for her, but Nahilya said she had Nix for company, and Torryn promised they would always be nearby.

Filgaryn stepped forward and picked up Ayrahylse's body in his front claws. "I'll dispose of this for you. The kraken could do with another doll."

Much to Pyrah's surprise, the kraken, Tavia, followed them up along the coastline. Daerys assured her the sea monster wasn't staying. She would return to her nesting site soon. She was curious to see where the dragons, the children of air, planned to settle.

"You're always welcome in our home, Filgaryn the Unseen," Pyrah said.

Filgaryn smiled once more and took off.

"The emperor is in an interesting position," Pyrah said at length, watching Filgaryn's form disappear.

"How so?"

"If the story that Rhodys unfairly murdered Rivyr is circulating Artroth ... maybe we should be expecting more dragon families to flee or rebel against Artroth. Your father's family is an ancient, almost sacred bloodline."

"This is the beginning of the end of Artroth," Torryn replied.

It was strange. As a young girl ostracised and exiled from her homeland, she had spent months dreaming of returning to court. She dreamed of being fawned over, of being able to manifest and fly anytime she wanted to. As a princess in her uncle's court, she never appreciated how much of a prisoner she was. She didn't need power or riches or status.

This Ramyr was her sanctuary, a land of safety.

A crown wasn't meant for her. Ramyr was a wild land, open and free for exploration. In these mountains she heard the Wing Song clearer and louder than she had ever heard in her lifetime. Here with Torryn, a dragon with human ancestry, she could spread her wings and experience freedom.

Pyrah tightened her grip on Torryn's hand and drew him closer to her. Everything she needed was in him. His dragon heart was her home, and she burned with an all-consuming fire for him. The flames of her growing passion would be eternal. Never would she yearn for another as she did for him.

Torryn bent his head, brushing his firm lips against hers. She reached up, twining her fingers in his hair, and deepened the kiss. He tasted of freedom and hope.

Thank you for reading my work. If you enjoyed Fires of Retribution, why not help an author out and leave a review on either Amazon or Goodreads?

All reviews are helpful and I am sincerely grateful to all my wonderful readers willing to take a chance on me.

 amazon.com/author/kjburrage

 goodreads.com/author/show/22623993.K_J_Burrage

Character Guide

Ayrahylse (AIR - ah - lease) – yellow dragon, life-mate to Torryn. Fancies herself queen of the northern parts of Ramyr.

Balyin (B – al – yin) – an old healer loyal to General Rivyr's family.

Bryn (BRIN) – A salt-rat aboard the 'Wyn-Tyn' who has power over land.

Charyss (CARE - riss) – Pyrah's twelve year old daughter. She has some healing and power over plants.

Cilvryn (SILV - rin) – Pyrah's uncle, the Emperor of Artroth.

Corinah (COR – in - ah) – One of Rhodys' sisters in Artroth.

Daerys (DAY - rees) – A young newly manifested dragon, who has an earth moving power.

Duryl (DOO – rill) – A young male dragon that Pyrah's mother hoped she might have married. Duryl did have feelings for Pyrah and when she left Artroth he tracked news of her.

Elryk (ELL - rick) – Also known as Elryk the Empty. Pyrah's twin brother, born without a dragon.

Filgaryn (PHIL - gah - rin) – General Rivyr's lieutenant. Dark grey dragon whom Ayrahylse made an enemy of.

Gahryk (GAH - rick) – An ancient dragon of Artroth. Known as the all-knowing one. When he saw the demise of Artroth he left, even though he was secretive about what he saw.

Galvrayne (GALV - rain) – Filgaryn's brother. Was to be Ayrahylse's life mate.

Hael (HAY - el) – A black scaled dragon with golden horns. Filgaryn's uncle, a great commander of Artroth.

Izzur (Is - zur) – One of Rhodys' bodyguards who flies into Wymeria with him.

Jilearah (JILL - ear - ah) – Mysterious medicine woman who lives in the swamp. Torryn often trades some of his snapdragon meats and products for companionship and help.

Laelyth (LAY – lith) – rose gold dragon who first appears at Pyrah's dragon summit. She comes with Gahryk.

Latunya (LAH - too - nah) – The mother of Pyrah and Elryk. She has stayed behind in Artroth.

Luthur (LOO - th - er) – The Chieftain of Wymeria and husband to Pyrah.

Mairtyr (MARE – tee – er) – Xavryn's favourite, sent to Ramyr to spy on Rhodys.

Melayah (MEL - ay - ah) – A young manifested dragon with the power over the wind.

Nahilya (NAH - hill - ya) – Empty of a dragon, Nahilya is a healer that lives a reclusive life in the forests.

Neo (NEE - oh) – A human child that Torryn watches over.

Nix (N – ix) – Elryk's blue and green parrot.

Parlyn (PAR - lin) – The father of Pyrah and Elryk. Was a renowned healer.

Pyrah (PIE - rah) – The heroine. She is also known as the Green Lady and the Mistress of the Sea.

Rhodys (ROW - dis) – Pyrah's cousin. A dragon prince famed for his cruelty.

Rivyr (RIV - ver) – An Artrothian general who takes over the Stronghold.

Ruryk (ROO - rick) – The young son of Yirys, a female battle dragon.

Rygard (RIGH - guard) – A human chieftain known for his wealth and prosperity.

Sussette (SUE – set) – Empress of Artroth and Rhodys' late mother.

Tavia (TAY - vee - ah) – Known as the sea witch or the Kraken.

Torqui (TOR - key) – The dragon name of Pyrah, the Green Lady of Wymeria.

Torryn (TOR - rin) – A dragon who lives a reclusive life in the northern mountains. He was betrayed by his life-mate and is known as the father of lies or the deceiver.

Tya (TEE - ah) – A young dragon that manifests under Rhodys. She attacks Torqui during a battle and runs away.

Uxhyn (UH - x - in) – A gigantic black dragon known for his gentleness. He has kept his human name 'Hyn'.

Vallah (VAL - ah) – Pyrah's ten-year-old daughter.

Virrow (VEAR – oh) – A soldier dragon loyal to General Rivyr. Grandmother to Nahilya.

Xavryn (EX - av - rin) – Rhodys' elder brother.

Yirys (YEAR - iss) – A female dragon that Rhodys brings into Wymeria as a bodyguard.

Ythryr (YITH – ear) – A dragon of myth, believed to be the dragon who first rose against human invaders, he was the very beginning of Artroth. The first white dragon.

Language Guide

Aluel (AY-l-ool) – Father

Araae helphelwyn. Terini gorthorawyn (AH-ay HEL-fel-win TE-ree-ne GOR-thor- A-win) – Live Valiantly. Die Honourably.

E birelle'n ion tryth garah (EH – Brigh – ell'n I-on – TRIGH -eith gah -rah) – I burn with an all consuming fire

Elt (EL-t) – My

Kairn (K-AIR-n) – Two meanings – a) bastard/ illegitimate or b) mongrel

Ketur (KET – er) – Beloved (used for life mate only)

Lullah – (LULL – ah) – Dragon word for mother.

Mynrell (MIN-rell) – has many meanings son, daughter, heir, fosterling, adopted. All the same and all equal. Dragon use only

Ramyr (RA - mer) – Artrothian word meaning safety. This is the ancient name for Rama

Ri Rshon hanoch (RI R-ish-on HAN-ock) – Considered coarse language – Old Dragon's Genitals

Rokun (ROO-k-un) – Word for a human not worthy of dragon respect. Also used for a wicked person

Rshon Aluel (R-ish-on AY-l-ool) – Dragon Father

Rshon Lullah (R-ish-on LULL - ah) – Dragon Mother

Rshon mahthyt (R-ish-on MA-th-at) – Dragon Dung

Sais-levly (SACE - LEV – ee) - flying lizard an insult in Artroth

Shakhyr - levly (SHAR – k – her LEV – ee) - corpse lizard. The term in Artroth to describe the corpse of a dragon who has been executed. It is also a term to describe a double death. If a dragon has a human heart, their human is tortured and executed first. Once the dragon remains, they are tortured and killed a second time.

Sudunah (SUE-dun-ah) - Sister

Sudunyn (SUE-dun-en) – Brother

Tieryn-myn (T-air – in M-in) - Death for young - an ancient Artrothian practice - when one offers to die at the hands of one's enemy in exchange for their offspring's life.

Vehyl (V-hay-el) – Word for a human that is worthy of dragon respect. Often used affectionately.

E vydel el taldyn (EH VI-del EL TAL-din) – I love you fiercely

Elt rshon desn tollah hy el (ELT R-ish-on DEZ-n TOL-ah HI EL) – My dragon heart beats for you

Location Guide

Avhyl (AV – hill) – Rygard's Fort, where Rhodys kept his forces.

Artroth (ART – roth) – The dragon empire, Pyrah's country of origin.

Ayr-Rouhella (AIR – ROO – hell – ah) – An ancient nesting sight, the home of thousands of bones of unmanifested dragons killed by human hunters. Also said to the be the home of Ythryr the Blessed.

Dunnharrow (DUN – HA – Row) – An island that Daerys and Torryn build together.

Garrowmyth (GAR – row – mith) – A seaside town that Pyrah and her company attack.

Green Isle – An island to the south of Wymeria, where Elryk and Pyrah spent time together away from the humans.

Gyptumm (GIP – Tum) – An island that Daerys and Torryn built. The name means Lizard Mine, in the tongue of the people to the far north.

Levly Peak (LEV – lee) – Translated to Lizard Peak. This is where Torryn had a little accident and built these mountain.

Lorlyn (LAW – lin) – A trading port town in Trader's Bay.

Ramyr (RA – meer) – A large land mass that is home to various people groups. The Artrothians call it 'safety'.

The Stronghold – Torryn and Ayrahylse's palace home in the north.

Stonethaw Range – A mountain range that this sheltered from the elements and provides Pyrah and company shelter.

Swamps – Torryn's hunting grounds in the north.

Tamaryn (TAM – ar – in) – A large port city in Widow's Bay.

Wymeria (WHY – meer – re – ah) – A village in the south of Ramyr. Pyrah's home.

Wyn -Tyn (WIN – tin) – The island that Daerys rises from the ocean bed.

The Historical Inspiration Behind Fires of Retribution

Fires of Retribution is a fictional work set in a fantasy world. I have a great love of history, especially ancient history, and so I couldn't help but use one of my real life, all-time favourite historical figures to rewrite her story. My story is a creative piece so should not be used as 'fact'. If you want historically accurate literature, try non-fiction.

Boudica/ Boadicea

(Pyrah)

'Win the battle or perish: that is what I, a woman will do; you men can live on in slavery if that's what you want.' - Boudica

Boudica was an ancient Celtic queen of the Iceni Tribe. She was made famous after her rebellion against Rome (AD 60). Her husband, Prasutagus, hoped to curry favour with their Roman overlords and signed Emperor Nero—yes, that Nero—as co-heirs with his two daughters. This was no minor action. This was a considerable sum. He hoped by doing so that his people would not be attacked.

Unfortunately, Boudica's husband died, and the Roman governor of the land, Suetonius Paulinus, decided that he would take the lands and household for himself. Boudica was publicly flogged and her daughters sexually assaulted by Roman slaves. Humiliated, Boudica was exiled.

Boudica was not a woman to back down. She saw that other Celtic chiefs suffered the same mistreatment from Rome. The resistance grew.

She captured Camulodumum (Colchester), where the imperial agent had fled. The Britons showed no mercy. Camulodumum burned, and there were reports of desecrating cemeteries and mutilating statues.

Boudica then took Londinium (London) and Verulamium (St. Albans).

The Roman historian Tactius gives an account of the final battle in 61 AD. Historians believe it took place in Mancetta near Nuneaton. The Britons attacked the Roman defensive line, but their great numbers worked against them. Lightly armoured against the Romans, they must have suffered horrendous causalities against the volleys of heavy javelins.

The Romans attacked using their tight formation, stabbing with their short swords. Their cavalry encircled Boudica's army, and the slaughter from the back began. Tactus estimates that 80,000 Britons (men, women and children) died during this battle.

Some sources say that rather than being taken alive by the Romans, Boudica took poison. Others say she died from her wounds shortly after. To this day, she is remembered for her courage. In 1902, a statue of her was erected in the Old Roman capital of Britain, Londinium (London), next to the Houses of Parliament.

Cartmandua and Venutius
(Ayrahylse and Torryn)

In order to retain their throne, Cartmandua and Venutius were in the pro-Roman camp and made several deals with the Roman overlords.

In 51 AD, another British king, Caratacus, who had been leading a resistance against the Romans, tested the couple's loyalty to Rome. He had been defeated in battle and sought safety from Cartmandua. Instead of sanctuary, she put him in chains and offered him up to the Romans.

Cartmandua may have been rewarded by the Romans, but her actions were turning her own people against her. She made a further mistake in 57 AD, divorcing poor Venutius and having an affair with his armour-bearer.

Venutius was to have his revenge. Using the anti-Roman sentiment among the people, he began to build alliances.

Rome sent some back-up, and Venutius suffered an initial loss. Cartmandua escaped thanks to the Romans.

Venutius waited for the right time. In 69 AD, Nero died, which resulted in a time of political unrest in Rome. Venutius attacked. This time, when Cartmandua appealed to Rome for help, they were only able to send auxiliary troops.

She fled to the newly built fort at Deva (Chester) ... but what happened to her after her arrival remains a mystery. Queen Cartmandua simply disappeared

Acknowledgements

To my dad, Glenn Stevenson, who fostered my great love and respect for history. His own love of history encouraged my obsession with Boudica, who inspires this story. He also passed on his dry humour and wit, so if you find anything funny between the pages of my story—that's his fault as well.

To my mum, Jacki Stevenson, who proofread hundreds of pages of kiddie scribbles. (That takes dedication and love.)

To my MIL, Kaye Burrage, who has read everything I'm willing to release and tries to sell to anyone she talks to.

To my critique partners, Janine Burger and Holly Cline. Thank you for all your helpful insights and encouragement to make this story the strongest book I could write.

To my fabulous editor, Katie Wolf, for her endless patience, diligence and encouraging my enthusiasm. She doesn't seem to mind all my annotations to my own work and backstage comments.

And oh, isn't the artwork gorgeous? Thank you to Chicklen Doodle (instagram) for helping me make *Fires of Retribution* a little bit more special with artwork. It has been fabulous working with you.

And of course, to you my readers, for taking a chance on me and reading my work. Without you there would be no stories.

About KJ Burrage

KJ Burrage currently calls tropical North Queensland, Australia, home. She has been developing her craft since she was ten years old. Alas, the original floppy discs from 1995 have disappeared!

She lives with her three young daughters, an exuberant pug-cross and a cheeky blue parrot.

Growing up she had grand visions of becoming CS Lewis. When she grew up a little more, she decided she was going to be JRR Tolkien. Now, she's learnt to be proud of her own voice and the pen name KJ Burrage is perfect for her.

She has a Bachelor Degree in Primary Education with a major in literacy and worked as a primary school teacher. She has also been a co-owner of a laser engraving business.

Life can be unpredictable (and unfair). After the sudden and tragic death of her husband, she returned to her passion of the written word.

You can read more at www.kjburrage.com.

facebook.com/profile.php?id=100071328683512

instagram.com/kjburrage_author/

tiktok.com/@kjburrage_writes

goodreads.com/author/show/22623993.K_J_Burrage

amazon.com/author/kjburrage

https://twitter.com/KJBurrage

Also By

The adventure continues with the Dragon's Heir Trilogy. Set 3000 years after Fires of Retribution, it's full of dragons, found family, battles and sassy characters.

1. Son of the Crown

2. Prince of Scales

3. Herald of the Dragon King